JOHN BRATBY

Breakfast & Elevenses

Also by John Bratby BREAKDOWN

Breakfast & Elevenses

HUTCHINSON OF LONDON

HUTCHINSON & CO. (*Publishers*) LTD
178–202 Great Portland Street, London, W.1

London Melbourne Sydney
Auckland Bombay Toronto
Johannesburg New York

First published 1961

*This book has been set in Scotch Roman type face.
It has been printed in Great Britain by The Anchor
Press, Ltd., in Tiptree, Essex, on Antique Wove
paper and bound by Taylor Garnett Evans & Co.,
Ltd., in Watford, Herts*

With unshed tears and sodden sentimentality, to L.B.R. who would have been pleased now, but who did not wait to witness. To L.B.R. who did not really think there was that reason for staying around, and to whom I would like to show the present—a far better present than the only other—fifty Players, which seemed to mean so much at the time, in that dearth of affection. To L.B.R. who didn't know my love, because I did not know it either, I dedicate this book on a page containing a dedication dripping with dismalness and miserable with morbid matter.

Contents

1

Before Breakfast

LIKE most boys of three he was small, and his name was Peter. He lived in Grandpa's house across from the field of tombstones. Looking back through the decades, the earliest thing that Peter could remember was the little matter of the jar of cold cream. 'If you are a naughty boy the Sandman will get you'; and the Sandman was big Grandpa, apparently. The memory was blurred and dim, like a certain type of Sickert painting, but he never forgot it. Daddy was gay then, because Daddy was young; and Daddy's complexes had not created a rot in his nature as they did in years afterwards. Mummy was young too, ten years younger than Daddy, and at that time, at the end of the 1920's, she was not yet soured by too much of Daddy. Grandpa and Grandma had had many offspring, as Grandpa, a monumental mason, was big and virile; and in the Victorian house that faced the cemetery there were always many people, with Grandpa presiding in the background. The corridors in the house were dark, and the rooms were dimmed by the heavy hanging curtains even when they were drawn back, and the Victorian clutter helped to add to the darkness in the rooms. The room Peter slept in was a bit more modern of course, and that was where the pot of cold cream was. There had been another little matter that he had remembered, but that was a confused memory: it was to do with a bottle of ink in the kitchen. He remembered that the kitchen was the darkest room in the house, with a dark-wood table; and it was in there, as he looked out of the window, that he first heard about 'the blackbird pecking off her nose'. The kitchen was so

9

dark that it depressed him: all tall dark cupboards and gloom. All he could remember about those tender days were his crimes, and the rest of his experiences were for ever obscured in a dark emotional mist.

Peter could remember the garden, and the circular seat round the trunk of the tree. He could remember the green grass in the sunshine, leading past the trees to uncles and aunts in the sun-blur at the end of the garden, that was so far away to a small boy with small legs. But as he looked back from the Lunchtime of his life he could remember very little, and only the cold-cream affair stayed in his mind as the decades passed and the experiences accumulated to millions and more. Why was it all so dark when he was three?

Apparently, Peter had smeared the cold cream all over the bedroom. He could not remember doing that, but he could remember the wrath that followed. He could remember the sound of a voice telling him, from the dark regions above his head, that he would have to be reprimanded by Grandpa, as if this was a hell in store for him, and he remembered being frightened. Grandpa had never spoken to Peter, apparently, and Grandpa was like London—all remote, unknown, and therefore terrifying. London remained that way until he was well into his teens, but Grandpa became a little less terrifying as he and Grandpa got older, and Grandpa began to speak to him in a ponderously friendly way. Grandpa got to like children very much during the Supper of his days, and he spent his time making them toy railway-stations.

Peter had to walk into the back room where Grandpa was; and it seemed a long way from the doorway, across the carpet, to the vast grey and indistinct height that was Grandpa, standing in front of the mantelpiece and fireplace. Peter remembered the curtains, and the window on to the garden, with more clarity than he remembered Grandpa: perhaps the French windows were easier to look at than Grandpa, who at that moment was the Supreme Terror of All. For the first time in his life Peter felt on his own. He was focused, and his little soul was forced into self-awareness. This is probably why he remembered the experience. Grandpa was not enjoying

10

the part he was being obliged to play either, for being temporarily made into God on Judgement Day by the rest of the family was rather a strain. There was not anybody so suitable in the family for the part of the Sandman as Grandpa, so he was being used, used because he was remote. Peter's daddy was not remote enough from Peter to enable him to play the Sandman part. The cold cream was a big crime and the telling-off had to be of an appropriate magnitude. A policeman would have done if the family could have got hold of one, but there was not a policeman available. And so it was left to Grandpa, and, somewhat unwillingly perhaps, Grandpa consented to impress upon Peter that cold cream should not be smeared all over the bedroom furniture. It does not need pointing out that Peter's crime was big only in comparison with the rest of his good little acts: Peter was normally a minute saint, even if the family did not realize it because of the high standards they had regarding children's behaviour.

Outside the door of the room stood members of the family; inside the room stood only the Sandman and Peter. Peter looked at the grey blur in front of the fireplace, and quailed. The Sandman spoke his piece and Peter listened with the appropriate amount of respectful terror. It was an awful experience, and the voice, that merely told him not to do it again, was terrible for Peter to listen to. There was nothing more to the punishment than having to listen to the voice from the height, but that was quite enough for Peter, and he never smeared cold cream over his parents' bedroom furniture again. After the Talking To, Peter's soul, no more focused by terror and isolation with Grandpa, merged into obscurity again, and it was quite some time before he became aware of himself again.

.   .   .   .   .

Peter's golden curls had gone with his chubby baby face, and now, at the age of nearly five, his hair grew straight and brown, and his face had an anonymous and smooth look. Peter had a sister now, and he was playing with her by the side of the dining-room table, at which Daddy and Mummy were finishing their breakfast. Toys were on the floor by the legs of the modern, extendible dining-room table, and the sun was in the room. Peter was happy.

Peter's parents had moved from the Victorian house in Wimbledon, by the cemetery, to a new house on a mortgage in a new suburb near to London. Peter's mother played a lot of bridge with the neighbours in the evenings, made dresses, smiled a lot, and did gardening. Peter's father was earning only ten pounds a week, but that was a lot before the Second World War. The father was beginning to isolate himself from his fellows, and his persecution complex was beginning, but he had not started rowing Peter's mother every evening yet, and there was still a certain amount of sunshine in the marriage at this time, even though the smile of Peter's mother mainly asserted itself when she was out of the house and walking down the road between the fresh new houses.

Peter's father was drinking his after-breakfast cup of tea at the table above Peter's head, and Peter's parents were talking seriously about something. The dining-room was in the front of the house: it contained a sideboard, a bookcase, and a thick and comfortable carpet. Peter did not know that he was out of luck that day. When the father turned his head, smiled, and looked down at Peter, telling him gently that the boy must go into hospital for a long time, Peter only felt a vague cloud descend over him, for he did not really realize what he was in for. Peter had a gland in his neck that was filled with poison, and he would have to have it cut out.

·　　·　　·　　·　　·

The new house, with its Saturday- and Sunday-tended back garden, with its features of the 1930's, and its chrysanths in the small front garden, had been full of sunshine for Peter, who had not yet gone to school; but in contrast the hospital was grim, and there was no sunshine of the sky or soul. A bed in a ward was no substitute for the small room of his own that he had slept in before, and there was no freedom, and nobody to play with in the hospital. His parents did not seem to visit him in the hospital very often and he was there for an interminably long time. He remembered the room where the nurses and the doctor were, and he remembered his mother telling him outside the room that it would not hurt when they operated on him. A nurse told him that he must breathe in deeply when they put the pad over his nose, and before he knew where he was he was lying on a bed or table, and breathing the stunning smell from the pad over his nose. He could not remember, when he tried to as a man, anything about the wound in his neck afterwards in the hospital, and only a few incidents could he recall that happened during that time of hospitalization. He did remember, however, that it was a long time full of sadness and loneliness.

When he was convalescing in the hospital his mother sent him a comic every week. When the post came he was eager for the tube that was his rolled comic. At the end of the ward, in which there seemed to be no other children, there was a letter-rack that he could see by the big door through which the sister and the nurses came. One day he saw his familiar rolled comic in the rack, but nobody brought it to him. His long sad stay in hospital was not as long as the waiting for that comic to be brought to him from that rack that he stared at for so long. It was all a blur of sadness at that time when he tried to remember it as a man.

A few incidents stayed in his mind—incidents that happened during his grey stay in the hospital.

One day some of the beds were moved to another ward, and the monotony briefly ceased. The metal beds were wheeled through the corridor, beds with children in them. In the corridor, which was grim like everything else, Peter's bed came alongside that of another boy of his own age, and while the beds were left together the other boy, who was more forthcoming than Peter, gave Peter some exciting advice, which Peter thought was rather daring. If Peter's middle-class mother had only known—what would she have said? Peter's mother was always so keen that he should be clean. The man of the world, in the cot-like bed by Peter's similar bed, spoke to Peter through the bars of the bed, and told Peter to pick his nose, and eat from the tip of his probing finger. To the nicely brought-up Peter it was like being told to steal from his mother's purse. It was evil: probably the first really evil thing that Peter had ever done. He did it then, and he did it for many years afterwards. For an hour of comparative enjoyment Peter and the man of the world were temporarily left together in a small room, both of them in their cot-like beds. After that they were both put in the same ward, but the man of the world was a long way away from Peter.

Exactly at this time Peter had another experience, that was of such a kind that it disturbed the hospital. It was the only time that the character of Peter was brought to the notice of the hospital staff, because for the rest of the time Peter was an uncommunicative and charmless child. Peter had been charming when his face was baby-bulgy, and his hair was all golden and curly, but he distinctly lacked charm when that stage was passed. When that stage in his childhood was passed he lacked character also. Peter left his cot-like bed and went to the lavatory. The cell was grim again, and it was high, with a small window high above the bowl. When Peter closed the door after him, and stood in the privacy of the lavatory cell, he slid home the little golden and shiny bolt that was below the handle of the door. After he had sat in the little room for a while, he got up and went to open the door. At first he could not open it, and then the thought that he could not get out made him nervous and quietly hysterical, and he became vastly unintelligent at the task of pulling back the bolt. There was a confusion of hand-worn gleaming brass on the door where the bolt was, and to the feverish and scared eyes of the young boy in his pyjamas, the exact situation of the bolt became hard to find. Eventually they came to see why he had spent so long in the charmless room: they no doubt realized that something must be amiss, also realizing that the cell had not enough charm to make a boy stay in it for so long. They accumulated outside the tall door and called instructions to him, half amused and half worried. At long last Peter managed to release the bolt. The man of the world laughed uninhibitedly when he heard about it.

The experiences that Peter could remember across the decades were few, and these related ones are all of them.

For 'afters' every lunchtime the children in the hospital had rice. Peter was this time in a smaller ward with lots of children, but he was a solitary child, and the proximity of the children did little to alter his loneliness. He dribbled down the side of his cot-bed just for something to do to relieve the monotony, but the chiding nurse did not seem to sympathize. And he had rice, and rice, and rice. He hated the white, boiled, and tasteless stuff, and it stuck in his unwilling throat when he tried to get it down. His stomach heaved with revulsion, and he had to eat it many many times. For the rest of his life he hated rice, and even when he was thirty, and when he had it with curry, he would leave most of it on the side of his plate.

One more thing he remembered about the hospital. One sunny day they put the children out in a courtyard in wheel-chairs with rugs over them. Peter went to sleep in the sun, and they left him out there so as not to disturb him, and they brought all the other lively children in. They remarked on this to Peter when he awoke, and this focused him for a brief moment. The point is that Peter was essentially one of a mass in those days, hardly existing as an individual at all, and the few experiences mentioned gave him his only rare moments of self-awareness. For much of the time until puberty, the great time of self-awareness and awakening, Peter was unaware of himself as an individual or as a separate entity. From the age of five to the age of ten, when he was at a private school, he lived most of the time in a daze, unaware of the world around him, and unaware of himself. The experiences that will be recounted, that Peter had when he was at that school, were the only times that the sunshine of awareness shone through the clouds of Not-Being.

2

The Beginning of Breakfast

PETER'S mother examined the scar on his neck after she had made sure that he had been washed properly. The mother was very careful about cleanliness, and the scar periodically got dirty, making it necessary for the woman to clean it by the process of squeezing its edges with her fingers. The needle-holes, where the thread had been, got filled up with dirt, and Peter found the squeezing pain of his mother's prying finger-tips part stimulating and part irritating. His mother told herself that her son must be wholly clean before he went to school.

Peter had been out of hospital for some time now, and had been to school for a slightly lesser time. He had a blazer with a badge on the breast pocket, and a cap with a peak and a smaller version of the badge on it. He went to a private school that had the preposterously imposing title of The Percival-John Preparatory High School. The T, P, J, P, H and S were incorporated in the badge, and Peter felt a bit of an ass when his aunts asked him where he went to school and he had to reel off this fantastic conglomeration. He wore long socks with coloured bands at the top, black shoes, and short grey trousers. One day he would wear long trousers, and that would be the day indeed.

Across the road from Peter's house lived Martin Maryland, who was dark and mystical-looking, even though he was not very much of a mystery to anybody. Martin liked cap pistols as much as anybody else, and he only had the appearance of mystery because he had dark shiny straight hair, and dark eyes in a dark-skinned face. Martin was a friend of Peter, if their relationship could accurately be called a friendship: it was better describable as a relationship, because like most children they had their quarrels. Peter and Martin merged outside their houses and went off to school together. Next to Peter's house was a bare patch of land, a break in the row of houses, that led to the main road that ran some distance behind the back fence of Peter's back garden. The male commuters, who lived in Peter's road, used the unbuilt stretch of land as a short cut to the railway-station that was some way along the main road, and there was a path worn by many polished shoes through the middle of the waste ground. Half past eight in the morning saw a stream of newly breakfasted and spruced-up business men striding up the slight incline to the main road to catch the train to town. Peter's father had been one of the stream somewhat earlier in the day.

Peter and his friend went up to the main road, along the main road, past the traffic-lights where Vernonsdale Drive crossed the main road, down the hill to the railway-station, and a little further on they turned into a foliage-bordered road of some privacy which led them to the road where their school had its location. The school was merely a Victorian house in a row of such houses, of which the lower floor was used as the school; there being two classrooms, a long room where they sometimes played when it was wet and where they hung their coats, and a yard at the back of the house where they played when it was fine. The two classrooms were full of desks, and they were front rooms looking on to the mostly deserted road. There were two teachers in this private school, one of them—the headmistress—a grey-haired and ageing lady called Mrs. Percival-John, and a younger, be-spectacled, and rather stern female, who had less to do with Peter's education than the headmistress.

Peter was in love. She was dark-haired, pretty-featured, with large brown eyes, and her abundant curly hair and soft ways tore Peter's heart into shreds. But Mary-Jane did not notice Peter, because Peter was not an interesting boy, and Martin got most of her notice. Peter played with a yellow-haired girl called Esther, who treated him without the disdain of Mary-Jane, but he was not attracted to Esther whom he called Es for reasons of linguistic economy. There was also Semantha: she was a sharp-featured girl with straight black hair, whose brother went to the school too; and Semantha and her brother lived at the corner of the road in which the school was. But although Semantha was not as stand-offish as Mary-Jane, Peter's heart was not stirred by her.

As Peter and Martin approached the school, they saw the accumulation of children waiting outside because it had not yet opened. They joined the group, Martin mixing readily and Peter standing on the outside of the group casting sheep's-eyes at Mary-Jane. Everybody accepted the fact that Mary-Jane was the prettiest girl in the small school, and she wore, always, long brown socks that came up to her slightly nobbly knees. Peter, even at his tender age, was aware of the lack of aesthetics of Mary-Jane's knees, but though he often looked down when she was near him, he was far more conscious of her long curly hair and large brown eyes. It is debatable whether Mary-Jane knew he was in love with her, and probably nobody but Peter knew the full extent of his feelings towards the self-confident little charmer.

Harry was unique in the gathering of schoolchildren outside the school. Harry was worldly. Far more worldly than the boy in the hospital. He had an atmosphere about him that none of the other children had, and he wore a suit, which was enough to put him apart on its own, for none of the other children wore suits. Harry had not started at the age of five: he had come at a later age, and there was a suggestion of a lack of permanency about his relationship to the school. Harry had a waistcoat, and a watch that was in a pocket in the brown waistcoat: this struck the other children as fabulous. He wore his suit carelessly, in great contrast to the other children, who were carefully clothed by proud mothers who used the iron a great deal. Harry was a creature from another world, and he vaguely suggested racetracks and Soho. Probably Harry was aping a father who lived in such an atmosphere. He had a careless grin, and he knew he was

19

different from the other children. He was not middle-class, and heaven knows why he was at the school for carefully brought-up little children. Harry knew that if you went into a telephone kiosk and pressed button B you might be lucky and get a couple of pennies coming into the trough below the coin box, coins that some impatient person had not bothered to retrieve. He successfully demonstrated this to a group of the children outside the sweet shop by the station on one occasion, and he was a hero in their eyes because of that, for they were all so carefully brought up that they could never know about such things except from Harry. Another thing that there was about Harry was that he always had a sixpence or some pennies on him, unlike the other children who had no financial position whatsoever. Harry was respected by the other children, but he did not seem to respect himself very much, although he enjoyed showing off his particular talents of comparative worldliness. And finally it must be said that Harry was good-natured and not at all stand-offish. When he talked to Peter he did not make him feel inferior, as the other children did when they spoke to Peter. The other children despised Peter because Peter had an inferiority complex and stood on the outside of the clique.

Why was Peter so inhibited? Why was he unsure of himself?—so unsure of himself that he spent a great deal of those early days in a daze, escaping from the realities by daydreaming? Even his daydreams were blurred as was his personality—if you could say he had such a thing as a personality. Peter *was* a dream, afraid for some inexplicable reason to wake up and live. He was unsure, unintelligent, dull, and uninteresting, wasting those years that could have been so full of life.

The reason might have been this: The bridge parties had stopped at his home, and nobody ever came to call. Auntie Margaret came infrequently, but Auntie Maggie and Auntie Myrtle, or the neighbour housewives, had stopped coming to play bridge in the dining-room in the evenings. Arthur, Peter's father, was getting rather difficult, and he put people off when they came to visit. The marital rot was setting in.

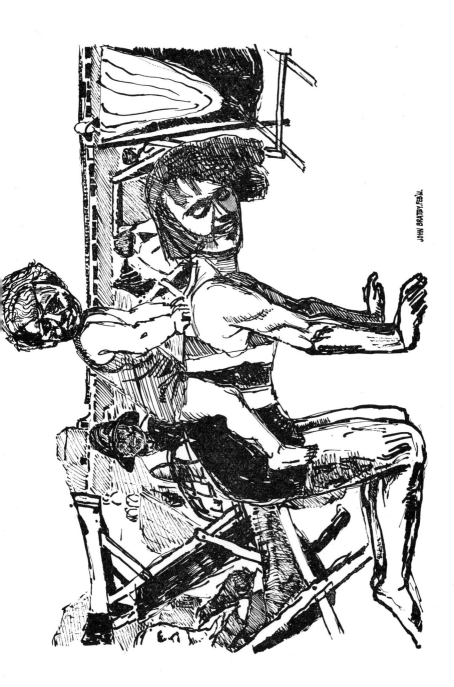

Peter knew that the atmosphere in his home was rather queer, and perhaps he felt his inferiority complex because of that. He knew for instance that Martin across the road had a more normal home life than he had, and as he knew that his father was getting odd he felt different from the other children because of these things. His mother was protecting herself from the strain of her husband's wearing aggression by becoming reserved and within herself, and her face was becoming expressionless and grey. The good years had passed, and her flapper days were just a memory. The days when she flapped around with the chaps with her sister Bella were a long way away, and a living death was taking hold of her. She put a scarf round her hair to protect it from the dust, and grimly ran the vacuum-cleaner over the dining-room carpet, with a perpetual cigarette in her still-handsome face; and with a weary acceptance of her lot she did the daily chores and resorted to smoking her fags. She came alive when they went on their annual holiday to Little Landow by Sands, but when Peter reached the age of nine the holiday snaps showed her frowning into the sun, with six tramlines across her grey forehead, the sun-drenched beach-hut they had rented photographed in the background. But Peter was not nine yet.

Peter's father had begun to 'jaw, jaw, jaw' at Peter's mother in an aggressive way for long unceasing periods when he got home from work in the evenings, letting out the results of his maturing persecution complex upon the poor woman, who just stood and unwillingly listened, afraid to walk away or to utter. Peter would look at them standing in the centre of the room, as his father went on and on, and Peter lost his respect for his parents. Children who believe in their parents as people to respect have a confidence in themselves that Peter had not got. The children at the preparatory school sensed Peter's lack of confidence in himself and they made his life a misery because of what they instinctively knew about the boy. Such is the cruelty of children in the jungle world of the very young.

Peter stood on the outskirts of the group of children who were waiting for the doors of the school to open, and silently he remembered the jawing voice of his father, and the scene that had occurred the previous evening and the evenings before that: the evenings were always the same, loaded with his father's incessant monotonous and complaining voice. Arthur had black hair that was in tight and minute waves on his head. He was very proud of his hair, and he set the waves when he was in the bathroom before breakfast every morning. He had heavy horn-rimmed glasses, behind which dark aggressive eyes encircled with shadows and dark bags beneath were magnified by the heavy lenses of his spectacles: he was extremely myopic. His skin had darkened as he grew older, and his strong body and face had an aggression to them that was a manifestation of his aggressive nature, the powerful urges of which were frustrated completely. As a result of this complete frustration he was very irritable, and his nature became twisted, as his marriage grew older, and the stupidity of his life impressed itself upon him more and more. When he was younger he had not been frustrated, because he had been able to express himself, and his urges, in the activities that are those of a young man. But as his married life wore on and on, his urges piled up inside him unreleased, they went sour within him, and he became like a caged and unexercised dog spiritually, yapping angrily to be freed. Peter's mother had been a very good-looking woman in her happy and youthful days, but now she was prematurely grey-haired, and strain was lined indelibly upon her visage. She was still a handsome woman, above middle height, bespectacled, heavy-boned, and with livid great birthmarks over the backs of her hands. She dressed well. Certain phrases and parts, from these one-sided rows, impressed themselves upon Peter's mind, so that he always associated his father with them. 'I'm not going to have anybody browbeating me,' and, 'I'm not going to have people talking about me behind my back,' said Arthur, and his persecution complex was revealed in such complaints that he forced into the ears of his weary wife. When his home-life was of this nature, it is no wonder that Peter felt ashamed, and developed an inferiority complex. Arthur suspected that people ridiculed him, and although they might not have done at first they did afterwards, as a result of his aggression born of the suspicion that they ridiculed him. Arthur felt that people thought that he was below them, and because of that Peter lost the respect that a boy usually feels for his father; and without a father to look up to he felt at a disadvantage with the other children in the pompously named preparatory school.

· · · · ·

Mrs. Percival-John sat her at desk by the window, and the children wrote in their exercise books, while Peter cast sidelong and admiring glances at the fair Mary-Jane. Mary-Jane could even draw better than anybody else in the class, and when she drew a floor-handbrush from imagination the groups of bristles were drawn at angles to each other, just as they should be, while all the other children drew their brushes from imagination with the bristles drawn all wrong. Mary-Jane was obviously deserving of Peter's enraptured admiration, even though she was perhaps just a little bit spoilt and just a little bit conceited and uppity.

The children had a plan, and it was directed against the boy Peter. He sensed that there was something in the air and he was wary. Some of the glances that were directed at him as he sat at his desk made him aware that the others were up to something that might be to his disadvantage.

When the breaktime came in the middle of the morning all the children went out into the small enclosed playground and waited for Peter to follow, but Peter stayed in the classroom where he knew he would be safe: the classroom was holy ground and the children would not dare to harm him there.

It was Peter's reserved nature that they resented, and all the extroverted children banded together to persecute the isolated introvert. It is not safe to be a lonely one if you are a child amongst children. They will attack the lame duckling. It was just a matter of animal instincts: one of the primitive laws of instinctive behaviour of the child jungle. Peter had not done them any harm, it was just that they resented his

24

difference. Later on, in his next school, when he had changed from 'bullied' to 'the bully', he was to lead the crowd in the persecution of a boy who was isolated, a boy who was in the unenviable position that Peter found himself in at that time, in the classroom of Mrs. Percival-John's school for little primitives posing as dear little things.

Peter sat in the deserted classroom and was apprehensive, to put it mildly. The two teachers were off the scene, and his only defence was the sanctuary of the room of learning. The persecutors sent a representative to try to get Peter into the playground. She was a nice little girl, with a false smile, who did not deceive Peter when she asked him sunnily to come into the playground. If he had not been suspicious before, her request would have aroused his suspicions, because nobody ever asked him to join them at play, and he was accustomed to stand alone watching the others play. The little girl returned to the persecutors without success, and they decided on another approach, while Peter stared unhappily at the large map that hung on the wall behind the rows of desks. They decided that charm would not lure Peter into the arena, so they wholeheartedly abandoned that line and sent in Semantha, who was a girl not renowned for her charm exactly. She came with a threat. She came into the classroom and threatened Peter, her dark eyes wild with fury beneath her black lank fringe. For some reason her threat had the desired effect, and unwillingly the boy Peter followed her through the dark corridor, through the coat-room, and into the yard, where all the children were waiting, and where the bicycle-racks were. They were watching him as he walked on to the stretch of concrete.

'Let's play leapfrog,' said somebody to Peter. Peter was never asked to play leapfrog, and he knew that he was in for something, but he was resigned to it by now, and he had not the ability to resist the combined wills of the children to persecute him. They all bent down in rows, and the frogs at the back stood up and leapfrogged over the others. 'Kick me,' said the notice that one of the jumpers pinned on Peter's backside before jumping over him, and unaware of the notice

Peter wondered why they all started to kick him. It was not the kicks that made him cry, it was the exhibition of hate.

The children were called in to class, but the weeping Peter stayed out of sight in the playground. When the back door into the house closed after the last child, Peter ran out of the playground, through the alley by the side of the school, and all the way home. He felt it was a desperate thing to do, because to desert school in the middle of the morning was just not done, but he was prompted by an extreme misery.

When he got home he went into the dining-room where he found his mother in a corner looking most unattractive with the vacuum-cleaner. She looked up with anger from the misery of housework, and he received no sympathy from her: perhaps she did not understand the situation.

When afternoon school had finished, the children, afraid of what they had done, or instructed by the headmistress, came to make amends. Only one or two of them came, and they stood at the front-garden gate of Peter's house, as he watched them from the dining-room window. They smiled at him, and beckoned for him to come out, but Peter did not trust them and they went away again.

Peter went to school the next day, and the children acted as if nothing had happened. The young teacher with the grim face came into the classroom, where the children were milling preparatory to the entry of Mrs. Percival-John, and she said: 'Good Morning, Peter,' in a manner that Peter found unsympathetic. But perhaps the poor grim lady was trying to be nice, but had just lost the knack as it were. She certainly would not have said 'Good Morning' to him on any other occasion, and Peter knew that she had spoken to him because he had run away. He felt that he was being briefly reprimanded.

3

The Second-hand Bike

BALHAM was feverish some way past the railway-station
which was called that of Balham Minor; and far up the hill,
on the other side of the area in which Peter lived, was an
area called Shamber Hill. Further up the hill lived the rich,
and it was there that a millionaire scrap-dealer lived at a
later date. The golf-course, called Shamber golf-course, pro-
vided a nice walk for Peter and his father on Sunday mornings; but when Peter's father went for a walk on his own, and
Peter asked him where he had been, he would say enigmati-
cally: 'There and back to see how far it is,' which seemed to
Peter to be a completely unnecessary piece of subterfuge, in
view of the fact that Peter was well aware his father's journey
had been completely innocent and not worth making a
mystery about, even though Peter did not know exactly
where his father had been. Arthur took an absurd delight in
enigmatic answers for no justifiable reason whatsoever, and
when asked his opinion about anything he would smile a
stupid personal smile to himself and say: 'It all depends,'
without giving any clue as to what it all depended upon.
Such an attitude, by a father to his son, was sure to cause
a sense of acute bafflement in the son's mind, and no doubt
this explained a great deal.

In the Shamber Hill area lived Hugh Hambledon, a boy
a year older than Peter, the son of a rich father, owner of an
undersized two-wheeled bicycle, and a boy who possessed a
great deal of self-assurance. He was a peculiar child, who

27

pushed boys who were on roller-skates to make them fall down, until a stray milkman told him that it was not done to push a man on wheels. Hugh had small calculating eyes and was domineering. Peter, on the other hand, possessed only a three-wheeled bicycle, because he had not graduated to a two-wheeled one. Arthur bought Hugh's undersized two-wheeled bicycle for Peter, and painted it, until it looked so nice that Hugh regretted selling it. Arthur was not a practical man, and the painting of the bicycle was uncharacteristic, the generosity of the act being uncharacteristic also.

Peter rode to school on the two-wheeled bicycle, and it was a status-symbol. However, the fact that he now possessed such a bicycle was not impressive enough to make Mary-Jane fall in love with him. Sometimes he bicycled to the preparatory school and sometimes he walked. One day he was with Martin at the top of the waste stretch of ground that led to the main road, and Hugh came upon the scene, Hugh's house being some distance away up the main road. Peter and Martin were being quite friendly at that moment, not because Peter was worth being friendly with, but because Peter was the only boy Martin could find to play with and walk with that morning. Peter, and the boy across the road called Martin, were making their way down the incline of waste ground towards their respective homes, and they could see Peter's father in the garden of Peter's house. Peter's mother used to say that Arthur did his gardening in his vest because he wanted to attract the widow-woman next door, and it was true that Arthur liked talking to the widow-woman over the garden fence, but whether or not Arthur's deltoids were big enough to cause her to feel amorous about him is a debatable point, because Arthur was not athletic-looking. However, Arthur was gardening in a pure white vest, and he was so middle-class that it looked positively indecent. Arthur was the private sort of man who would manage to look positively shocking in the street if he was dressed in shorts and sandals: that was before the Second World War. But Arthur only went so far as to garden in his vest, and he only took to walking down the street in sandals (with socks) when he lost his job at the gin company and started to crumble. It is significant that when Arthur started to disintegrate at a later date, the chief sign of his disintegration was the fact that he had taken to walking down the street in sandals; all the road knew then that something was seriously amiss, because Arthur in sandals was as decadent as Scott Fitzgerald. Before he crumbled, when his marriage broke and he started living on his Savings Certificates, Arthur was respectable, respectable and private. He was so private that he hated the fact that the commuters, on their way to and from the station, could look over his garden fence: he wanted a garden with high brick walls, although perhaps he did not mind the fence between him and the widow-woman being only five feet high.

As Arthur was raking over a patch of bare earth for the eighth time—Arthur was meticulously neat, and he loved making bare earth look precious, with all the lumps of earth made all tiny—he saw the three boys meet at the top of the incline, and then he went on making the earth lumps smaller and smaller so that the patch was covered over with minute neat particles, even smaller than the carefully tended waves of hair on his head. When Arthur wrote a letter he would take half an hour to write a page, for his writing, done with a thick gold nib, was terribly neat, with small, thick, and round letters. When Arthur wrote a letter it was a ceremony and an occasion, homage to the god of Preciousness, whoever that might be.

Hugh came up to the two boys, domineering as usual. He ordered them to fight each other, and reluctantly the two boys obeyed because they were frightened of the older Hugh. They lunged at each other without much heart and then they saw Arthur climbing over the garden fence. Now this was a preposterous sight. Arthur played cricket in the back garden with his son, but there was a strict sense of decorum present when he did it, and it was characteristic of him that he did physical things with a restraint in accordance with the laws of middle-class behaviour. Climbing fences was wild. Climbing fences was just not Arthur, and Peter was somewhat shocked in the centre of his soul by what he saw. Perhaps this

29

experience had a profound effect upon him in his later life, and perhaps it did not.

Perhaps Arthur had been waiting for such an occasion as this. Perhaps he had imagined himself defending his son from danger. He certainly ran up to the boys with an unusual alacrity, and with a gleam in his eyes that was rare. Peter felt that his father was not interfering for Peter's sake so much as for Arthur's sake. Perhaps it was for Arthur the chance to play a part. And then, alternatively, perhaps the motivation was that Arthur loved his son; but as Arthur never showed such a feeling towards Peter, Peter did not feel that that was the motivation that caused his father to sternly wave Martin away down the well-trodden incline.

Arthur had misinterpreted the situation: understandably. Arthur thought that Martin had attacked Peter, for he was unaware of the fact that the evil one was, not Martin, but Hugh, the calculating boy with the pig-like eyes set in the wide flat face. In fact Arthur talked in a friendly way to Hugh, and pointed a straight imperious arm down the incline, as an order to the perplexed and quivering Martin. Peter, being an idiot, did nothing to put things in their correct perspective: he was not verbacious by nature, and was not used to communicating with his father. His thoughts were whirling, and they remained unuttered as he went with his father down the incline, past the brick building where the boys let off their catherine-wheels in the daytime in November, and through the side gate into the back garden.

It was only then that Peter found his tongue—it had been in his mouth all the time—and dizzily explained to his father that the villain of the piece was really Hugh Hambledon, the boy who now owned a brand-new, undersized, two-wheeled bicycle. Arthur did not like to find that he had made an idiot of himself, and in a remote manner he explained that to his son. Arthur never apologized to Martin, for he resented the family across the road, as he resented everybody, especially his wife's brothers and sisters when they came to call, which, as a result, they did not do any more if they could possibly

JOHN BRATBY FEB 61

help it. Arthur's aggressive attitude was a bore to them, and he was an outsider in relationship to his wife's kin and to his own. It was hard to feel sympathy for Arthur, but if one tried hard enough no doubt one could find grounds for sympathy somewhere—if one tried terribly hard, and knew some of the causative factors that made Arthur twisted after the first years of his marriage.

Arthur had been a wine-taster when he was twenty to thirty, and then he got married to a younger wife whom he treated in those days in a fatherly fashion. He was charming at that time, and when he had been in the Royal Flying Corps he had been one of the boys. Iris, Peter's mother, had been one of many children produced by Peter's small grandmother, and she had been truly beautiful in those days. Arthur's mother had been a Jewess, but this had been kept a strict secret, just as a few more things were kept a strict secret. Arthur was secretive, a hereditary trait. Arthur's father had made sporting guns; and had lived in a big house, with a horse and open carriage for the transport of the family. Iris had not loved Arthur, but he asked her to marry him with such persuasiveness that she gave in to him, and then after they were married the usual thing happened, and Arthur gradually, as the years passed, took her for granted. Arthur's parents and brothers and sisters were all fine and nice people, but, seven generations before them, the family had been as loose as a sheet on a clothes-line moved by the slightest chance breeze. Great, great, great, great, great, great-grandfather had been a wild one, and English to the core. So had that ancient gentleman's brother, and so had his sister. Arthur's great, great, great, great, great, great-grandfather had liked low ladies, and as he was rich, they had liked him.

Arthur's great great-grandfather had been as sane as a Freudian analysis and in the following generations sanity had been a predominant feature. But insanity could occur, just as in every other family, and when it did, it was in Arthur. Arthur's madness was in such a diluted form that it was hardly noticeable, but it was enough to make him twisted

32

—just a little twisted. Arthur knew about this weakness in himself, but he prudently did not tell Iris about it until he got her to the altar and well married to him. When Iris found there was something amiss she remembered the tale of Arthur's ancestor and wrongly jumped to the conclusion that his wild forbear had contracted venereal disease. Letting her imagination run riot, in a way that was very unlike the normal Iris, she looked back in time and saw the doctor put him in a steam-tub, with his head projecting from the tub, and when this did not cure the trouble, fancied the poor man rotting away in a rather unpleasant fashion. Then, before he died— some while before he died—he would have given his wife a child, and the child would have had the germs within him, and been mad. The child would have borne fruit eventually, with the aid of the woman that he married, but the fruit would be infected by heredity and even his son in turn would have inherited a degree of madness, although the germs would be less by then. As the generations passed the madness, caused by the hereditary V.D., would become more and more diluted, and a few generations would be skipped. But she made up her mind that the madness had recurred in Arthur, and she was very angry at the thought that he should have married her knowing this, never forgiving him. She even went to a general practitioner, and asked the lady if Peter might inherit it. The lady doctor ridiculed her fears, but Iris was still angry, and persisted in nursing her imaginary grievance. This caused a breach between her and Arthur, who had a twisted force within him that he was afraid of. He was afraid to allow this force to be active, and he suppressed it with disastrous results, for it could not be contained satisfactorily. He was afraid of his temper, and he never hit his son for fear he would lose his self-control. Afraid of losing his self-control, Arthur continually stuffed back his urges into himself, and he imprisoned the life-force within himself, a life-force that had a vitality born from the twist in his nature. This is probably why Arthur never allowed himself to be ambitious, and why he stagnated in a frustrated fashion for most of his married life, only letting out his frustration by rowing his wife evening after evening, in a monotonous fashion. Arthur became suspicious of the whole world, and looked out at life with a peculiar self-conscious and mirthless smile in his be-spectacled eyes, eyes that looked golden, but were not.

Before, Arthur was all right; but when he was some time married, had bought a house to hide in and to brood in, and the monotony of his married life had established itself firmly with its nine-to-six job from Monday to Friday, and its lack of horizons, he began to rot, slowly and undramatically, finding no means of self-expression, except in polishing his shoes before work in the mornings in the car-less garage, writing his meticulous letters with their handwritten dupli-cates, and raking bare earth until the particles were as minute as the waves in his thick black hair.

Surely somebody sympathized with Arthur? But Arthur was so difficult to sympathize with, for he was so aggressive, and he hated pretty extensively. Once, when he was in his twenties, he had had friends, and nobody had thought that he was queer; but as he grew older, and the skin on his face grew harsher, and lost its freshness, he came to a time when he had not a friend in the world, except his hair with its waves, and his thick golden fountain-pen nib—they were firm friends and they always gave satisfaction.

Iris, on the other hand, developed after her marriage in reaction to her husband, rather than as an individual. Iris would have been a different woman if she had married some-one else, while on the other hand Arthur would have developed in the same way whomever he had been married to. There is more to say about Arthur than there is to say about Iris, because he was the stronger character, and she spent most of her time adjusting herself to him, or protecting the sensitivities of her soul from the onslaught of the overpowering man with the dark Jew face, by becoming hard, and by becoming remote. In his way Arthur was as remote as Iris. He was afraid to love his children, and so was Iris. The two children were brought up in an atmosphere that was to a certain extent inhuman. There were kisses at bedtime, it is true, but mani-festations of affection towards the children by the parents

were nevertheless rare. It must be admitted that as he lay in his bed at night Peter would receive a kiss from a cigarette-smelling mouth that was his mother's; and he would at times be expected to kiss his father's leathery and pipe-tobacco-smelling cheek; but these were formal gestures, and, if such an unexpected thing as a passionate clutch to his mother's bosom by her had happened, he would have been as surprised as he would have been if he had been given an electric-train set. Her bosom, though adequate in size, was not motherly anyway, and it did not matter how big it might have been, it still would have been remote, now sexless, and not what you would describe as motherly. Iris had not the disposition that would have been necessary to make her bosom motherly. It can be readily understood why Peter grew up unable to make friends. Friendship and demonstrations of affection were foreign to him: he had never come across them in his experience. Peter grew up remote from his parents, in the same way as they were remote from him, and he grew up remote from everybody. He was not a lovable child because he did not know how to love. When his mother died he had to force himself to cry. And when his father died he felt nothing at all. When his mother died he was in his teens, and he felt ashamed that he did not cry instinctively. He felt that he ought to love his mother enough for the tears to come, but he had to use a device to make the tears come, and even then they only came once, and never came again. He sat in the empty house and looked at the doorway of the room, the doorway through which his mother had come with the dinner and tea so often, and in the shadows by the door he tried to see the memory of his mother, and summoned up all the emotionalism that he could muster. He tried so hard that he did eventually see his mother standing there, and as he dwelt hard on the realization that he would never see her ever again, and that he was now alone in the wide world, the black surges of emotion swirled around him, and with his eyes on the vision of his brave, near-blind mother, he cried; but the tears were of self-pity because he was alone in the world. His mother had loved her children in her reserved kind of way, but as she had never told them that, they never found love for her. Long afterwards, when he was a man, and he could understand what had been going on inside his mother, Peter felt affection for the woman who had tried so hard to see him well educated, the woman who had so wanted him to make a success of his life, but he could never feel love.

. . . . .

There was a girl at the preparatory school called Camellia. Camellia was a big girl, and she was not in Mrs. Percival-John's class, but was in the class in the other front room, taught by the younger woman who was a bit grim, and who also looked as if she did not know how to love. Camellia lived in a road that was at the end of the road that Peter lived in, and although she was under ten she was adult to the younger Peter. Very soon Camellia would leave the preparatory school to go to a secondary school. Camellia was of a commanding disposition, and she was looked up to by the younger children because of her maturity. Her face was broad, her eyes big, and she felt that she should act in a responsible manner. She had a younger sister, and Peter was a little bit in love with the younger sister, although he loved Camellia the best, for they did not come any better than Camellia, who did not think that Peter was worth looking at or talking to.

One day, when Peter went to school on his second-hand, undersized, two-wheeled bicycle, the machine with the child-size wheels, he pedalled up to the waiting group outside the school, and Camellia, for want of anything better to do, came over to Peter, attracted by his bicycle, and not his personality. She wanted to ride the bicycle, but Peter was reluctant to let her do so. There were so few things he cared about in his life that those things that he did care about he cared about to an extreme, and the small-wheeled bicycle he cared about deeply; a treasured possession. But Camellia knew how to compel Peter, for she was of a commanding disposition. Peter gave in, but he had to ride behind her on the tiny luggage-rack above the back mudguard; he would not let her ride the bike on her own, for he had horrible visions of her riding away round the corner and off for hours and hours. Camellia started off down the road, and Peter clung precariously on the back, watching the road speed past below him. There were millions of nasty little stones on the surface of the road, and Peter was afraid that he would fall off, for his position was not very safe. He was so sure that he would fall off that he almost helped himself to do that, and as the machine went down the road, away from the front of the school, he slipped down, hung on to the bike with both hands, and was dragged along the small stone-covered road on his bare knees. Camellia stopped the bicycle and Peter found his feet. From both knees issued blood, and in the wounds were embedded tiny stones. Peter's mind closed up with fear and he felt very terrified. He had not been wounded as bad as this in his life before. Becoming the comparative adult, Camellia took him into the school where his wounds were attended to by the headmistress. Camellia felt frightened underneath her composed, big-girl exterior, for she felt that she was to blame for what had occurred. Camellia took Peter home to his mother, for he was not expected to attend classes that day. Peter felt rather important because of the attention he was receiving, also pleased that he had been given the honour to walk all the way home with that big girl Camellia, and, in addition, dizzy with fear because of the accident and the vision of the horrible racing road. He also felt that he was a wounded soldier which was rather nice. His mother did not regard the incident as very important, however, somewhat to the disappointment of Peter, but he felt rather proud when his mother told his father, when his father came in from work that evening. Such incidents were the highlights in his uneventful and somewhat grim little life. He could still just see the scar on his right knee amongst the curly hairs when he was thirty-three, and he was still rather proud of it when he was twenty, the reason being that he was Peter, and Peter was like that.

.   .   .   .   .

It was cold that winter, and the water froze if it was out-side. Peter pulled the garden wheelbarrow to the kitchen door, and filled it with water. The next morning the water had frozen, and Peter was pleased. His mother poured cab-bage-water into the wheelbarrow, on top of the frozen water, and when that froze it made the ice a lovely light-green colour, which made Peter ecstatic, and he almost loved his mother for the cabbage-water contribution. The wheel-barrow, with its lovely load of transparent green, stayed out-side the kitchen door for days, and Peter loved the ice that he could stare at, and he loved it with a contained passion. It was important to him.

Peter was walking home with Martin, Camellia, and Camellia's sister, but they were not talking to him because he was not interesting enough: he was only with them because he went home by the same route. There was a long fence opposite Peter's house, that led from the turn in the road to Martin's house, and this fence bordered the garden that be-longed to the house where the B.B.C. organist lived: he had a big car and seemed very glamorous to Peter. The organist was very much out of place in the road, because he was not middle-class, because he was not a nine-to-six man, and because he was famous. Organists were popular just before the war.

Peter had an inordinate respect for famous people, and he had never talked to one of them. If he had had the chance to talk to a famous person he would have been scared out of his wits by the magnitude of the occasion. The great organist had been by his car in the road one day—his car was always out in the road, looking dusty and magnificent—and Arthur had actually had the cheek to talk to the great organist, while Peter stood fearfully in the background, feeling thoroughly ashamed of his father for presuming to make contact with a member of the mighty class of people who got into the papers. In Peter's mind there was a vast breach between the ordinary people and the famous, and he did not feel that it was at all proper for that gap to be bridged. The famous were like royalty, and you did not just go up to royalty and speak to them. But that was just like his father, thought Peter—his father was quite abnormal, and positively embarrassing. His father had said afterwards that he would get the organist to take Peter up to see the B.B.C. one day, and even Peter's mother was shocked at the presumption of this. Peter's father never did go so far as to ask the organist to do that, however, and Peter was glad. Peter liked the idea of having a look at the B.B.C. or the Mint as much as any little boy, but to ask the organist to take Peter to the B.B.C. with him was so improper that Peter would have been ashamed to go. After all, royalty and the famous were not any good unless they were unapproachable. If Peter had written to the Queen, and the Queen had answered his letter, Peter would have been a quietly hysterical mess for a year. The famous and royalty were gods, gods were up there in the sky somewhere, and you just could not walk up into the sky, and that was that. Only an abnormality like his father would try to walk up into the sky. But there was one thing to be thankful for: his father did not make a habit of such transgressions.

The little group of schoolchildren walked along by the organist's fence, totally unconcerned by the fact that Peter would be leaving them at any moment to go to his house. Peter was thinking about his wheelbarrow of transparent green ice, ice that had unfathomable depths of wonderful shades of green down to the bottom of the wheelbarrow, and he had been thinking about it all day. He was terribly proud of his green ice, and the properties of cabbage-water were positively marvellous to him. He desperately wanted to show the ice to Camellia's sister. Trying to conceal his emotions about the cabbage-water, Peter asked Camellia's sister if she would just come for a moment and look at the ice. Grinning at his idiocy, the girl refused at first, but she could see that he wanted her to so desperately that she then acceded to his request, and, while her big sister and Martin waited impatiently outside, she went with Peter to look at his world of green wonder. Needless to say, she did not see in the ice what Peter saw in it, and she left Peter by his wheelbarrow feeling that there was something not quite right about life if a little girl could not see the amazing beauty that he saw in the translucent green ice. He asked his mother if she saw it was wonderful, and she said she did, but probably she did not.

4

The Rows were Stronger Now

THE rows were stronger now, and when Peter went to school he could hear his father's voice in his head: he could not hear the words, but he could hear the characteristic sound, and the monotonous, aggressive, relentless 'jaw, jaw, jaw', as his mother called it. Peter heard the noise every evening, and it stayed with him all day in his memory. The sound of his father's voice did not need to be consciously remembered by the boy: it came into his head without his wanting it to, and it would not go away. It was an unvarying, interminable, angry, and inescapable continuation of sound: the verbal manifestation of his father's frustration. Peter never ever listened to the words, even though they were said in his presence, and all he heard was the anger: the sustained, inexhaustible, and monotonous anger. The life-force of Arthur was not put into his work, it was put into his rowing. Arthur talked until he was tired, and then he went up into his bedroom, where only he slept, and he would sit on the side of the bed and think about how he was persecuted, until he had enough energy to enable him to go downstairs again and have another session, a bit quieter this time, while the children were in bed. Iris did not look forward to the evenings.

Arthur's aggression was even: there were no highs and there were no lows: it was steady. He never went berserk, and he never sat in fierce silences. He never hit his wife, and he was never violent, except on two occasions: one when he lost his glasses in the chrysanthemums and could not see, and two when Iris slapped his face. 'Jaw, jaw, jawing' was his métier, and he hardly ever departed from that line. On one very rare occasion he performed an act of hate, but that was isolated, for he did not do hateful acts, he only talked, and talked, and talked, with a stream of hate in it.

Iris went out to do her shopping, and sometimes she went to see relatives, but her social life had become poverty-stricken. When she was invited to go and see an old friend and his wife she hesitated, because she was not really allowed to do such things. He had known her before her marriage, but he was harmless, and only wanted to renew their acquaintance in the most proper fashion. Iris went.

He brought her back in his car that evening. It was in the late summer. Iris had taken Peter with her, and had spent most of the afternoon talking to her old friend's wife, and the old friend had talked to her when he got back from work. Arthur was waiting with jealousy.

Arthur was quite sincere: he really thought that he had to make a stand, and he really thought that the old friend was after Iris. Iris and the man found Arthur looking somewhat pale and exhausted when they entered the house. Arthur was not eager to do what he thought he had to do, and the nervous strain of waiting for them to return had exhausted him. Rowing a woman was what he knew how to do, but putting a man in his place was not what Arthur knew how to do.

At first there was a rather unpleasant verbal exchange in the doorway of the kitchen. The old friend of Iris was a pleasant man, who certainly did not want any trouble, and he was mostly silent. Arthur made accusations in a voice that had lost its usual body, and which was shrill. Iris told him concernedly not to be a fool; she was not so much angered by her husband's jealousy as touched: it was the nearest to a demonstration of affection for her that she had got from him for many years. She was wrong to interpret his jealousy in this way, however, because he did not love her now, and it was just that his pride was hurt by the thought that another man might be tampering with his property.

It was getting dark now, and in the half-light in the front garden Arthur rowed with the innocent man, as the innocent man tried to make his departure. Arthur raised his fists to the man and attacked him. Remembering that Arthur was very myopic, the man did not hit back but instead knocked off Arthur's glasses, thereby rendering Arthur somewhat ineffective in battle. The man was a decent sort, realized that Arthur was being more pathetic than anything else, and did not want to hurt Arthur. As Arthur floundered, the world around him indistinct, and as Iris prepared to make the supper in the kitchen in a state of some agitation, the man got into his car and drove away, never to be seen again—understandably.

It was unthinkable that Arthur should not go to work the next morning. The pattern of the family's life revolved around Arthur going to work five days a week and in the mornings on Saturday. If Arthur could not go to work that was a crisis. They were middle-class people, and middle-class breadwinners went to work five and a half days a week, except for two weeks in the summer when they went to the seaside, and except for Christmas and days like that. Daddy must go to work. But the following morning, from the sanctuary of the bathroom, where presumably he could not see to set his hair, the spectacle-less Arthur threatened not to go to work until his glasses were found in the front garden. It was a family crisis. Iris was distraught in a calm sort of way, and she and the two children went into the garden and looked. The front path led down to the front gate, bordered by narrow beds of chrysanthemums. To one side was the drive-in to the garage, and to the other side was a tiny lawn bordered on four sides by narrow flower-beds. Somewhere lay Arthur's thick-lensed, horn-rimmed spectacles, and the three members of the family bent down everywhere in the front garden. Peter found them, and normality was quickly restored, and the three of them would have given thanks if they had been religious.

This incident was uncharacteristic of Arthur: he was a 'jaw, jaw, jaw' man, and his aggression was even, consistent, and unchanging. He hit Iris once, but that too was uncharacteristic. One evening when she was standing by the dining-room table, being forced to listen as usual to Arthur's complaining voice, both of them standing as was customary on such occasions, an urge rose within her, and she slapped his face. It was a pathetic gesture, but it stopped the flow of verbiage —verbiage containing no swear words at all, for Arthur was middle-class, and he had his sense of respectability. (If the children heard their father swearing, they would use the words themselves, and that would not be nice. Arthur had been very careful to see that both his children went to nice schools.) Having received the slap, Arthur decided to slap his wife back. Peter, who was watching from the crescent of windows that looked on to the road, felt a desire to protect his mother, but he just sat immobile nevertheless. That was all there was to it: just a slap for a slap; and Arthur would not have hit his wife if she had not hit him first: he was not a violent man.

As has been said, Arthur did not act his hate either. Only once. Peter was in his bedroom and he had not yet gone down to breakfast. He heard his father calling him in a strangely urgent and commanding manner, and, wondering what the matter could be, he went apprehensively down the stairs. Halfway down the stairs Peter saw the figure of his father, his overcoat and bowler on, silhouetted by the light from the windows in the front door, and standing at the bottom of the stairs, looking up at him. His father looked different: he was holding himself uncharacteristically erect, and he looked almost handsome, with a slight trace of Lucifer in his eyes. The anger in his father's eyes was not the usual kind, and he looked as if he thought he had done something very wild indeed, and was just a little bit afraid of his daring. Another thing that was different was the way that his father spoke to him: it was in an unusually imperative and commanding manner. Arthur told him that he had better let his mother and sister out of the kitchen. Peter did not quite understand the situation. There were cries coming from the kitchen. He was being called by his mother to open the kitchen door, and his young sister was crying hysterically. Perhaps his father had tried to murder them, or perhaps his father had cut off all his mother's hair. These explanations Peter had little faith in, because he knew that his father was not that kind of man. But he did not know the man who had ordered him to come down—his father was suddenly a changed man, and perhaps this new father had done something that his old father would not have done. Sure that his son would let the two prisoners out of the locked kitchen, Arthur let himself out of the front door, and went off to work in his black bowler hat, his black overcoat, and with his carefully rolled black umbrella.

Peter opened the kitchen door and was told by his mother that his sister wanted to go to the lavatory. Apparently, when she had found that she was locked in for a few moments, his sister had decided to get hysterical about not being able to get to the lavatory upstairs. His father was the same as ever that evening. That morning Arthur had briefly found the assertive spirit of his youth, but that evening he was again the deadened, middle-aged man who was tied around and around by the monotony of his existence, and who could only complain endlessly and hopelessly.

5

Clem and the Scaffolding

PETER was afraid to live. Peter was paralysed. Peter saw life through a blur of fear, and only now and again did things become focused. He was withdrawn, and he lived in a perpetual daydream, but even the daydream was fuzzy. Subconsciously he tried not to exist. Only now and again did he live in reality.

Why was this? Why was he so abnormal? Did the behaviour of his father have this extreme effect upon the child? Was the behaviour of Arthur so powerfully destructive to the child that Peter became a zombie? It seems unlikely that Arthur was completely responsible for the extremely withdrawn state of the isolated boy.

At the preparatory school, The Percival-John Preparatory High School, Peter's zombie state was most pronounced. He made no degree of contact with his fellow school-mates, and, afraid to be himself in the world of reality, he preferred to withdraw into a state of daze. On the other hand, he existed more as a person at home, for example, when he was playing with his sister Annabell. He was not so afraid to show himself to her, but when other people came near he would retire into his shell like the head of a tortoise will retire into the cover of its shell. It could not be truthfully said that he was known to his younger sister: he played with her, ran with her, made her cry, and talked to her a certain amount, but they were not intimate; and Peter was remote even from her, unknown to her, a mystery to himself and to her. But with her he opened up more than usual.

47

There was Trevor. But although he played with Trevor, and fought with Trevor, he was barriered off from him. Peter was still at the preparatory school when he went to stay with his cousin Trevor, but he was somewhat older now. The war was not yet, and Peter did not yet wear glasses. Cousin Trevor was a year or two younger than Peter, and when Peter beat Trevor in a wrestling match he apologized to his cousin because he felt guilty about the unfair advantage that he had in size and age and weight. But the courageous Trevor still wrestled with Peter. Peter did not fight with anybody else except his sister, and the self-assertion manifested by his fighting with these two smaller people was uncharacteristic, and only the embryo of the change that was to occur in his nature when he later changed from 'bullied' to 'the bully'.

Peter was nearly ten when he went to stay in the summer holidays at his uncle's house. Trevor's father was well-off, while Peter's father was not. Trevor's father was a company director, and had a large black car and a spacious house. Peter was impressed and he was in awe. Trevor had a sister called Trevorene-Lou, who was clever at school, and in addition to this Trevor was even cleverer at school. Peter, who was a dunce, felt a natural inferiority complex. Everything about his uncle's family made Peter feel inferior, and he was inferior. Trevor and his sister were not brought up in a twisted atmosphere, for all was bright, intelligent, and normal in that household.

Cousin Trevor and Peter slept in a large front bedroom on the first floor of the big house, where Trevor's electric-train set was always on display on the floor. There were two beds, and they fought on the beds. As they fought Peter came in close contact with the body of his cousin, and he commented on the discovery that from Trevor's body there emanated a harsh smell. Trevor politely replied by saying that Peter's body also gave forth a peculiar smell, adding that *he* had been too polite to mention it. Peter felt somewhat at a disadvantage after that exchange of civilities.

Next door to Trevor's house lived a thirteen-year-old girl

called, rather exotically, Catrina. Catrina had a younger sister but she was on the side. It was the maturing Catrina who awakened hitherto unknown feelings in the two boys, especially in Peter. Catrina had very dark straight hair, a mysterious oval face, a fringe, dark unfathomable eyes, and a yellow and greasy skin. Peter fell in love with her, and Mary-Jane, who had by now left the preparatory school, was quickly forgotten. When Trevor told Catrina that Peter was in love with her she said that she did not blame him. This reaction was completely incomprehensible to Peter. He sensed that pure and undiluted conceit in the girl could have been the cause of the statement, but he could not bring himself to think such an unpleasant thing about the girl he had chosen to be infatuated with, so he preferred to remain puzzled. The love affair was no more extensive, and no more eventful, than has been described: Trevor and Peter visited Catrina only twice, and as they wrestled in her garden most of the time, and as Catrina was completely concerned with herself, nothing more happened. In the friendly atmosphere of his uncle's house Peter opened up more than usual, but when he returned to school he was to close up once more, and to start living in a dream again.

Trevor and Peter read the *Beano* comic extensively, became very concerned about the adventures of a large character called Desperate Dan, and played Monopoly.

When Peter returned home from the sunshine of the home of his uncle he was impressed by the smallness and darkness of his parents' less wealthy home. Cheerfulness that he had experienced at his uncle's home was not in his parents' home, and he began to cry. When he told his father why he was crying his father felt a feeling of guilt, and went upstairs. In the wall of Peter's small bedroom was a little door that opened on to a storage space under the sloping roof. Peter's father took a large parcel from there and carried it downstairs to the sad boy. Peter had developed into an enthusiastic stamp collector, and he had a red album that he prized greatly. The parcel was opened and what Peter saw within it made his sadness disappear. Arthur had in past years collected all the

50

foreign stamps that came on the letters that passed through his hands at his place of work, and he had put them in the parcel and stored them away. It was strange that Arthur had not seen fit to give these stamps to his son before, for he had been well aware of the fact that Peter loved stamps, and would have been more than overjoyed to receive the fabulous collection that was stored in the dusty space beneath the sloping rafters. The treasure had been so near and yet so far. Every night Peter, the stamp collector, had slept only a few feet away from the parcel in the cupboard. The fact that Arthur had not given the stamps to his son at an earlier date shows that he cared very little for his son. While Peter was a stamp collector, birthdays and Christmases had passed, but Arthur had not seen fit to give the parcel to the boy. When he did eventually give the boy the stamps it was not an act of affection. The tears of Peter, and his explanation for them that he found the house sad after living in his uncle's house, made Arthur realize, more intensely than he found comfortable, the effect his constant rows had had upon the boy, and to relieve his conscience he gave Peter the stamps. The explanation and tears of Peter had made Arthur realize that the rows had created an atmosphere of gloom in the house that Peter became aware of by comparison. But soon after Arthur resumed his rowing, for his frustration was greater than his sense of duty to his son.

About this time a company began to build on the plot of waste land that adjoined Arthur's mortgaged house.

Peter had lived nearly ten years now and he had developed. He could now speak to people. He was still an extremely withdrawn child, and was to remain so for quite some time, but there were moments now of social contact. These moments were to become greater in number as time passed, and as he grew older and became more experienced at the business of living. His first real triumph as a social being was his friendship with Clem. Peter made more of a friend out of Clem than Martin did, and that was a triumph indeed, for Martin had been the social one, the boy who mixed well at the preparatory school. Peter had one advantage over Martin in the matter of acquiring the friendship of Clem, and that was that Peter lived right next to the building site. The commuters walked no more across the waste patch to the main road that led eventually to Balham Minor station. They had a long way to walk now. Arthur could not now expect his son to meet him at the station in the evenings, bribed into doing so by the reward of a penny every time, for the journey was too long. Foundations were laid, and Clem began to erect the scaffolding.

The children wandered on the building site, for it was mightily attractive to them. Clem seemed to be there more than the other workmen, and of the children Peter was there more than the others, because he lived only a few feet away. Clem was a quiet man with dark hair, and he liked the quiet boy Peter; perhaps they had something in common. Clem could mention the time he built the scaffolding for a church steeple, and Peter was entranced. Peter had a man-sized bicycle now, and he was allowed to go to another building site, and bring up a piece of earthenware angle piping, whenever it was wanted on the site next to his home, where the new house was being built. Peter was in his element and his life had begun, such as it was. There was a harsh Scottish workman, who carried a hod full of bricks up the ladders that were roped to the scaffolding that Clem had erected, and who had red hair and a vicious temperament. Peter learnt a lot of new words from him, and one day Peter used one of them to his mother: she was shocked to the core of her being, and deeply hurt: so hurt that she did not do anything about it. To add to the joy of these days, Peter found another friend, who followed him wherever he went, even followed him if he was riding on his bicycle, or riding on his bicycle with a small wad of paper wedged against the front wheel, so that when the wheel revolved a burring sound would result. The new friend was a young Alsatian dog, who had come from nowhere.

But Martin scored over one thing. Trust Martin to score somewhere; Peter might have been more of a success with Clem than Martin had been, but Martin's father helped Martin to score where Arthur could not help Peter to do so.

Martin's father made his son a miniature hod for carrying bricks in, and it was well made and it did not break when two bricks were carried in it. Martin proudly carried the hod on his shoulder and Peter felt inferior again. Peter told his father about this, and Arthur felt that Martin's father was trying to prove that he was a better father to his son than Arthur was. Arthur brought this matter extensively into his rows with Iris, and felt persecuted about it. But Arthur was not a practical man. Arthur decided to make a hod for Peter and he went into the garage and looked at his work-bench reflectively. Arthur had a few tools, and he had a vice on the work-bench, but they did not signify that Arthur was a handyman. Not that Arthur did not try to be on occasion. Only Arthur always made a mess of his little jobs. Arthur would have liked to be efficient in this field of endeavour, but endeavour was all he achieved, and there were quite a few of his follies round the house and round the garden to testify to the fact that Arthur was a botcher. One day Arthur had decided to make himself a bedside-cabinet, out of a nice wood and just as high as the pillow level. He made the cabinet after a fashion, and he put it by his bed with pride. It remained there for as long as Arthur lived in the house, but the thing was that the pieces were not joined together, and if you knocked it it would fall apart. Still, Arthur tried. It was neatly done, what there was of it, and it was nicely varnished. Peter had a faint suspicion that the joints did not join, and that was why it was never put together, but he could not test his theory, because he could not get to examine the cabinet, his father's bedroom being forbidden ground: Arthur believed in privacy. Arthur got his bedroom privacy, because by then he never shared his bed with Iris: their relationship had become so strained that such intimacy was out of the question. Lack of sex made Arthur even more sour, and it had the same effect upon Iris. Arthur made a hod for Peter but it disintegrated when Peter put two bricks in it. Martin looked expressionless as usual but he felt inwardly very triumphant. Heaven knows what Arthur felt.

Clem said that when he went out he turned his working coat inside out and then it was all smart. Peter did not know whether to believe him or not. Peter believed Clem when Clem told him that the Jaguar was the best car there was.

Clem grew fond of Peter and Peter grew even more fond of Clem. When the house was near completion, and the children had climbed the ladders many times, and walked along the trestles that seemed so high above the brick-strewn ground below, Clem wanted to show his liking for the boy in some way, and so he invited him to the pictures. Peter was excited, for he did not go to the pictures, and to go with Clem would be a wonderful thing. When Arthur heard about the invitation he thought dark thoughts. Arthur knew about Life and he had heard about men who liked young boys. He could understand Peter talking to Clem on the building site, but the idea of Clem taking Peter to the pictures seemed very suspicious to him indeed. He introduced the subject into one or two of his rows with his wife. Arthur did not have an opportunity to investigate Clem, until the Saturday afternoon came when Clem was to take Peter in to Balham to the film. Clem came in his smart suit, told Peter that it was his working clothes reversed, and Peter was all dressed up for the occasion. Arthur saw Clem at the side gate, and the investigation began, much to the embarrassment of Clem, who realized what Arthur suspected. Arthur was condescending to Clem, because Clem was lower-class and Arthur was middle-class from upper-middle-class parentage. Peter had never seen his hero embarrassed before, and the sight of Clem colouring as Arthur investigated his character made Peter rather sad; for he respected Clem far more than his father, and it was not right that his father was making Clem feel ill at ease. Arthur asked Clem what his name was, and Clem answered 'Clem'. 'Clem what?' asked Arthur unsympathetically, and Peter felt it was all awful. But they eventually saw a wonderful film called *Barricade*, that Peter did not follow at all; but there were soldiers climbing over the barricade right into the cinema, or so it seemed, for they were in the front seats, and Peter had a wonderful time.

Clem moved to another building site when the house was finished soon after, but as it was not far away, and Peter had his big bicycle, Peter was able to go to where Clem was working, and his happy days continued. Peter saw the harsh Scotsman accidentally break his hod, which was expensive to replace, and Peter learnt a few more nasty words, and he learnt a more powerful way of saying them, for the Scotsman had been very angry indeed. One day Clem took Peter quite a long way away to another building site, and they went in a big hut where there were many workmen: they had a cup of tea, but Peter felt that he was out of his depth and he was glad to get back to the building site. But the happy days with Clem were to end. Peter was to need glasses, and he was to sit for the entrance examination to the secondary school in Balham, a school called St. Elevenses Boys' School, founded long ago by two brothers. 'In days of old, when knights were bold, the founding brothers flourished. Good men and true, the will to do, the arts of peace they nourished. . . .' But Peter was not to nourish the arts of peace at St. Elevenses Boys' School.

.　　　.　　　.　　　.　　　.

Sexton Blake came in a floppy paper-backed booklet, and he was Peter's next hero. Peter was passionate about reading of the great detective who bore such a striking resemblance to Sherlock Holmes, and he read avidly. The sun was shining in the back garden, the grass on the lawn was green and well mown, there was nobody in the garden but Peter, and Peter sat on the roller in the middle of the lawn reading about Sexton Blake. Peter looked up at the backs of the houses, and the sun blurred them with shimmering heat. He was reading about a lovely lady who had a calculating nature. Peter was old enough to absorb the fact that the lady was terribly nice physically. He was also reading about a man who was in a difficult position, a man who was surrounded by a collection of damning evidence that pointed to the fact that he was a murderer. Actually the man was innocent. The lady was in possession of the damning evidence, but Sexton Blake was not, and she wanted the man, who was rich, to marry her. Very alluring, the lady suggested to the man that if he married her she would not make the damning evidence known. Peter shifted his short grey flannel trousers on the massive cylinder of the garden roller, and read, absorbed. He read what the lady said to the man: ' "Would you like my arms around your neck, or a noose?", and she put up her soft, white, curving arms invitingly as if to embrace him around his neck.' Peter was stunned. Waves passed swirling in his head and he could read no further. Himself, he would willingly have gone to the gallows if those arms could be put around his own neck. He had never felt like this before. Sex was rearing its ugly head into his consciousness for the very first time, and the hot sun did not help matters. Peter was not acquainted with the feeling that had entered into him from those words in the book, and he felt weak. Dazedly he read the words again. He got up and walked unsteadily round the garden roller, wishing with all his heart that those arms would form a noose around his own boyish neck. Was life really like that? he wondered. He had no knowledge of the facts of life because both his parents were too shy to tell him, but he knew that those arms would give him ecstasy divine. He did not read that book any more that day, and when he next saw his mother he felt she must know the thoughts about the soft white arms that were still feverishly roaming in his mind, and he looked away from her guiltily.

.   .   .   .   .

The situation was the same. On another occasion Peter was sitting on the roller reading in the hot sun, and nobody else was in the garden.

Peter was facing the backs of the rows of houses; the heat was blurring his sight of the back-bedroom windows of the houses, and there was a peculiar silence and stillness at the backs of the houses. Nobody was at home in Peter's house, and nobody seemed to be around anywhere. No lawn-mowers

whirred, and he could hear no cars on the roads that were out of sight.

Peter looked up from his book and stared at the row of bedroom windows that stretched down the block. He felt that somebody was looking at him. But there was no sound and no movement. He stared at the two bedroom windows of the house that was on the other side of the widow-woman's house, two houses away, and although he could see nobody at all, he felt that someone was watching him from one of those windows on the upper floor. The haze of heat seemed to envelop him and the silence was intense. Peter could feel that there was someone there. He did not know the people who lived in that house, and he could not seem to remember their appearance. He had stopped reading now and was just staring at the upper-back of his own house. From the direction of the bedroom windows of the house two houses away his name was called, in a long and drawn-out female voice. He stared in terror at the windows, just below where the roof of the house came to the top edges of the bedroom windows, but he could see nobody. Then, as he stared through the haze of heat, his name was called eerily again, and he was paralysed. He rushed indoors and wished his mother would come home.

Somebody in the house had been playing with the boy. That somebody had realized that Peter was a sensitive boy and had amused themselves at his expense. They could not have done the same thing with Martin.

6

Marital Discord and Discourse

ARTHUR, the influence upon the boy Peter, was getting worse, and as a result the marital discord and discourse were getting worse, and the consequence was that the influence, the formative influence, upon the boy Peter was getting worse also. The result of being brought up in his formative years in close contact with the aggressive creator of discord was already clearly manifest, and would continue to manifest itself for years to come—in one way or another—subtly or obviously. When Peter passed the age of ten, went to St. Elevenses, and entered his teens, the complexes caused in him by Arthur's conduct would influence Peter's behaviour in some ways that were different from the ways his behaviour had been influenced at the preparatory school. Peter would for a long time hence be remote and introspective, because of the early effect Arthur had had upon him; but changes were to occur, and new behaviours would be added. He was approaching puberty when the war started, and puberty is the stage of change. But he was not yet at that stage. Peter had glasses now—steel-rimmed ones. Hitler was a German god; and Peter rode to the preparatory school on his adult-sized bicycle. He was all set to fail the entrance examination to St. Elevenses, and he knew nothing that the ageing and good Mrs. Percival-John had taught him. She regarded him as one of her failures. But Martin, who would take the entrance examination at the same time as Peter, would compensate, because Martin was sure to pass, and he did.

Many of the children at the preparatory school had left by now for one reason or another, and the number of children in the school was decreasing. But Semantha was still there, although her brother had gone to St. Elevenses long ago. Semantha, who would probably change into a ravishing beauty after puberty, just as her brother was to do, was a mean-looking and sour girl at the preparatory school in her last years there. Charm was not her strong point.

Peter did not manage to get the children at the preparatory school to come to tea at his home. Martin always had a girl or boy to tea at his home—tea followed by play in the garden, and tea preceded by play in the garden. Peter longed to succeed in this, and he asked Semantha to come to tea. Semantha reluctantly accepted with a minimum of grace, feeling trapped. Playing with Peter was regarded by the children at the preparatory school as a distinct bore.

Peter did not understand politics at that time in his life: in fact it was a long time before he really did understand politics with any real clarity. He lived in a personal, local world full of an acute lack of intelligence of the outer world for all of his teenage years, and during all that time politics were incomprehensible to him. At the age of seventeen he had grasped the difference between capitalists and the workers, but that was strictly all he understood at that age about political issues. And his awareness of the difference between capitalists and the working classes was caused by having to listen to the speeches of his friend as they walked home together after the end of school at St. Elevenses, his friend being a member of the Socialist Party of Great Britain, the principles of which the friend would defend heatedly at every opportunity. Peter was still an unintelligent youth at that time, and, although he did not understand much of what was thrown at him by his friend, Peter did absorb one thing, and that was that the unscrupulous money-makers were the Capitalists, and that the backbone of the country, the capitalist-misused masses, were the Glorious Working Men: Peter's friend was rather like Gulley Jimpson in that respect, for he thought that all the capitalists should be killed and all the wonderful working men should be sent to heaven. Peter's friend was called Splay-foot Sam.

While he was at The Percival-John Preparatory High School, Peter was just about aware that Adolf Hitler was a dirty word or two, and that was the complete extent of his political knowledge and knowledge of world affairs. Peter had absorbed one other thing about the outside world from his father's *Daily Mail*, when he was at this stage in his life, and that was that Tommy Farr was going to fight Joe Louis for the heavyweight title of the world.

Peter was bored in the preparatory-school playground one day, and he stood on the dusty concrete by the fence idly watching the other children play. For some reason Peter decided to liven up his life somewhat by shouting 'Heil Hitler' a few times. He had heard this phrase so much that it had stuck in his memory, although he did not know what the phrase meant. Children do repeat things that they have often heard, without quite knowing what they mean. Even art-school girls of nearly twenty will use phrases that they have heard used by the art-school boys, without being aware that the phrases are not suitable for use in the home.

Peter shouted 'Heil Hitler' without knowing what it meant. But the other children knew what it meant, and they knew that it was improper. They angrily told Peter to stop, but Peter felt that he must defy them by persisting, so he went on shouting 'Heil Hitler' into the air. They could not stop him, and Semantha, the girl with the black fringe of hair down to her eyes, resorted to threats. Her mean, sharp face glared at Peter, and she issued out the biggest threat she could find. She had sensed how much Peter wanted her to come to tea, and she knew that if she threatened not to come it would catch him where he was least protected, and it did. Peter said 'Heil Hitler' once, rather weakly, after the threat was issued, and then he became quiet. When Semantha did come to play with him in the garden it was a most unsuccessful social occasion, and Semantha did not seem to be interested in any of the things that Peter suggested that they should do. Peter showed her the things that he felt quietly passionate about, but she just stared at him with dislike, and they went in and had a glum teatime. So much for Peter's first acquaintance with the dangers of politics and foreign affairs.

Arthur's only interest in politics, that Peter had been aware of, had occurred some time previously, when Arthur had been grumbling about Lloyd George one day when the family were out on a Sunday outing.

Arthur made a gesture of contempt for his neighbours, every time the family went for a walk round the houses, near their home, at the week-ends. Arthur's end at the weekends. The gesture that Arthur made was not in keeping with his middle-class behaviourism, and it was rather surprising in that respect. Just as it is considered more gentlemanly to leave a tear in the trousers than to sink so low as to mend it, so perhaps Arthur thought that his little habit or gesture, while walking round the houses slowly, was the act of freedom befitting a gentleman. In fact it was not gentlemanly at all. But Arthur did it; it was a further manifestation of his complex character, the character that had such an important bearing upon the development of the boy Peter, so it must be mentioned. The walk round the block on Sunday afternoon was an institution, and it was performed at a slow and leisurely pace, with Arthur walking on ahead, trying to separate himself from the other three as much as possible, and being totally taciturn. Arthur walked with self-consciousness on these walks, as he did on all of his walks. Arthur seemed to regard his walks as public appearances, and he was convinced that everybody watched him, as the people passed, and from their windows. The family would go out of the front door, and Arthur would dawdle, looking carefully at the flower-beds, while the others walked out of the front-garden gate. Then the promenade would begin. Regularly, at intervals of an eighth of a mile, Arthur would stop, with an air of being on a stage, and, with an expression of contempt for the world around him on his face, mixed with an expression of middle-class dignity, and a firm conviction that he was doing the right thing, he would scratch his anus through his trousers, and then walk on. Peter felt that this was positively disgusting, and, no doubt, so did Iris. Iris thought that another thing that Arthur did was disgusting, and she told Peter so. While Arthur was in the bathroom in the early mornings, and while the other three members of the family were sitting down to cornflakes in the kitchen, the sound of Arthur blowing his nose into the wash-basin after he had washed his face would be heard throughout the house. Iris winced every time she heard it. Peter was brought up by his mother to think that this was appalling. One day Peter would react to all this concentration upon what was nice, and what was clean, and he would revel in dirt and bohemianism. He would react just as vicars' daughters invariably react to their upbringing when they become loose ladies from the age of sixteen. There is no exception to this rule: vicars' daughters always do it.

There were week-end shopping expeditions to crowded Balham. Fernando's vast store, where you could get everything, and if you could not get it there you could get it at Algherti's by the market, was a favoured place for Arthur and Iris, who would become part of the milling throng of shoppers until it was time to go home to tea. In Fernando's Arthur would invariably wander off on his own, and sometimes they never found him, and they would have to go back on the bus without him. The market place was a good place to lose the absorbed Arthur too: but, make no mistake, they did not have to try to lose Arthur, for he just got lost without any help. Sometimes the shopping expedition would start off from the home at Balham in a sunny manner, but sometimes there would have been a row over Saturday lunch, and the expedition would be clouded over with bad feeling. In this latter case Iris would get the children with her, and Arthur would be shopping with them three against one. The two children saw more of their mother than they saw of Arthur, and as a result Iris had more opportunity to get them on her side, and the three of them treated Arthur as an ogre in his absence. And also, when there was a row, the children were passively on their mother's side. She always seemed in the right to them, because Arthur was more obviously the aggressive one.

Arthur came home at lunch-time on Saturday, feeling tired after the week's work, and a row started, and matured. Sometimes, if the meal was a success, Arthur would go into a trance as he sat at the table, coming out of it to eat, or to rush to the window of the dining-room if a car passed. Arthur seemed to resent the intrusion into the otherwise deserted road of cars at the week-end, and he always rushed to have a look through the window when they roared round the corner where the organist lived. But this Saturday Arthur was not in a trance between courses, and he was not interested in the occupants of passing cars. There was a row, and his eyes were dark with anger behind his horn-rimmed spectacles.

The expedition to Fernando's Department Store after lunch began in an atmosphere that was far from pleasant, and in their minds the children sided with their mother as usual, and thought of their father as an ogre: their mother looked martyred and silent as they went out, and their father looked beastly and unpleasant. Their mother's attitude suggested to the children that, if it had not been for their father's attitude, the expedition would have been full of sunshine. In actual fact, when their father was not present when they went out, their mother was neurotic and harassed in the crowded streets by the shops, and there was not sunshine just because Daddy was away at work. But it was true that when they went out with Daddy, and Daddy was angry and rowing, no shopping outing could have been more unpleasant. Daddy insisted upon being called 'Daddy', even when Peter was ten: Daddy told Peter that to call one's father 'Daddy', when one was a boy of ten, was not babyish; but Peter felt that he was too old to call his father 'Daddy' at the age of nearly ten. Arthur wanted to be loved, but you don't love a gun-bristling tank just because it wants to be loved. Arthur wanted Peter to be habitually and lovingly at the railway-station to meet him, when Arthur got off the train at the end of the day, because Arthur wanted the 'loving son' set-up, but Arthur knew that there was no hope of such a habit establishing itself naturally, and the only way that Arthur got his son to wait for him at the station was to bribe

IRIS AGED BY
MARRIAGE

him. Arthur was lonely, and Arthur wanted a wife who loved him demonstratively, and children who did the same, but he had killed the chances of such things being—he had killed them long ago by his repetitive rows and jeopardizing 'jaw, jaw, jaw'.

Arthur rowed his wife all the way down the road, and all the way to Balham: the pressure was on this day, and the rowing was not to be just confined to the house. Their journey to Balham was interrupted by a stopping-off halfway down a hill, for a purchase had to be made at a shop there. After the purchase had been made the four of them waited at a bus-stop, and it was a wild bit of waiting, because Arthur was rowing all the time, and the combination of the harassing influence of the Saturday-afternoon street, and the wearing effect of Arthur's now-wild complaining, was making Iris inwardly distraught. When Arthur rowed in the street his rowing became disintegrated and ferocious: Arthur preferred to row on home ground, where his rowing was not interrupted by distractions, and where he felt master of the situation. When he was rowing at home, Arthur rowed in a composed fashion, but when he rowed in the street, he felt afraid, and his aggression became thin and sharp. He felt at a disadvantage when he was being aggressive to a woman in the street: he was perhaps afraid that one of the passing males would interfere. Realizing that Arthur felt at a disadvantage, Iris took the initiative, in a way that she would not have dared to do in the house in Balham Minor. Iris suggested with angry composure, her face white with strain, that she intended to carry out the shopping expedition without Arthur that afternoon. She said that she would take the children with her, and that Arthur had better shop on his own, as she could not stand any more rowing. Arthur suddenly felt lonely as he heard himself being dismissed, and he resented the fact that she should have the company of the children while he was expected to go off solitarily. The bus was a long time coming, and the four at the bus-stop were each of them standing isolated, each member of the family on its own, separated by the atmosphere of strife and strain. They were standing by a high pole that had a bus-stop sign halfway up it, and they were a short distance away from a T-junction, waiting for the double-decker red motor-bus to come down the main road, that curved up over the hill, on the other side of them from seething Balham.

Arthur angrily said that he would go with Peter, and that Iris could go with Annabell, Peter's younger sister. Peter was on his mother's side, and the idea of spending the afternoon with his irritable and undignified father was horrible to him. Iris, unsure of herself to the extent that she did not know whether Peter would choose to go with his father or not, told Arthur fiercely that he could have Peter if he wanted to, and moved away from the bus-stop with Annabell grasped by the hand: Annabell had no choice in the matter at all—she was just a pawn in the game, a pawn with no will. Annabell existed by the skirt of her mother's coat, connected to her mother by clasped hands, and that was all there was to Annabell's role. Peter realized, as his mother moved away, that a critical point had been reached, and he realized that, unless he acted quickly, he would be left with his father for the afternoon. Most probably, after a while with his son, Arthur would have resorted to the thing he had done once before in similar circumstances. Arthur would have tried to buy his son's friendship, by buying him something and taking him to the Charles Cord restaurant to have a nice tea. But Peter saw only misery ahead of him for the afternoon: even if his father did buy him something and give him a tea, he would have felt unhappy in his father's duplicity-filled company. His mother moved away, and Peter was on his own: his mother did not seem to want him, and he did not want his father. So he ran: he ran round the shops that were on the corner, set back from the road behind a large curving area of grey pavement, and he ran down the smaller road as fast as he could. There were no people on the pavement, surprisingly enough. He felt as guilty as if he had robbed a bank, for he had never done this before. He was very afraid now of his father. He heard his father shouting his name, and he knew that his father was running after him. Arthur had loved cricket, and still did, and he ran as he had run on the cricket-field when he was twenty to thirty years old. Peter did not stand a chance. Peter hid in the entrance to an alley, but that was rather futile, because seconds after he saw his father's face dark before him. Arthur was deeply hurt that his son had run away from him, for he liked to deceive himself into thinking that his son liked him as other sons liked their fathers, and this demonstration of dislike was painful to the man. His anger passing now that he was away from Iris, Arthur asked his son perplexedly why he had run away, and Arthur concealed that he was hurt. Accepting that he was caught, and accepting the fact that he was in for an afternoon with his father whether he liked it or not, Peter weakly said that he did not know, which was to a certain extent the truth.

The Charles Cord restaurant was on one side of the bridge that spanned the River Limber, and Peter and his father approached it through the confused and congested centre of the town. After the tea Arthur bought Peter a present, and the dupable boy had by now begun to think that his father was not such a bad chap to spend a Saturday afternoon in Balham with, as he had thought he was by the side of the pole with the bus-stop sign on it. The afternoon was full of the particular atmosphere of Arthur, and everything in Balham had seemed to Peter to be enveloped in a kind of psychological semi-darkness: Peter's will and personality were easily taken over, and when he was with someone of strong personality he saw life through their eyes, and not through his own: when he was with his father that afternoon he saw life through his father's eyes—devoid of gaiety, emotional, furtive in a peculiar sort of way, and anti-social. Arthur was pleased with the cupboard love that he had created in his son towards him: as he could not get the real thing he had to be content with an imitation. Arthur pretended to himself that the imitation was the real thing, and he was sure that Peter really felt affection for him that afternoon. They returned home, and Arthur and Peter entered the kitchen, where they found Iris making a meal for Annabell. Iris could see at once that Arthur had won over his son in a fashion, and she resented this. She said to Peter, in a voice that suggested that he had done something underhand: 'Did you enjoy the afternoon with your father?' Peter showed her the present, but she did not enthuse over it with him as he had expected her to. Iris felt that Peter had betrayed her, and she would have been happier if Peter had returned in tears after his outing with the evil Arthur. To Iris, Arthur was the Great Offender, and she expected her children to treat him as such, and not to find the ogre tolerable on any occasion.

.   .   .   .   .

Auntie Maggie lived in a dark Victorian house that was joined to another, and the kitchen window looked on to a minute yard, the view from the kitchen table being one of brick walls, high and oppressive. The hall to the dark front door was gloomy, and hardly any light shone into the hall through the stained glass in the front door, a front door that was flanked on the inside by hanging coats, so that one could not see properly as one approached the front door from the kitchen at the end of the narrow hall. Maggie did not live there from choice.

To get to Maggie's house you left the tram in the main street in Balham-Far, walked down a few drab streets, and came to the Victorian road, halfway down which was the narrow residence of the prematurely grey-haired and stocky woman. Even the road in which Maggie lived was narrow. The houses were high, and a dirty dark red. Maggie gave herself to her two daughters, and to her husband who liked fishing on a Sunday. Maggie lived in an atmosphere of housework and making meals. Once upon a time Maggie had been gay, young, and full of hope—once upon a time. She did not assert herself, and she had a placid nature unlike that of any of her brothers and sisters, none of whom was mild as Maggie was. Her sister Iris could never be described as mild, and neither could her brother, the father of Trevor. Maggie was the eldest of the children, and she had had to be the responsible one in her childhood: somehow this had deadened Maggie, and she remained for all her life restrained, unemotional, stolid, phlegmatic, stoical, and rather stodgy. Way back behind her exterior Maggie had a soul, and somewhere she had feelings, but nobody would know. She was kind, but her kindness had no obvious warmth. Maggie had missed the boat somewhere, and she knew it. There were millions of women like Auntie Maggie, living for others, sacrificing for others, and looking martyred all the time. But Maggie would endure: Maggie would probably live until she was ninety, though goodness knows why. She never strained herself, her nerves never dominated her, there was a sameness to her all the time, and she looked the same at the age of thirty as she did at the age of sixty-five. Her two daughters married very well later on, when they grew up, and then Maggie lived through them, looking at photographs of her grandchildren, and feeling proud of her two daughters. Her two daughters were lively and vital, and it was as if they had taken all her vitality and used it for themselves. Maggie's husband was often in the house, upstairs somewhere, but you hardly ever saw him. Maggie's eldest daughter was at that certain stage in her life, and she went round the house singing 'There's a yoo-hoo in your eyes', but that did not alter the gloom in the house by the smallest degree. Wherever Maggie kept house there was a stodginess—a stodgy gloom that hung on the walls and in the kitchen cupboards, and it was powerful and undisturbable. Maggie had a presence, and she imparted it to everything around her—without hope it was, heavy and dead. No wonder Maggie never died, for she was already dead. But you could not dislike Maggie: there was nothing active enough in her to dislike, just as there was nothing active enough in her to like. Maggie had just never got going.

It was Saturday again, and Arthur and Iris, Peter and Annabell were on their way to visit Auntie Maggie. It was not an exciting prospect. But the brothers and sisters of Iris were a clan, and they kept intermingled. Iris had to see Maggie now and again. There was anger, and Arthur was high-pressure rowing at Iris, as the family made their way to Auntie Maggie's. It is irrelevant what the row was about: the row was the thing, and it did not matter what it was about. The important fact was that the row was outdoors, and that it was a high-pressure row. Arthur's outdoor rows had a special quality: they always made Iris act. At home Iris just let herself be rowed, and she just stood in the dining-room or in the kitchen, letting the row go on and on. Arthur always got rather desperate and weak, when he was rowing in the street, while they were going somewhere.

As they approached the road wherein Maggie lived her exciting existence, Iris began to run away from Arthur, the children with her. Arthur was so surprised that he just watched them, following at a walking pace. Iris and the two children were let into the house by Maggie, and they felt they had found a sanctuary, but a feeble sanctuary it proved to be. Iris told her sister that Arthur was outside in the road, and Maggie looked worried, the atmosphere being tense, expectant, and uncomfortable. Arthur began to bang on the door, and demanded to see his wife, shouting in a loud voice. The trouble was that he felt neglected, and he wanted to join the others. He did not want to spend his Saturday afternoon on his own: he did not like his own company any more than anybody else did. It was rather a horrible prospect for Arthur to be left alone with Arthur. All he wanted was to get inside with the others, and have a nice long row all through the afternoon. But he did not get inside, and eventually he went away. Peter was ashamed of his father for shouting in the road, and hammering on the door.

In such earth the plant Peter grew, and he was formed accordingly.

7

Entry to St. Elevenses, 1938

ST. ELEVENSES BOYS' SCHOOL, Philippa Road, Balham.
Situated opposite the Grammar School. The Grammar School
boys wore red caps and grey blazers, and the St. Elevenses
boys wore striped caps, striped blazers, grey flannel trousers
(down to the shoes), a house tie that was striped with angled
stripes denoting the particular house, a huge embroidered
badge on the blazer's pocket, and they were allowed a reckless
freedom of self-expression concerning the pullover and the
shirt, although a boy could not go too far regarding his pullover or shirt—a pullover knitted with a design that was of
Betty Grable would not last long at St. Elevenses Boys'
School. The stripes on the blazers of the boys who went to
St. Elevenses were dark-blue-cum-purple and alizarin crimson: the two colours clashed horribly, but you could see a St.
Elevenses blazer a hundred miles away, and one supposes that
that was something. The St. Elevenses boys, as they were
invariably called, were the élite, and the Grammar School
boys were not up to their standard at all. St. Elevenses just
missed being a public school regarding its snob status, but it
was an excellent school, and, even if it was not quite a public
school itself, it made sure that it never played rugby matches
with anything lower than public schools. The St. Elevenses
boys all looked the same until you looked closely, or weighed
them, or measured them. When you looked closely you could
just see that each boy was different from the rest. En masse,
in the playground, at lunchtime or at breaktime, they looked
like a vast collection of tastelessly coloured blazers, all of the

boys the same, except for a bit of weight here or a bit of adolescent height there. But, if you dared to get anywhere near the terrifying horde, you would be surprised to notice that one boy had ink on his trousers and a fringe on his brow, that another boy had Brylcreem loaded on to his hair, that another had awfully long and conspicuous feminine fingers hanging against the grey flannel of his trousers, and that another had a long neck and fuzzy hair: the fact of the matter was that they were all different from each other, and they were not just a collection of tasteless blazers, as one had at first thought when one walked into the school surrounds. Very rarely a boy would have a suit on, but he would not last long—a master would get him eventually, and then his number would be up. Dirty books were not allowed in the school either. Dirty books and suits were out. But they got in just the same. Talking to girls in a gay way was frowned upon by the masters in those days, but it went on in the streets quite extensively nevertheless. When the school-caretaker's daughter began to walk through the school grounds, on her way to school, there was bedlam: she was stopped eventually, of course, but only after three whole months of the most awful disturbances in the craniums of hundreds of the boys. Allowing a girl to walk through the playground when it was full of blazers was positively improper: if she had been ugly things might not have been so electric, but she wasn't ugly at all. You could not get away from it: once inside the gates of the school you were on male ground, and only old charladies could walk therein without busting the place apart—old charladies, masters, and boys. It was like the Rotary Club: male sanctuary. You could tell the mashers apart from the other blazers: they combed their hair all the time, made the most of themselves by kiss-curls, water-waves, fine pullovers, and carefully selected shoes. And there were the heroic ones: those with their colours for being excellent at one sport or another. There was usually only one boy in the school who had his boxing colours, and he walked undisturbed, and was never barged into: he was the God of Aggression—usually a nice quiet chap, the type vicars liked.

The front-entrance gates were open on weekdays, and they were made of wood, unpretentious and ordinary: the school did not have to show its class by having assertive wrought-iron gates, for the school had a quiet, gentlemanly confidence in itself, it had a full complement of boys, and it turned away multitudes of hopeful boys every year. You had to pass the entrance examination to get to St. Elevenses, and that was where Peter showed his inadequacy. Peter could not even spell 'St. Elevenses', let alone get into it on merit. The school was so sure of itself that it did not mind what the outside world saw, when the outside world looked momentarily through the gates, as it passed on the pavement outside the wide-flung, open gates. What the outside world saw, as it looked in, was this: a bleak, brown, wooden hut, with a roof of asbestos, and no windows, that was the Scout hut before the war, and which housed soldiers during the war; and a concrete and narrow road, bordered by bare earth-flats for playing marbles on, that led, after one hundred yards, to the Junior School building, which was a Victorian house that housed the Juniors, the school dining-rooms, and the tuck-shop, and which backed on to the cycle garage. A few miserable trees were also visible from the road, and if you were lucky you might see a couple of undistinguished Junior School boys, blazers and all—a glorious sight to see. If you looked in, and saw no blazers, you might very well come to the conclusion that the place was anything rather than a school for boys that narrowly missed being a public school. To one side of the gates was a spiv second-hand-car sale-yard; and on the other side was a long, grim fence of some height, behind which was impenetrable forest, in the middle of which stood a white thing of antiquity, unvisited and strange, called Our Lord's Little Place.

For a boy, at nine o'clock in the morning, the walk up the narrow concrete road from the open gateway was a miserable and gloomy thing, and you had to think of Mars bars if you wanted to keep your morale up—Mars bars, or what you had heard on the wireless the previous evening, when you were supposed to be doing your homework. The school was too proud to care what people thought about its appearance. But, like the gentleman who has a nice suit on underneath his threadbare overcoat, the school looked better when you had passed the Junior School and came in sight of the main building of modern red brick, by the side of which was the playing-field of grass, where the cricket was played and where the races were run. But even so, the school was completely unpretentious; the classroom desks were old, stained with ink, and carved with initials; the science laboratory was gloomy; and there was nothing very new anywhere except the boys. However, as you looked at the mass of the main school building, it seemed to complain to you that it ought to be a public school, and that it was not fair that it was not quite that. Far and wide stretched the reputation of the school, and the lucky boys came even from remote localities to study there, and to have their characters developed, as they absorbed the fine tradition of the school. It was like the universities of Oxford or Cambridge: you just had to exist in the atmosphere for years and you came out a better person, a cut above the rest, a potential Prime Minister or a great artist, but never a potential dustman or a potential bricklayer. It might have been, but was not, for reasons of tact and restraint, the proud boast of the school that none of its boys had ever left to become a professional dustman or bricklayer. You went to St. Elevenses and you ended up good, just as much because you had been to St. Elevenses as because of your own endeavours. Plant a young plant in good earth, and it will grow up fine. Juvenile delinquents very rarely got into the school to become Elevensinians, but if they did they were fine young men before they left, such was the influence of the school. Even Hell, with his spit campaign, was tamed in the end, although that did take some time: making him a corporal in the cadet-force of the school was a clever move, and that helped to transform the brutal boy who so appropriately was the bearer of the surname Hell: one did sense that he had felt that he had to live up to his surname—it must be difficult to be a boy whom the vicar likes when your surname is Hell. They made him a corporal, and he felt a sense of responsibility that gradually changed him for the good. Perhaps he will become Prime Minister one day.

.   .   .   .   .

Peter stood waiting in the sunshine, while the headmaster sorted out the boys who were to take the entrance examination. The congregation of mothers and boys was in front of the Junior School building, and some distance away from Peter stood his mother, feeling for her son. If Peter passed the examination he would be in the Junior School for one year, and then he would enter the Senior School. Peter's meagre intelligence was ready to be put to the test, and the little idiot really thought that he might pass. Iris had high hopes too. Peter had never used his brains before, and that day it showed—showed on blank pieces of examination paper, with his name written in ink by himself at the top of the page. One day Peter might distinguish himself, but not that day, the day he had been anticipating with mixed feelings since he was eight. It was an important day, and here it was: Peter felt numb, but the sunshine was so nice that his spirits were high. The examination was to be held in a classroom in the main school building. Peter was impressed with the place, for it was magnificent in comparison with The Percival-John Preparatory High School: he very much wanted to go to this wonderful place where the boys wore *long* trousers: if he got there he would not be a little boy any longer, for only big boys wear trousers that don't show their bare red knees.

Peter stood in a line of boys outside the Senior School building, and he stood on sacred ground, outside the main entrance to that building—sacred ground that only prefects, parents, and masters were normally allowed to walk on. Batteries of big windows stared from the face of the inhuman edifice, and Peter looked, from the line of boys he was a part of, to see if he could see his mother. His mother watched him looking round for her, and she knew that Peter could not see because he had not got his glasses on. Peter took his glasses out of his spectacle-case, and put them across his face: suddenly the world looked terribly clear, everything in perfect definition in the glorious sunshine. Peter saw his mother, and she smiled a beautiful smile at him, a rare thing for her to do. Peter was happy because of the smile, because he could see properly now, and because the sun was gently warm and making the grass glow a beautiful green. Before he knew where he was, the line began to move into the entrance of the building, in response to an order by the ageing, dignified, and stout headmaster, in his ground-length black robe, with the pleats across the back of his shoulders. The chill and severe interior of the building enveloped Peter, and he went to his fate. While the examination was on he just sat and dreamed, the blank paper in front of him, while the other boys bent over their desks writing furiously. When his parents heard some weeks later that he had failed, it was no consolation to them to remember that Winston Churchill had been a dunce at school. Perhaps because Winston Churchill had not yet made God-rank at that time, just before the beginning of the Second World War. Iris never did respect bricklayers anyway.

Iris was hurt. Her life had become a waste, and she was determined that her son was not to become a waste as well. She was determined that he should go to a good school. She went and saw the headmaster on Peter's behalf. She was the only parent of a boy who had failed the entrance examination that year to go to see the headmaster about it afterwards, and this impressed the headmaster. Iris put on all the charm she could rummage up—she had not used her charm for a long time, and it was getting a little rusty, but it worked— and she pleaded with sincerity. As a result, Peter started in September at the Junior School. Iris must have loved Peter in a way, for she had tried very hard for him, in the headmaster's office, to the side of the main entrance to the main building. The most she ever did for Peter was what she did in the headmaster's office during the hour the ageing teacher saw her. The headmaster respected the sincerity of Iris that day.

·   ·   ·   ·   ·

The boy was being persecuted, and Peter watched. The boy was tubby and bespectacled, and like Peter he was an outsider. Because he was an outsider, the other boys in the Junior School that breaktime attacked the tubby boy. They had to do something at breaktime, and conkers were out of season. Each boy had either a small attaché-case, or a satchel, in which he carried his books, pen, pencil, rubber, and pencil-sharpener: most of the attaché-cases were frayed and grubby: a brand-new attaché-case stuck out like a sore thumb, and the tubby boy had a new attaché-case that was obscene in its light-brown, cheap-leather newness. The new case made the other children hate the tubby boy even more, and they darted at him and tried to provoke him. Woe betide the tubby boy if he should dare to attack, by fighting forward from his position in the Junior School doorway, for then the horde would have leapt upon him and dragged him to the ground for the 'kill'. Peter respected the tubby boy for what he did, in the face of the overwhelming odds, to protect himself. Peter thought that what the tubby boy did showed considerable initiative, and as a fellow outsider Peter felt for the tubby boy in his predicament. Boys would dart forward at the persecuted boy, and poke at him, and hit him, and then they would stand back and jeer. No doubt it was all very character-forming for everybody concerned. What the tubby boy did was to raise his head high, look wildly at his tormentors from his glass-faced eyes, toss his fair straight hair desperately, raise his obscene case, and swing his case round his head in circles, so that the tormentors could not approach, for fear of being hit by the corners of the fast-circling case. Peter thought it was rather heroic. It was in Peter's first term at the school. He was learning to become a potential Prime Minister.

8

Before the Marriage-break, and
before the War

WITH reference to the future—when, after this stage that
we are still dealing with, Peter's father left his job at the
request of his employers, Iris left him, the result being that
Peter was free of the influence, and paralysing atmosphere, of
his father. Advancing puberty, plus this new-found freedom,
caused an awakening in Peter, but in his first year or so at
St. Elevenses prior to that awakening Peter lived in a state of
the negation of his personality, and it is this period that we will
endeavour to describe, despite the fact that the best description of that period—a description of too much brevity—is
simply that it was *fog*. How does one tell of months in a child's
life that were essentially uneventful? Peter's life at the preparatory school had been one essentially of paralysis, and all
we have been able to do is to relate the times when Peter
had infrequent moments when the paralysis disappeared. Do
not make the mistake of thinking that Peter's life, up to the
age of ten, was fairly eventful, just because you have been told
only about the awakenings from sleep when they occurred:
unfortunately one cannot write about sleep, as it is a state of
negation. In his teens Peter did become more part of the
world around him, and his periods of reality were more
frequent than they had been before; but the effect of having
been brought up, during formative years, in the company of
his twisted father was to show even when he was sixteen, for
even then he escaped into daydreaming more than most boys

of that age, and had periods of fog or daze. Peter had been frightened into himself by his father's behaviour, and only when he was an adult did the effect of living with his father, when he was young, begin to wear off.

Ten years of age, bespectacled and unintelligent, Peter was bottom of the form when he was in the Junior School. The desire to fight was manifesting itself to a certain extent at that time, and sexual awakening was manifesting itself also, in a number of strange ways, although Peter did not know the facts of life until Smithers told him after a rugby match, when Peter was older. It may seem peculiar that a boy should feel aware of sex for years, prior to that moment of truth, despite the fact that he had no idea that the act of sexual intercourse existed.

At St. Elevenses, while he was in the Junior School, Peter joined the Scout troop. The Scout meetings were held in the Scout hut, wherein Peter was in awe of the big Scouts, who were decorated from head to toe with proficiency badges of one kind or another. Peter longed to be covered from head to toe with so many proofs of intelligence, successful endeavour, and skill. There seemed to him to be nothing better in life than to be able to walk around emblazoned with honour like that. But it was reef-knots and granny-knots, the latter not to be made, that occupied Peter, and by the end of the school year Peter had not even passed his Tenderfoot. Scouts who made granny-knots were a disgrace, but Peter made them all the time.

Peter went to Scout camp that summer, and came back from it with impetigo and his Tenderfoot. That summer, Iris spent her first summer holiday unaccompanied by her husband: the marriage break-up was beginning.

The tents were pitched in a field, and at first Peter slept with two other older Scouts in a small tent, behind a bigger, full-size one. The entrance to the small tent was partially blocked by a pole of wood that held up the top-front of the tent. Peter, for some reason, had a fight in the tent with one of the older boys: the area of combat was so small that hardly any harm was done to either of the combatants, but the

aforementioned pole was broken, and as a result of that Peter moved into the big, full-size tent that housed eight Scouts. The Scouts in the tent were undistinguished Scouts, Peter being the most undistinguished of the lot, and the youngest. Peter's sleeping head rested, at night-time, very close to the ground, and the ants swarmed over his face as he slept. And the ants bit Peter's tender, washing-weakened skin. Iris had made Peter wash so frequently that his skin had become tender, and it had no resistance to the poison in the bitten areas. Peter scratched the irritating bitten parts of his face, and his skin became infected, impetigo developing, and spreading, until his face was covered completely with sores that ran with pus. Peter enjoyed that summer immensely. By the following September Peter had got a clear face again, but not before that.

After an open-air breakfast of porridge on a tin plate, and scrambled egg with tiny bits of bacon in it, Peter took his Tenderfoot test for the third time: there remained only the firelighting test, and then Peter would have passed. Luckily the examiner was a Scout who had a kind heart. Peter made his fire by piling lots of lighted matches on top of each other, and this was not permissible: and even then the fire went out. Peter's intelligence was abysmally small, but he had a certain pathetic quality about him that touched the heart of the older Scout who was taking the examination, and, glancing from right to left, to make sure that nobody was looking, the examiner passed Peter in his firelighting test. Peter was vastly proud when, at the full-uniform ceremony on the field, he was given his Tenderfoot badge to sew on his shirt.

. . . . .

His face covered with running sores and pink ointment, Peter was dropped off at the farm, from the coach-load of Scouts, on their way back to London. His mother and sister were at the farm, his mother working very hard in the fields to pay for the holiday she and her offspring were having there. Iris felt that she had to work like a slave to pay for her keep, although this was not quite true. Peter and his sister were supposed to work in the fields also, but Peter spent most of his time falling desperately in love with Gwendolene, and did not get very much farming done. Gwendolene was the farmer's daughter, and she had dark eyes, rosy cheeks, and lovely dark hair. She was younger than Peter. Peter was not looking at his most attractive at that time, because his face was covered with sores and ointment, but he could not help falling in love with Gwendolene nevertheless. Gwendolene was about nine years old and friendly. The furthest that Peter got with Gwendolene was to make the polite and friendly little girl say that she liked him: if she had asked him how he felt about her, he would have asked her to marry him.

The 'farmer' who owned the farm was a business man, who was away from the farm during the daytime, except for the week-ends. He was a sad man who had diabetes. His wife was a plump and attractive woman who had three little daughters, and they all lived in an antique farmhouse. Peter, not content with his impetigo, got what his mother called 'plum spots', through eating too many plums on the farm, and they came out in red blotches all over his body. He slept in a room with a low ceiling, a wall mirror, and a bespectacled and uncommunicative university student: Peter spent much of his time smearing ointment over his face, so that it mixed with the blood and made an even texture of pink that he naively hoped would look like healthy skin. The 'plum spots' were periodically anointed with a white, quick-drying lotion. But Peter was happy, because of the sunshine, the holiday atmosphere, and mostly because he was in love with dark curly hair and friendly, cheerful, dark eyes in a rosy face. Peter was not so happy when the 'farmer' caught him climbing a carefully brought-up young apple tree one evening, and it did not abate the man's anger when Peter tried to explain that he did not know that it was an apple tree. Peter was neither happy nor unhappy—merely astounded—when he and Gwendolene entered a barn and found six little piglets lying on the straw on the ground by the doorway, pale in the sunlight shimmering against the pale wood of the side

of the barn, their necks severed, and the blood bright and
fresh: Gwendolene did not seem to be surprised, but Peter
thought that murder had been committed, and that he had
better tell the 'farmer'. Gwendolene's sister was very proud of
the fact that, by straining herself, she could make her face
fill with blood, as her face quivered tensely with the effort,
and Peter learnt to do it too. Gwendolene had an elder sister
who was a blonde, but Peter liked dark hair, for he was a
romantic, and dark-haired girls seemed to fit into romantic
daydreams better than yellow-haired girls. One day, when
Peter was in the bedroom of the three girls, with them and
his sister, Iris came in, and was enraged to see Peter in such
an improper setting. Peter, who had only been talking to them
of course, was chased out of the room, and he went and cried
under the plum tree at the back of the farmhouse. The three
little girls looked down at him from their bedroom window
and said: 'We thought you said that you did not cry.' Peter
did not reply to them. They had not been mocking him: they
were just surprised that his boast to them previously had not
turned out to be true.

.   .   .   .   .

Peter got off the train at Balham Minor station, with his
mother and younger sister, and there was his father waiting
for them, in a dark suit, and with a dark expression on his
dark face: Arthur immediately noticed the state of Peter's
face, and naggingly asked Iris why she had not taken him to
see a doctor.

Back at home again, still thinking of Gwendolene in a
dazed sort of way, Peter did what the doctor told him to do,
and every now and again, during the course of the day, he
would spray a colourless liquid, from a perfume-spray adapted
for the purpose, on to his face: the liquid dried up the sores,
and one day Peter pulled off the last yellow scab from his
face and the impetigo was no more. It had been a nasty time.

Auntie Myrtle had asked Peter what he would like her to
bring back from the United States of America for him, and

he had said that he would like a sheath-knife, as he had decided to start a collection. When she brought back the knife it remained for ever the only one in Peter's collection, and also its life was very short. Peter was rather disappointed in the sheath-knife, for it was undistinguished, and cheap-looking, and he had expected better from the vast land across the sea.

Arthur saw the knife with its slightly curving blade, and its yellow handle with a cowboy stamped upon it, and he could not make out why Peter had wanted his aunt to buy it for him: Arthur was unaware that Peter had decided to collect sheath-knives. Arthur's suspicious and persecution-complex mind started to work overtime, and eventually he darkly came to the conclusion that Peter proposed to murder him. Arthur was sure that everybody was against him, and it made sense to him to think that his son proposed to stick the knife in him one night, when he lay asleep by the side of his unassembled and home-made bedside-cabinet.

Peter came down early as usual, before the others in the house had risen from their beds, and in the cold, grim, early-morning light in the kitchen he made a cup of tea, which he would take up to his mother, as she lay in bed: the tea-making for his mother had become a habit, and he enjoyed it as it made him feel that he was a very good boy. He put the kettle on the gas-ring of the gas-stove by the boiler, hurrying because he knew that very soon his father would be down in his dressing-gown, to perform his habitual ritual of drinking his effervescent Andrew's Liver Salts: a ritual of opening the familiar green tin, stirring the spoon in the glass, and making the white powder mix with the water, so that a buzzing sound would fill the kitchen.

After his mother had drunk her tea in bed—it was the most pleasant moment of her day—Peter went to his bedroom to dress himself. Peter found that his pyjama-trousers were not what they should be, for the cord that held them up had, at one end, slid back out of sight into the curving and long tunnel of material that contained it. When this happened it always presented a very difficult problem, for the hidden end could not easily be brought out into the open again, and it was imperative that both ends of the cord should be projecting, because otherwise the two ends of the cord could not be tied, and the trousers would fall down: Peter was very particular about being well dressed in bed. Peter spent three-quarters of an hour squeezing the tunnel of material that ran round the waist of the trousers, so that the tunnel rucked and the cord was worked forward to the opening of the tunnel: when he could see the end of the white cord he got a safety-pin, dug at the frayed end of the cord, and pulled it out into the open: the sense of achievement that he felt was enormous, and he stood with naked legs, and a pyjama-coat on his torso, looking delightedly at the two ends of the white cord that projected from the top-front of the striped and light-blue pyjama-trousers in his hands. He sat back exhaustedly on the bed, above the headboard of which was hung a large map of England. He heard his mother calling him from the kitchen, telling him that his breakfast was ready. He dressed hurriedly.

When he arrived in the kitchen downstairs his father had gone off to work, and his mother had just finished raking out the ashes from the bottom of the boiler that had been alight all night. She pointed down to the bottom of the boiler, and Peter saw his sheath-knife: it had no handle now, and the metal of the blade was dulled with the effect of fire: from the end of the blade a spike projected that had once been covered by the handle.

Arthur thought that prevention was better than cure—especially when you cannot cure death. 'Your father thought that you meant to kill him with the knife,' said Iris to Peter, with contempt for her husband in her voice, as Peter stared wonderingly at what was left of the knife in his hands. Peter had a dark vision of his father coming down in the night and putting the knife in the boiler, after lifting the circular plate off the top of the boiler with the bar supplied with the boiler for that purpose; and Peter was surprised that his father could have thought that he would plan to kill him. Peter had been brought up to be a nice boy, and patricide was as foreign to his nature as was the idea of wearing in bed pyjamas, the

86

trousers of which were round his feet, in a crumpled mess below the sheets, and at the bottom of the bed, when he awoke in the morning.

.   .   .   .   .

Arthur's bedroom contained a wardrobe that was facing the end of his bed; a dressing-table, with a pair of brushes and a collar-stud on the flat surface below the tiltable circular mirror—this dressing-table standing by the windows that looked on to the garden; a chest of drawers that stood by the door; and a carpet. The room was usually dark, even in the daytime, and whenever Peter trespassed therein he felt the room had an atmosphere that suggested that no joy was ever felt there at any time. Arthur's wardrobe had a few clothes in it, and they were good clothes, because Arthur had a theory that if anything was worth buying it was worth getting the best. Even though there was a carpet on the floor, of some once-warm pattern and colour, and even though Arthur had a Paisley dressing-gown that hung on the door, the room had an austere quality that was lacking in Iris's bedroom, that was next door to Arthur's bedroom: perhaps this difference was because of the fact that nobody could go into Arthur's bedroom, whereas anybody in the house could go into Iris's bedroom if they wanted to. There was a freedom to Iris's bedroom that there was not to Arthur's bedroom. Peter, when he later learnt the facts of life, could never imagine his mother going to her husband's bed, because the atmosphere of his father's bedroom was so grim that Peter felt that even the grimmest type of sexual intercourse could not have taken place there. After he had learnt the facts of life from Smithers, on the way back from the rugby match in Public Fields, Peter often wondered where his father had found his sex.

Between his father's bedroom and his own bedroom was his mother's bedroom, that contained his mother's and his sister's beds. In his mother's bedroom was a tall mirrored wardrobe, and Peter would use that mirror if he came home for his lunch in the middle of the day. Peter grew very familiar with that mirror. Peter had discovered hair-cream: he used it very liberally, and his aim was to get his hair to lie perfectly flat and gleaming round, and on top of, his skull. After lunch, and until it was time for him to walk to school, he would spend the time in the empty bedroom, in front of the mirror, combing and combing, and looking and looking, until his hair was perfectly straight and perfectly smooth. On his way to school he was, by school law, supposed to wear his school cap, but he did not do this, because the cap would mess up his hair: school prefects passed him on their bikes as he walked to afternoon school, his thoughts entirely on his hair gleaming creamily in the sunshine, and they would call to him to put his cap on. Until they were out of sight he would fumble with his cap, as if he was going to put it on, and then he would put it in his pocket again, folded in two. It would have ruined his afternoon if he had been forced to mess up his hair by putting on the cap, for there was not much chance in the afternoon of getting to the long mirror in the school cloakroom. It was calculated that Peter spent as much time on his appearance as Auntie Maggie's teenage working daughter did. One lunchtime, Peter tried to look on top of the wardrobe by lodging his booted toes on a ridge at the base of the wardrobe and clutching with his hands at the moulding that ran round the high top of the vertical piece of furniture: before he had a chance to raise himself sufficiently to look on the top of the wardrobe he had pulled the wardrobe over on top of himself, splitting one of the polished mahogany side-panels on his polished and slightly pointed head. The wardrobe was very heavy, and he was not very strong yet, and there was a horrible collection of tense moments, during which time he tried to stop the wardrobe falling flat on top of him. Eventually his quivering hands settled the leaning wardrobe in a vertical position again. His mother was very angry, but not as angry as she would have been if the wardrobe had fallen over completely, for then it would have been broken more seriously. Peter was glad the heavy wardrobe had not fallen over completely, because he did not relish the thought of being underneath the giant mass of wood. As it was he had to comb his hair again, and was nearly late for afternoon school.

Arthur had misinterpreted the International Situation. He could not settle down that night. He thought that the aeroplane passing overhead might be a Hun, despite the fact that war had not yet broken out; and just as he had to see the cars that passed his dining-room window, while he was having his Saturday lunch, so he had to see the plane in the dark night sky. There was a full moon that night, and perhaps that accounted for the strange behaviour of Arthur that terminated when the police came to the contemporary suburban house in Balham Minor, in Hastershire.

Arthur looked at the plane in the sky, from the windows of his back bedroom, and watched the plane until it went out of sight over the top of his house. Peter was in bed, and so were Iris and her daughter Annabell. But Arthur had to see the plane from his wife's bedroom window, after it had passed out of sight from his own bedroom window. In his pyjamas he rushed wildly into Iris's room, and stood staring from her bedroom window at the passing plane droning slowly and high in the sky, a strange figure in the moonlight in his striped pyjamas. Iris was angry at this intrusion, and she said a few things from her bed to Arthur, who took no notice at all. Arthur was allowed to row evening after evening, but he was not allowed to waken his wife and daughter from sleep, and he had never done this sort of thing before. Eventually he retired again to his room, and Iris's bedroom door was closed again, and they all went to sleep—except Arthur, who was rather unsettled for some reason that night—probably because there was a full moon.

It was rather unfortunate that Arthur heard another plane in the moonlit sky some time later that night: Arthur rushed into Iris's bedroom again, and it was then that Iris became distraught. Iris needed her sleep very badly, and when she turned out the light in her bedroom, at the end of the evening of wearing rowing, she expected to find peace: the intrusion into her bedroom caught her at a time when she was not prepared for it, and when her nerves were frayed. Another row started, and Arthur was in and out of Iris's bedroom, rowing intermittently: night-time rows were unheard of by Iris, and this one roused her to action, in a way that the evening rows never did. During one of the moments when Arthur was walking up and down in his own bedroom, preparatory to another entry into his wife's room, Iris got out of her bed, opened one of the windows, leant out, and tapped on the nearby bedroom window of the house next door. Arthur had not allowed a phone to be installed in his house, otherwise Iris would have phoned up the police herself that night. Iris asked the next-door neighbour, who leant out of his bedroom window in response to her knocking, and who had replaced the widow-woman in the house next door, if he would phone up the police: the man obligingly did as she asked.

Peter remembered his father standing on the stairs in his Paisley dressing-gown, Peter himself higher up on the stairs than his father, and his mother standing in the hall below with the dark-uniformed policeman looking up at his father. Arthur said nothing as the police officer told him not to do it again. Arthur had also said nothing when he had been in the hospital, for a voluntary period of observation by doctors of his mental state, and so he had not revealed his twisted mentality, and they had been forced to discharge him as completely sane. Arthur had agreed to go for this period of observation at the request of Iris. He was aware that he was twisted, and he was intelligent enough to say nothing when the police or doctors were present.

.   .   .   .   .

His long grey flannel trousers were baggy and stained, but that did not single Peter out from the other boys at St. Elevenses: the boys might comb their hair, wear special shirts or gleaming white collars, neat and cleaned blazers, oft-pressed ties, and clean underwear, but there were two articles of apparel that they allowed to reach a disgraceful state, and they were the trousers and the caps. The caps were worn as little as possible, and they were greasy inside and out, as well as being invariably too small. The trousers had bicycle-grease stains near the turn-ups, and were pressed once in a blue moon. It was a peculiar thing, but the boys felt that they were sufficiently well attired to talk to girls if their hair was combed carefully into waves, and if their collars were respectable, and they would venture into romances quite happily with trousers that a tramp would be ashamed to wear. But the trousers had to be grey: that was the school law: woe betide a boy who wore brown trousers. There was no precedent for such a thing, but if a boy had come to school in red trousers he would probably have been expelled on the spot: his chances of being made a prefect, when he got into the sixth form, would have been non-existent if the judgement of his crime had been lenient enough to allow him to remain at the school. But the fact was that no boy would have been stupid enough to come to school in red trousers: it would have been better if he had come to school naked. But make no mistake: there were no naked boys at St. Elevenses—that was just a figure of speech. St. Elevenses was not a nudist colony, as we think we have already made quite clear: St. Elevenses was blazers, blazers, blazers—striped all over with purple and blue—hundreds of them, with boys inside them —boys who had hardly felt the stirrings yet of sex, boys who were perplexed to find they were changing, boys who did not let Mummy bath them any more, and boys who knew exactly what sex was about—in theory, that is. And scattered around the school somewhere were a small number of boys who knew what sex was about in practice, disgraceful as it was.

Peter, before his father and mother had split up, and before the war came, had reached the stage where he bathed himself, where he was aware of girls—thinking that kissing was the last step—and where he titivated himself, as his mother called his vanity, in front of the wardrobe mirror. And it was at this stage that Peter thought that silk stockings were the most exciting thing that he had ever seen. One night he put one of his mother's silk stockings—the left one—on his own leg, under the cover of the bedclothes, and in a state of pure ecstasy he slept through the night with it on, returning it furtively in the morning when his mother was not in her bedroom. Adolescence was on the way.

. . . . .

The war came, but it did not affect Peter very much. Peter never heard the wireless, because his father was suspicious of such things. One day Arthur had practically purchased a wireless, and he was about to pay for it when he was asked to sign something by the salesman. Arthur was even more suspicious of signing things, and, refusing to sign, he sent the wireless back to the shop. They had the wireless on approval for about two glorious weeks, and then they started living without communication with the outside world again. In those days the wireless was an important part of middle-class life, just as the television is these days, and Peter felt that his home life was very queer in that it was less a wireless: this just added to his feeling of inferiority because of the unique situation he found at home. He thought that no other parents would row: it was inconceivable to him that the parents of the other boys at his school had rows at home.

Peter never had a chance to read the *Daily Mail*, which was the paper that his father took with him to work every day, or, if he did get a chance, it was the strip cartoons that he read. So as a result of this, and as a result of not having a wireless, Peter's knowledge of the progress of the war was limited. Later on he was impressed by the existence of the war by gas-masks, air-raid shelters, his call-up, and the doodle-bug that brought his bedroom ceiling down on his head; but if it had not been for those things, and a few more odd things, Peter's awareness of the war would have been small indeed: his state of daze was hard to penetrate. But what did penetrate later on was the fact of *girls*: that got through his daze all right; but Shakespeare, mathematics, geography, and all that never really got through to him—until the headmaster told him, when he was about fifteen, that unless he did better at school he would have to go out and sell peanuts, and then Peter tried. Peter regarded selling peanuts as so utterly below him that he did everything he could to avoid doing so: but we have not come to that yet, for the hair had not begun to grow under his arms at the stage in his life with which we are now dealing. That was a disturbing occurrence by the way—Peter was very surprised to find the first hairs growing under his armpits: he had expected to grow bigger, but he was not prepared for things like that.

Auntie Myrtle was the most attractive sister that Iris had: she was unmarried, and she had a freedom about her that her married sisters did not have: she was the glamorous one. Myrtle had a man: he was something or other—nobody could tell just quite what—but there was a feeling that he was a dentist—a dentist without a practice. He was Irish and dark, slightly too unconventional for Iris's family—they liked gentlemen who had settled jobs—and they thought that he might have been a bounder, although he was not for as it turned out he loved Myrtle very much indeed.

Myrtle and her man came to visit one Sunday: visits by relations were rare and they livened things up for Peter when they occurred. It was like Christmas to Peter when someone came to visit. They all sat in the lounge at the back of the house. It was in the lounge that Peter played the few records, playing them on the 'His Master's Voice' gramophone that wound up and that had a little dog on it who was listening to a gramophone horn: Peter was not playing the gramophone on the occasion of the visit, but when he did he avoided playing the very black record that told sadly of Old Virginie: Peter felt that the sound, and appearance, of that record was so utterly depressing that he avoided it like the plague. The difficulty was that there were so few records to play, and now and again his sister and he were forced to play the big black record with the black label to cause a little variety: they usually quarrelled before it was put on the turntable. As the adults talked, the gramophone closed up on a side-table, Peter wandered from the kitchen to the lounge: and then Myrtle's

93

man gave him sixpence. When Arthur found out he asked Peter to give it back, and much to the embarrassment of Myrtle's man, and much to the disappointment of Peter, Peter handed it back: sixpence was a lot of money to Peter in those days. Arthur had thought that no one should give his son money but his parents. His parents never gave Peter any money, but apparently that was beside the point the way Arthur saw it. Arthur had a peculiar and twisted pride.

Talking of sixpences—Peter was given a sixpence by someone for services rendered, and this Arthur did not seem to object to. Peter was very thoughtful about the sixpence, and decided that he would give it to his father for safe keeping. Peter thought that if he himself kept the sixpence he might lose it. Arthur put the sixpence in the tiny pocket of his waistcoat—the waistcoat that was decorated by the watch-chain that hung in two loops across his flat stomach —and determined to justify the trust given to him. Arthur thought that he had been given the sixpence so that Peter would not spend it at the first opportunity. Arthur was wrong: Peter had given it to him only because he thought he would lose it in the garden—that it would fall out of his trousers pocket while he was playing with his sister Annabell.

The Wall's ice-cream tricycle came round every now and again, and when it did that was an event in the road—to the children in the road, that is. The ices that Peter bought were the cheapest, as he was never given enough money to buy the more expensive kinds: the twopenny ices were not for the likes of him. The penny ices were sticks of frozen fruit-water, triangular in section, encased in thin white and pale-blue cardboard that you tore away as you licked, likely to last as long as ten minutes if you licked all the time and were very careful and did not succumb to the temptation to chew, and were positively heavenly—at least Peter thought they were. With a penny Wall's ice in his hand Peter was in his Seventh Heaven, to use his mother's phraseology.

There stood the ice-cream man by the fence that bordered the garden of the organist. It is of no importance to mention that actually it was not the organist's garden any more because he had left the house and it was now empty. Martin was buying a twopenny ice, and so was Oscar, the brutal boy who lived up the road, whose bedroom was scattered with records that the boy had broken in a fit of temper, temper being his main character-trait. When Peter had seen the broken records he had been astounded, because he would never have dared to break any records himself—not that he had any records to break.

Peter ran and asked his father for the sixpence. But Arthur intended to protect the boy from himself: Arthur would not give Peter the sixpence to squander on the frivolity of ices. Peter had felt the ownership of the sixpence acutely, and when the sixpence was withheld from him he had a fit of temper. He had to do something that would make his father see how deeply he felt about being prevented from buying the penny ice-cream.

It was a Saturday or a Sunday: very little happened between Peter and his father on Monday to Friday weekdays, because Peter did not have the opportunity of seeing his father much on those weekdays. Arthur had been raking some earth preciously that afternoon, and out in the garden was a precious patch of earth in which Arthur intended to plant seeds. Arthur would probably never get round to actually planting the seeds, but that did not really matter, for it was the excuse to rake the earth that was the thing. Not a lump of earth bigger than a sixpence lay on the light-brown patch in the garden. Peter trampled over the patch viciously, stamping on the holy ground for a few demoniacal moments, and then he rushed into the house, and in a wild and provocative fashion told his father what he had done, adding something about it being because he had not been given the sixpence that was his by rights. Arthur, as has been stated, was afraid of his temper. And he restrained himself from chastising his son whenever he felt like chastising him. But when Arthur saw the stamped-on earth he saw red. He had been happily fiddling with that earth all afternoon, and that patch had become more dear to him than life itself. How wonderful it had been to rake the earth until all the particles were as small as he could make them: mowing the lawn had nothing on raking earth. Arthur chased his son up the garden and down again. Round the young apple tree that was planted in the lawn, and across the paths that traversed the vegetable patch. Down the garden again, and up the garden again: across the paths that divided the vegetable patch at the end of the lawn. Peter was electrified with fear, and he ran, his feet hardly touching the ground. He ran with short steps through the vegetable patch, and with racing strides across the lawn. He knew that if his father caught him the result might be of unprecedented terror. His father had never been so angry with him ever before. So Peter, given speed by his terror, saw to it that his father did not catch him, and eventually his father walked back into the house. In the house Arthur thought about his anger and was afraid of himself: so he controlled his ferocity intensely and determined that he would do no more about the matter. Arthur gave the sixpence to Iris, and when Peter came in at last, and his father was behind the closed door of the lounge, reading his paper, a pipe in his mouth, Iris gave the boy his sixpence. But by then the ice-cream man was far away.

9

Cousin Trevor

PETER rode on his adult-size bicycle for a whole day: the cars swarmed round him in the roads, he stopped at the traffic-lights, and he lost his way five or six times. His uncle had given him a list of towns to pass through on his way to his uncle's house. It was as good a way to direct the boy as any: Peter made his way from one town to another and as the light was failing he came into the familiar environs of his uncle's house and a feeling of relief came over him: he cycled down the familiar roads and then into the road in which his uncle lived. Very soon they were welcoming him, and the long-awaited holiday had begun. There was no point in thinking about the long journey home—that was two weeks away.

.   .   .   .   .

His cousin Trevor was bigger now, as big as Peter was, and Cousin Trevorene-Lou, though dressed in plain schoolgirl clothes, and not of a glamorous disposition, was now a big girl in the very best sense: Peter eyed her chest with wonder. Trevorene-Lou was fifteen or sixteen then and Peter was twelve.

It all started when Peter and Trevor went to the nearby town. They made their way to the bus-stop two roads away, and on their way to the bus-stop, by the side of some hedges, they had a fight: it was not a sporting fight—it was a fight with some anger in it—and Trevor fell on to the pavement.

When they got to the town they went into Algherti's, and walked down the long aisles looking at the wonderful variety of things on the counters. The war was on, and the book buyer of the store must have been a substitute who was careless and bought books without reading them, for Peter found some paper-backs for sale there that should not have been there at all. Those particular books were not there for long, and no replacements were made: somebody must have told the managers of the chain of shops that those particular paper-backs were undesirable. Peter, being older than Trevor, who had not developed a liking for such books yet, bought one of the books. It was bought with the money his mother had given him for the holiday, and he had not much money left after he had bought it. The book was not lavishly covered: it had a pale-pink cover of bad-quality thick paper, and on it, in rough capitals, was printed the title of the book: *You take me, you keep me*. It was all about a lorry-driver's mate who had once been an overworked seamstress, and who seemed to change lorry-drivers every five minutes. Peter thought that the title was rather enigmatic.

When they got back to Trevor's home Peter's aunt asked him why they had had the fight. Peter said nothing, as he so often did, and went away furtively to read the book with perspiring hands. That evening, when all the family were in the sitting-room, playing a word game, Peter left the book on the seat of a chair, and Trevor reached for the book with a peculiar expression upon his bespectacled face. Peter took the book before Trevor could get it, and Trevor relaxed into his chair with yet another peculiar look upon his young, but very intelligent, face.

Later on, Trevor and Peter went into the bathroom to wash before going to bed. The bathroom was not very spacious, and they stood near each other, shirts off, and vests on show. There was a desultory exchange of words about the book, Peter justifying his interest in the book, and Trevor being rather nicely brought up about it. Peter asked Trevor if he knew what breasts were for, Peter being informed on this matter, and Trevor said stiffly that he did not want to know.

Peter wondered if Trevor did know or not. After that the conversation became rather heated, and a fight began in the confines of the bathroom, between the bath and the wash-basin. Peter took off his spectacles so that he could fight without the danger of their getting broken, but he forgot to put them down anywhere, and fought with them clasped in his hand. He soon forgot that his spectacles were in his hand, and hit Trevor on the top of the head with the closed hand that contained the spectacles. Peter looked with great distress at the shattered spectacles in his hand, realizing that he would have to spend the rest of the holiday in a myopic blur, and, understanding the magnitude of the tragedy, Trevor said he was sorry with sincere feeling and with no regard for the fact that it had been Peter's fault entirely. They spent some more time in the bathroom, hostilities completely forgotten, and then Trevorene-Lou came in, having felt that she had been waiting far too long for her pre-bed wash. Trevorene-Lou said nothing as she went straight to the wash-basin, put down her washing equipment, and began to wash, her back to the two boys. She, too, had only a vest on her torso, a rather unglamorous garment of brown wool, and Peter stared unbelievingly at what he was being allowed to see. He could tell that Trevorene-Lou was not being brazen, partly because she was not acting in a brazen way—she was completely concerned with getting her face washed—and partly because he knew that Trevorene-Lou was a girl of the utmost purity, whose eyes just did not register sexual awareness at all. Trevorene-Lou had been so annoyed at being kept waiting for the bathroom that she had decided to barge in despite the fact that the boys were still there, and her concern with her determination had made her forget that her torso was not properly covered. Peter was very impressed with this incident, and he valued it, for it was the most he had ever seen, to that date, of a girl or woman. He read his book in bed afterwards with a swirling mind until his cousin in the other bed asked him to put out the light.

Peter went into the town to go to the optician's. As he had expected, the optician told him that his glasses would not be repaired until the last day of the holiday, and Peter left the optician's seeing everything in an approximate way.

Rationing was at this time making housewives frustrated, and Trevor's mother was finding it difficult to feed all the people in her house. Peter had brought his ration book with him, but such things as shop-made cakes were hard to come by. In the town there was a shop that sold one cake to every customer, and Trevor's mother hit on the idea of sending Trevor and Peter into the town, so that they could each buy a cake at the shop. Peter felt rather an idiot without his glasses on, and he did not like the idea of going into the shop to buy the cake, because he was afraid he would not be able to see which cake he was supposed to buy, and he would be embarrassed to ask the shop assistant to help him, and to have to explain to her that he was too blind to see the cakes on the shelf: Peter always felt embarrassed when he went into shops anyway, spectacles or no spectacles, and if the shop assistant was a girl it only made things worse, and his face was liable to go a horrible red colour.

Trevor went into the shop first and Peter waited outside. Trevor was not embarrassed by anything, for he was too intelligent for that sort of thing. Peter waited on the pavement, and near him was a queue of people, a characteristic of those wartime days. In the queue were two nice young girls, and Peter began to stare at them through a mist, thinking that as he could not see the expression in their eyes they could not see the admiring expression in his. But they could see the expression in his eyes, and Peter was very disconcerted to find that they were laughing at him.

Soon Trevor came out of the shop with his cake, and it was Peter's turn to go into the shop. But, despite the contempt manifested by his cousin regarding his cowardice, Peter would not venture into the shop, and they got on to the bus with only one cake. When they got to Trevor's home the aunt was furious with her nephew. They all had tea together, Peter being very silent, and Trevorene-Lou told a funny riddle, her face crimson with embarrassment. She had to be greatly encouraged by her brother to tell the riddle, and did so with some reluctance. The story concerned the similarity between missionaries and prunes, and the answer to the riddle was that prunes, like missionaries, go down into dark places and do good. Peter thought that it was surprising that such a sensitive girl should have displayed her merely vest-covered chest to her cousin in the bathroom.

. . . . .

Peter's holiday at his uncle's house was nearing its end, and he went into the town and collected his repaired spectacles: the town was in definition again, and he felt that the sun had broken through the clouds for the first time in nearly two weeks. The following day he put his precious and lurid book in his pocket, and rode away, the list of towns that his uncle had given him a fortnight previously in his other pocket: Peter would read the list of towns from finish to start this time.

The journey seemed interminable, and the hills that he had freewheeled down on his first journey now forced him, on his return journey, to dismount from his adult-size bicycle, and, holding the handlebars with one hand, walk slowly in the gutters up those hills that had once seemed so sweet. He stopped wearily in the middle of nowhere—as it seemed to him to be, so far from anywhere familiar to him—by some shops, and listened to the sound of a lady's silk slip as she walked past him: his senses, so tired by the journey, reeled at the sensuous sound, and with a feeling of frustration and yearning he began to walk up yet another hill. He had nearly reached the top of the hill, and was dragging his feet over the concrete of the side of the road, his legs so tired that they seemed to be unnaturally light below his body, when he saw a girl on the other side of the road. She had come out of a side turning further up the hill, and was firmly walking in a direction that was at an angle to the road: Peter saw that she would soon step off the pavement, walk across the road diagonally towards the pavement on his side of the road a yard or so ahead of him, and mount the pavement on his side of the road, after which she obviously intended to go on walking down the hill. Peter further realized that by the time she had crossed the road diagonally he would have come up the hill to the point where she would mount the pavement from the road. His excitement was intense in a tiredly light-headed sort of way as he prepared for her to come nearer and nearer to him, finally to walk past him very closely. There was no one else in sight, and Peter felt that they had the hill to themselves. He felt that she must feel the sexual tension of the approach as he was feeling it, and the Approach was an experience that was terribly sweet to him: how he wished that he had this girl as his girl—to go to the pictures with, to walk in the fields with, and, ecstasy of ecstasies, to hold, and to kiss. She was his own age, pretty, with young adolescent charms, and a budding chest swelling girlishly beneath her blue top-coat. She wore no hat, her eyes were perhaps smiling and perhaps just always appearing to smile, and those eyes half pretended not to be aware of him, and they were trying to hide their expression in a light sparkling mist that was in them. Peter trembled as they approached each other on the hill, his legs dragged, and the bicycle bumped against his side as he walked with it. Poetry, love, sweetness, and desire sang in his mind, as the moment of their paths almost crossing became imminent. She looked neither at him, or from side to side, and he wondered if she liked him, or if she thought that he was not attractive. She passed him without showing a sign that indicated that she realized that he was there, and a feeling of disappointment came to him as he thought that perhaps she had not realized that he was there. She walked out of his life down the hill, and as he went on to the top of the hill and remounted his bicycle he could not bear the realization that he would never see her again. He had wanted to speak to her—to be like the bold boys and to have said something confident, flirtatious, and charming—but he had not had the necessary courage. He despised himself for his lack of heart, and all the way home he thought of what might have happened if he had spoken to her: she might have become his girl eventually he thought despondently, his mind full of dreams, and as he pedalled home he thought of walking with her, talking with her, holding her, and kissing her. How he hated his weakness in not being able to speak to girls like the other chaps did. How he hated to think of what he was missing. But he never learnt how to approach a girl, not for a long time, until he was sixteen or thereabouts, when he plucked up enough courage to ask Hilda if she was going to wait for her bus, when they both knew perfectly well that he knew that she was. There were going to be some long years before that day when he spoke to Hilda for the first time—years full of yearning—years full of the inability to speak to a girl—girlless years—years when his senses cried for a girl of his own. But, as he cycled home from the hill and his uncle's, he did not know that he would have to wait so long before he was able to make his first contact with a girl: if he had known then he would have not believed that it could be possible: every day, from that moment on the hill to the time when he actually spoke to Hilda, he thought would be his last one without a girl. And even though Hilda, when she eventually came into his life, was a dream of flirty eyes and femininity—all that he had ever wanted, in fact—his association with her was not enough to compensate him for his long yearning years of feeble-hearted waiting: not that he ever really thought of her as his girl when they were together anyway—she often mocked him—although it must be admitted that she stayed up until one in the morning with him, waiting at the bus-stop for her bus, watching the buses stop and start, without getting on one, until after the last bus had gone.

10

Auntie Maggie's House

PETER was in the Senior School building, studying there day after day, at the time when Arthur lost his job, and began to walk around in sandals—presumably to save the cost of a new pair of shoes. Peter never found out exactly why his father lost his job: it was something to do with Arthur becoming too difficult to work with—something to do with Arthur having been for too many years at his place of work acting in an obstreperous and vociferous manner, and it was something to do with Arthur being dismissed with reluctance because he had been with the firm so long. Presumably Arthur had not only rowed at home with his wife.

It was Iris's chance: she felt no obligation to stay with Arthur any more, and soon after he lost his job she went to her mother's house. Arthur obviously did not intend to try to get another job, and he began cashing in his Savings Certificates, and living on the money that was thereby realized.

Peter was sent to Auntie Maggie's house—she had moved by now to a house opposite a flower nursery—a house that was nearly as gloomy as the other one, and Iris and Annabell went to stay at Grandma's and Grandpa's modern little house that they now occupied in the years of Grandpa's retirement. All the strays ended up at Grandma's and Grandpa's house, and it was even used as a store for the dental equipment that belonged to that man of mystery—Myrtle's man.

Iris found this break-up a strain, and she developed shingles on her face: Peter visited her from his aunt's, and he felt his mother was remote from him when he went up to her, as she sat in a deck-chair in the garden in the sunshine, smiling self-consciously at him through the mess on her face. When the shingles disappeared, Iris prepared to get a job to provide the money necessary to pay for the maintenance of herself and her children: Arthur was not sending her any money. Iris began to train at Remington's, learning to operate a Remington's accounting machine. When she had learnt how to do this, she got a job at Fernando's store, operating one of those machines in that vast store in the accounting department.

In the back garden of Maggie's house—there was hardly any front garden, because as the house was built just where the road turned the front garden was cut back to the front of the house by the curving pavement—was an air-raid shelter, projecting grimly from the surface of the ground, and it was within this that Peter slept, in the company of his auntie Maggie, his uncle, his two female cousins, and the school-teacher lodger. At the end of the garden was a railway track, along which noisy trains passed periodically, and the garden curved round the side of the house to a pair of large wooden gates, as well as being at the back of the house. The garden was in direct contrast to the nursery across the road, for it was not an example of horticultural splendour: dour, and not splendour, being the operative word in the mostly bare-earth garden. A few yards away from the shelter was a garage with a hopeless car in it, the garage being situated on the piece of garden that was by the side of the house. It was outside this garage that Maggie's husband prepared his fishing tackle and tried to service his hopeless article of transport: Maggie's husband was on view more these days than he had been at the other house. He was often to be seen during an air raid, his head unprotected from the danger of falling shrapnel, standing outside the air-raid shelter, staring at the sky in which a dog-fight was taking place, while in the shelter were clustered the other members of the family, Peter, and the curly-headed lodger who possessed a wonderful bicycle that could make forty miles an hour down a hill when there was an air raid on and when he was racing back to the shelter. Peter regarded the bicycle with enormous respect, for it was new and shiny, and had a fine three-speed gear in the hub of the rear wheel.

Maggie's older daughter was going to get married, and the younger daughter was about seventeen, at work in a factory—glamorous, and all covered in lipstick: Peter regarded the younger cousin with some respect for her clumsy sophistication. The younger cousin, who was called Betty, had a boy friend called Charlie, who insisted on saying 'Le da de da de da' in a fatuous voice when the door of the house was opened to him by his girl. Betty informed Peter one day that Charlie was 'slightly screwball', and she pointed her finger at her head, twisted it round, and looked up at the sky significantly and exaggeratedly, showing a large amount of white eyeball as she did so—all this being a pictorial attempt on her part to indicate the state of her boy-friend's brain. One day Betty quarrelled with Charlie, who was a very nice chap really, and instead of going to the pictures with him on that Saturday afternoon, she took Peter with her. Peter thought that this was very romantic indeed, but of course it wasn't. Peter spent some of his evenings with the others in the dining-room-cum-sitting-room, sitting sprawled out in a chair by the fire, meditatively staring at his pullover-covered stomach that moved as he breathed: he could not understand why his stomach should move when he breathed, for he understood that his lungs were further up and in his chest. Peter spent a great deal of his time doing peculiar things of this nature, and the rest of the time he thought about girls he had not got.

One night they were all lying out in the shelter, some of them asleep and some of them trying to sleep. The floor of the shelter was well below the bottom of the entrance-way, and a raised bunk on the wall opposite the doorway contained Maggie's eldest daughter. On the floor slept the others, in separate wrappings, and that night Peter was sleeping beside his young-man-conscious cousin Betty. Just previously, as the elder daughter was stepping down into the sunken shelter, her feet poking down to the floor, and her body and head half in the entrance-way and half in the garden, Peter had inadvertently stepped hard on her foot. This had annoyed the elder daughter considerably: Peter did not care overmuch about that as he did not think that Betty's elder sister was glamorous, although many men older than she was thought that she was very exciting: the fact of the matter was that Peter liked girls who were exaggeratedly feminine, with lots of black hair, and lots of make-up, and, whereas the elder cousin did not fit this description, Betty did.

Peter lay in the darkness by the side of Betty, and he thought of her romantically as he stared into the impenetrable and sightless blackness above him: he knew that Betty was awake, and that one of her hands lay by her side a few inches away from the blankets of his bed. After much deliberation and consideration, Peter put his own hand on that of his cousin Betty, and she let his hand hold hers for a while, saying into the darkness that wasn't it romantic. The school-teacher, who wanted to go to sleep so that he would be fresh for school in the morning, said into the darkness that he did not think that 'romantic' described the situation in the shelter very well. Nobody could see anything at all, nobody but Peter and Betty were aware of the hand-holding, and Betty was merely being kind to the adolescent boy in an older-sister kind of way. Soon she withdrew her hand from his, and she and Peter went to sleep. It had been a profoundly moving experience for Peter when he had held that hand that had felt so expressive of the mysteries and charms of the opposite sex.

. . . . . .

Peter slept for a while in Betty's room: this was not as bad as it sounds. There was a period when the shelter in the garden was not occupied solidly throughout the night, and during this time the members of the Auntie Maggie family either slept on the ground floor within easy distance of the cupboard under the stairs, which they used if the sirens went, or they slept in the bedrooms on the first floor. Betty's bedroom was a tiny room in the front of the house that was situated just above the front door and which had a high and small window:

if Peter stood on a chair and looked out of the window, his eyes hardly higher than the bottom of the window because the window was so high, he could see the front-garden gate directly beneath him, the road viewable at a less-acute angle, and in full view was the nursery across the turning road. But Peter did not stand on a chair for Betty's bed was below the high window and Peter stood on that. Peter would watch the young ladies walking by from his awkward vantage point in Betty's bedroom. A few feet from the bed, against the wall opposite the windowed wall, stood a dressing-table, the glass top of which was loaded with Betty's cosmetic equipment—a lipstick, tubes and round and decorated boxes, a carelessly and temporarily abandoned stocking, and a layer of scattered face-powder. In one corner of the tiny and narrow room was a thin wardrobe, and above the aforementioned dressing-table there was a mirror. But Betty slept in the big bedroom next to this room, sharing her mother's double bed, leaving her tiny bedroom for Peter to sleep in. Betty dressed and made herself up in the tiny bedroom when Peter was out of the room, because all her clothes were there and her cosmetics were there.

Peter, who, as time passed, had been growing older all the time—peculiar as that might seem—had the typically confused and turgid state of mind in relationship to the phenomenon of sex of the younger adolescent. The very thought in his mind of a petticoat would cause dark currents to swirl within the confines of his cranium, and a love scene on the cinema screen would make his collar seem too tight, and make him glance uneasily from side to side, to see whether anybody was observing the expression of idiotic ecstasy that was on his face, or the leer that was curving on his young red mouth: he was convinced that people were looking at him when he was emotionally disturbed in the cinema in this way.

It was torment for Peter to sit in a bus opposite a girl of about his own age, and on such occasions he would not know where to look: as he was almost as embarrassed to have to look at anybody facing him in a bus, he did not find very easily anywhere to fix his gaze that caused him to feel unselfconscious: empty seats and windows were the places that, if he was lucky, he could look away at, if a pretty girl sat across from him. Buses were agony to the over-self-conscious Peter, and after some time he developed a technique that helped him to ride on buses with the minimum of nervous and emotional strain. He would endeavour to sit, not on the long seats that faced other long seats, but to sit on the smaller seats that faced in the direction that the bus was going, and to sit on the inside of such double seats, so that he could stare out of the window for the duration of the journey. Even paying for his ride was a torment for him, and when the bus-conductress asked him what fare he wanted to pay he would shout the amount in a choking or emotionally charged voice. But he felt comparatively protected and secluded when he was on the inside of a double seat, staring for all he was worth out of the bus window at the rapidly passing scene, doing his best to pretend that he was not there at all. On one occasion he had been unfortunate enough to get on a single-decker bus that had no choice of seats offered: he was forced to sit in the lower half of the bus, where the two long seats faced each other, and opposite him, and beside him, sat a crowd of young girls, laughing, and talking in voices that to Peter were full of sexual awareness. For all of that journey he sat with his hands between his knees, his bottom half off the seat, and with his blushing face bent down so that he was looking at his knees. When he got on a double-decker bus he would quickly look into the lower deck, and if it was crowded, or contained any laughing girls, he would mount the stairs to the upper deck, in search of some comparative safety. If he was on the inside of a double seat, looking out of the window, his safety would not be assured, because if a girl was sitting in the seat in front she might turn round, look past his face, and converse with her girl-friend who was in the seat behind him: this was a comparatively rare occurrence, and only happened when the bus filled up with factory girls, or even worse—for they were sometimes nearer his own age—schoolgirls; but when it did happen, he would be petrified, as he tried not to look at the girl's face so close to his and looking past his ear—an ear that was, on such occasions, invariably a very deep crimson, his ears blushing a deeper red than his face did.

Walking in the streets was not a free and easy thing for Peter to do: if a person approached him walking in his direction, passing by him, and walking on—a thing that happens to pedestrians a million times a month or more—the approach, when Peter and the other pedestrian were facing each other, would be an agony of self-consciousness for Peter. He preferred to walk behind people, and did so if he could; he preferred not to walk on the outside of the pavements, where everybody could see him if they wanted to; and he preferred most of all to walk alongside a fence, so that if someone approached in his direction he could pretend to be studying fence-construction until the pedestrian had passed: Peter studied fence-construction in this way to a vast extent, but his intelligence being what it was he never ever found out how fences were constructed. He was not a happy pedestrian.

Peter wanted to see a film that starred Carmen Miranda and Betty Grable. Both of these ladies were symbols for Peter, and he had a newspaper photograph of Carmen Miranda, printed blotchily on the poor paper of the newspaper, that he used to take to bed with him. To watch Carmen Miranda on the screen singing 'I, I, I, I like you very much—I, I, I, I think you're grand' and 'Would you like my hips to hipsnotize you' had an effect on Peter that nothing else on the silver screen was capable of having upon him: Carmen Miranda's silk-covered, astoundingly mobile, rumbaing hips, rhythmically pounding into his senses from the screen, made Peter squirm, and he wondered if what he was seeing was decent, so completely disturbing did he find it. He had written to Betty Grable, and had received in reply to his passionate letter only a printed order-form for photographs of her: in view of the fact that he had asked her for the light-blue woollen cardigan that she had worn as she danced in *Down South American Way* he took a dim view of what he received in reply to his letter, as he did not find the printed order-form at all sexually exciting. He filled in the form, however, and sent it off to Hollywood, enclosing enough money for two

large photographs of Betty Grable, but all he received, after
the post-office had finished with Betty's return, was one
photograph of Betty looking rather glum and far less
glamorous than usual. But Peter continued to admire Betty
unreservedly. Peter was going to see the latest film that those
two ladies had made, and he stood nervously outside the
towering and expansive façade of the Odeon cinema, not even
daring to go near enough to inspect the photographs that were
displayed outside the building. Peter kept his distance from
the cinema so that nobody should know that he wanted to go
inside to see the film. It seemed obvious to Peter that if anybody knew that he wanted to see the film they would immediately understand how he felt about Carmen and Betty,
and that they would straight away know that Peter would
have the sexual experience of his young life when he was
inside the cinema: Peter did not want to reveal himself, so he
pretended to be looking at the passing cars, casting sweaty
sidelong glances at the façade that kept Betty and Carmen
from his eyes. It must be understood that Peter was—in this
pre-adolescent period in his life, when his sexual awareness
was just beginning, and when he was experiencing the
difficulties of biological changes occurring in him—unbalanced,
and had a distorted perspective on all things to do with girls
and women. He was convinced that the few passing people
knew that he wanted to go inside the cinema, and he sweated
with embarrassment at the thought that those people knew
his turbulent inner thoughts: seeing Betty and Carmen in this
film meant so very much to him, and he had been looking
forward to it for a long time. After a while of watching the
cars he thought that he would not have the courage to go and
see the film—he thought that he would not be able to dare to
label himself as lustful by the act of entering the foyer and
buying a ticket. There was the terror of buying a ticket from
the girl cashier also: that was an added horror. He decided to
walk up the road a little first, so that he could muster all the
tiny bits of courage that perhaps he possessed somewhere, preparatory to an assault on the cinema on the way back from
his walk: he went quite a long way from the cinema, however,

111

and met two of the boys from his school: he was sure that the two boys knew what was happening in his mind, even though he was far from the cinema, and did not tell them that he hoped to go. With faltering steps he made his way back to the cinema, then stormed it in a kind of rush, glanced with extreme embarrassment at a picture of Betty Grable displayed outside as he rushed inside, and, crossing the entrance-hall rapidly, he blushed through the cashier's grille, and let the coins slip from his fingers, tender with much perspiring, on to the tiny area of counter in front of her seemingly taunting face. He paid for his cinema tickets under this grille many times after that, and the girls who took his money changed periodically. He did not know, when he paid for a ticket at a later date, and received his ticket from a girl with flirty eyes, that that particular girl would remember him, and that he would, at a still later date, wait with her at a bus-stop, until all the buses had stopped running, and until the clock on the corner struck one in the morning. The girl with the flirty eyes was Hilda, and while she was serving as a cashier in that cinema she had some rather restless rest-periods in the projection room, warding off the advances of the young projectionist. But Hilda was still to come, and at the time we are dealing with Peter got his sexual experiences second-hand from the silver screen at the local Odeon cinema, when he saw Don Ameche kissing Betty Grable.

Peter spent a lot of his time wishing in the little bedroom that really belonged to his cousin Betty, the daughter of Auntie Maggie. He would sit on the edge of the bed, the picture from the paper of Carmen Miranda in his hands, and he would wish: he felt rather an idiot as he did so but he kissed the soiled piece of newspaper once. He had handled this piece of paper with sweaty paws so often that it had become greasy and brown: but it was still very precious to him.

Peter stood up from the bed, the picture of Carmen Miranda fluttering on to the upper sheet, and he stared down at the collection of cosmetics on the glass top of his cousin's dressing-table: the cosmetics thrilled him, and he looked at them with awe as they lay scattered amongst the layer of face-powder. After a while he picked up the lipstick and began to smear his own lips with the red grease, looking in the mirror as he did so: he was hoping that he would derive a feeling of excitement from this, but the main feeling that he did in fact derive from the act was a feeling that he looked positively absurd in the mirror, his full lips loaded with red grease under his emotion-dark eyes behind the lenses of his spectacles. The lipstick did not all come off when he wanted it to, and sure enough his aunt asked him what was the matter with his mouth when he next saw her: he muttered something about the cold wind making his lips sore and red, but he did not feel that he had convinced her: in his feverish attempt to get the stuff off he had rubbed too hard, and his lips had become sore, making them look red with soreness, the remainder of the lipstick caught irremovably in the tiny crevices in his lips.

But this was not all that Betty's bedroom had to offer: there was another erotic experience—to be found from the silk stocking that lay on the floor beside the dressing-table, discarded by Betty during a hurried changing act before she had gone out with her boy-friend the previous evening. But Peter betrayed himself by keeping the stocking for two days. Betty was heard to complain that she could not find one of the two stockings that she had left on the floor of her bedroom, and she looked over the breakfast-table at Peter, and said, half teasingly and half kindly: 'Perhaps Peter has taken it.' Peter refused to believe in his mind that Betty was sure he had taken it, and he told himself that she was just making a shot in the dark. He did not reply to her teasing remark, and sat with a buttoned face, a mist of perspiration in front of his eyes.

11

The Senior School

PETER spent the first two years in the Senior School in the classroom of Mr. Chalk. Mr. Chalk was the form-master, and he also taught French to boys throughout the school. There was another French master in the school, a man by the name of Mr. Cheese, a man with well-greased silver hair—hair that had a sticky, mat, and lustreless surface to it, which made the authority on hair-dressings—Peter—think that the hair-grease used was vaseline—who played the violin at morning assembly, the sound of which was completely submerged beneath the massed singing of the five to six hundred boys in the hall. Mr. Chalk on the other hand was not musical, although he also had silver hair, Mr. Chalk's silver hair being rather sparse and glittering, the main feature of his hair-style was that of a carefully combed kiss-curl that adorned the top of his forehead. Mr. Chalk wore steel-framed spectacles, had a subtle and sheepish sense of humour, and was addicted to the use of the cane—to the using of the cane on the hand that is. Caruthers was a boy in Mr. Chalk's form, and this dark-haired youth, though no older than the other boys in Peter's form, was enormous. Mr. Chalk was not only addicted to the use of the bamboo cane on boys' hands, but he was also addicted to the use of the cane on Caruthers's hand. Caruthers's hand had been caned by his form-master many times, and he had thought about the act of being caned on the hand many times, when he thought of an idea that would introduce a little humour into his next caning. Caruthers always sinned in little ways, not big ones, and he was caned for such minor

114

crimes as talking in class and not doing his homework. The cane on the hand was not as bad as the cane on the rear, but it hurt quite a lot nevertheless, and even putting one's hand in the snow afterwards did not cause the hot pain to go away very quickly: if one was caned just before the breaktime bell one could rush out into the open air, and if there was snow on the ground one could bury one's hand, or hands, in that. Sometimes the cane was banged on one hand, and if the offence was somewhat greater the cane was banged on the other hand as well. Usually Caruthers had only one of his hands hit with the bamboo stick that had been taken ceremoniously from behind the teacher's desk, but on the occasion we will relate he was in for the double treatment. Caruthers's crime was probably that he had not done his homework for the last two times: he waited in front of the class for his punishment as Mr. Chalk bent down to get his cane. Mr. Chalk called some of the boys by nicknames that he had invented, and which he thought were rather humorous. The boys all laughed when he used the nicknames, but that did not indicate that the boys thought that their form-master's humour was good: the boys were only allowed to make a noise when the teacher made a joke—then they were allowed to guffaw for as long as they liked—and when their permitted opportunity arose they would take full advantage of it with relief, regardless of whether the joke made by the teacher was funny or not: many teachers had the mistaken idea that they were humorists as a result of this phenomenon. Caruthers was called 'Mother's' because he was rather sheepish about his preposterous size and gave soppy girlish smiles when spoken to by the teacher. As both Mother's and his teacher had a natural tendency to act in a sheepish, smiling manner, they had a certain fondness for each other, a fondness that the teacher did not allow to influence his treatment of the boy in front of the class, or not in front of it for that matter.

Mother's stood waiting for his two swipes, and he was prepared to put his little plan into action. He was so familiar with the habitual act of being caned that he knew the process in every detail, the process being completely unvarying. His plan was based on this knowledge. Usually Caruthers, who was much taller than his teacher, would instinctively lower his hand so that it was at a level with the navel of his teacher, a level that Mr. Chalk found suitable, for he could then wield the cane in an arc to the boy's hand without any difficulty.

We have said before that Mr. Chalk was sheepish, and it was with a sheepish smile, hiding his delight in the prospect of the caning, that he walked from his desk to Caruthers, with the cane in his hand and his eyes on the floor: Chalk never looked a boy in the eye when he caned him. Chalk had caned Mother's so many times that he could do it in a dream, and it was in a dreamy state that he neared his victim, preparatory to performing the habitual and unvarying action. Chalk raised his cane as he stood in front of Mother's and then said: 'Raise your hand please,' which was the unvarying instruction on such occasions. Mother's raised his hand so that it was on a level with his own shoulder, his arm outstretched in front of him. Chalk raised his cane sleepily, prepared to strike, and raised his weak blue eyes to where he expected the hand to be, namely on a level with his invisible navel. When Chalk realized that Caruthers's hand was not at its usual level, he did not have to look higher to know where the hand was, for he immediately realized the joke that was being played on him, and that the hand was on a level that would necessitate his having to stand on tip-toe to cane it. Chalk smiled as he still kept his head slightly bent down, and above him Caruthers was grinning all over his brown face, while the rest of the class slowly began to laugh. Chalk was obviously not angry, and it was obvious to the class that their teacher appreciated the subtlety of the joke that had been played on him, so the laughter of the class increased into a delightful merry roar. It was a pretty incident. Chalk did not cane Caruthers, but sent him back to his desk in the third row from the windows. There was something very charming about Chalk sometimes, and he appreciated subtlety even it if was contained in a joke at his expense. But the joke had to be a good one: if it had not been Chalk would not have been so nice about it. Combined with this small virtue, Chalk took a small delight in the caning of boys' hands, although it must be admitted, in all fairness to him, that he only caned when there was a justification for the chastisement. Chalk was a self-absorbed man, and self-absorbed men do not make good disciplinarians: he was unable to keep discipline without the use of his cane, but with the use of it he was respected by the boys, and he was able to remain self-absorbed without any attendant loss of order in the classes to whom he taught French verbs.

.   .   .   .   .

Peter was reacting to what he had been at the preparatory school. There he had been bullied, and now he was gradually making a name for himself as a fighter. He was still an isolated boy, unintelligent and remote, but he distinguished himself in one way—one way only—that of being a scrapper.

Peter's change, from being the boy who was bullied to the boy who was now almost a bully himself at times, was perhaps caused by the fact that he was no more under the influence of his father, and the fact that the upheaval of adolescence was in its very early stages within him. There is nothing that changes a boy more than a physical change within him, and, if there is, then perhaps it is the release from a dominating parental influence. Peter had lived in the shadow of his father's dominating anger for a long time, and that had stunted the growth of his individuality. Now he was free of his father and the restriction was removed. However, the influence that his father's behaviour had had upon him was to affect him for a long time yet, and to be the reason for his introspective and shy nature in the years to come.

There was, in each form in the school, an accepted ranking of the fighters, which became changed only when a fight between two boys proved that ranking to be inaccurate. This ranking in his own form was known to each boy, and it was a very exact and clear ranking. No boy in a form was in any doubt about the relative physical prowess of the boys in his form. Peter was ranked second from the top in his form regarding fighting—fighting out of the boxing ring that is—

fighting in the school playground, fighting in the cloakrooms and classrooms when the masters were out of the way. The most formidable boy in Peter's class was Caruthers: if you tried to fight Caruthers he would just smile, hold your arms in a vice-like and slow manner, and play with you gently, squeezing until you asked for mercy. Caruthers was not violent, however, and funnily enough he was bullied by boys who were two years older than himself, and whose attacks he would not resist: if attacked by older roughs, Caruthers would look soppy, and let them hit him, putting up no resistance to their attacks at all, even though he might be slightly bigger than they were. Caruthers was an enigma. And Caruthers seemed to attract persecution of himself by older roughs in some indefinable way: they seemed to resent his size in relation to his age.

Unlike Caruthers, Peter was violent—dangerously violent: in fact Peter's fighting was of no skill or intelligence, and depended for its success solely upon its unrestrained violence. But he was helpless against Caruthers.

In the school there were unwritten laws appertaining to scrapping: and if these laws were contravened goodness knows what would have happened: the fact was that the laws of fighting were adhered to strictly. These laws sprang partly from the Marquess of Queensberry rules. But wrestling was of course part of the fighting technique that was allowed. Things that were definitely not cricket or British were kicking, scratching, punching below the belt (not to do this was a firm rule), using weapons (knives, if used, would have caused a scandal in the school, and the activities of our present-day teddy-boys would have been despised utterly by Elevensinians in those days of fairness and individual bravery), cruelty (boys fought with a certain restraint even though they might fight violently, and it was not done to want to break your opponent's arm, to want to disfigure your opponent for life, to want to make your opponent scream with pain, or to want to murder or maim your opponent), and fighting two or more against one. These laws did not perhaps make sense, in much the same way that boxing does not make sense, but there was a humanity and logic in these laws if you cared to perceive it.

The boys were not filled with the maniacal hate that is in the youth of today, and which is responsible for the kind of fighting that the youth of today indulges in. The boys then did not have a despairing death-wish, and they wished to preserve themselves, while at the same time they wished to prove themselves physically. Boys in those days—Elevensinians or other boys—did not take a carving-knife to the cinema and afterwards slide it into another boy's stomach outside the cinema. And boys in those days did not make a habit of killing policemen, or beating up aged people. There was a sense of fair play (the term provokes laughter these days, and it is out of date) existent in those days, but the youth of today is too aware of the horrors of war to be able to live with the cricketing virtues. 'Live fast, love hard, and die young' was never a motto of a boy in those days, when there was hope in the future, but that motto is held by much of the youth of today.

Digglewick was not liked. Digglewick's father was an artist, and the rest of the boys in his class thought that Digglewick thought too much of himself. Despite the discordant colours of his blazer, which was a rather faded one and a rather unclean one, Digglewick had a personal colour that was like the colour of uncooked pastry: his face was a pale and hilly presentation, with more features to it than most, and his hair, which was a buttery-grey colour, squiggled abundantly and in a closely waved manner from his pale forehead: you were somehow forced to look at the colour-scheme of Digglewick's face and hair, and that stayed in one's mind. Digglewick was more of an outsider than Peter was, and he was in the same class as Peter. Cocksure was the nature of this boy—an aggressive cocksureness—and cocksure boys were not the thing at St. Elevenses—in fact there was nothing more unfortunate than a cocksure boy at St. Elevenses, for he was sure to come to grief at some time. Elevensinians would sooner or later take a cocksure boy down a peg or two, to use a phrase that the boys themselves used. A year afterwards things came to a head, and all the boys converged on Digglewick, took hold of his hands and feet, and 'bumped' him rather hard a number of times on the classroom floor. Digglewick showed a hitherto unperceived sense of his own dignity and a surprising element of courage, because while he was being 'bumped' his thin lips remained set and closed and he uttered not a word, despite the fact that his posterior was hitting the floor more than ungently: most boys would have yelled their heads off. But that day of reckoning came later on.

Digglewick was not a fighter, and he did not seem to be aware of the ranking of the fighters in his class, for he would taunt, not only the physical weaklings in the class, but also he would rashly taunt the fighters such as Caruthers and Peter: it was obvious to all that Digglewick would get his 'come-uppance' fairly soon. And as it happened Peter was to give it to him with the full approval of the rest of the class. Digglewick received his 'come-uppance' a year before he received his 'bumping'. It must be pointed out that 'bumpings' came in various sizes: there were friendly 'bumpings', just as there were friendly 'debaggings', but also there were unfriendly 'bumpings' which the whole class helped to execute, and these were the result of a class conference and were most unpleasant, occurring very seldom indeed.

Now and again Digglewick would tire of the strain of restraining his exuberant nature, and he would start taunting the other boys, or hitting them with exercise books. Digglewick was tolerated, the boys being so surprised by his presumption, and so astounded by his rashness, that by the time they had collected their wits after an attack by him Digglewick would be out of the classroom and halfway down the corridor, whistling tunelessly and with much spirit. But a spirit of resentment towards Digglewick existed in the mind of the class, a resentment so far unmanifested.

Caruthers, afraid of being called a bully, absorbed Digglewick's attacks on him, in much the same way as the U.S.A. absorbed the non-military attacks of Cuba in 1960 and 1961 —without a crushing response, without retaliation, and with control and restraint; and, like Cuba, Digglewick reacted by taunting the giant even more. Caruthers was so often being accused of being a bully by the smaller boys in his class that he had inhibitions and complexes about retaliating physically when the midgets attacked verbally. This was a peculiar and hitherto unmentioned phenomenon: Digglewick was not the only comparative midget who would taunt Caruthers, knowing that the giant would not retaliate because he was afraid of being called a bully. But, just as Cuba would not go so far as to drop a bomb on the U.S.A., so none of the smaller boys would go so far as to hit Caruthers on the nose: they knew just how far they were going to be allowed to go. But Digglewick had not even this degree of discretion, and although he never went so far as to hit Mother's on the face he did punch Caruthers on the shoulder once or twice. It was obvious to everybody in the form that Digglewick was a blithering idiot, for no smaller boy in his right mind would hit Caruthers. But Caruthers put up with Digglewick's hit-and-run attacks, because he was still afraid to retaliate for fear that the form would rise up and call him a bully again: he did not seem to realize that the whole form was waiting expectantly and hopefully for him to rise up and crush the little horror called Digglewick, and that if he had done that the form would have been wholeheartedly behind him. Caruthers was in a difficult position: older boys resented his size in relation to his age, and when they attacked him he was wary of their strength—the strength of older boys; and smaller boys resented his greater size, tended to taunt him, and knew that he would not retaliate because he was afraid of being called a bully. It was only boys like Peter that Caruthers could defend himself against, and they were too prudent to attack him: Caruthers knew he could defend himself against such as Peter, because if he did the class would not call him a bully, such as Peter being considered to be strong enough to defend themselves against Caruthers, even if they were obviously not strong enough to beat him in combat. The result of all this was that Caruthers did not attack anybody, and he suffered insults and attacks with a stupid smile, boys like Peter regarding him with a healthy respect. Digglewick, like Cuba, continued to play with fire, but Caruthers never did retaliate.

Peter was a different kettle of fish to Caruthers: if Peter

fought Digglewick, after Digglewick had attacked him, the class would not have considered that Peter was being a bully. Peter knew this, and he also knew that if he squashed Digglewick the whole class would be morally on his side. But Digglewick seemed completely to lack a sense of discretion, and like a fool he rushed in where angels had feared to tread. Perhaps his success in plaguing Caruthers, without injury to himself as a result, made him think that he could do the same to the strong and silent Peter. Digglewick made a false judgement. How could Digglewick have thought that he could go on for ever, plaguing everybody in his class, without one day getting what he deserved? Digglewick was foolhardy— not brave—and he acted in a manner that was not in accordance with his fighting ability.

Peter sat in the row of desks by the aisle, the same row of desks that the seemingly seldom sagacious Digglewick sat in: the row ran from the front of the mass of desks to the back, and Peter sat two desks from the front, while silly Digglewick sat somewhere behind. When the bell rang clamorously down the corridors, indicating that the class was at an end, the boys would feel relieved, collect their books together on their desks, put the exercise and text books together in an attaché-case or a frayed leather satchel, and then, when the master dismissed them and departed, taking authority with him, the boys would begin to talk and then to shout, rising from their desks, preparatory to vacating the classroom. It was Digglewick's habit, when the master had left the room, and the boys were just about to rise from their seats, to get up quickly and march down the aisle to the front of the class, hitting the seated boys on their heads with a collection of exercise books: Digglewick usually hit every boy in the row but Peter—he would hit the four boys before Peter, and the boy in front of Peter, but not Peter, for somewhere it seemed there was in Digglewick a small particle of discretion. But it was only a very small and transitory particle, for one day, after the bell had rung, Digglewick rose from his desk, having collected his books together more quickly than the rest (he was a boy characterized by quickness in most things, especially in

122

mathematics), bubbled with released energy, and went up the aisle to the front of the class, hitting all the boys in the row that bordered the aisle on their heads, *including* Peter. Peter was so astounded that he sat there, white with fury at the indignity of it, for such a long time that Digglewick was out of harm's way, and out of the school building, before he could even pull himself together enough to get out of the confines of his seat and overlapping desk. Peter was the second-best fighter in the class and he was jealous of his position: after all, the only thing that he could do well was to fight—he was hopeless at studies, no good at mixing, and futile with girls. Peter knew that if he allowed the weaker boys to see him being struck by Digglewick, as they were, those smaller boys would soon lose their respect for him, and might even start to treat him rather as they treated Caruthers—and Peter certainly did not want that. Peter began to long with all his heart for the time when Digglewick would hit him on the head with a group of exercise books again: he would be prepared the second time—by God he would! Peter's face was expressionless, and his mind icy with condensed anger, as he walked out of the classroom on his own.

It was all so absurd, thought Peter: Digglewick had not even had a single fight with anyone. But Peter had his dignity. The swipes that Digglewick made on boy's heads with exercise books did not really hurt, but that was hardly the point: Peter regarded himself as rather holy ground in some ways, and it was inconceivable to him that a twerp like Digglewick should dare to desecrate. Peter's thoughts were profane, and he thought about his biceps: Peter was rather conscious about his biceps: there were few things that Peter was conscious of—girls were one of those things, and his and Primo Carnera's biceps were two more of those few things. Peter regarded the measurement round Primo Carnera's biceps as being as astounding as Digglewick's temerity. Only idiots ignored the ranking of fighters in a form, and only idiots failed to realize that the second-best fighter was holy ground to all except the best fighter in the form: you just did not hit the second-best fighter in the form on the head—especially if you were a non-combatant type: it just was not done at St. Elevenses: you could not expect to get away with it. But Digglewick seemed to think he could get away with it, and he seemed blissfully unaware of the danger.

Peter did not think about many things, and when he did think about something it occupied his whole hole-like and usually empty mind exclusively and continually: if any thought did get into Peter's mind it dominated, because there was no competition to it for prominence from other thoughts, simply because there were no other thoughts. The thought about Digglewick's behaviour found itself in a vacuum above Peter's glasses, and it was king of an empty castle. Peter thought about Digglewick's temerity throughout the day, throughout the evening, until he fell asleep in Betty's bed, and throughout the morning. Peter's supremacy was in jeopardy, and that could not be. Max Schmeling knocked out Joe Louis: Louis was astounded at such impudence: Louis waited with fury in his heart. You could not dethrone a king! The next time that Schmeling dared to enter a ring with the dethroned king Louis he was taught the enormity of his daring in having floored him, for the black boy did not give Schmeling a chance, and knocked him out early in the first round. Digglewick should have known that you are in danger if you jeopardize a fighting man's supremacy: Peter's anger as he waited to avenge himself was as fierce as the anger that had been in the heart of the greatest heavyweight since Tunney and Dempsey. Poor Schmeling and Digglewick.

The French lesson bored Peter to tears: he did not know any French words, and he did not understand French verbs. Chalk caned a boy or two in a perfunctory manner, and invented a nickname for another of the boys. The lesson dragged on, and Peter existed in a daze as usual. And then it was all over, and the bell was clanging away down the gloomy and vast corridors. Chalk left the room, and Digglewick started down the aisle, raising and lowering his collection of exercise books: there were yells of ineffectual protest. Digglewick had done it before and nothing had happened, so he hit Peter on the head again, smiling with that cocksure smile of his, his curly head in the clouds. Peter was on Digglewick before the unfortunate and much surprised boy had got out into the clearing in front of the desks. Peter threw a multitude of punches, but as usual only a few of them landed where they were supposed to land: the terrifying thing about Peter was not so much the injuries he inflicted, as the look of fury on his face. Unlike the other boys in the form who came from settled and calm homes, and who were as a result not filled with disturbances and tensions, Peter came from a background of insecurity that did not make him a boy whose spirit was at rest. Peter's spirit was never at rest, and when he fought this showed in the violence of his attack. Digglewick backed away from the flurrying fists, his exercise books in confusion in his hands. He crashed against Chalk's desk. The rest of the boys crowded around, and Digglewick began to realize that to fight in front of an audience that was wholeheartedly for the other man was not very good for the morale: as the other boys urged Peter on Digglewick's face became ashen with discouragement. Digglewick never hit Peter on the head again after that, and Peter's position as a respected fighter became even greater than it had been before, but Digglewick remained undaunted and he did not change his ways except with regard to Peter.

Peter had been very surprised to find that the most encouragement during the fight had come from the intellectual of the form, whose excited face had bobbed in and out of his vision while the fight was in progress, and whose voice had betrayed an enthusiasm Peter had thought ill-befitting a cranial type: Peter at that stage in his life expected his intellectuals to be unphysical, bad at games, and disgusted with blood-sports such as boys fighting and foxhunting: but this particular intellectual apparently profoundly enjoyed watching fights, and that was a revelation to Peter. Now, unlike Digglewick, the intellectual of the form was intelligently aware of the ranking of the fighters in the form. The intellectual took a non-participant interest in the fights that occurred, and he studied form in the form very carefully. If Peter had lost the fight the intellectual would have given the phenomenon much careful thought. Chalk viewed the intellectual with a certain amount of humour, and he nicknamed him 'Not-so-Green' because the intellectual's surname was Green. Not-so-Green did not give the appearance of being a physically active lad; and the slack and curving outline down his back, from his shoulders to his seat, indicated clearly that he was a sedentary boy. Not-so-Green was aware that he was the intellectual of the form, and his manner towards the rest of the boys more than betrayed this awareness: Not-so-Green had a superior air and a deprecating manner. He was the only intellectual in the class, and he did not find it difficult to play the part to the other boys, for it was a C type class as opposed to the A and B type classes, and the boys in it were the brainless ones of their age-group in the school, the clever ones all being in the A form, and the middling ones being in the appropriate B form. Not that Not-so-Green should have been in the A or B form, for Not-so-Green was not particularly clever at his studies—he just philosophized a bit and talked 'imitation-adult'. Not-so-Green had long straight brown hair that did not grow down his neck, but which was very thick at the back of his head, so that his head looked very long horizontally from his forehead to the back of his head: the weight of the hair at the back of his head seemed to weigh the back of his head down, and his face was always raised: when he walked the back of his head bounced gently up and down. He was often to be found in deep philosophical and pretentious conversation with boys older than he was; and, when a member of his class passed him while he was occupied with such pseudo-intellectuals, he would give that member of his class a look of aloof and devastating scorn. Not-so-Green thought that he was a genius; the thing was that you did not have to be a very advanced boy to feel you were a genius if you were in Peter's form. Every boy was forced to do P.T. (physical training), which was done in plimsolls, white shorts of thin material, and a singlet. Not-so-Green looked ridiculous when he was on the school field, running round or doing physical jerks, and he looked like a fish out of water. Physical activity was all right he felt if someone else was doing it, but that to expect him to do it was absurd. He did not think that such activities were befitting to an intellectual: he felt that one could not retain one's dignity when one was so attired and running round the school field. The teachers should have realized that he was an intellectual and excused him from P.T. But then that was how it was—nobody seemed to realize he was an intellectual except Not-so-Green himself. It was very unperceptive of the masters not to have realized that they had an intellectual in one of the classes of younger boys in the lower school.

Garsterhome had not entered the Senior School at the same time as Peter had entered it: Garsterhome had come into Peter's class at a later stage. As a result of this Garsterhome's position in the form as a fighter had not been established. In such cases it was always rather stupidly assumed that the newcomer was not a dangerous man with his fists. Peter assumed this and regarded Garsterhome carelessly. Garsterhome came from a farm that was some distance from the town of Balham, and like most new boys he was silent and reserved—unsure of himself. But within Garsterhome there lurked a restrained and undemonstrative aggression: it was as if he had the heart of a fighting animal hidden behind his reserved, young-boy exterior. Peter and Garsterhome tangled one day. Why they came to fight each other is shrouded in mystery: the fact is that Peter treated Garsterhome with a certain lack of respect—the lack of respect that Peter gave to the physical weaklings in the form— and Garsterhome, who had his pride, and knew that he could fight, resented being treated without the respect due to him as a fighting man. The cause of the fight might have been as small a thing as Peter barging past Garsterhome. Peter was surprised as, during the fight, it became clear to him that Garsterhome had the spirit of a fighter: Peter had not bargained for that. But what was really distressing to Peter was that Garsterhome was fighting with a considerable formidability—so formidable was Garsterhome, in fact, that Peter began to realize that, unless he fought very hard indeed, he might lose his position of being the Number Two fighter in the form. They wrestled against the desks in the almost empty form-room, and quietly in the background Not-so-Green watched with an absorbed and intelligent interest. Not-so-Green could see that the ranking might be changed as a result of this fight, and he was eager to keep himself well informed on such matters. Peter began to get the measure of his opponent, and his opponent obviously measured a great deal. Peter now knew that Garsterhome had a fighter's heart, and that the farm-boy was not to be beaten easily, if at all. Usually Peter's violent method of fighting met with no equal violence, and so his violence usually won him the fight; but he found that, in a stubborn way, Garsterhome was countering violence with violence. Garsterhome did not seem to be dismayed by the ruthless jerks of Peter's body as they wrestled together— in fact he did not seem to be dismayed by Peter's fighting ability at all, and he seemed to take all that Peter could give in his stride. Peter had not met this kind of opposition before and he was at a loss to know what to do: he was becoming tired: stamina was not one of Peter's strong points. Lack of stamina had not been a disadvantage in combat before for Peter, because his violence had decided the matter fairly quickly in past encounters. Both boys finally decided to lay down their arms so to speak, and an unspoken draw was decided upon, with the dignity befitting two fighting men who respected each other's prowess. It was not in Peter's nature to dislike a boy because that boy could beat him, or because that boy could draw with him, in fact Peter would feel only respect for such a boy, and, as Peter and Garsterhome decided to call an armistice, Peter felt almost a liking for the farm-boy. Garsterhome had not beaten Peter, just as Peter had not beaten Garsterhome: it was obvious that the position was that there were now two second-best fighters in the class. It had not helped Peter any when, during the later stage of the fight, Not-so-Green had shoved his face forward and said, trying to pretend that the fight was something heroic from a novel of heroes: 'I think you have met your match this time.' But, as it turned out, Not-so-Green was right.

12

An Act and its Motivation

ARTHUR was lonely in the empty house in Balham Minor outside Balham; and his wife Iris was training to be a Remington accounting-machine operator, living at her mother's house some miles away. Iris's father, the 'Punishment' of days that were past, was now an old man with a bald dome and long white hair round his ears. He was a rawboned, giant man who wore a long woollen cardigan indoors, and who spoke very rarely. He had not been pleased when Iris had come to live in his house, and he would rather have not had her under his roof, but the family ties were strong: Grandfather understood about Arthur, and sympathized with his daughter Iris, because he himself had been attacked verbally by the quarrelsome Arthur. When Arthur had rowed at Grandpa it had been like a bad-tempered terrier yapping at an old, silent, and weary lion. Grandpa's rowing days were over, and he had stood silently waiting for Arthur to stop. But Grandpa himself had been a great wife-rower in his younger days, only he had done his rowing in the bedroom: now he was, in contrast, a man renowned for not speaking.

Peter had been brought up to think that his father was essentially wrong. So in his subconscious Peter thought of his father as a man who had no rights: his father was not like other fathers who had certain rights—his father was to be treated without respect, and as worthless. Iris had, by her constant attitude, taught Peter to regard his father in this way. Not that Iris had said anything that made Peter feel in this way towards his father: it was something that he had learnt from her attitude towards Arthur. Before the family had split up, but after Arthur had lost his job, there had been a short period in which Arthur had been treated as a man who had no right to hold up his head in pride: the fact that he had lost his job made Iris treat him as a loafer and as worthless, and the two children had caught on instinctively to this new attitude in the house towards their father, and they had begun to treat him in a disgusting way that even he did not deserve. Arthur himself at that time had not felt that he had any right to dignity, in view of the fact that he had lost his job—a thing no self-respecting middle-class man should do—and he allowed his children to abuse him. Peter had called names at his father without mercy and without restraint, and the dignity of middle-class-family life had been completely collapsed. And, to make matters worse, Arthur at that time resorted to jeering at his son, even in the presence of Martin.

At the time that Peter was in the company of Caruthers, Digglewick, Garsterhome, Not-so-Green, and his form-master Mr. Chalk, and at the time that he was staying with his auntie Maggie—when Iris was training, and staying with her aged parents, and when Arthur was alone in the semi-detached Balham Minor house—Peter did a thing the motivation for which can only be understood by reference to a period in Peter's past life: the period we refer to was in fact the time after Arthur had lost his job, and before the family split up—the period when Arthur's position in the family as a respected father had so rapidly and pathetically deteriorated. Before we continue our story in its correct sequence—before we tell of the thing that Peter did that was motivated by his experiences during that unfortunate period—we must describe that period when the family was just about to break up.

Arthur had lost his job and he would go out for walks now and again. One day, when Arthur returned from such an aimless walk, Peter leant out of the dining-room window, and as his father came up the front path, trying to look as if he still had his self-respect, Peter launched a tirade of insults at his father: 'Wall-face, fence-body, table-face . . .' shouted Peter,

JOHN·BRATBY·
FEBRUARY 1961.

inventing, wildly and extensively, insults that he thought were wonderful in their originality. Before Arthur had lost his job Peter would never have dared to shout at his father in this way, but now the restraint was gone; and Peter's attitude to his father was so extreme that it was unjustified, for, bad as Arthur might have been, he did not deserve such treatment. Iris was to blame for this sudden change in the attitude of the two children to their father: when Arthur still had his job Iris had felt bound to preserve for him his correct place as a father in the family, but as soon as Arthur lost his job she felt justified in breaking up everything: she had lived for so long imprisoned in the strain of his constant nagging that, as soon as she felt that she had a right to break free, she did so, more than drastically, and her children followed her lead. If Arthur had kept his job she would have felt bound to continue bearing her burden, for she lived according to the laws of middle-class behaviour: but for the father to be without a job was not middle-class, and when this happened she felt free of middle-class obligations to her husband like champagne bottled for years, when the cork was removed she burst free unrestrainedly, and family dignity was ruined by the spouting liquid of her self-righteousness. The family life had not been ideal, but it had had many good qualities, and it was tragic to see it destroyed so utterly, the father of the family brought to ridicule by his children.

On another occasion during his period of no employment, Arthur was having an undignified row with Peter, the result of which was that Peter locked himself in his bedroom in the front of the house. Arthur, feeling that, if he was to be treated as a being with no dignity and no rights, he might as well act not in accordance with middle-class-behaviour laws, went out into the street, called Martin over to him, and began mocking Peter who was staring down at the street from his bedroom window. Arthur tried to get Martin to mock the self-imprisoned Peter as he was doing, and he pointed up at Peter with a jeering laugh on his face. But Martin could not understand the phenomenon of a father mocking his son in the street, and he stood there by Arthur, with embarrassment on his face, reluctant to join in the mockery—mockery that was itself a mockery of middle-class-family life—a way of life that had not been undermined for Martin. Arthur had in a short time been reduced to this sort of behaviour, and it was an awful and pathetic disintegration of the man. He had now nothing to live for: his whole world had collapsed around him, and the family he had worked so long for had turned against him. There seemed to him to be no point now in keeping up pretences: all was lost: and so he allowed himself to collapse without caring. It killed him in the end. Arthur lived in his house for some time after his family had moved out, and then he went up to York and took a job as a wine-waiter, leaving the house to be taken over by the building society who had not been paid their regular mortgage repayments. His life in York was only a waiting for death, for he had nothing to live for. He did a few peculiar and unbalanced things while he was there. He had an accident: he fell down some stairs and broke his leg: it mended, but he made out an insurance claim for twenty thousand pounds. And then he became ill, and went to hospital without the heart to fight his illness. His daughter visited him and saw him in a state of disintegration. By then Iris had died, and Arthur asked his daughter if Iris had spoken of him on her death-bed. Arthur had wanted Iris to love him, and he thought that in spite of his treatment of her at Balham Minor she might have loved him on her death-bed. But of course Iris had not mentioned him at all. Soon after Iris died Arthur died too. But it was not the illness that had killed him: it was the break-up of the marriage. If Iris's loyalty to her husband had been greater, Arthur would have lived longer. The house in Balham Minor was in the hands of the building society, but a great deal of the mortgage had been paid off while Arthur was working in London—when his family life was in existence. So on Arthur's death the major proportion of the house became the property of his heirs— namely Peter and Annabell. But we are leaping ahead in time, and the chronology, although not parachronistic, is becoming muddled.

We have committed the author's crime of flash-back

chronology, so that the following event in Peter's life, while he was in Mr. Chalk's class, will have its motivation explained. Sometimes an author cannot show the bearing of one event upon another in a character's life, if those time-separated events are described in the correct sequence.

Peter liked to wear his shirt-sleeves rolled up in great balloons of shirting round his biceps. There was a small boy, in a younger class than Peter's, who was in awe of Peter, for he knew that Peter was a fighting man and strong. Peter liked to wear his shirt-sleeves rolled so much that he wore them that way even if he had his blazer on; and when he had his blazer on there would be huge bulges on his upper arms, caused by the rolled shirt-sleeves beneath the arms of the blazer. The little boy regarded Peter's arms with amazement in the playground, and ventured forward to ask if the bulges were caused by Peter's biceps: the little boy knew that Peter was strong, and he thought that it was just possible that Peter was like Popeye the Sailor-man with spinach in him. Just as Peter was a hero to the smaller boy, so some of the older boys—boys in the school rugby team for example— were heroes to Peter. One of Peter's heroes was Potter—a tall boy with blond straight hair and light-blue eyes—and this giants sports hero was nicknamed the Empire State Building. Then there was Inkacious and his curly hair—a wonder to behold; and dark and satanic Plathit, towering, and with shoulders so broad that they were almost unbelievable— Peter longed to have shoulders like the sixth-former Plathit— Plathit the menace of the boxing ring. What a day it was in Peter's life when Welling, a younger boy than Plathit, but as heavy, weathered the storm of Plathit's blows in the ring in the eliminating bout in the assembly hall. Of course Plathit won, but Welling's courage was the talk of the school, for Welling had given only a little less than he received. Ciganter was another sixth-form hero. Baby-faced and not so tall: Ciganter with the blond hair and the cherubic and pretty face. Peter would never forget that time in the park when the school rugby team was playing another school, and Ciganter had started to run with the 'pill' in his hands, his acceleration so amazing. Ciganter had run almost into two husky forwards of the opposing team, who were waiting to tackle him. What did Ciganter do? Hero of heroes that day was he: he kicked the ball—it bounced ahead between the two forwards, to be caught again in the hands of the astounding Ciganter, who had run empty-handed between the two forwards, to catch the bouncing ball after he had passed between them. How the spectators had cheered such presence of mind, such speed, such skill. But that was not all. There was the time that Ciganter fought Plathit in the boxing finals, before the whole school, on the stage at the end of the assembly hall. Ciganter, though smaller than the marvellously built Plathit, was so heavily muscled that he was in the same weight division as Plathit. Nobody expected Ciganter to stand a chance against Plathit: well, after all, Plathit's prowess in the boxing ring was a legend. Ciganter might have been good at boxing, but he could surely not make much of a show against the great Plathit. The bell went for the beginning of the first round, and Plathit backed away from Ciganter until he was against the ropes. Ciganter slung his padded fists upwards at Plathit's face in a dynamic flurry. That was all there was to it: Plathit fell to the canvas beneath the ropes and was counted out. It could only have taken a fraction of the three-minute round. Ciganter got his boxing colours for under a third of a minute's work in the ring. Oh what heroes they were! But when Peter was in the sixth form Potter was in the Navy, and Ciganter and Inkacious were in the R.A.F. Peter was sure that they all must have got the V.C.: after all, heroes were heroes, weren't they?

Peter told the truth to the small boy. Peter would have liked to have had biceps that bulged in his blazer. Then into the school grounds came that dark-faced and dark-clothed figure, the sight of which, amongst the boys, made Peter feel ashamed. At this time Arthur would sometimes come to see his son, and these visits embarrassed Peter enormously. Other fathers did not wander into the school grounds at all hours to see their sons. And also Arthur looked so peculiar—or so Peter thought.

Some days afterwards Peter decided to go to the house in Balham Minor after school dinner and in the dinnertime break that lasted from half past twelve to two o'clock. Peter wanted the belt that he knew that his father kept in his bedroom. Peter felt he had a right to the belt: his father never used it for one thing, and for another Peter wanted it so much. It was a lovely leather belt—strands all intertwining: a belt dark and proud. Peter longed to wear the belt round his grey flannel trousers.

Peter first made sure that his father was away from the house, and then he broke in. He knew the house better than he knew the back of his hand, for he hardly ever looked at the back of his hand, and so he made his entry without very much trouble. But when he got into the gloomy and depressing atmosphere of his father's bedroom he encountered some difficulty. When Peter had been living at the house, and when he had then sometimes ventured into his father's bedroom in his father's absence, the belt had been in the dressing-table drawer, easily accessible. Peter went to the oval-mirrored dressing-table, that was bathed around by the light that shone through the window into the otherwise dark and miserable room, and found that the belt was not in the drawer any more. He searched everywhere, but he could not find it. Then he knew that it must be in the chest of drawers that stood against the wall that faced the window. But all the drawers in the chest were locked. Peter wondered if his father had anticipated that he would come after the belt. Peter looked at the tiny keyholes in the fronts of the drawers, and his lust for the belt, which he knew instinctively was in one of the drawers, mounted in his mind. On the face of each drawer was a small brass handle, and Peter pulled each handle strongly until each drawer broke open, the lock-tongues breaking from their holdings under the strain. Arthur told Peter afterwards that he had not believed that Peter could have been so strong, and Arthur said that that was why he had brought the police in, for he said that he had thought that a man had made the burglary. The police had told Arthur that his son had done the crime, for it was obvious to them, if it was not obvious to Arthur, that the theft of a belt indicated that Peter had called. Peter often wondered afterwards if his father had delighted in the chance to get the police on to him.

Peter was not being intelligent about the burglary: he had gone into the house in an emotional and not calculating state. The belt had called to him and he had blindly gone after it: that was all. He did not realize that he would be bound to be discovered afterwards. This gives some indication of the state of Peter's mind at this stage in his life. Daze, emotion, and the impulse to fight ruled his mind at that time at St. Elevenses. And a want for girls was there as well. But intelligence was not with him, and clear thinking was a thing that Cousin Trevor did—not what Peter did, unfortunately.

Peter ignored the National Savings book in one of the drawers, and left the house with the belt round his waist. He would not have thought for one minute of stealing the savings book and trying to cash the certificates at the post-office by forging his father's signature: Peter was not a criminal. The theft of the belt did not seem to him to be a crime. Dizzy Peter.

Time passed, and then Arthur came up to Peter in the school grounds and asked him if he had broken into the house in Balham Minor. The belt round Peter's waist gave him away, and Arthur insisted on depriving him of it.

Some time after that Peter was sitting in a school dining-room eating his dinner. It was a subsidiary dining-room that was on the ground floor and at the front of the house that contained the Junior School, a house called Mannock, and it was presided over by the biology master, a strange man who was also in charge of the school Scout group. Two long tables ran down the room to the bay window that looked across at the cricket nets and the Scout hut, and at the other end of the room was a table at right angles to the other two tables, at which sat the presiding master, a few prefects, and a few privileged boys. Peter was eating his sweet course amongst the other boys, and he was at the end of the room near the bay window where it was light, the other end of the room where the master sat being shrouded. Opposite Peter sat the son of the biology master, and the tables were crowded with boys. Peter was happy as he ate and talked with the biology master's son, even though he no longer possessed the belt and never would again. And then he glanced up the room and saw his father. It was one thing for his father to come into the school grounds, but for him to enter the dining-room was a terrible thing: or so thought Peter, anyway.

When Iris got to hear that Arthur was visiting Peter at the school, and causing the boy to be much troubled by his visits, she went and saw the headmaster, asking him to forbid Arthur to do so: the headmaster did this, but not before Arthur went into the just-described dining-room. Peter froze in his seat and saw his father out of the corner of his eye. Arthur asked the biology master if he could talk to his son very briefly, and the master seemed very displeased at the interruption, and his face coloured. But Arthur asked with an undercurrent of forcing aggression in his voice, and the master knew that he could not refuse, unprecedented as the request might have been. Arthur walked down between the tables towards Peter, and Peter did not move the spoon that was in his hand. Arthur came up behind his son, and then leant over him, speaking loudly into his ear so that the boys nearby could hear. He said: 'If the police ask you, don't lie: tell them the truth.' Arthur seemed to be almost smiling, as if he felt he was exercising some enjoyable power over his son. And then he left the room. The police never came to see Peter, and Peter was sure that his father had only come to embarrass him in front of his school-fellows. Arthur had nothing to do at that time, and his visits to his son were merely something with which to occupy his time. He knew perfectly well that Peter hated his visits, and he seemed to enjoy tormenting his son in this way.

Peter would not have broken into his father's house if it had not been for the time when he had lived with his father, at which time his father had become a thing of mockery to him. It was because his father's position as a respectable middle-class-family head had been undermined at that time, when he had just lost his job, that Peter could even go so far as to conceive of the idea of stealing from his father, let alone perpetrate the theft. Middle-class morality had been inculcated into Peter so much, during the time when the marriage and family life had been comparatively sound, that he would have thought it wrong to steal from his father, even if his father was separated from his mother, and it was the period of ridicule of his father that made him regard the matter differently. If it had not been for this period of the undermining of parental authority, Peter would never have thought for one minute of acting in such an un-middle-class manner as to steal from his father.

13

Bully for Peter

PETER was an introvert behind the exterior of ferocity: not that he bared his teeth all over the school playground, for his ferocity was not quite so demonstrative as all that. But apparently he did have a glaring and frightening appearance at that time: he continued to have this kind of appearance, on and off, for the rest of his life until middle-age, despite the fact that he finished fighting people on a large scale from the age of about eighteen, and was, from the age of thirty, a person of a considerable degree of gentleness.

Like many adult boxers and wrestlers, Peter, while he was in Chalk's form, had a shy soul beneath his exterior of acts of violence and stern, oft ferocious, appearance. There was this contradiction: he was afraid of life in many ways, but also he frightened some of those around him. This contradiction is often to be found in similar types of people to Peter as he was as a lad: their fear makes them defensively aggressive, for they feel that they have to pretend they are not frightened by acting in a brutal manner. In fact, human ferocity very often springs from fear: those who are not afraid do not have to pretend that they are not.

The soul of a lad of Peter's age is often amazingly primitive, just as the soul of a boy of five will be jungle-like and terrifying in many of its manifestations. Peter, while he was in Chalk's form, was not like some of the boys of his age, who have a few adult sides to their natures by the time they have reached that age, and whose primitiveness has been modified by those elements of sensibleness in their nature: Peter was a moron, without any scrap of developing adultness at all, and his primitiveness was completely 'unadulterated' by the admixture of finer ingredients, and sometimes not limited in any way by reason, rational thinking, or a sense of propriety. So therefore he had in him the pure primitiveness of the bully: he was not often bullying, for mostly his fighting was clean, but on one or two occasions he acted in a way that was not a credit to him. Usually Peter's innate, Elevensinian sense of fair play eradicated his bullying impulses however. But Peter was an emotionally ruled animal who was often non-objective about his own behaviour, and when occasionally the lust to bully rose in his prehistoric mind there were no adult thoughts there to suppress that lust, and it motivated him, unfettered by self-discipline or self-control.

Seaver was a younger boy. When he got older, Seaver became a strong, dark-haired, bespectacled boy, of a reserved nature, whom nobody dared to abuse; but when he was a year or perhaps more younger than Peter he was just the reverse, for he was then the sort of boy who seems to invite persecution by an apparent sense of his own inferiority, unjustifiable though that sense of his own inferiority might have been. As he grew older, Seaver had a reaction inside himself that was similar to that experienced by Peter, who reacted against being bullied at the preparatory school by becoming a fighter later on. There came a time, when Peter was in the sixth form, when Peter would not have dared to fight Seaver, and at that time Peter wondered at the memory of the time when he had bullied the boy. At that later stage, Peter observed Seaver walking heavily and darkly round the playground, and Peter was amazed at the change that can occur in a boy in a few years: then adolescence had made Seaver into a creature as big as a man, and a transformation had been effected by the forces of Biology.

But Seaver was, at this time in our story, a boy who seemed unwittingly to invite bullying. Peter had had his dinner and was idling, waiting for the afternoon classes to commence. Boys were sparsely scattered about the school grounds, and soon the grounds would be crowded by boys returning from

141

having dinners at their homes, until, just before the bell rang at the beginning of afternoon school, the two closed doorways into the main building would be surrounded by about two-and-a-half hundred boys, shoving and pushing, waiting for the doors to open, leaving the rest of the grounds fairly empty. When the doors would be opened by prefects, the boys would crowd in through them, stamping on each other's feet, and squashing some unfortunates rather painfully against the door-jambs. But it was three-quarters of an hour to opening-time, and Peter decided to break the monotony of idly strolling round by endeavouring to make Seaver kiss the ground by bending his arm up his back. This disgusting performance was enacted without much success in the small enclosed square in front of the tuck-shop. On other occasions this small piece of enclosed concrete would be packed with boys endeavouring to buy squashed-fly biscuits and like delicacies from the multi-purpose charlady the other side of an open window.

Peter had another try at making Seaver kiss the ground a few minutes afterwards, and this occurred inside the Junior School building, just outside the entrance to the main dining-room. The boys had all had their dinners in the dining-room by that time, and the room was empty except for the masters, who were dining in peace.

Peter had almost succeeded in achieving his uncommend-able aim, and was bending Seaver, the staircase to the first floor beside him, and Seaver resisting as well as he could, when a master came out of the dining-room, having finished his dinner. The master was off duty, and all he wanted to do was to continue to enjoy the sensations of a full stomach without interruption: he was not eager to act in an authoritarian manner at that moment. But he could not just pass by the scene of torture without doing something about it, so he told Peter to come and see him in his classroom when the two o'clock bell went, saying this in a very uninterested manner, and quickly walking away and out of the Junior School building.

The master's name was Matchmart, and he was, of all the masters, the one who seemed to be most remote from the boys themselves. All the other masters were in varying degrees involved with the lives of the boys that they taught, but this man, although he was involved in the activities of the school, was not involved with the boys as persons. He taught the boys; and spent a lot of time helping the school secretary, in the office next to the headmaster's room; and he was a figure apart, humourless and self-absorbed. He was often to be seen behind the counter belonging to the office, where stationery was sold before morning assembly in the large hall. He would on these occasions help the female secretary to provide the boys with their needs. His only claim to humanity while he taught his subject was that he had an obsessive condemnation of clichés, but apart from such moments of feeling he taught efficiently and without humanity. He was neither soft with the boys, nor stern to the point of harshness like the music master: it was difficult for Peter to know in advance what would happen when he went to the master's classroom at two o'clock. Peter found the master's remoteness frightening, and he expected to get a caning, although his expectation was not based on any knowledge or past experience. Mr. Matchmart was famous in the school as the teacher who managed the school-dinner service, the biology master being only in charge of the small dining-room. Once, when Peter was waiting at the end of one of the crowded tables, in the vast main dining-room in the Junior School building, preparatory to going and queuing for his first course, Mr. Matchmart came into the room, surveyed the assembled hundreds of boys waiting patiently in their seats, and then went over to where Peter was sitting, right at the end of the first table, asking Peter to lend him his chair to sit on while he was speaking to the assembly. Peter lifted his bottom off the seat of the chair as Mr. Matchmart pulled away the chair: but then Peter, finding that he was not rising steadily, put down his bottom again, preparatory to rising in a steadier fashion the second time. Unfortunately the chair was away by the time Peter lowered his bottom, and Peter fell sprawling at the master's feet, the master looking at him rather oddly, and the multitudes of boys laughing gigantically. But that was some

143

time before the torture of Seaver was witnessed by Mr. Matchmart.

Peter made his way up to the first floor where Mr. Matchmart's classroom was, his heart pounding, feeling very frightened. He had never been caned on the seat of his trousers before, and as he expected this to happen to him in Mr. Matchmart's room he entered the room with much trepidation and misgiving. But Mr. Matchmart could not be bothered with the matter, and he cursorily dismissed the astonished boy, telling him not to do it again. Mr. Matchmart was not a sadist.

Every now and again the syllabus was changed, and it came as a surprise to Peter to find that the P.T. period was the first in the afternoon's block of three lessons. He did not feel that it was right that they should go into the school after dinner-break, only to take their clothes off and go out of school again: he felt that apart from taking their clothes off they might just as well have stayed outside. If P.T. was after a period, or periods, of monotonous book-learning, and if P.T. was then followed by some more classroom monotony with Mr. Chalk or Mr. Grate, it served as a welcome and refreshing break, much looked forward to, and after which the boys sat in class all pretty-fleshed from the cloakroom showers and with eyes that were like dewdrops from the green green grass of Ireland in the morning. But Peter thought that it was silly to have more physical activity, straightway after the rough-stuff indulged in during the dinnertime break: usually, when the crowds came into the playground, just before the bell that announced the start of afternoon school, there would be a scuffle or two, or a chase, or a game of jumping hard on a joined row of bent backs—although, until the crowd mounted, the dinnerbreak time in the school grounds was a fairly lonely affair.

After Mr. Matchmart had let him off, Peter went to his locker, number two hundred and sixty-four, the one that had the busted lock, and extracted from it a smelly and moist bundle that consisted of a pair of earth-stained P.T. shorts; a wrinkled and equally earth-stained vest; and a pair of never-cleaned plimsolls; wrapped around by a wet towel that saw the air just enough times to keep it from becoming mildewed: the plimsolls were inside the bundle, and the rest was wrapped around that central core—a traditional thing with most of the boys. If Peter did not hurry he would be late for P.T. But the P.T. master, who had been a public-swimming-pool attendant in his less dignified days before he became a temporary war-time master of physical training at the school, did not turn up for some time, and the boys idled around in the cloakroom amongst the hanging clothes.

During the war many things were in a state of mild confusion, and some of the masters had been called up to fight for the glory of their land of bits of green grass, hedges, and trees, mixed up with factories, jerry-built houses, and chimneys. In normal times each class had P.T. on its own, but at this time the C class, that Peter was in, had its P.T. with the A class of that age-group. In the A class was Martin, the boy who had once lived opposite Peter in Balham Minor, the boy who looked like a miniature and darkened version of Lyndon Brooke the actor, the boy who had now become remote from Peter. As the boys stood around in the cloakroom in their P.T. kit (the high, dark-brown frames of wood, that held numerous clothes-pegs and coat-hangers, dividing the long room into aisles; and assemblages of clothes bulging out from those frames, pants and vests visible on the outsides of the assemblages, and blazers and overcoats hidden from sight) Martin was doing acrobatics on the end-vertical of one of the frames, with a group of admiring boys around him. Martin was not so strong—it was the balance of his body that enabled him to hold on to the vertical bar with both hands and raise himself until his body projected out vertically. Peter watched this display with admiration, for his legs were too heavy for that sort of thing.

Chipperoy had come into the A form at about the same time as Garsterhome had come into the C form. Chippleroy soon proved himself unworthy of his class, and later on he was demoted into the C class where Peter was. An A form boy, not good enough for the A form, who was demoted to the

C form, instead of being put in the B form, would be one of the cleverest boys in the C form. Chipperloy had straight blond hair, of some brilliance, that flopped over his eyes, a smallish figure, and a skin of a surprising whiteness. He had a girlish way with him, and that was fatal, for girlish boys were persecuted by the other boys. Chipperloy was extremely good at cross-country running in the park, but that was because he had a good stamina rather than because he was strong. Chipperloy, later to develop a spirit, and to become what he called a 'lone wolf', was at this time rather afraid of his new school, and he had even had advances made to him in a bus by a homosexual gentleman. When later he developed his spirit he would taunt the boys who had formerly persecuted him, yell to them defiantly that he was a lone wolf, and when they advanced upon him, enraged, he would send a girlish laugh into the playground air, and run away on his swift and slender legs, knowing that they could not catch him. But Chipperloy had not come to this yet, and he was undressing in the cloakroom in a modest way, casting frightened glances, as Martin put on his little circus. The P.T. master was obviously being rather slack, and he had not yet come to take control of his class. Chipperloy had got to the nude stage in his changing, and the whiteness of his girlish body was so china-smooth that it struck the other boys as positively obscene: they began to stare, and to jeer, at the boy who stood in the shadow cast by the high clothes-hangers frame; and Chipperloy stood frightenedly watching them, looking like a strip-tease dancer at the most crucial stage in her act. Perhaps Chipperloy was one of those developing boys, who are half girl and half boy: he had no female forms, but there was such a girl-look about him that the other boys felt they were looking at a nude girl, and they hid their embarrassment beneath their jeers. Peter had not been the first to look, or the first to jeer, but the obscene look of Chipperloy's body stirred him, and disturbed him so much, in a way that his unintelligent brain could not understand, that he became the chief jeerer, and advanced upon Chipperloy, with a snaking and cracking whip of a moist towel: Chipperloy backed away,

146

running whitely round the clothes-hanger frames, and the sense of Elevensinian fair play in the rest of the boys made them call Peter off.

When the P.T. master came they all went out of the building and on to the school field. The war had come, and the school field was not what it had been: encircled by a cinder running-track, the field was disfigured, at its far side, by a gun-emplacement, surrounded by sandbags and manned by two bored soldiers. The master left the boys to play with a ball, and it might have been an accident that it hit Chipperoy below the belt: the boy doubled up, his face creased with pain, and he began to cry and scream with pain in a rather frightening way. A kindly and bored soldier, who had had nothing better to do than to watch the boys at play, came over from his pit by the running-track, and, realizing the seriousness of the situation more than the stupidly staring boys, held Chipperoy kindly, spoke to him soothingly, and eased the pain with massage.

14

All Responsibility Abandoned

ARTHUR, with all sense of responsibility abandoned, left the house in Brushdean Walk, Balham Minor, Hastershire—the mortgage payments not paid for some time—to be dealt with by the building society as they thought fit, after they later found out that the house was no longer occupied. Arthur just left the house and all it stood for. He could have sold his share of the house, and lived for some time on the proceeds, but for some reason he did not do this, his mental state at that time causing his motives to be confused. Arthur went north, and found a job as a wine-waiter in York, using to some advantage his earlier experience as a wine-taster. When the building society found that the house, on which the mortgage repayments had not been paid for some time, was abandoned, they carted off all the furniture in it, and stored it in a warehouse in London, intending to sell it to pay for the mortgage payments that had become due. The building society did not know that the furniture in the bigger front bedroom did not belong to the owner of the house, but belonged to Iris, being a wedding present to her from Arthur. They had no right to this furniture, and as a result Iris made a visit to the warehouses of the building society to identify the furniture which was hers. And at about this time Iris made a visit with Peter to the now-empty house at Number 27 Brushdean Walk.

Iris had started to work in a big store in Balham, where she operated an accounting machine in an ill-lit room in the building's basement, where, after some time, she developed a cataract over one of her already short-sighted eyes, the eye trouble being a result of the bad light in the accounting-department room. Before she developed the cataract, she made the visit to the house she had once lived in. At that time Peter was still living with his auntie Maggie, going for evening walks, with Betty and her boy-friend, that should have been an education to him, but were not; and visiting his mother at his grandparents' home at intervals, to collect his weekly sixpence-a-week pocket-money, and ostensibly to renew his acquaintance with his hard-working mother. At the end of these visits he would be forced to kiss his younger sister on her big forehead, a thing that he did with undisguised reluctance, and as rapidly as possible, leaving the house as quickly as he could, with his auntie Maggie, in an attempt to forget the taste of his sister's sexless brow. Peter had no use for money at this stage in his life, actually finding it quite difficult to use up the weekly sixpence; and when his mother suggested that, as he was a big boy now, he could have his weekly stipend increased to one shilling, he actually refused, a thing that his mother, who thought that all boys liked money, found very peculiar.

Leaving Maggie with Grandpa and Grandma, Iris spent her afternoon off by visiting Brushdean Walk with her son. When they came to the familiar roads a feeling of nostalgia dazed the ever-dazed Peter, and when they walked down Brushdean Walk, Peter felt that he was walking in a dream, so deeply affected by the attack of memories was he. Before he got to the house he remembered how he had left an air-gun, that he had just got in exchange with Martin for a repeater cap-gun with a revolving six-chamber cylinder (a rare and wondrous toy in those days, made of cast iron), at the pavement end of the alleyway that led to the back-garden gate, and in a swirl of nostalgic dizziness he recalled how, when he had gone to get the air-gun after his dinner, he had found it had been stolen. This memory swirled with a re-collection of a verbal investigation into the creation of babies, carried out while sitting in the gutter with the little girl from further up the road, the little girl's conclusion being that babies fell into the lavatory pan. Peter remembered that he had dismissed this theory as being too unlikely, because of its lack of hygiene, and he had been left with the more pleasant theory concerning the gooseberry-bush, a theory that he was highly suspicious of, after frequent inspections of the gooseberry-bush at the end of his garden: as he walked down by the side of the familiar houses with his mother, he wondered how babies really did come, but he was not too worried about his ignorance, his desire for a girl at that time not being caused by any medical knowledge, kissing to his mind being the ultimate ecstasy—not that he had yet achieved that delectable goal.

Light-headed with nostalgia, Peter waited at the front door, while his bespectacled and grey mother inserted her key in the lock. They toured the empty house, and Iris said very little, her emotions being rather too much for her. When they left the house Iris closed the front door, and, standing just by it, she looked for the last time at the house in which she had spent so many years: they might have been years that contained much unhappiness, but she had managed to find some secret happinesses in those years too, and as she looked round at the face of the house that was hers no more she began to cry, in full view of anybody who might be watching. Peter had never seen his controlled and hard-faced mother cry before, and he stood there by her weeping figure in considerable selfish embarrassment, not thinking to say something that might console her. 'They' had been watching the tragic visit, watching from their windows as neighbours in a middle-class road will, making deductions, and thinking about things that are none of their business. When the man and woman next door saw Iris crying on the doorstep, they understood the reasons for her tears, and, remembering that someone had once called Iris the 'woman who was always smiling', they felt sympathy for Iris, and the woman next door rushed round the two adjoining front gardens, and in a flustered way invited Iris to come and sit with them for a while. The woman led Iris into the house, and, as Iris recovered her composure in the next-door sitting-room, Peter eagerly looked through the film magazines that he found there.

15

3 Technical

THE old man had been something of a philosopher in his old age, and he saw the war as proof that the evil and hate that is in men will always exist, flourish, and cause wars: he could not accept this realization, though he knew it was true, and so one day he died. Peter went with Auntie Maggie to the house of his grandmother and grandfather, and saw his dead grandfather lying cold in the bed, that was, because of the air raids, in the back, lower room: Grandfather was very long, and his toes projected bare from below the end of the blanket that covered him. Peter had never seen death before, and he wanted to get away. As he was leaving, obviously eager to do so, his grandmother, little, yellow-haired, wrinkled, and surprisingly calm, told him to touch his grandfather's feet, to feel how terribly cold they were. Peter could not conceal the distaste he felt at the idea, and his grandmother, who was usually so mild (suppressed by her husband), taking Peter's reluctance as an insult—for she felt that Peter's distaste was a distaste for the body of the man who had been a part of her in life, rather than a distaste for the death it contained—suddenly shouted at Peter in the gloomy, Victorian-crowded room, in a voice that made it impossible for the boy to avoid doing what she told him to do: he touched one of the ceiling-pointing and massive bare toes, and felt it as cold as ice.

After the funeral the scavengers came, filling the house and taking away the books that the old man had collected in the tiny front room at the top of the house.

There was now room for Peter in his grandmother's house,

and he left Auntie Maggie's house, and went to live with his grandmother, his mother, and his sister. Peter liked girls, but his sister was his sister, and that was a different thing altogether, especially in view of the fact that she was too young to be sexually formed. Just before his grandfather had died, Peter had tried on some new trousers that his mother had bought for him, and he had innocently confided to her, with genuine alarm, that his phallus had grown enormously while he had been staying with his auntie Maggie: his mother, not realizing that her son was uninformed about the facts of life and genuinely puzzled about his growth, had treated him coldly. Now, after his grandfather's death, Peter was legally an adolescent, the legal age-period of male adolescence being, perhaps surprisingly to some, from fourteen to twenty-five (women: twelve to twenty-one). He was big and strong, but useless at games; and he water-waved his hair so that it formed two waves on the top of his head, the ridges of which ran straight and precisely from his hair-line to the back of his head, the waves waving from the side-parting rather than from the hair-line: he was inordinately proud of the appearance of his hair, and after wetting it with Brylcreem and water, which made it black, he would press in the waves and dry his head in front of the fire, combing it out afterwards into gold-touched brown waves, the mirrored result giving him tremendous delight in the privacy of the bathroom in his grandmother's house. The hair-dressing was carried out in the strictest privacy, behind the locked door of the tiny bathroom, and, when he dried his watered waves by the fire in the lower backroom, he would put his head as near to the fire as possible, and pretend to be reading a book. The attention he gave to his hair was secret, and it would have embarrassed him if he had thought that his mother really knew how much his waves meant to him: as a result of his hair-attentions, which took hours and hours, and because of his natural lack of intelligence, he was bottom of his form after the Mr. Chalk period. Other boys of his age neglected their homework because they went out with girls: Peter neglected his homework because he loved his hair. Not

152

that he would not have loved girls more if he had been able to —it just happened that his hair was all there was to love in his life.

Peter had now moved into Mr. Grate's form, which was called 3T. Peter had been in 1C and 2C; and now he was in a form called 3 Technical, as opposed to the brighter classes in the same age-group which were called 3A and 3B. Why the dunces of their age-group should be put in a form that had classes that had a technical bias is a mystery, but no doubt the wise and experienced staff of the school knew what they were doing. 3T had as its form-room the room of Mr. Grate, who taught English to various forms in the school as well as acting as a form-master. Mr. Grate had a stomach that bulged and bulged until at the waistband of his specially made trousers there was a strain on the trouser material that seemed to be dangerous. Mr. Grate was over middle-age, over average height, far over average weight, and possessed of a humorous disposition that was far merrier than the average school-teacher's disposition. He had a bald dome, white hair in wisps round his ears, and he dressed in grey. Merry though he was, he was a stern disciplinarian. He was a little tempera-mental, and sometimes a whole lesson would go by without a joke being made by the king of fun, although many of his lessons were laughter all the way. As with Mr. Chalk's little jokes, so it was with Mr. Grate's jokes, and, regardless of the quality of the humour, the class would laugh, for the sake of laughing, and for the easing of monotony that it represented. But, unlike Mr. Chalk, Mr. Grate sometimes made good jokes. However, he was the only one in the room allowed to make a joke, and that did tend to make him seem funnier than he really was: he had the monopoly on fun, and he could manu-facture whatever quality material he liked, knowing that his consumers would accept it because they had no alternative. But he was a nice, fat, jolly man generally speaking; and far more of a character, and a person with boy-loving humanity, than the other members of the staff: there was only one Mr. Grate in the school. He used the cane on occasion it is true, and used it on the bent bottom whenever he used it, but he did not give six of the best very often, and on one occasion he showed great mercy to Peter, who had never been caned in his life. Seeing that Peter was scared out of his wits, Mr. Grate asked him if he had ever had the cane before, and on learning that Peter had not, and that Peter was paralysed with fear, he let the cowardly bully fighter go back to his desk uncaned. It seemed unbelievable that Mr. Grate had been a great tennis-player in his university days, and had been an Oxford blue. Mr. Grate was a great humanist, and he not only knew every boy by name (one other of the masters achieved the wonderful feat of always knowing the name of every boy he taught), but he knew details of their home life and parenthood, as well as understanding each boy as an individual apart from the anonymous mass. When Mr. Grate taught a class he taught a collection of individuals (many of whom liked him a great deal, with a few reservations). A character as great as Mr. Grate seemed wasted in the school, for one felt that he should have done better things with his life than just teach boys, commendable occupation though it may be to do so. There were some teachers in the school who were hardly known by boys they did not happen to teach, so large was the school, but Mr. Grate was known to every single boy in the school, whether he taught them English or not.

Mr. Grate's room was different from the room of Mr Chalk. For one thing it was on the upper floor of the building, a classroom away from being directly above Mr. Chalk's room, and, for another, the desks were arranged differently. The desks faced three walls of the room, the boys sitting with their backs to the centre of the room, and in the large central space were two or three short tables. Two desks faced the fourth wall by Mr. Grate's front-facing and massive desk, and in those two desks sat the form-captain and the form vice-captain: the form-captain, elected by the class, was a miniature and younger version of Mr. Grate physically, staid and humourless, dependable and reliable; and the vice-captain was a conscientious, wiry, and swarthy youth, who had been chosen because he was the hero of the class—terribly good at athletics and games. Time had passed, and, although 3T was what 2C became, the constitution of the dunce-class had changed considerably, partly because there had been an influx of new boys displaced by the war. Peter was no longer definitely the second-best fighter in the form, even though Caruthers had left the school by now, because in the form there were now some rather hefty boys, one of whom was sixteen. The best fighter was without dispute the vice-captain, and second place remained undecided, Peter having almost as good a claim to it as the others, because of his peculiar violence.

Cushumph, although he could run like a rabbit, had considerably more courage than that fugitive animal. Cushumph was, it is true, somewhat fugitive in his nature, wary and touchily alert, but he was a boy who was prepared to fight against great odds, and a boy who made himself felt. Cushumph sat at a desk that was next to the classroom door on one side, and next to the desk of the form-captain on the other side: Cushumph was very popular with the other boys, for he had a certain charm and was the form hero, and he had been elected to be the form vice-captain. He would have been elected as the form-captain if he had been more of an intellectual, more staid, and a typical product of the petty-bourgeoisie: the boys felt certain pressures on them, when they were electing a form-captain, that made them choose one who would be approved of by the form-master, and Cushumph was too much of a boy's boy and not enough of a teacher's boy: this does not mean, however, that Cushumph was not liked by the teachers, for he was universally popular—it was just that he was too thick-headed about studies despite his phenomenal earnestness regarding those studies, and that there was about him a faint suggestion of an insecure background. However, the election of form vice-captain was another thing altogether, and having chosen a captain who would be approved of by their teacher the boys felt entitled to let themselves go regarding their choosing of a vice-captain. They unanimously chose Cushumph, who would have been captain if the electors had not felt fettered.

Cushumph was the stuff heroes are made of. Like others in

the form who had come in at a later stage, because of the disruption in their education caused by the war—boys who had been held back in their studies by being moved from one school to another, partly because of the war and partly because of parental instability and wanderlust—Cushumph was older than Peter, being well into his fifteenth year. Cushumph was successful with girls, more because of his real charm and fineness of character rather than because he had a smooth, public-schoolboy approach veneered over with careful grooming and an easy and over-confident manner; and Peter, who was honoured to be a friend of his, was very impressed by the fact that Cushumph went out with shop assistants and factory girls, for, to Peter, such girls were far more attractive and worldly, as a result of his telescopic view, than schoolgirls. Cushumph was a very earnest and sincere boy who would have been distinguished for these qualities alone. He was slightly built, wiry, possessed of a great degree of stamina, and hard-muscled if not bulge-muscled. Cushumph, who excelled at cross-country running, fighting, boxing, rugby, football, cricket, and goodness knows what other sport, was, unbelievably, not what we would call a natural athlete, for he was good at those things rather more because he tried so hard than because he could excel at those things as a matter of course: he was comparable to the Mighty Atom, Jimmy Wilde, in that he excelled physically because he tried and had heart rather than because he was blessed with muscles galore. Cushumph, though not tiny by any means, was below the average height for his age. Boys did not tangle with him, not because they were frightened by his size or muscles, which were not frightening, but because they were afraid of the fact that he never gave in during a fight, that he had extreme courage, and that he forced his slim arm muscles to deliver a very hard punch. Never ill like Jimmy Wilde, Cushumph nevertheless had much in common with the world champion of long ago.

Peebles, the form-captain, who sat at a desk next to that of the form-master, and whose desk was next to that of Cushumph, was a stout, solid, staid, and essentially sober character, in direct contrast to his right-hand man Cushumph. Peebles, not being a terrible fighter, left the disciplining of the class, when the master was out of the room, to Cushumph, who would reluctantly bang a ruler on wayward boys' knuckles as those boys sat at their desks, the reluctance being born from the element of kindness in Cushumph's nature.

Peebles was a studious boy, though not a boy with a facile talent for learning: like Cousin Trevor's sister, Trevorene-Lou, he was good at his studies because he was conscientious, and not because he was brilliant. But Peebles was an essentially good boy, a very suitable representative of the teaching staff when that authority was absent. Peebles would have startled everyone if he had laughed at a dirty joke, or if he had sung a popular song in the playground: Peebles did not go out with girls (heaven forbid), and he was the personification of sanity, proper conduct, and discretion amongst the boys in 3T: if the class became wild, his calm and steady voice would remind them of the dignities of adult behaviour, and they would settle and resume work again. Perhaps Peebles was a little bit of a prig, although it must be added in his defence that he was a kindly boy. He was the Judge of the form, judging with a strong sense of his own personal goodness, and judging as fairly as he could. He did not fight or degrade himself by acting with the slightest degree of abandon—partly because his weight made it difficult for him to move very fast, and partly because he had an instinctive belief in the advantages of dignity. He was a quiet boy who was liked by his fellows with restraint, making most contact with boys of a disposition that was similar to his own, namely boys who believed in acting in a dignified and pseudo-adult manner—Not-so-Green being such a boy, although Not-so-Green felt he was too superior for anybody but the pseudo-intellectuals of the A forms. There were two factions in the form 3T: there was the group that believed in fighting, school sports, girls, and a careless attitude to lessons; and a group that believed in trying to be adult and doing their homework. It was surprising how clearly divided these two factions were, although there were of course boys in the class who were good at sports and at lessons, and boys who loved girls and mathematics at the same time: it would have been difficult to find, however, a boy who scrapped who was interested in being a staid imitation adult at the same time. Cushumph, the fighter, was regarded as something of a traitor by the careless faction, because he tried earnestly to learn, and because, to their surprise, he had become, upon election as vice-captain, an upholder of authority. There were the boys who would fight in the class room when Grate was out of the room, and there were boys who would disdainfully ignore such disturbances: divided as the two factions were, there are exceptions to every grouping, just as there are to every rule, and some boys, Cushumph being one of them, walked in and out of both camps.

Martin had been transferred to this class from the A form, because he intended eventually to study building, and the technical-bias course was more suitable for him than the arts-bias course taught in the A and B forms. But by now, their homes in different places, Peter and Martin were remote from each other, Martin regarding Peter as a bit of an enigma now that he had changed from a bullied boy to a violent fighter.

There were three boys who had recently joined the class that Peter was in, a class that was fundamentally a continuation of the form 2C, and these three boys were older than the average age of the form, and each one a character in his own right. The most peculiar one was Arthur, that being his surname, a thing that caused Peter much perplexity. Arthur was the oldest boy in the class, being sixteen years old, if not more, although his ability at lessons was, if anything, slightly below the average, this inability also puzzling Peter, who felt that a boy so old should be much more knowledgeable than boys much younger. Arthur looked like a man to Peter, for he was tall and large and had a mature-looking face, a face above which sprouted straight yellow hair, uncombed and falling in a cow's-lick of some rigidity over the left side of his forehead: Arthur played cricket left-handed, a thing that stayed in Peter's memory, and because of his size was better at sport than most of the other less-developed boys in that class. Arthur was, like Peebles and Cushumph, though not like Peter, a kindly boy, who had a mild temperament. He mixed with the other boys in his class as though they were of his own age, and it was rumoured that he had more than one smashing shop-assistant girl-friend—girl-friends of a mature, developed, and desirable seventeen. Girls of sixteen and seventeen were to Peter the ultimate attainment, girls of eighteen being untouchable sex goddesses: if Peter had had a girl of seventeen he would have gone barmy with pride: but, as it happened, Peter did not even have a girl of twelve, the poor blushing nincompoop. Cushumph showed Peter a grubby photograph of a sixteen-year-old girl in a bathing costume, a picture of Cushumph's girl at that time, and Peter's respect for Cushumph was unbounded, and his mind swam as he tried to put himself in Cushumph's place. How Peter longed to have a place in the world of boy-girl relationships that existed for other boys outside the school. Peter often told himself that faint heart never won fair lady, but that did not seem to make any difference to him.

The second of the three older boys who were recent acquisitions to the school and to Peter's class was Tabbot. Tabbot was the Robert Taylor of the class—all pretty hair, oft-combed, and pretty girls. Lessons and school itself were on the side for Tabbot, Girls being the only worthwhile thing in life for him; and how right Tabbot was to think in this way, thought Peter. Tabbot was always talking about girls; always combing the tiny quiff of waves that lay, short-cropped, for only two inches from hair-line backwards; and always staring into space in the classroom during lessons, with a faraway look in his pretty blue eyes that suggested that he was only waiting for the school day to finish, releasing him into the world of off-work, gay, and uninhibited, working girls outside. Tabbot would hardly attend to the classes at all, and he would sit, alternately dreaming of kisses and skirts, and alternately putting a small comb through his precious and over-neat quiff of blond and tiny waves, with an effeminate air, followed by a little patting of the quiff with the soft, moist ends of long graceful fingers. He thought that he was

159

God's gift to women; he suggested by his appearance that he was; and it was also obvious that quite a number of girls thought that he was. He was the tallest boy in the class, thin, and carefully dressed; with a small and pretty-featured face way up on top. And with his long, slender arm he could throw a tennis ball to a vast height in the playground, so that it came down in the street outside, a feat that made Peter worship. Tabbot sat at one of the short tables in the centre of the room, next to his intimate friend who was the third member of the trio.

Boogter was the ugliest boy in the class: perhaps he was the ugliest boy in the world at that time—it was quite possible. But he was as great a womanizer as his friend Tabbot, a fact that Peter could not begin to try to explain, as he thought that girl-catching was a matter of good looks. Boogter was short, had a preposterously big and bumpy nose, a huge head, wore glasses only when he had to, and had a grotesque, completely non-athletic body. He told dirty jokes, was clever at his studies (as a boy of his age should be in a younger form, according to Peter), seemed to come from a background that was completely un-Elevensinian and spivish, looked even older than he was, was horribly worldly, was a veteran in experience with the opposite sex (Peter, who was completely inexperienced, admired him reluctantly for this), and looked very very wrong in a Elevensinian blazer. But, to cap all these preposterous features, Boogter had a feature that prevented him wearing a cap—a feature that was his only claim to beauty: Boogter had the most beautiful head of large-wave, brown hair—hair that had been allowed to grow unchecked for years, except for a little trim at the neck now and again. Of course Boogter got into occasional trouble with the prefects, because he could not get his school cap over the abundance of waving beauty, but only army authority would make Boogter relinquish his sole claim to beauty, and the thought of the army barber cropping that lot off simply made Boogter determined to avoid his call-up by some underhand means or other. Once, in the science room, when the science master was out of the room, Boogter combed his hair down, preparatory to combing it back again, and many of the boys cried out that he looked like a girl, for when combed down Boogter's hair fell almost to his shoulders. Boogter and Tabbot did not fight, for they were too old, and it would have been considered unfair if they had fought the younger boys in the form: they were outside the fighter ranking. Arthur fought boys of his own age if forced into it, but he was also considered above the ranking of fighters. Peter and Cushumph were part of the ranking of fighters, however, and Peter often fought Cushumph, though in a friendly way. The class was bigger than it had been when it was called 2C, and considerably changed in its constitution since then, although the nucleus was still the same as it had been, with the exception of Caruthers, who was now in the outside world, working on a farm and being a sudden success with all the landgirls. Peter would have loved to be a success with all the landgirls, but that was not to be his lot in life. Peter observed, and he wished weakly; dreamed through his lessons; was exactly bottom of the form in the examinations; and came to life when he spasmodically fought. His was not a full life, and he was wasting his adolescence—unlike Cushumph, who was living his to the very full: a life of sport, girls, endeavour, and success. The only things that let Cushumph down in Peter's eyes were that he did not seem to wash, and that he never pushed his cuticles back, allowing them to grow halfway up his finger-nails, frayed, glutinous-looking, and unpleasant.

Smithers had come from 2B into 3T, and he became a friend of Peter at this time. Smithers was mad about toy trains, and trains of any kind, and he was good at geography because he knew all the railway-stations in the country. Smithers was greasy; with an olive complexion, dark eyes, and black greasy hair that fell in a thick fringe over his forehead. He was a conscientious boy at his studies; fairly successful in the terminal examinations; a very fast runner (this made him useful at rugby as a wing three-quarter, Peter being a myopic forward if anything); and just above average height for his age. He was the same age as Peter, entering into the period of adolescence. His eyes were remarkable: they looked like those of a frightened Negro boy, being liable to roll mysteriously at times; and in their clouded and dark-brown depths moved multitudes of sensitive feelings, some of them frightened, some of them wildly angry, and some of them just caused by extreme sensitivity. Smithers was a physical type, quite able to take care of himself in a fight, and often to be found locked in mortal combat with Peter, wrestling being his method of fighting: but the peculiar thing about Smithers was that he was prone to cry. He would cry if he received angry words from Grate, and he would cry in the midst of battle; but he was as good a fighter as Peter, and often to be found wrestling with much aggressive feeling. He felt enmity very deeply did Smithers. When Smithers got hold of the rugby ball his olive-skinned powerful legs would spring into supple action, and no one could catch him. He had his own running-spikes, and always won the two-twenty and hundred yards in his age-group in the school sports. Later on, when Smithers had just had a birthday and Cushumph was nearly going to have one, they both found themselves in the same age-group, and they raced in the same race. The headmaster, aware of the speed of Smithers, was surprised to find that Cushumph could beat the olive-skinned, feeling-full, and dramatically emotional Smithers, for, though Cushumph was considered to be fast, Smithers was considered to be faster: actually Cushumph was the prince of the longer races in his age-group, and it was his earnestness that had enabled him to beat Smithers, Cushumph's earnestness enabling him to do almost anything if it was concentrated hard enough. It must be understood that friends in a boys' school at that age do not love each other all the time, and although Peter and Smithers were friends and intimates they often disturbed each other's emotions in an unfortunate manner, and emotionally charged wrestling would be the result, friendship being temporarily a thing of the past, and Smithers losing his temper absolutely. It was all because Smithers felt things so much, so emotionally, so dramatically: he was really a very nice boy as boys go—and could he go when he was on the running-track!

162

16

Bully for Peter again

THERE were all kinds of gas-mask cases: everyone had an identical gas-mask that they had to carry around with them all the time, but one could express one's personal individuality by one's choice of a gas-mask case, if not by the gas-mask itself, which was a grotesque, long-snouted, black thing with 'evil' written all over it: it was amazing how soon children tired of wearing the gas-masks as a plaything. You could buy all kinds of gas-mask cases in the shops, or if you were uninterested in your appearance, or poor, or a schoolboy, you could wear the cardboard case that was issued with the mask by the Government. Boys at St. Elevenes either wore the Government-issue case, suspended by a strap from their shoulders, so that the case lodged against their hips, or they bought cases of a restrained and unobtrusive colour: flamboyant gas-mask cases were OUT at St. Elevenes, and they were considered to be girlish: the manly thing was to be grim about your gas-mask case and not gay about it. There were long shelters submerged in the ground on two sides of the school's smaller playing field, and other air-raid shelters. Practice alarms were rung, and the boys would all put on their gas-masks and run into the shelters in an orderly manner.

It was hard enough for a boy to join the school at the proper time, i.e. to enter the Junior School or to start in 1A, B, or C; and if a boy joined the school after that, and went in at the beginning of a school year, or the beginning of a term, entering a form the body of which was unknown to him and the nucleus of which was already formed, joining a second, third, or, in exceptional cases, a fourth form, he would find cliques and suspicion, and life would be very hard for him at first. But if a new boy to the school joined a second or third form in the middle of the term, when all the other boys in the form already knew each other, he would be completely isolated, and rehabilitation would be hell for him. Boys who entered the school at the proper time—at the beginning of the six-, seven-, eight-, or nine-year course—would join in company, and they would not feel outsiders so much as if they joined in the middle of the course, in company with only one or two others: but if one solitary boy joined, not only in the middle of the course but in the middle of the term, he would be treated worse than an outlaw, and he would feel that he was as queer as a coot.

Femme joined 3T, coming from another school, and he joined it not only in the middle of the term, but in the middle of a lesson. The whole class was in Mr. Grate's room when the headmaster ushered the frightened Femme into the room and explained the position to Mr. Grate. For a new boy to join the form in the middle of a lesson was a very unusual thing, and a great awareness of the new boy was created. It would have been unfortunate enough as it was, Femme coming in at this stage, right in the middle of things, but Femme's appearance made the whole form view him with utter loathing. He was a nice, frightened, clean, well-brought-up boy, but that did not help him at all.

Femme sat at the first table in the centre of the room, his gas-mask case still hanging from his shoulder, and his face tense with fear, as the lesson was resumed: hostility was like an electric charge in the room. Femme was effeminate; and he had a long, uncut lock of yellow hair that trailed across his wide, white forehead and dangled over one eye: did he think that he was Veronica Lake then?—Femme with his peek-a-boo bang. His fingers were long, white, and like dead fingers; and they were immobile with fright as they lay on the brown wood of the table-top. The reaction of the whole class was unanimous: Femme was horrible, as horrible as something from under a stone—or so the rest of the class thought—and hostility battered silently at the poor boy, who was really quite a nice boy, but had unfortunately committed the crime of entering the school in the middle of the many-year course, in the middle of a school year, in the middle of a term, and in the middle of a lesson. But what made Femme provoke a feeling of absolute loathing in the minds of the watching class was something far more to his disadvantage than the things just mentioned: cuboid, and gleaming in a slimy manner, hanging just over a foot from the floor as he sat in his chair, was a gas-mask case of bright-green, shiny plastic: it was as revolting as if Femme had entered the room naked except for the wearing of a bright-green, plastic, transparent mackintosh.

The effect this all had on Peter was illogical, soul-disturbing, and dangerous for Femme. Peter hated the boy with a hate that was all-consuming and primeval. And a group of the other boys felt the same way about Femme in a slightly less violent degree. Did Grate sense the terrible hostility to the new boy?—Grate showed no sign that he did. Femme was in need of protection: once the mob got at him he was for it.

The behaviour of men is sometimes without rhyme or reason, but the behaviour of schoolboys is sometimes purely animal in its violence, hate, persecution; and viciousness. Just as animals will tear one of their own to pieces because he has some peculiarity, so schoolboys will do the same. Femme was the lame duck, the owl in the daytime, the Eton boy in the public bar.

Peter was not a leader, but he became one just once, when he led the Persecution of Femme: then he became the leader because his loathing of Femme was the most intense.

When the bell went for the mid-morning break, Femme knew he was no longer protected. He wandered out of the classroom before the others, because he had, as yet, no exercise books or text books to collect up together; and he slid his long, cold, and white fingers gently under the sloping lock of uncut, yellow hair and pushed its end away from his eye. Later on, well after the awful initiation ceremony, Femme lost the longness of that lock of yellow hair that so distinguished him from the other boys in his class, and which looked so odd. The mathematics master who took Peter's class for that subject was a queer young man, who was not on intimate terms with the boys and who taught mathematics by speaking terribly fast, assuming, wrongly, that the boys were intelligent enough to follow what he was saying. Digglewick was the only boy in the class who really followed everything that the mathematics master said: the master would talk nineteen to the dozen, his back to the class, as he wrote complicated algebraic formulae, in white chalk, on the blackboard, the chalk powdering on the black slate. He was an austere man: but one day, after having noticed Femme's long lock with irritation on many previous occasions, he did a thing that was uncharacteristically unconventional and gay, completely regardless of Femme's feelings or of Femme's parents' feelings, a thing that consisted of taking the law into his own hands. With a queer, slightly mad smile in his dull, light-brown eyes, the mathematics master beckoned Femme to come from his desk to the front of the class: Femme peered from his large, watery-blue eye—the other being covered by the end of the sloping, yellow lock—slid his fingers girlishly under the end of the lock to push it up, walked to the open space in front of the class, and stood there apprehensively, waiting, the long lock having fallen down again. The initiation ceremony, yet to be described, had been rapidly forgotten by the boys, and Femme had wisely changed his girl-type gas-mask case for a sober one: as a result, Femme had become part of the class, only distinguished from the others by his straggly peek-a-boo bang: it only needed the lock to be cut, and Femme would merge into obscurity. Before Femme knew what was happening, the mathematics master had produced a pair of scissors and had deftly snipped off the trailing end of the single yellow lock of hair on Femme's wide, white forehead: Femme now looked completely normal —slightly girlish perhaps, but apart from that he was now an integral part of the form 3T. But to return to the initiation ceremony, an initiation the ceremonial aspect of which was as beastly as anything that was carried out in the Chefalu abbey of Alistair Crowley, the Beast 666.

Femme was lost in the corridor, and the other boys in Peter's form were out of the school building before Femme was. Femme wandered round the rapidly emptying corridors; while outside the big doors at one end of the school building —a massive, wingless block of red brick—congregated a menacing mob, in the centre of which was Peter. Peter was not a person, as he stood amongst the mob that was waiting for Femme to come out of the building: he was the most intense part of a feeling of hate, that was so powerful that it obscured the personalities of the individual boys. He felt he was the core of the body of hate, and he knew that what he did the others would back up and imitate. It was the crowd versus an individual: a matter of crowd psychology, mass-madness being the most insane and violent of all.

Femme appeared in the gloomy doorway, and he stood there with his shiny, bright-green gas-mask case bumping gently on his girlish hip, suddenly aware of what was to come. Peter advanced on the boy, and the others followed. Femme rushed round the corner of the building, and stood cowering against the towering, unsympathetic, and monotonous red-brick wall, as small stones were thrown at him. He did not retaliate. Why had the poor inoffensive boy received this cruel punishment? His crime had been threefold: he had come to the school in the middle of a term, he had affinities with a famous sex-symbol of the time called Veronica Lake, and he wore a girl's gas-mask case, bought for him in a hurry by his mother. No greater sins than those were committed in a boys' school: the jungle knows no mercy if you contravene its laws.

· · · · ·

Coffee found he had haemophilia when he was thirty, but the first time that Peter ever set eyes on him, when Peter was in 1 or 2C, and when Coffee was in an A form, much the same age as Peter, Peter saw him as a boy with jeering eyes and a great, red, full mouth that was all lips—in fact Coffee was then mostly a pair of blood-filled lips. When Peter was in 3T and Coffee was in 3B, Coffee's preposterous lips had become only slightly less dominant because he had grown older, his face had developed more character, and he was known as a joker and a jeerer. He was below the average height for his age, unathletic, intelligent in a bright way, and the owner of two large, alive, mocking eyes, eyes that were always waiting for the time when they would light upon a boy who could be made fun of in front of the other boys. There was no malice in the nature of the boy Coffee—he just thought that his purpose in life was to present idiots to the rest of the world, a thing that he did with resounding success. If you were vulnerable in any way it was best to keep out of Coffee's way. Peter was vulnerable, for Peter was a dunce, and in that respect fine game for the mocking, jeering Coffee. Coffee developed into quite a character when he was in the fifth and sixth forms; and when he was over thirty he became a valuable and hard-working member of society, surprising as it may seem, though his contribution to society in his adult years did not consist, needless to say, of presenting idiots to the masses.

Again the war caused a disruption in the school curriculum. Some of the teachers were at war and there was a shortage of staff. 3T and 3B were to have their biology lesson together. It must be added in passing that reproduction was taught to the boys when they were in their fourth forms. When he was in 4T Peter learnt about Amoeba, Binary Fission, and Spirogyra, and it was only when he was in 5T that he learnt 'officially' about the human reproductory processes, and by then he had learnt about them from Smithers, coming back from rugby in the park.

The two rival forms, for that was what they were, crowded into the biology lab., their usual hostility subdued by the proximity of the biology master. Peter held his attaché-case in his hand, and dreamed about nothing, as he struggled through the door. Coffee, who had not heard of the formidability of Peter, flipped his hand against Peter's carefully set hair, and then, before Peter could do anything about it, Coffee darted to a seat at the back of the class. Peter went to his seat at the front biology bench, and sat in his usual place next to his dark friend Smithers. We will not try to pretend, for the sake of variety in our narrative, that Peter's reactions to the same stimuli were other than completely consistent and monotonous: Peter was an essentially boring boy, living in a comparatively uneventful grey mist. His reaction to the head-taunt of Coffee was exactly the same as his reaction had been to the head-taunt of Digglewick: cold fury, waiting for revenge, and a feeling that his reputation as 'a fighter not to be tangled with' was in jeopardy. Stamens, petals, osmosis, and plant reproduction failed to interest him during most biology lessons, but this time he was so preoccupied with thoughts of revenge that he did not even hear what the Scoutmaster-cum-biology master was saying. Peter sat bolt upright on his high stool, and the biology lesson swirled around him, penetrating to his consciousness not to one degree. At the back of the class, his eyes smiling as always, Coffee attended to the lesson intelligently, completely unaware that he had put electricity into a non-insulated wire, a wire that was normally fully loaded, and which was now, because of Coffee's addition, overloaded, and liable to cause a fire. The bell rang, heralding the dinner-break, and the biology master shut off the class from his mind, even though it was still in his room, milling and shouting: Peter forgot his attaché-case and books, left them on the long bench, and walked rapidly to the end of the room. Coffee was packing his satchel, and he grinned mockingly when he saw Peter approach him, taunting words on his red lips ready for delivery. Peter stood one side of the back bench, and Coffee stood on the other side: Peter swung his fist at Coffee's face in a wild arc, failed to make contact, and even more wildly swung his arm back, preparatory to making another fistic swing: Peter's elbow hit Coffee on the nose, Coffee's nose began to bleed, and Peter rushed from the room, suddenly deciding that flight was the best thing in view of the inattentive biology master's presence in the room, leaving his books and case on the front bench.

Coffee was in the habit of returning to his home for dinner, unlike Peter, who stayed to school dinner. Just before the bell rang for commencement of afternoon school, Peter was told by an intermediary that Coffee wanted to speak to him. Peter followed the intermediary to where Coffee was standing in front of the lavatory block. Coffee looked spiritually uncrushed but remarkably subdued, and his eyes smiled at Peter with only the weakest trace of mockery in them. Coffee told Peter that his father had thought that perhaps Peter had broken his nose, but Peter did not think that the nose in front of him looked broken. Peter thought that it was surprising that Coffee's nose had been so affected by an unaimed, and unintentional, elbow blow, and Peter was surprised that the boy's nose had even bled, Peter not being prone to nosebleeding at all. Coffee had hoped to make Peter feel a fool by handing him the case that Peter had forgotten to collect in his frantic moments, and Coffee had collected the case and its contents after Peter had left the biology room, having taken it home and back again with him. Coffee handed the case to Peter, explained with cautious restraint why he had possession of it, considering that under the circumstances more mockery would be inadvisable. Peter had not even realized that he had forgotten his case, and he took the case from Coffee with an expressionless face.

17

Peter and Commerce

PETER stayed in the form of Mr. Grate for two years, while he was in 3T and while he was in 4T. Adolescence was upon him with a vengeance, and change was the operative word. Boys at this age are transformed from horrible little 'Just Williams' to sexually aware, blossoming youths, whose hair begins to curl where it was formerly straight, whose complexions become fresh and beautiful instead of grubby, whose eyes become beautified by thoughts of pretty young girls instead of being filled with thoughts of the *Beano* or the *Dandy* comics, whose bodies become fine with the beauty of young manhood instead of being merely sexless and utilitarian, and whose back trousers pockets contain combs instead of envelopes of stamp swops. The transformation, wonderful as it was at this stage, was only just beginning; for at the later age of sixteen moustaches would begin to grow, voices would be self-consciously gruff, chests might even bear a single and proud hair, girls would be in their wallets, muscles would be well defined, and they might be capable of fighting a grown man.

It would be difficult to say with certainty that Peter was becoming beautiful, however, even though his appearance was changing, because he was so unsure of himself and had glasses: a boy of that age looks more attractive if he is sure that he can attract girls, and Peter's adolescent looks were marred by his conviction that he was not up to standard in his appearance. He had beautiful hair, he was sure of that; but he was convinced that he had a receding chin, although he had not; was sure that a bespectacled boy was an ugly one; was disgusted by his facial spots; and was sure that the reason he could not get a girl was because he was ugly. In actual fact he was quite a nice-looking, shy, pretty-haired boy, but with inhibitions, complexes, and with a few spots on his chin.

In desperation, Peter became a business man—or, more correctly, a business boy—and he entered the bakery trade, in spite of the fact that he remained at school. Some boys deliver papers at this age, but Peter was afraid of the outside world and he earned his extra money without leaving the protected atmosphere of the school. Times had changed, and he now felt the need for money: he had a shilling or perhaps two from his mother every week, and that represented his capital, capital with which he founded his bakery retail business. He had no overheads, had a credit system, and had a regular clientele: his business was a resounding success. Peter also went into the publishing business, making a fair income out of that too, but we will deal with that later.

COMMERCIAL ENTERPRISE ONE: THE BUN TRADE

At eleven o'clock it was milk-time: each boy had half a pint of milk, the cost of which was paid for by the Government, the milk being for the purpose of keeping the country's youth healthy in the wartime days of rationing. Peter, something of a health-fiend at that time, drank as much of the white liquid as he could, drinking the milk that the other boys did not want, as well as drinking his own share: one time he drank a quart, and felt very pleased with himself, because he was sure his health would increase enormously.

The milk was consumed in the classroom, and at that time the boys tended not to go out of the school building as much as they had done before the milk-issue was instituted. The tuck-shop was a long way away from Grate's form-room, and only boys whose form-rooms were on the tuck-shop side of the massive school building were able to eat bakery with their half-pint of milk, and even those boys found it inconvenient, for the tuck-shop was part of the Junior School building and

172

milk was drunk before the boys left the building, because the empty bottles had to be collected up systematically.

Peter travelled to school in the mornings on the trolley-bus that ran from Balsham, where his grandmother and mother lived, to a bus-stop just outside the school. Peter's sister now spent each school term at a boarding school, a school run on charity and being one of the aspects of a club to which Arthur belonged; the children of members of the club who had fallen on hard times, and the children of other members of the club, being able to belong to that school: as a result of this, Peter only saw Annabell during the holidays, when she came back to live with Peter, her mother, and her almost senile but harmless grandmother, who dropped sugar all over the place and who slept throughout the afternoons. The double-decker, red, 37 trolley-bus, with its overhead conductor-rods, and its inside conductor-lady with her ticket-roll printing machine lodged on her flat, dark-uniformed stomach, was an institution at that time in Peter's life, and it was in fact, as a result of that 37 bus, that Peter met HILDA later on when he was in the sixth form. Just before the bus got to the school it passed through a minor shopping centre that included a baker's shop, and one day Peter got off the bus at the stop before his usual one.

Peter, dressed in the dark-blue mackintosh that was the usual overcoat worn by the boys at St. Elevenses Boys' School, a plate of porridge and some bacon in his stomach, and feeling freshly washed and sleep-renewed, his hair set with careful fingers, walked into the empty bakery shop, after having inspected the penny plain buns displayed in the window. He bought one bun, and carried it along the road with him in a small white paper bag: he passed the shop that did a roaring trade in Tizer and acid-drops; passed the hair-dressing shop where the hair-dresser had manhandled his head and cut off too much hair, so that it had been difficult for Peter to make it into waves for a week afterwards; crossed the road by the spiv second-hand-car yard; and walked into the school grounds, with the usual dignity of an Elevensinian boy when he is in the view of the public. The bun went very well with his milk, and Peter realized, with embryonic business acumen, that he was enjoying something that the other milk-drinkers were not. The next morning Peter stopped off at the bakery shop again, and this time he bought twelve penny buns, currantless, brown-skinned, compact, and austere. But, austere as they might be, they made milk-drinking a luxury. When milk-time came, Peter opened the flap of his desk, pulled out the bulging bag of buns from amongst the text books therein, and opened shop. The profit was minute on the sale of each individual bun, but custom was enthusiastic, and Peter made a rapid five pennies and one half-penny—nearly sixpence—and that 50 per cent profit seemed a lot to Peter. Peter, his shop closed, ate his bun with his milk and a feeling of contentment and prosperity, and gave much thought to the business of selling one-penny buns at three-halfpence each to a ready market, and with no competition. There were five school days in the week, and at that rate Peter eagerly calculated that he could make two-and-sixpence a week: there were thirteen weeks in a term, and that made . . . Peter got out an exercise book and did calculations on the last page . . . that made One Pound, twelve shillings, and sixpence a term: three terms a year, and so nearly Five Pounds a year—clear profit—a great deal of money for Peter. However, Peter was still the dunce of the form, number thirty-three in the terminal-examination results.

Peter's financial position flourished and he sometimes bought fifteen buns each day: he had a regular, luxury-seeking set of customers, that he could absolutely depend on, and sales were very rapid indeed. If he failed to sell the last bun he would take the cost off his profits quite happily, and eat it himself, having two buns with his milk: he felt he could afford it. One day he ploughed some of his profits back into the business, and bought twenty buns, but that was a mistake, and he had to eat more buns that day than he was happy to eat. Arthur was his best customer, for Arthur bought two buns each day. Peter bought a tiny, red-covered notebook, and started a credit system: happily the boys always paid up in the end—after all it must be remembered that Peter had a mighty fist, a very useful part of his shop equipment. Grate cast a blind eye on these business proceedings fortunately. It was inevitable that competition should arise eventually, and at one stage another boy—was it Digglewick?—started up a rival shop ten desks away. But he had not the patience that Peter had, and he soon got fed up with buying buns before school started in the mornings; and also he found the profits too small, probably because he got more weekly pocket-money than Peter did—one of the boys getting ten shillings a week pocket-money. For some reason Peter terminated his business after a term or two: we think that was because he thought that he had by then made enough money to retire on, a pound or two being a fortune to Peter at that time in his life. Now this commercial enterprise was an important milestone in Peter's life, for it was the first time, up till then, that he had publicly shown any character and individuality, apart from that concerned with his scrapping. Before this he had been known by his fellows as a fighter, as a boy who yearned for girls, and perhaps as the boy who was the dimmest in the form: but now he had shown initiative and business acumen, unlikely character traits for the dreamer called Peter.

COMMERCIAL ENTERPRISE TWO:
THE PORNOGRAPHIC-LITERATURE TRADE

Can a boy who does not know the facts of life write porno-graphic literature? Take a boy who knows that girls are kissable, who knows that girls have breasts, who knows that girls have different genitals from those possessed by boys, and whose adolescent emotions become turgid and feverish at the very thought of a girl. Is it conceivable that that boy could write sexually exciting literature?

Peter's most profound piece of knowledge to date of the anatomy of the female human species was obtained years ago, when he had been living with his mother, with Arthur, with no wireless or pets, and in the same house as his younger sister Annabell. Annabell had been just a child then, but she had been a girl-child, and Peter had learnt from her. Young children will talk to each other, without embarrassment and with innocence, about their bodies; and one day Peter had been talking silly nonsense, about lavatories and the like, to his giggling sister in the house in Balham Minor. Peter was running up the stairs, his sister laughing at him from the top, and as Peter stumbled after his sister their conversation was innocent, but not what the vicar would condone. Annabell lifted up her skirt high, giggling as she did so, and Peter saw her bare. It was then that he realized that girls were different to boys somewhere below the waist. But he only thought that urinal discharge was differently achieved by girls than it was by boys, for he had no idea that reproduction was anything to do with what he had been privileged to see.

Some time after the bun-selling period in his life in Mr. Grate's room on the upper floor of the Senior School building, Peter sat down at his grandmother's dining-table, placed some foolscap pages on the polished bare wood in front of him, and secretly began to write. It was in the evening, and he should have been doing his homework, studying *Much Ado About Nothing*, but Peter was embarking upon a literary career instead. The table he wrote at was used for meals, after which it was carefully cleared, and the tablecloth removed. It was the same room in which Peter's grandfather had lain in his bed, dead and cold; and it was a dark room, filled with the smell of old people, and old things. Heavy curtains hung over the French windows behind the seated and crouched figure of Peter; ornaments crowded the mantelpiece; and a proud stag looked down into a valley, on the wall against which the table was placed. The battered old wireless, that the old man had hit when it refused to utter, stood on a small table by the side of the French windows; and in the corner by the wireless was the armchair that only the old man had sat in in days of yore, and in which Peter sat nowadays when he wanted to listen to Geraldo—Peter loved listening to Geraldo, Glen Miller not being on as much as Geraldo was. Peter liked listening to the recordings of Bob Hope too, because sometimes he heard the voice of Betty Grable at those times. Sitting, small, clothed in black Victorian clothes, her skirt down to her shoes, her sparse yellow hair in strands across her pink and nearly naked skull-top, steel glasses on her face, bent over her sewing, was Peter's grandmother, looking exactly as grandmothers should look, a remnant of a past age, soon to die. Across the none-too-large room, behind the figure of the grandmother sitting in front of the fire, sat Peter's mother, in the third armchair in the room that was full of decaying creature-comforts. Peter's mother's eyes were full and clouded with tiredness behind her tortoise-shell-rimmed glasses; her grey hair was thinning slightly at the hair-line; and in her birthmarked hand was a welcome and rest-giving cigarette: she found it hard to work in the big store all day, and then to have to come home and cook and mend for her thankless son Peter, who was selfishly self-absorbed all the time. Her clothes, though scrupulously clean, were new long ago; and in the evenings she would put on what she called her 'slacks', which bulged unpleasantly over her stomach. She was now living only for Peter, and, to a lesser degree, for her daughter. She longed for Peter to be a success, and she had a blind faith that her son would one day become one. The fact that Peter was an ignoramus and bottom of his form pained her immensely, and it was with shame that she compared Peter's scholastic achievements with those of her brother's children, Trevor and Trevorene-Lou. But she interpreted Peter's withdrawn, morose, introspective nature as being a sign that he had potential powers that would one day be released. Peter did indeed one day become a fairly famous figure in his profession, but before that happened she died, and she was not able to see her son in his success as she would so dearly have liked to do. When she died her son was still up to nothing in particular.

Peter wrote with his pen, and covered up the part of the page that was written upon, so that neither his grandmother nor his mother should by chance see some of the things he was writing about. He wrote in a painstaking hand, and he wrote in an emotional frenzy, letting out all his sexual frustration into his narrative. He wrote about a lovely girl in a theatre-box, whose dress had come undone; and about a man with a

sub-machine gun, who entered the box and sprayed the audience with bullets. He wrote about the man escaping in a huge, thundering, American car; and he terminated his tale by describing dramatically how the car power-housed into the Grand Union Canal. He did not know where that canal was, in fact he thought that he had invented the name, and he used the name because it sounded so powerful, evocative, and titanic. Two foolscap pages were covered with heavy, inky, curly writing: he looked with a feeling of achievement at the two ink-laden pages that had formerly been virginal. Secretly he took the two pages out of the room, muttering evasively as his mother asked him kindly what he had been writing.

Peter showed the story to Smithers, and then to the form's literary critic Not-so-Green. The story was read by a number of the boys, and, although the literary critic had not thought much of it, Peter was pleased with some of the reactions that he had received, and, encouraged, he went home and wrote another story. This story was concerned not with drama or crime, but simply with eroticism: it was concerned with a lovely girl and an amorous gentleman, who were sitting in a suburban sitting-room, the man's temperature rising rapidly as the evening wore on, and terminated with the gentleman switching off the electric light and advancing across the room towards the delectable, much-described girl. At the end of the two foolscap pages Peter drew a ring with his pen, and inside the ring he wrote in capitals 'NICE WORK IF YOU CAN GET IT', this becoming his trade-mark, and occurring at the end of all his future pieces of pornography. He charged his form-mates 'one penny a read', and, although he did not make as much money at that as he had done with the buns, he was very pleased because the money he did receive represented literary appreciation of his work. He would no doubt have made more money, and had more readers, if he had known the facts of life.

18

The Farm-camp

SOMEBODY had to pick up the potatoes after the mechanism drawn by the farm-tractor had unearthed them. Most of the farm-labourers were at war, and somebody had to pick the potatoes up. There were the landgirls, dressed in shorts and well-filled pullovers, and with their hair tied up in silk squares: but there were just so many landgirls, and there were a vast number of potatoes, lying just underneath the earth, below the coarse, short foliage above each family of them, as yet unseen by the outside world. Somebody had to pick up the potatoes. So England asked its schoolboys.

The biology master was put in charge of the farm-camp because of his experience in organizing and running Scout-camps in the past. The summer sun shone happy and warm, and the holidays had arrived: the school was empty, and the farm-camp offered to the boys money, a holiday occupation, the open air, and the company of their fellows. A large number of boys went that summer, including Peter. It was perhaps surprising that they did, for nobody could say that it was fun picking up potatoes fast before the tractor came round again and dug up another row: it was all bending; putting spuds into sacks, one boy holding the mouth of the sack open, and one boy emptying the basket of spuds into it, the mouth of the sack sometimes closing accidentally, and the spuds falling on the ground; clearing the foliage away; and not a moment to talk before the tractor came round again, with the thumbless farm-labourer in it, and they had to start doing it all over again. The work was hard and grim, and the Elevensinians, now free of their blazers, had to get up at an unearthly hour in the morning, so that they could start work on the earth in the half-light. But there were the evenings at the camp; the scrumping industry organized by the rugged spiv Elevensinian; the money; and the group from the girls' school farm-camp, that sometimes picked up potatoes on the field next to the one the boys were in: compensations. There was Cushumph's girl that he kissed behind the tree—blonde, buxom, sixteen, and chesty; and of course there was Lulu as well—Lulu, the seventeen-year-old landgirl, who seemed to be on her own, and on whose rolled-shorts-topped thighs the boys wrote their names with their fountain pens, as she screamed and giggled girlishly in the open back of the lorry. And there was the troop of landgirls, rather too old for the boys, but nice to watch. Compensations for potato-picking: but not for Peter. 'Lulu, Lulu . . . bash away Lulu' sang the boys, as she stood in the back of the moving lorry with them, one girl amongst so many boys.

Peter was in love with Lulu—naturally—although he had never spoken to her, and never would. He was in love with one of the landgirls too, but she was twenty-three, and never knew of her admirer. Lulu had a peculiar effect upon the earth-smeared Elevensinian boys: they were all in love with her, but at the same time they seemed to hate her too—to hate her because they could not have her, and because her appearance disturbed them. Lulu was not part of the troop of landgirls and she would work with the boys: unlike the other landgirls, who came from London, she lived nearby the market-gardening farm. The boys would come to the farm from the farm-camp site in the back of an open lorry; and in the late afternoon they would return in the same lorry, a lorry that had been used for carting anything, including manure, small bits of the manure still being in the lorry. In the mornings the lorry, crowded with fresh-washed and combed boys, including Cushumph, Peter, and Peebles, would stop on the main road, and Lulu would climb over the back-wheel mudguard, over the side of the lorry, and into the mass of laughing boys, some of whom had eagerly helped her up. And in the late afternoons she would be returned in the same manner. One late afternoon, after Lulu had alighted from the lorry of excited boys, and was walking away by the side of a barn to her home beyond, her back to the boys, the boys showed their admiration of her in a peculiar manner. The last load the lorry had carted had been one of potatoes, and at the feet of the boys were a number of those vegetables. Yelling with a certain amount of derision, the boys pelted the figure of Lulu with the missiles; and as she hurried away the potatoes clattered against the dusty side of the barn, none of them hitting her because they had been aimed badly on purpose. Lulu did not tease them, but her appearance did, and the boys resented that. It annoyed them to be constantly shown something that they liked, but which was something that apparently they could not have: none of the boys went out with Lulu, probably because she had a farm-labourer boy-friend. Ah, but she looked a fine sight that day when she went home with her fleshy and bare thighs covered with Eleven-sinian signatures: Peter would have loved to have put his signature there with the others, but he would not have dared: in fact he found the whole business rather lewd. Needless to say, Lulu was pretty, and comely of figure, and not really called Lulu. Lulu, the sex-symbol of the potato lorry.

Sometimes the boys travelled to their place of work by bicycle; and often when they went to other farms they would get their steeds from the big tent where all the bicycles were kept on the camp-site, and ride away, feet encircling happily. Peter would, on these occasions, come bemusedly home with two of the others, in the soft late afternoon, all three cycling along the green-sided lane abreast of each other, and singing romantically 'Blue champagne . . . purple shadows and blue champagne' or 'Just Molly and me, and baby makes three . . ., we're so happy in our, blue heaven,' the happy, work-freed young voices floating clearly, and with a great deal of feeling, down the lane. Peter felt nearer to some of the boys that summer; the communal life of the farm-camp, and the sleeping together, bringing even the most introspective of the boys out of themselves. Peter had journeyed from his grandmother's

house to the farm-camp on his bicycle, a full-sized second-hand machine, and he would return on it. Early in the mornings there were races down a hill that came upon them suddenly, as they rode to the farm where they would work. The hill would turn the wheels, and the wheels would turn the pedals; and Peter, eager to win by going faster, would hit his feet down at the flying pedals, crashing them down jerkily, in an attempt to make the dizzy, blur-chrome pedals go faster than they were going on their own: Peter got to the bottom of the green-walled hill-road first, for he knew his bicycle better than Cushumph knew his. During the term times, in the evenings, Cushumph would have been cuddling girls, but Peter would have been cycling aimlessly round the roads, getting to know his cycle, and wishing that he was getting to know one of the laughing-eyed girls that he passed.

Peter swore at the camp, swearing uninhibitedly and constantly, until one day the biology master took him to one side, and told him in a kindly manner that, although one was entitled to swear if one hurt oneself, one was not entitled to swear just for the sake of swearing. Peter had felt adult saying 'bloody hell' and worse after every sentence, and he had felt more confident because of that method of speech, but after the master had told him off he cleaned his conversation, but by only 50 per cent.

The field that the St. Elevenses camp was on was covered by big tents supplied by the Government, and at the end of the residential and sleeping quarters was a huge tent that was used for the dining-room: the biology master had a thing about scrambled eggs with chopped bacon in it, and they had that for breakfast every morning. At the week-ends parents would come down, and sisters too, and that was very gay, but Peter had told Iris to stay away, for a visit by her would have embarrassed him. In the evenings Peter sometimes took a rugby ball to the edge of the field, and he would kick it vertically into the air as high as he could, run forward a step or two, and catch it, as he had been taught, deep down into his stomach: he became very good at this, but he remained useless in a rugby match nevertheless.

The boys at the farm-camp were of all ages from ten to eighteen, and members of the same form would have chosen the same tent, the result of this being that two tents were occupied by very big boys, some of whom were heroic figures in the school rugby team. In the mouth of one other tent, in the evenings, scrumped apples were sold from a potato sack, and weighed on a pair of scales from the cooking tent, the spiv Elevensinian who had stolen the apples making a good profit until he was discovered by the biology master.

Fights were far more frequent at the farm-camp than they had been at the school itself, and Cushumph and Peter had many part-friendly skirmishes, to keep themselves in good trim, to let off frustrated aggressions, and so that they could see who was the strongest. Peter had grown bigger by now, while Cushumph had seemed to have stayed the same size as he was when he entered Grate's form. Peter could now almost beat Cushumph, and one day they mutually decided to go away from the camp and have a fight in private, to decide once and for all who was the strongest. The whole thing was planned and premeditated in a friendly way, and this took the aggression out of it completely. The accidental skirmishes had had a healthy ferocity, but this over-organized and self-conscious fight had too much mutual agreement about it for it to have any spice of ferocity, and it ended in a very odd manner, much to the embarrassment of Peter. Peter and Cushumph were good friends, and Peter admired Cushumph immensely: in fact it would be true to say that in a healthy manner Peter loved Cushumph, a thing that apparently Cushumph instinctively realized. Peter's love was unexpressed and completely proper: merely the admiration of one boy for another. Cushumph was not a conceited boy, despite the fact that he was good at so many sports, and, although Peter was not up to his standard in getting girls or in sports, Cushumph was very friendly to Peter. Cushumph must have been tired that evening as they walked out of the camp together. They came to a deserted and seemingly suitable spot and prepared to do battle. They stood apart and faced each other, Peter hoping to have a fine, hard fight with his friend: but as they looked at each other the necessary aggression did not seem to come into them. Peter looked at the feeble, friendly eyes of his friend with some perplexity, because he did not understand the look in those eyes, a look that should have been alert, bright, hard, and challenging. They tangled and rolled in a devitalized way on the grass, and then Cushumph got on top of Peter, held his arms down, and, embarrassment unparalleled, Cushumph kissed the helpless Peter. Peter was staggered. He certainly did not like this sort of behaviour, and they walked back to the camp in an embarrassed silence, as the sun sank away, and the darkening sleepy evening blurred the forms of the trees and made the edges of the fields hard to see.

.　　　.　　　.　　　.　　　.

Welling was at the camp, and he slept in a tent with some other members of his own form. Next to Welling's tent was one of the sixth-formers' tents, containing one or two heroes and other less-distinguished sixth-formers. Welling slept in the entrance to his tent, and his bed was visible from the outside, as was his bottle of lemonade, the sight of that bottle giving one of the sixth-formers an idea for a rather horrible practical joke.

In the sixth-formers' tent was a hero who has as yet been unmentioned, and his name was Tiger. Tiger was a short boy, but that was his only physical disadvantage, for he had shoulders like slabs of rock, thick well-muscled arms, bulging legs that he used for football and running, and big hands that he used for boxing. Tiger's brother went to an art school where, it was rumoured breathlessly in St. Elevenses, he drew nude girls, and Tiger himself was very good at drawing. Tiger had a shock of blond, slightly waving hair, that flapped as he ran; and he moved his squat and powerful body with the grace of a boy instinctively concerned with aesthetics. He was feared and respected. There were more heroes in the sixth form at that time than there had ever been before at the same time in the school; and the rugby team that played other schools was the best that St. Elevenses had had: a seven-players team was formed from the heroes, and it swept the country, winning all its seven-a-side matches. Tiger was one of the heroes needless to say—no less than Plathit or Ciganter. Like the great cat in the best-seller he was born free, and looked it. But Tiger was not the sort of boy to perpetrate a practical joke like the one that Yatchjohn perpetrated, and it was mistakenly that Welling, the fighter of Plathit, blamed Tiger for the injustice of the vulgar joke that was played at his expense.

Yatchjohn slept in the same tent as Tiger. He was a bright boy, and, though younger than the average age for the sixth form he was in, he was so clever that he was in that sixth form. He was a little too young, and not quite developed enough, to be one of the heroes; although afterwards, when they had all left and entered the Services, he became captain of this and captain of that. However, he was not built in the heroic manner, having enormous calves, an enormous bottom, and sloping and narrow shoulders. He had a smooth, greasy, oval face; straight dark hair; ever-smiling eyes; and an olive complexion: facially he looked a little like Smithers who was younger than he was. His eyes were the eyes of a joker and a humorist, bearing a slight resemblance to the eyes of Coffee: both boys' eyes were ever-smiling. The other sixth-formers treated him as something of an oddity among them, and they tolerated the younger boy: later, Yatchjohn matured with the ageing of two more years (he stayed in the sixth a long time), and became serious, responsible, and dignified, as befitted a school-captain, head prefect, and captain of soccer and rugby. But at this time in our story Yatchjohn was never serious, and nobody would have thought that he would later have become head of the school, when there was a shortage of heroes, and he was the best there was in the days of shortage of so many things.

Yatchjohn, treated at that time by his fellow sixth-formers as a bit of a joke himself, was forever on the look out for likely material for a joke, although, unlike Coffee, he did not ridicule other boys. He came out of the sixth-formers' tent one day and saw the lemonade bottle that belonged to Welling, the bottle standing by Welling's bed. Yatchjohn emptied the bottle, and quickly took it with him into the deserted sixth-former tent, where he filled it with a yellow liquid identical in appearance to lemonade. He stoppered the bottle again and replaced it by Welling's bed.

Welling came back to his tent feeling thirsty, and took a long drink from his lemonade bottle, a drink that he did not find as refreshing as he had expected it to be. Welling spat out the obnoxious liquid, his face white with fury, and he ran across the field to the water-tap to clean out his mouth. Any other boy in Welling's form would have accepted this joke, when they got to know that it had been committed by a sixth-former, for sixth-formers were big, and the rest of Welling's form were not. Welling was not as mature and developed as the sixth-formers, but his courage and pride were from one of Homer's works. By then all the sixth-formers had been told about the joke, and Welling met Tiger who laughed at him. It was considered senseless for a boy of Welling's age to tangle with a hero like Tiger, but when Welling heard the laughter he thought that Tiger had been responsible for the joke, and he leapt upon the tough, hard-muscled, and obstinate sixth-former, the two boys falling, legs splayed, between their respective tents. Welling was tall for his age, and Tiger was short for his age, so they were about the same height; but Welling's muscles were unformed, while Tiger's were those of a man, hard, defined, and familiar to him. Boys came out of their tents to see the struggle, and it was obvious that Welling was causing Tiger some difficulty. Watching boys wondered at the courage of Welling, and spoke about it amongst themselves with awe. Wild as Welling was, he could not combat the quality in Tiger that would not give in. There was one supreme heroic virtue in Tiger, and that was that he did not know the meaning of defeat. Eventually Tiger got on top of Welling, and with his short arms pinned those of the younger boy to the grass: Tiger stayed in that straddling position for some time, regaining his breath and emphasizing his victory; and then he rose from Welling and the battle was over. Three things were remembered by the watching boys: one was the courage of the younger Welling; another was the proof that they had witnessed that heroes are not to be beaten; and the third was the nature of the practical joke played by Yatchjohn. Yatchjohn wisely kept out of the way while the fight was on, and watched from behind the sloping side of a tent. What would have happened if Welling had fought Yatchjohn might have been another story, for, though Yatchjohn became a hero after the other heroes had left to fight a real war, he was never any good in the boxing ring—he with his narrow shoulders—whereas Welling in later years became the heavy-weight-boxing champion of the whole school, unchallenged, except by Peter, in what Peebles scathingly called a stupid moment. Peter, years later, became a student of boxing, and read the *Boxing News* every week. When Peter heard that there was nobody to fight Welling in the school boxing finals, he volunteered to fight the champion, despite the fact that he was short-sighted and lighter than Welling. His challenge was accepted by the sports master. Peebles leant over his desk in geography and told Peter that he thought he had no boxing wisdom because he had agreed to fight an obviously superior fighter. This hurt Peter, who considered himself to be a boxing authority, especially in view of the fact that he knew by heart all the heavyweight-boxing champions of the world, from John L. Sullivan to Joe Louis; but Peter had a mad suspicion that he could beat Welling, and he still wanted to fight him. But the sports master was informed of the inequality by the interfering Peebles, and Peter was not allowed to give himself to the slaughter, St. Elevenses being an essentially humane place. But that last incident was in the future.

19

The Facts of Life

GINA was presumably the possessor of some animal magnet-
ism, although Peter did not think about it in quite that way
when he craned his neck over the wooden school fence in the
hope that he might see her coming down the road on her way
to work. The road she came down was at right angles to the
wooden fence; and between the wooden fence on the school
side, and the concrete where the boys were allowed to walk and
run, was a bushy and treed strip that was out of bounds: but
Peter climbed over the wire fence edging the concrete, struggled
through the green entanglements, his hair in ridges of carefully
set waves, and stood on tip-toe by the wooden fence, his eyes
pleading that the empty road would soon fill with the delightful
figure of his beloved Gina. Gina walked up the road towards
the school fence slowly: she was a dark-haired girl with dark
introspective eyes, and she was about sixteen years old. It
must be understood that Peter did not on any occasion make
any contact with Gina; Gina probably did not think much of
the raw-faced, cow-eyed, and bespectacled youth, who stared
at her with a pounding heart, as she walked by on her way to
work in the mornings. But Peter thought all the time of the
dark little Gina. Gina was admired by other Mr. Chads than
Peter, for Arthur watched over the fence in the mornings
before the school doors let the boys in, and Cushumph
watched too. Until Arthur asked her what her name was, she
had been known by the three boys as Mary, a fact that made
Peter listen to the song on the wireless that was popular at
the time with great romanticism and daydreaming: the song

190

was 'Mary, Mary . . . sweet as any name can be . . .' When the experienced Arthur had asked her her name, she had stopped for an instant, and said quietly, so that they could hardly hear: 'Gina,' and then walked on. That was all the contact that was made by any of the three boys with Gina. Watching the girls go to work in the morning became an institution for the three boys, and an older blonde lady, of a flashy appearance, was admired a great deal as well as Gina; and then there were three schoolgirls, one of whom had a lecherous look and a big chest: the schoolgirls were very young, and only the prematurely developed one received any attention, Cushumph theorizing that girls who thought about sex a lot developed quicker. But Peter reserved his great love for Gina, and sometimes he would stand on the concrete, away from the wooden fence, and stretching himself would try to see if she was coming, it being uncomfortably possible just to see her and avoid standing on forbidden ground at the same time. Peter would watch the road that was empty, his heart pounding because of the knowledge that soon he would see her at the end of that road, minute because of perspective, after she had turned the corner into view. It is impossible to describe the effect the sudden sight of Gina at the end of the road had upon the boy: his head would thunder with passion, and do that until she had walked all the way up the road, that was at right angles to the school fence, crossed the road just by Peter, and walked out of sight, close along by the other side of the school fence. Neither the older blonde lady nor Gina responded to the encouraging looks given to them as they passed by Arthur and Cushumph, but the prematurely developed schoolgirl with the lecherous eyes responded overmuch, by calling to the two boys (Peter watched the most, but was out of the rest of it) and giggling with her two friends. Arthur made a date with the young schoolgirl, age differences ignored in the cause of sex, and Arthur waited at the rendezvous for some time before he walked away, the girl having stood him up, regardless of the fact that Arthur was a good-looking young fellow.

There were two occasions during the school day when the three boys watched over the fence, their feet scrabbling on

191

large stones at the foot of the fence amongst the weeds and
entanglements: there was the time in the morning, and the
time just before the school doors opened for afternoon school
—the time when the working girls came to work after going
home for their dinners. It was at this latter time that Arthur
and Cushumph did most of their bird-watching. Being a
forward and enterprising lad, full of initiative in matters
connected with the opposite sex, Arthur, who liked the blonde
lady, decided to carry things a bit further than just watching
over the fence: he got the sheepish Peter to go with him, and
they both followed the blonde lady after she had passed the
watching point. The two boys went out of the second pair of
school gates, and followed her all down the side of one school
fence, and then all down the side of another school fence, past
the main school gates, past the second-hand-car yard, and
into the small shopping centre beyond. Peter felt he was acting
uncharacteristically and he felt guilty, for he knew that he
would not have dared to follow the flashy blonde if he had
been alone: but he tagged along with Arthur, quivering with
a sense of the excitement of the occasion. They watched the
blonde lady go into an entrance-way, and then they returned
to school, having achieved very little indeed.

.   .   .   .   .

Peter could not understand it when he heard about it. It
seemed so undignified: he could not imagine the music master
lowering himself to participate in such a ludicrous activity.
Peter tended not to believe it, in fact, rejecting it as an in-
accuracy. But he could not get away from the facts. He had
to think more about what Smithers had told him on the way
back from rugby practice in the park, and he wondered how on
earth his mother could have got up to such nonsense.

Peter had learnt the facts of life. He now knew; and, as has
been stated, he did not accept the knowledge very readily.
What Smithers told him, as they both walked to the park
gates in their rugby kit, preparatory to catching a trolley-bus
to the school, their rugby boots covered with caked mud, and

their rugger shirts moist with sweat and smeared with dirt, was no less than a Revelation to Peter. He had had no idea it was like that: it had not occurred to him that respected and proper adults could act in such a base manner. He felt that if what Smithers had told him was true, then all the dignified act that adults put on, especially to young boys like himself, was to his mind a fraud. He felt cheated: the untouchable supremacy and respectability of adults was false, if they acted, as Smithers had said, when the bedroom curtains were drawn. And yet he still could not quite believe it all—it was all so preposterous. Could his mother, so aloof and so completely unanimalistic, have acted in this way with his father? Could his father, with all his act of adult supremacy, have acted like some animal when his watch-chain and waistcoat were hung in the wardrobe? Impossible—surely it was impossible. And then there was his headmaster—could he do such things—such base and vulgar things? But it was the music master he could least imagine doing the things that Smithers had said that people did to make children: the music master—so stiff and stern, all clad in black, and so correct in his manner—could he really have done those funny things with his clothes off? Presumably he must have done, for Peter knew that he had a young son. Peter had learnt the facts of life, and his world was shattered. Peter had learnt about the act of love, and the propriety of the adult world was split asunder. The behaviours of the middle-classes were a lie if this was what those middle-classes got up to in their spare time. Oh, for Pete's sake, thought Peter—royalty could surely not do it too!

Sometimes the boys went from the park to the school without the aid of the trolley-bus, and they would run through the town in their rugger kit, tearing past and through the startled shoppers on the pavements of the busy town, running in the gutters mostly for it was a clear way there. But this time Peter had the cost of the fare, and he rode with Smithers at the top of the trolley-bus, his mind in a turmoil. He had to check. Smithers might be inventing all this, although that did not seem like Smithers. Perhaps, thought Peter, Smithers had got it all wrong: Smithers had admitted that he had not had any personal experience of this peculiar performance. But how could Smithers have got it *so* wrong? Where there is smoke there is fire, and that suggested that Smithers's account must have had *some* truth in it. The Act must then be something like Smithers had said it was; and, if it was, that was bad enough. Could the music master possibly . . . ? He could not have done—surely not. Peter stared out of the trolley-bus window, and looked at the females in the town below with complete puzzlement: were all those people capable of such ridiculous behaviour? He had thought until then that girls were merely for kissing and for cuddling, and that to see their bare chests was the final intimacy. Now he knew that that was only the half of it, and he just could not believe that life was like that. His mind cried with disbelief as he thought of his mother doing such things. Adults had always acted towards him as if he was inferior to them because he lacked their decorum: if they acted like animals in their bedrooms what right had they to expect boys to act in a nice and proper manner? Why, adults were as bad as boys; and Peter felt that they had been playing a trick upon him. The adult hierarchy was not of unimpeachable conduct any more: hitherto he had thought of the adult hierarchy as impregnable, but now he began to despise the untouchables. In the ensuing days Peter checked Smithers's story, and he reluctantly accepted the fact that his music master bounced up and down in bed with what Peter thought was a complete lack of self-respect, completely contravening the laws of decorum. Peter was ashamed for the adult world. And then, some time later, it occurred to Peter that he too would one day get up to that particular lark, and he nearly had a black-out with the emotional disturbance that those thoughts brought.

.   .   .   .   .

If you overslept they would come and get you: the post-office van would be waiting outside the house, and you would be hurrying into your clothes, preparatory to driving off with them without having any breakfast. Then, when you got to the sorting-office, they would send you off with your bag of letters, and there would not be any time for any elevenses, either, for it would be Christmas cards in letter-boxes all the time till midday dinner.

But that Christmas, when he was working at the post-office as a temporary worker, with a post-office armband on his upper arm, Peter did not oversleep, and it was the Christmas after that when he did.

There were St. Elevenses boys that he knew working at the post-office, and they all started work in the cold early hours. First they would sort the letters, standing in front of the honeycomb of boxes and putting letters in appropriate boxes; then they would tie all the separate bundles of letters with string, put them in a post-office sack in a special order, and leave the post-office. After this they would wander round the roads, the load in the sack getting less and less, and if they were lucky they would get a Christmas box, one that the regular postman ought to have got.

The St. Elevenses boys broke up a number of days before Christmas, the boys who were going to work at the post-office breaking up sooner than the rest of the boys. Then the temporary post-office workers would work every day until, and including, Christmas Day, while the rush was on; and halfway through 'the Day of Days in the year' the employment would suddenly stop, leaving the boys free to enjoy their holidays until the Spring term started again. It was a hard grind working at the post-office, but there was money in it, foreign stamps to steal from the envelopes, and it represented a change from the tedium of study.

Temporary workers from schools were not only male, and this livened things up a lot. Early in the mornings there were schoolgirls in the sorting-office, and this was very exciting indeed. Peter, who sorted and delivered the mail for one area, was given an assistant, who arrived at the post-office every morning, just at the time that he had got all the letters sorted and was ready to go out and deliver them: Peter was to give his assistant a proportion of his mail, and the assistant was to deliver that. As Peter and his assistant delivered letters in the same area, they sometimes met on their rounds, and any delivery difficulties would be discussed at those times. When Peter was shown his assistant the world turned upside down, to use a vulgar colloquialism, for the assistant was a schoolgirl—pretty, with red-smeared, bulbous lips and a short but voluptuous figure under her winter clothes and overcoat. Her name was Sally Charles, a Roman Catholic, nearly as old as Peter. Naturally Peter fell deeply in love with her: how could it have been otherwise?

She was nice, friendly, unsuspicious of men, quiet, and charming; and she did not make Peter feel that he was hopeless with girls. Perhaps the fact that he was in a sense her boss gave him a feeling of confidence; and as he had to explain the distribution to her this gave him something to say, and untied his tongue. Peter looked forward to the times when they would meet on their rounds: then she would put down her sack on a low wall round the front garden of a suburban house, and talk to him for a few moments about such subjects as how washing up for her mother made her hands red. Peter thought her little-girl hands looked positively divine; and as for her cherry-smeared full lips—they were in his dreams at night. Peter was talking to a girl for the very first time. He knew that this was his opportunity. He had waited for so long to have a girl of his own—to take to the pictures and so on, and here was his chance. There seemed to be no competition; the girl did not show any dislike of him; and he saw her often: he would ask her to come out with him. It needed courage for Peter to do this, but he knew that as he must take his opportunity while it was offered he would eventually ask her. He procrastinated until Christmas Eve, and then he asked her to come to the pictures with him: she said 'yes', as if he had asked nothing extraordinary, and rode off on her bicycle with her empty sack. A bit puzzled by the lack of feeling in her reply, and amazed at her casualness, he rode off on his bike to deliver his last few letters. He had been given two new roads to do that day, and he was not familiar with them. He posted a lot of letters in letter-boxes all along one road, and then asked a man in a garage where the other road was. It turned out that he had got the two roads mixed up, and had posted twelve lots of letters in the wrong road. The garage man realized that Peter had done this, and called to another man in the garage, to tell him what the stupid boy had done. Peter quickly left the garage, posted all the remaining letters, and left the people in the houses to redeliver the wrongly delivered mail, for he had not the courage to go back, explain his stupidity at every door, re-collect the mail, and deliver it properly. His stupidity never caught up with him, for the next day was his last day, the complaints did not reach the post-office in time, and anyway the people were not likely to complain until after Boxing Day.

Peter spent that evening at home with his mother, sister (she was home on holiday), and grandmother, in a state of expectancy and happiness. The next day was the half-day—Christmas Day—and then he would arrange a date with Sally Charles who was to become Peter's girl. Peter delivered his Christmas Day mail, feeling that he had already received all his Christmas presents. When he had finished, he went back to the sorting-office to make his date with Sally, but he found that she had gone home, having finished work early. Unless he saw her again he would not be able to make his date, and he felt that she did not seem to care much about the date or she would have stayed at the sorting-office until he returned. Visions of having a girl began to slip away from him, and he wondered how on earth he could make contact with her, for their employment together had finished. Peter could not understand her casual attitude to their proposed date: she had said 'yes' to his request after all. He got her address from the post-office, and leaving his bicycle there he walked down the street of shops, his raincoat unbuttoned at the front, and his house-tie flapping on his chest in what he felt was rather a rakish way. He was determined not to let her slip from his grasp.

He walked through the shopping centre of Balsham, and on down the main road into the residential area, feeling light-headed with enterprise: he was venturing, and he was frightened of the thought that he would knock on a door that would probably be opened by one of her parents. But temerity and initiative were forced upon him, for he just had to hold on to his only chance to get a girl of his own. He sat down on a seat under a tree by the side of the road, and tried to assemble the pieces of his courage: some way away was the opening from the main road into her road. Then he heard a call, and there she was, riding along on her bicycle with a girl-friend of hers: before he could tell her to stop she had passed him with a smile and a wave. Peter wondered how she could have forgotten about their proposed date, a thing that had been occupying his own thoughts ever since he had asked her to come out with him. Did she not realize that she would not see him again, and that he would not have any opportunity to make the date with her? He went on and walked down her road: it was a lovely road, with laurel trees in the gardens and lime trees in the pavements, and it was called 'Tilly Lane'—a road that he thought was a fitting place for such a sweet girl as her to live in. His head full of romance, he wandered along beneath the trees to her house. With trepidation he knocked on the door, and after a while the door was opened by his love, breathless, friendly, and with full lips parted. It was the first time he had seen her without her overcoat on, and she looked wonderful to him. Also she was not as restrained as she had been when she had been doing the job at the post-office: here she was in the freedom of her home. She told him that they were taking the Christmas pudding out of the oven, her enthusiasm about that being very intense. He asked her about the date, and she told him that her mother had said that she could not go out with him. She did not seem to realize how that hurt him. After some more brief and friendly talk she bade him good-bye, wished him a Merry Christmas warmly, and he found himself walking down the front path. He looked around at the world, and it was in little pieces.

His uncle, the father of Trevor and Trevorene-Lou, had his sisters and brothers and their families to stay for Christmas, and it had become an institution to stay at his house over Christmas. In years before, the family had assembled at the home of Peter's grandmother and grandfather at Christmas-time, but since the old pair had moved to the smaller house in Balsham a transference had occurred. Now that the old man was dead, the old lady stayed over Christmas with her son. That Christmas, Peter, Iris, Annabell, and the old lady went to join the family gathering at the home of Peter's cousin Trevor. They got there in the evening of Christmas Day, Peter's work at the post-office having prevented them from going earlier, and Peter was remote from the festivities, his mind black with pain at the thought that he had lost Sally. Normally Peter would have enjoyed the visit immensely, for he loved the atmosphere of his uncle's house, and the company of his cousin Trevor, but this time things were different. The house was crowded, and he had to sleep on a mattress laid on the landing: as he got into bed he felt alone with his all-absorbing misery: nobody knew how wretched he felt.

The Christmas festivities over, and Peter and the other three back in the old lady's house, Peter decided to try again. His inhibitions had been partly banished by the fact that the girl had said 'yes', for he had found that encouraging. He knocked on her door again, and this time he was confronted by her mother who looked disapprovingly at him. She would not let Peter see her daughter, and ruthlessly told him that her daughter obviously did not want to go out with him. Peter wondered if this was true, and he felt that the girl was doing what her mother had told her to do, and not necessarily doing what she would have done if it had not been for parental authority. He protested, but the mother was angry and adamant. Dejectedly he went away.

Telling himself that Sally was acting under instructions, and that she would not mind going out with him if it was left to her to decide, he decided to communicate with her directly. He wrote her a letter, a letter that told her of the advantages of being taken to the pictures by a boy: he explained to her, thinking that by doing so he was reinforcing his case, that she would be getting a back-row seat, the most expensive in the cinema, for nothing. But he waited for her reply in vain. He brooded for many weeks about Sally. The next Christmas he worked at the post-office again. She was there, now sorting and delivering her own round. But she had grown confident, aware of her charms, assuredly flirtatious, and just a little brash. She was no more the quiet, nice little girl. She ignored Peter, and seemed to have a lot to do with another Elevensinian who was working there, a very tall, waving, white-skinned boy, with blond hair and a small head, who looked like Dan Duryea, the film star. That made Peter, who still loved her, a very miserable temporary post-office worker indeed.

20

Battle

4B and 4T were rivals. And there were some substantial fighters in 4B, Packagger being one of them. If the two forms clashed, and once they did, 4B could depend on the full support of its members, whereas 4T could not depend on the support of its older boys, who felt they were above that sort of thing: so that left 4T with a battle strength consisting primarily of Smithers, Cushumph, and Peter, with the half-hearted backing of the rest of the form, with the exception of such as Arthur, Tabbot, and Boogter.

Cushumph and Peter were respected as fighters by the fighters of 4B. Peter was respected especially because they found his violence rather terrifying in view of its primitive qualities: they found that Peter fought with none of the inhibitions of a human being, and with all of the basic fury of an animal.

Stig, or Stiggo, as he was called by members of his form, was the leading element in the form 4B. He was not primarily a fighter, but he led the others into battle, retiring somewhat when the battle that he had instigated was in full swing. George Stig, the Instigator, was not a big boy; and he had that peculiar whiteness of skin that one or two of the other boys in the school had: he was one of the types of boys who were transitional between albino and normal in colouring. He had a round, smooth-formed head and a slippery-formed body; with light-yellow, straight, fine hair, that was plastered down on his spheroid head by much use of comb and hair-oil. His eyes were light in colour. He was the life and soul of the form 4B, the mischievous element, the cause of all the trouble. If it so happened, and it never did, that members of another form attacked Stiggo, they would bring down upon them the full might of Stiggo's supporters: Stiggo was the soul of 4B, and sacred to them because of it.

Apart from the gang-leader Stiggo, 4B had some fighters, some of them rather below average height but formidable nevertheless. The fighters in 4B were more numerous than those in 4T, but smaller, and as a result of this, and taking Packagger into consideration also, the two forms were evenly matched: if Tabbot and Arthur had supported their own form the balance of strength would have favoured Peter's form.

Finally we must describe Packagger. Packagger was about Peter's age; as big as Peter; yellow-haired; a law unto himself; and separate. Separate, but loyal to his form as well. Packagger was undeniably the first fighter of 4B. His father was a bookmaker, he spent a lot of his time at the races, and once he and Stiggo organized a book, bets being taken, and winnings being paid, a business enterprise somewhat larger in scale and far more ambitious than Peter's bun-selling business. He wore the school clothes, and he had been long at the school, but he was not an Elevensinian in the true sense, for he was more of the world of fast money, races, and no principles than of the world of pure Elevensinian morality.

4B had their form-room at the other end of the school building to Grate's room, the home of 4T, and as a result of this the two forms did not come into contact with each other much, breaktimes being spent by the two forms on different sides of the school grounds. But there was this rivalry, because they were warlike forms of the same age-group. If you are surprised that 4A did not have an aggressive, warlike rivalry with either 4B or 4T, we will explain that 4A was composed of boys who were good at lessons, and had more sense than to be interested in fighting in the dust, dirt, and on the concrete stretches round the school building.

Peter had had a skirmish or two with Packagger, but for the most part they respected each other's physical prowess, and usually passed each other in the playground with set and tense faces: as yet there had been no major battle between the two. But a major battle was to come.

If 4B and 4T had had form-rooms that were both at the same end of the school, they would have spent their break-times in the same part of the school grounds, and if this had happened much blood would have been spilt, and many full-scale wars would have been fought between the two forms.

. . . . .

They should not have done it, for, just as Stiggo was sacred to the other members of his form, so Cushumph was sacred to Peter.

4B were clustered outside the big doors at their end of the school building, Stiggo in the very centre of whatever was going on, and it was at mid-morning breaktime. Cushumph was perhaps being unwise, but he strayed to the 4B end of the school grounds on his own. If a fighter member of either form wished to circumnavigate and circumambulate the school building he was usually sensible enough to do it in the company of another fighter of his own form, for to pass through the alien camp alone was asking for trouble. In a sense 4B owned the area outside one pair of the doors of the school building, and 4T owned the area outside the other pair of doors. Cushumph had gone some way round the school building on business—he had to discuss matters of rugby with his house-captain—and after he had completed that business he thought that he would take the quickest route back to where his own form were congregated, this route passing through the 4B camp. No doubt Cushumph had realized the danger of the route, but had felt that he would have lacked courage if he had taken the longer and safer route back, the route that did not run through the enemy camp, and which encircled the garden area in front of the staff and prefects' entrance to the school building. At mid-morning break the building was emptied, and prefects stopped any boys from going in the building, but as the break was so short in time the two pairs of doors at either end of the block were left open. Close to their pair of doors clustered 4B on the narrow concrete path, and between the doors and the school playing field was a wire fence: between the wire fence and the doors there was no easy through-way, because the path there was full of clamouring 4B boys letting off steam. Cushumph walked towards the 4B cluster; and between the 4B group, and the mass of boys playing and talking away from the building, there was a comparatively empty stretch of path. 4B did not see Cushumph while he was walking amongst the crowd, but when he approached them across the empty stretch of pathway, they saw him and tension developed. Cushumph saw that he had become the focus of the attention of the 4B group, and he walked warily towards them: it was obvious to him from their expressions that they relished the fact that they were soon to have one member of the opposing camp alone amongst them and at their mercy, little though their mercy was. If he had been a man for peace at any price, Cushumph would have retraced his steps, but, although he did not look for fights, it was not in Cushumph's nature to turn back at that point, for the mocking jeers that would have accompanied such a retreat would have been too much for his pride. Cushumph saw that Packagger was looking at him with sadistic anticipation; and Cushumph entered the enemy camp, darting furtive and baleful glances warily to either side of him. They leapt upon him, and gamely he struggled against the overwhelming odds.

At this point Peter had wandered from his usual break-time haunt also, and he found himself near the woodwork building, amongst the crowd, and able to see the 4B camp. He walked towards them idly, not intending to go much further, and soon came into the view of the 4B boys who were struggling with the unfortunate Cushumph. Cushumph was being bent to the path, when his heated eyes saw Peter, and his call for help was long and urgent. Peter worshipped Cushumph, and the sight of his idol and friend being subjected to the humiliation of being persecuted by unfair odds, brought a surge of anger to his mind. Also the fact that he was called to the rescue made him feel that his position in life at that moment was heroic and Homeric, and this brought a light of fierce battle-lust to his eyes. He stood for a moment, eyes blazing, like a tiger about to spring, and the joyful anticipation of battle was clear on his face for the 4B fighters to see. He thrilled at the thought that he and Cushumph were to fight together against Packagger and the combined might of the primarily pygmy enemy camp. With a bestial roar of intense ferocity Peter charged. But Packagger and his compatriots were only in a mood for bullying with overwhelming forces on their side—they were not apparently in the mood for a sustained and earnest battle with two of the 'killers' of 4T. Because of this, and because Peter looked so terrifying as he ran towards them—Peter running straight at Packagger—

BRATBY

they let go of Cushumph before Peter got anywhere near them, and their ranks scattered sheepishly. Peter was disappointed: he and Cushumph walked away in contempt for 4B.

. . . . .

The war, the international war, had disturbed the school routines. There were shelter-practices, and also there were fast and orderly evacuations when the sirens went, at which times the curriculum was completely disordered. Boys missed classes that were important to their course of study, because they had been hiding in the shelters playing cards and entertaining themselves as well as they could. The staff tried to teach within the shelters, but this was soon abandoned for obvious reasons. That year the school photographs were taken on the minor school field, against a background of air-raid shelters. As a result of all this disruption discipline became relaxed sometimes, and during the dinner-break the boys wandered in the school building, and in their form-rooms, unmolested by the school prefects.

4T congregated in Grate's room one dinner-break after dinner had been consumed, and word came over the grapevine that 4B were preparing to attack in force. Word came via an excited emissary, a small member of the form 4T, that 4B were intending to come through the school to 4T's form-room where the proposed battle was to take place. Not all the boys of each form were on the school premises at that time, for some of them had gone home to dinner, but the principal fighters of the two forms were on the school premises, and that was all that mattered. 4T organized their forces, and sent scurrying members to find Cushumph, who was not in the form-room but somewhere outside the building in the school grounds. 4B collected their forces together in the same way, and at separate ends of the school building the two camps waited in their respective form-rooms, planning the battle that was to come. The aggressors were 4B. In Grate's room 4T waited tensely, wondering why the other form was taking so long to attack. 4T sent scouts from the form-room to go through the school to see if the enemy was on its way. One of the scouts came rushing in, and informed 4T breathlessly that the spearhead of the enemy force was halfway through the building: it appeared that the spearhead consisted solely of Packagger, this representing peculiar strategy to the minds of Smithers, Cushumph, and Peter. Packagger came into Grate's room and stood there unchallenged, a sneer on his white, hard face. Smithers stood by his desk, his desk being right by the door, and an unspoken challenge began to form between the two immobile boys—Smithers and Packagger. Bodies smashed against desks, and chairs were thrown to the floor accidentally, as Packagger wrestled with Smithers: Smithers's body was bent back over his desk, and an emotional wildness was in his eyes, together with the beginning of tears. Smithers had not really wanted to fight: it had just been that he had been standing nearest to Packagger when Packagger entered the room.

The room became filled with a surprisingly small number of 4B boys, and the remainders of both forms watched the fight between the two antagonists in silence. As the two boys fought, now on the ground by the door, legs kicking and bodies thumping, verbal skirmishes developed between some of the members of the opposing forms, resulting in lackadaisical struggles here and there. Peter and Cushumph watched, unmolested. Peebles watched too, standing in front of his desk by the master's desk, and he seemed silently to disapprove. It was not turning out to be the full-scale battle that had been anticipated, although Smithers and Packagger fought with no lack of earnestness by the door: Packagger did not fight in a proper Elevensinian manner, for he fought with a suggestion of cruelty; ruthlessly, silently, and with a vicious jerkiness to his hard body; and Smithers was hardly fighting in a lackadaisical manner, partly because he had to defend himself fully against the relentless attack, and partly because he had gone wild as he always did when he fought for longer than two seconds. Smithers fought gamely in his peculiarly emotional way, but Packagger was harder than he was; Packagger was on top of Smithers, pinning his arms to the ground, their heads at the base of Smithers's desk. Chairs lay overturned on the floor; and two desks, heavy though they were, had been jerked from their places by the heaving bodies, so that they were a little out of line: ink in the inkwells of those two desks had been spilled out, and lay on the writing-flaps of the desks; exercise books from the two desks had fallen forward from inside the desks, and lay on the writing-flaps amongst the spilled ink in disorder; a pen lay on the floor, its steel nib bent. Packagger had Smithers in a position that the emotional one could not get out of, but the controlling position that Packagger was in did not allow for any further action, a thing that Packagger found boring: to give the fight some more interest, without relinquishing his pinioning of Smithers, Packagger took his hands from Smithers's arms and placed his hands round Smithers's throat, squeezing cruelly in a decidedly un-Elevensinian manner. Smithers was not one to take pain in silence, unlike Packagger who could do that, and when in pain Smithers would tend to let the world know about it. As Packagger increased his cruelty by squeezing more viciously, Smithers screamed with pain: unrelenting, Packagger did not relax his hands, and Smithers's screams continued. Peter had an awareness of Elevensinian standards of conduct deep within his subconscious, and like most Elevensinians he would instinctively recognize any deviation from those standards if it was manifested in front of him in conduct that was below par.

As the screams of his friend pierced through his mind, he felt deeply that an injustice was being done, and he was surprised that nobody was objecting to Packagger's treatment of Smithers. The screams continued to ring across the room, and nobody moved or said anything. But Peter knew that most of the witnesses felt within themselves as he did, and he knew that they did not approve of the conduct of Packagger: most Elevensinians think as one on such matters. Also Peter felt as he had done when he had seen Cushumph persecuted by the form 4B: he resented seeing a friend of his treated in such a manner, and he felt that he ought to help his friend. But as things were he could not intervene in the fight: bad as the conduct of Packagger was, it would not be proper for Peter to side with Smithers against Packagger: it was

Smithers's fight. Peter's sense of the injustice that was being done mounted as Smithers's screams mounted. Then, with a look of contempt at the wailing Smithers, Packagger regained his feet, and unsteadily went to the centre of the room where his friends were. Peter knew what he had to do, and he crossed to the open door, where Smithers was regaining his feet, moaning. That seemed to be the end of the battle between the two forms, but Peter did not intend that hostilities should cease at that point. Apart from the fact that he had to avenge Smithers, Peter felt cheated that he had not been combatant. Packagger was tired, and because of that Peter's ensuing actions were somewhat unfair. But Peter knew that everybody would think it right if he avenged the cruel treatment that had been given to Smithers.

Packagger decided to return to his form-room, and, with the other members of his form behind him, he advanced towards the door, his eyes on the ground, feeling just a little bit tired, and feeling slightly heroic. Peter tensed, moved into the doorway, and blocked the door, standing there in Packagger's way, his face impassive, and resolution in his mind. Packagger told him to move out of his way, but Peter moved not a muscle and stared unflinchingly at the sadist. When Peter did not move as requested, Packagger understood Peter's intention, and he took his eyes off the ground, and looked at Peter with a wry and cynical smile of comprehension. Perhaps Packagger felt that it was unfair of Peter to fight him when he was tired and Peter was fresh: perhaps that was why he smiled that wry and cynical smile. But Peter told himself that Packagger had not had a very difficult fight with Smithers; and also Peter was confident in the knowledge that most of the boys would think that it was right that the cruelty to Smithers should be avenged. Smithers knew instinctively that Peter was going to fight Packagger to avenge him, and he watched the two tense boys, a feeling of thanks towards Peter in his tear-wet eyes. Peter and Packagger tangled, a chair crashed to the ground, and then Peter remembered his glasses: his glasses were his life, for if they were broken he would be forced to live in an approximate world until they were mended at the optician's. He carried a spectacle case in his pocket, in which to put the glasses before any fight that he might enter into, but there was no time or opportunity now to use that case. He extricated himself from Packagger, tore his glasses from his face, harshly told Peebles to look after them for him, shoved them into Peebles's hands, and then entered the fight again, unencumbered. The fight did not last long, did not change its location much, and Smithers was quickly avenged. After Packagger had left the room with his form-mates, Smithers thanked Peter, and Peter felt he was a hero: he felt that he had avenged Smithers, and protected the glory of 4T as well: he was so pleased with himself that he felt he would never forget that fight until he was fifty-five, and then it might slip from his memory, and be lost amongst the ghostly libraries of heroic deeds of man that are forgotten.

．　　　　．　　　　．　　　　．　　　　．

We have another story to tell of the battles at St. Elevenses Boys' School, a story that deals again with the wild emotionalism in combat of Smithers—a story that also deals again with that important aspect of Peter which was his spectacles. Peter was always breaking his spectacles, and Smithers was always losing his temper in combat. And before the conclusion of this chapter we have one other short story to tell, that deals with Peter's glasses again, and with revenge instead of avenging: this story deals with the revenge of Seaver, who had grown bigger, and was now a match for Peter. Both final stories in this chapter on Battles have their setting in and around the cloakrooms, where the boys left their overcoats, and where the boys changed before rugby and physical training.

．　　　　．　　　　．　　　　．　　　　．

The unfortunate thing about Smithers was that he could not seem to be able to have a friendly fight without losing his temper, and every time he had an unfriendly fight he would lose his temper even more, and he would get into a state of emotional wildness, at which times his judgements became completely distorted. One supposes that Smithers was sensitive to an extreme degree, and one also supposes that his upbringing had something to do with it, and that his parents were in some way responsible for his touchy temperament. When his temper was not alive, Smithers was an introspective boy, but not a retiring boy. One had to admit that Smithers had feelings: you could not get away from the fact that Smithers had feelings: feelings were one sure thing about John. And, by the by, another sure thing about him was that he was passionate about toy trains.

The P.T. master was late. The boys had changed into their P.T. kit in the cloakroom, and they were just mucking around. Not-so-Green was there, feeling a bit of a Charlie in his little white shorts, and trying to look aloof in spite of his attire. Some of the boys were mocking Edinburgh, because his undressing had revealed the fact that he was wearing one of his mother's woolly vests with a little tie-string at the neck with bobbles on it: it was understood that Edinburgh's mother had found that morning that she had put all her son's vests in the wash, and that one of her vests was the only thing to give to her son, but that did not prevent Edinburgh from looking absolutely sweet when he had taken off his shirt, Edinburgh being undoubtedly the prototype for 'Just William'—thick shock of hair, careless clothes, dirty face, and ragamuffin air.

The lads were getting restless. How the fight between Peter and Smithers started we do not know, but when it did Smithers lost his temper very quickly. The fight was brief, and took place in the deserted corridor outside the cloakroom: a furious fight indeed, witnessed by Not-so-Green. In all the rooms behind the closed doors in the long corridor classes were working diligently, and the corridor was deserted except for the fighters and the audience. If they had fought further down the corridor, by the classrooms, they would have been heard by a master; but as it was they were fighting by the cloakroom, and by the big open doors at the end of the corridor, through which doors the school field could be seen stretching green, and waiting for the boys to do exercises upon it. An occasional boy would come out of the cloakroom into the corridor, but nobody seemed interested in the fight, for they had all seen Smithers fighting Peter before, and they were familiar with exhibitions of Smithers's temper. Peter had forgotten to take off his glasses in the heat of the moment, for the fight had flared into being in an instant. For some reason, for ever to remain unexplained, Smithers suddenly went berserk in the middle of the brief fight, held Peter's head in the crook of his arm, against his waist, and punched Peter many times in the eye. The fight stopped there. Peter's eye had closed instinctively as the fist hit the lens; and pieces of glass were embedded above the eye and below it, but fortunately not in it. Peter wandered round in a daze; and Not-so-Green sneered at Smithers until the poor boy looked thoroughly ashamed of his wild behaviour. Not-so-Green's relationship to Smithers was a rather peculiar one: he was on fairly intimate terms with Smithers, but he frequently scorned Smithers for his clumsiness in a scathing way. When Smithers had trod on Peter's foot with his running-spikes, and one spike had gone through Peter's bare foot, Not-so-Green had acted like a virago, pouring scorn galore on to Smithers, like a scolding shrew. Peter often did P.T. in bare feet, and they had all been on the school field, when Smithers, not looking where he was going, had run on to Peter's bare foot. Smithers often did things like that, for he often did things so passionately, that he was unaware of other people when he did them. When Smithers acted in this thoughtless and careless way, it seemed to do something to Not-so-Green, and the intellectual of the form would become furious, battering verbally into the crestfallen Smithers, who would receive it all as if he fully deserved it. They took Peter up to the biology lab., and the biology master dressed Peter's eye. Peter swore then to get two pairs of glasses, keeping one pair as a spare pair, but he never did.

.   .   .   .   .

The doors had been opened by the prefect, the prefect was standing aside from the inpouring mass of rushing boys, and Peter and Seaver found themselves beside each other in the entrance to the cloakroom. Seaver had grown, and he had not forgotten the persecution he had suffered at Peter's hands. Peter had not forgotten that Seaver was a boy whom he felt aggressive towards. Hostility flared between the two boys and they began to fight, struggling together further and further into the cloakroom. Seaver seemed very sure of himself, and Peter found to his surprise that he was being manipulated against his will: in a short time Seaver had grown formidable, such rapid changes in physique being common in adolescent boys. Seaver had taken off his glasses, but he saw that Peter still had his on. Feeling that he could not properly defeat a boy with fragile glasses on, and being loath to risk breaking a boy's glasses, because he knew what they meant to a boy, he being a glasses-wearer himself, Seaver, without releasing his hold on Peter, took Peter's glasses from his face, lowered them towards the floor, and carefully slid them down and on to the tiled floor, so that they skidded away on the floor unharmed. Seaver knew that if he had dropped the glasses directly on to the floor he would have smashed them, and his treatment of the glasses was that of a boy who knew the value of spectacles to a myopic. The glasses were out of harm's way, and Seaver, now free of the worry that he might be the cause of the breaking of Peter's glasses, fought with a new freedom. At that point the prefect saw them, and he came into the cloakroom and separated the two boys. The prefect blamed Peter for the fight, for he had often seen Peter fighting, and thought that he was a regular fight-provoker, although Peter did not see himself in that way. Peter put on his glasses and followed the prefect, while Seaver walked away. The prefect took Peter into the science lab., that was at that time the gloomy form-room of the scientific section of the sixth form, many prefects being in that section of the sixth; and Peter found himself with three more prefects in the otherwise deserted room. A dirty plimsoll was found from somewhere, Peter was asked to bend down, and six from the sixth slapped hard on the cheeks of his tight bottom. Peter felt that he had been unjustly treated.

21

Cataract of Doodle-bugs

THE store in Balham, the eye-straining work that she was
doing there in the accounting department, and the nervous
strain attendant upon living on her own resources after years
of being a supported housewife—that nervous strain making
her tired towards the end of the working day, so that she
strained to see the figures on the accounting machine—all
combined to ruin Iris's eyesight. She developed cataract: an
opacity of the crystalline lens of the eye, or of its capsule, or
of both, producing impairment of sight, but never complete
blindness: and the milky film grew over both her eyes. When
she walked down the road she could not recognize people
walking on the other side of the road, and often, to her dismay,
she found that she had unwittingly ignored friends who had
passed her and smiled. What must Iris's thoughts have been
when she found that she had become a half-blind person?
That surely must have been the final catastrophe. If she had
not left Arthur she would have not had to go to the work that
brought on the cataract film. As a matter of fact the mar-
riage-split had been fatal for both of them, for neither Arthur
nor Iris lived very long after that. She must have thought,
after the cataract developed, that ever since she had married
Arthur her life had got worse and worse, till she became half
blind: she did not know that things were to get even worse
still, and that she was to die of a ruptured pancreas when on
a holiday in St. Ives in Cornwall. Did she ever think, as she
looked through the opaque films over her eyes, what her life
might have been if she had never married Arthur? She had

bccn an attractive woman before her marriage and she had had other admirers: what domestic bliss might have been hers if she had married for love—but, if she had, Peter would never have been born, and how would England have managed without Peter? (Very well, thank you.) Iris had indeed thrown her life away when she married Arthur. Iris gave up her job at the big store, and her lady doctor suggested to her that she might like to be a cook-housekeeper to a titled lady who had a daughter who was a professor. Iris was to fall from middle-class to working-class. The titled lady, an old, soon-to-die, bulge blue-eyed concerto-composer, who had yet to become famous, had the true artistic temperament, and her servants left her regularly. The house was always filled with the music from her piano: beautiful music that tinkled from room to room in the spacious house in Balham-Far, that had seen better days when his late lordship had been a king's adviser. The old lady's eyes were protuberant, but in a beautiful way, for the startlingly orbicular eyeballs were filled with luminosity, and the blue of her eyes was not suggestive of base and earthly things, but as divine as the sky. She had many cats, cats that had parcels addressed to them, and the cats were as important to her as people—more important in fact. She composed beautiful music; and as she was very old, it was not to be held against her that she was a little crotchety, for who is serene when the body is decaying and the cheering freshness of life is departing for ever? When Peter looked at her wonderful eyes, eyes that her daughter had to a certain extent inherited, he knew that the old lady must have been a very beautiful person before death began to drop hints to her. The house was on top of a hill, and filled with the memories of an aristocratic way of life that was still in the house to a certain extent, but which was becoming harder and harder to retain, as that way of life became out of date and the servants began to resent being treated as servants. Iris found the kitchen large, spacious, and gloomy; and the dirt she found on top of the high old cupboard appalled her, and she got to work straight away, and cleaned it all into one of the three battered old dustbins that stood outside the scullery door. Iris had a woman to help her, and Iris liked the professor-lady very much indeed. When Iris died, later on, the professor-lady cried, for the professor-lady was a beautiful woman.

Peter had moved from Grate's form-room, and he was now in the form 5T that was domiciled in the technical-drawing room, presided over by a hairy-bodied German mathematics professor, who wore a black plastic mackintosh to school, and who was a nice little thing in a foreign sort of way. 5T was the pre-General School Certificate form, and at the end of that year Peter would have to take his examination. Peter was fifteen to sixteen now; at a loss to know how to shave off the baby hairs on his chin without cutting himself, or cutting off the tops of his adolescent spots, because he had no father to show him how to use a safety-razor; and worried about the impending examination. He had been threatened with expulsion by the headmaster at the end of the yearly examinations in Grate's room, and he was scared. He was scared because he knew that if he failed the coming examination he would have to go out to work, and, although he was not afraid of work as such, he was afraid of leaving the protected atmosphere of the school, and going out into the outside world. If he passed the General School Certificate examination he would be able to continue on in the sixth form until he was eighteen, when he would take the Higher School Certificate examination, and this is what he wanted to do, because then he would postpone entry into the outside world for another two years after the G.S.C. examination. Peter was scared enough of the thought that when he was eighteen he would be dragged from the apron-strings of St. Elevenses, called up by the National Service order, and put in the Army amongst butcher's boys, boys who had left school at fourteen, boys who did not come from an academic atmosphere, and roughs of all sorts. Peter had had nothing at all to do with boys of that sort, and he was very afraid of them. Peter determined to pass the G.S.C., and that year in 5T he put a decorated cover on his report book, and applied himself to his studies in earnest. It was not too late at that stage to begin to study for the examination, and as a result of his work Peter became sixth in the form, instead of thirty-third, in the next terminal examinations: it must be remembered that the boys in the T forms were not very bright, and if a T-form boy worked (an unusual thing in that kind of form), he could get a good place in the form quite easily. Peter looked at his latest report in his report book with pride, and looked at the figure '6' that gave him confidence in the possibility that he might very well remain at the school until he was eighteen. He worked that year with a powerful concentration, for he was scared out of his wits by the threat of being shoved out of the protective walls of the school that had become his life completely by now: he could not see life beyond the wooden fences that surrounded the school, and he never wanted to: he would have been happy to stay there all his life. Peter did not fight very much that year, for he was growing up.

Peter looked slantwise from his bedroom window down into the next-door garden, after having had a session with the waves in his hair, and he drank in the sight of the woman who was sitting in a deck-chair, the grey skirt she wore giving Peter a thrill, for alternate pleats were of red, a thing that he thought was as glamorous as could be. He would often stare slantwise from the windows of the house at passing girls or at ladies in the gardens behind the house. That night he slept after lying in his bed conjuring up an impossible imaginary fantasy about himself and the lady with the coloured pleats. He was woken by the sound of the air-raid siren wailing and waving ominously through the night; and as he got out of bed he could hear the buzz of the doodle-bugs that had come over the Channel. He stood in the darkness of his bedroom, after combing his waves in the darkness and setting them, listening to the flight of a buzz-bomb, waiting for the sound to cut off, after which there would be an explosion when the bomb hit the ground. They were falling very near that night, thought Peter, as the terrifying buzz of a bomb increased in volume almost overhead: the sound ceased suddenly, and Peter knew that the bomb would fall very near to the house he was in, indeed if not on it. He waited, frozen, and then the explosion came from nearby and his bedroom ceiling fell on his head. Peter stood amongst the debris from the ceiling, the black window before him, and he felt a deep sense of tragedy: the falling plaster pieces from the ceiling must have ruined his hair-do and filled his hair with plaster-dust. Peter must have been tough, or the plaster on the ceiling must have been thinly applied or light, for he did not feel more than dazed by the ceiling that had fallen on him: but it was understandable that Peter's head was rock-hard, for until just recently his head had resisted the entry of knowledge exactly as a piece of rock would do. The ceiling had fallen only from that half of the room by the window where Peter had been standing; and above the bed the ceiling, though disturbed, was still up: he wished he had stayed in bed, for then his hair would not have got filled with plaster-dust. He found sleeping very annoying because his waves were always out of place in the morning: he had thought of wearing a hair-net, but did not because he could not get one without making a fool of himself, and he felt that it was not very masculine to sleep in one either. Halfway through a night his waves were still in a fairly reasonable state, and he often re-combed them when an air-raid siren woke him up. His comb was as important to him as his spectacles, but he did not keep a spare comb in case of loss, just as he did not keep a spare pair of spectacles. The importance of his hair in Peter's life at that time at St. Elevenses cannot be over-stressed. He hoped that his hair would get him a girl. All the energies that other boys put into going around with girls Peter put into the care of his hair. He loved his hair almost as much as life itself. With a hand-mirror and the wardrobe mirror he could see the side waves gloriously curving, as beautiful to him as the finest work of art. It amazed him that girls did not come running to him because of the beauty of his hair: he looked at his chin-line with two mirrors, and, telling himself that his chin receded, he blamed that. The house was in a state of confusion after the bomb had fallen nearby; and Peter, having dressed himself, went downstairs where the black-out curtains had been drawn, and into the lighted dining- and sitting-room, where his mother and grandmother were in a state of agitation. Peter crept into the kitchen, where there was a mirror on the wall, and with water from the kitchen sink he began to reset his hair, after having soaked it and towelled it in an attempt to remove the plaster-dust. Peter was more concerned about his hair than he was about the bomb that had fallen in the road, although he was interested in that latter phenomenon, as was to be expected. His hair black with water, and the waves set neat and tight, Peter went into the dining-cum-sitting-room, and sat by the heat from the fire, drying the wet waves of his hair, but pretending to be warming his body. Peter drifted out into the street with his mother, and as his mother talked in a serious voice, touched with an awareness of the drama of the situation, with a neighbour who had also come out into the street, Peter stood apart on his own in the gutter, looking into the night, and wondering how his waves were doing. They did not go to bed again, and, when some hours had passed, Peter felt his hair gingerly with tentative finger-tips, being careful not to disturb the set, and ascertained that his hair was dry: in the gathering light of early morning Peter combed out his hair, and felt pleased with life: everything was all right now that his hair was dry and perfectly wavy. But Peter's mother was still agitated, for she was worried about the damage the blast had done to the house.

Peter just managed to scrape through the examination in the summer of 1944, and learnt towards the end of the summer holidays that he had passed. In the autumn of 1944 he returned to school, entering a form called 6B: he was now over sixteen years old. He found himself in a form with boys he had not been with before, one or two of whom had been made into prefects when they entered the sixth form. In 6B he found himself with Coffee, Stiggo, and undersized friends of Stiggo; but only Coffee from amongst those boys stayed the course until the Higher School Certificate examination in 1946.

22

Hilda

BY NOW the heroes were in the Army; Yatchjohn was a
senior prefect, and on his way to becoming captain of nearly
everything; and Cushumph, Tabbot, Boogter, and Arthur
were lost in the outside world, Arthur joining the Army immediately. New blazers were in short supply; and as some
boys could not get them they were allowed to wear sports-
coats. Everything was going to pot because of the war. Peter
even wore no tie in his second year in the sixth. Peter's mother
bought him a new sports-coat, one that had too much padding
in the shoulders for Peter's taste. Peter thought that the
padded shoulders made false claims about the breadth of his
shoulders, as well as making him look like a spiv, and he made
his mother take out some of the padding. A new sports-coat
had he, but he still had to wear his old dark-blue raincoat
over it, his mother not being able to afford a new one, and
the raincoat was the despair of his life, for it was getting rather
short, and he felt that he would never get one of the girls he
saw on the trolley-bus if he continued to look like that: he
wanted a light yellow-ochre raincoat, with leather football-
buttons on it, but it was beyond the capabilities of his mother's
purse: so he travelled on the trolley-bus without an overcoat
on, even in the cold weather, his raincoat on his arm, so that
the girls could see his new sports-coat.

Buckets of sand were all the rage at this time. Sandbags
were to be seen everywhere; and all the best fathers were air-
raid wardens if they were not actually fighting the war:
Cousin Trevor's father was the chief air-raid warden in his

road—of course. Fire-watching was a popular occupation, and most buildings had to be watched at night. If you wanted to frighten an old lady you said 'Incendiary bomb'. The sixth-formers at St. Elevenses did fire-watching. There was a rota, and Mr. Chalk was in charge of the rota. Three boys would sleep in the staff-room every night; and when Peter was one of them he found it rather exciting, although no incendiary bombs fell anywhere near the school during the whole duration of the war.

Heroes sometimes came back to the school when they were on leave, looking very glamorous in their uniforms, and had chats with a few of the masters: they had not yet completely broken free from the influence and charm of St. Elevenses. After two years from the time they left the school, boys would have shaken themselves free, and then they hardly ever returned. High in the Small School, the Junior School building, was a room with a bar, where the Old Boys' club met, but considering the fact that nearly a hundred boys left the school every year the few old boys in the club-room did not signify very much.

Splay-foot Sam was in 5A, and he travelled home and to the school on the same trolley-bus as Peter did. For the rest of the time that Peter was at the school he got to know Splay-foot Sam very well. Splay-foot Sam would have worn a red tie if he had not felt bound to be a good boy and to wear his school house-tie, for Sam was a member of the Socialist Party of Great Britain, and talked solidly all the time about how badly the country was run: he had great verbal stamina had Sam, and Peter pretended to listen to billions of words with a red tinge during the time that he was associated with Splay-foot Sam. Sam was short, muscular, splay-footed, and brown-haired. He had an abnormally large head; beautiful blue eyes; and splendid, naturally waving hair, parted on the wrong side, which flopped down across one half of his forehead. Sam combed his hair and that was all: he was not the Narcissus-type fop that Peter was. Sam, who still wore a blazer, travelled home on the trolley-bus with a friend in his own form, a boy who was very tall, thin, and rabbit-faced:

they were an odd pair—one very tall and one not quite up to the right height for his age. When Sam put running-spikes on he could run like the wind despite his duck-feet, and because of this he was good at rugby and the shorter races. Sam was clever at his lessons; managed to write his history essays so that they became loaded with socialist doctrine; and was almost an all-round sportsman. He had enormous charm, and was good-looking in an off-beat manner, but his wide mouth would sneer: Sam spent a great deal of his time sneering: people who smoked were chimneys; girls with make-up on received a blasting from him as he passed them in the street; and petty officials always received an uncomplimentary word or two. Sam was all for being free and natural, and his parents had felt the same, because they had cut his pretty hair for the first time when he was four. Sam was a result of his father's teaching, and he related with pride how his father had thrown all his First World War medals over a bridge. Sam was sincere, and Sam had the courage of his convictions. Peter admired Sam, but mainly because his hair was so pretty. Splay-foot Sam was sensitive and artistic, and he treated flowers with the delicacy and respect that they deserved. When Sam's call-up came he said he was a conscientious objector, and he worked on the land for two years.

Hilda was the highlight of Peter's adolescence. She would never admit to being Peter's girl, but that was what she must have been. Hilda was the only girl that Peter had until he met the girl that he married, a girl called Priscilla, whom he met when he was twenty-five, the year that his adolescence came to an end.

It was odd that the only girl that the girl-shy Peter had was 'the Belle of the 37 Trolley-bus', coveted from afar by better Elevensinians by far than Peter, and encouraged to go to policemen's dances by all the policemen in the area in which she lived, for one would have thought that Peter's only girl would have been a wallflower at least.

When Peter first saw Hilda he never dreamed that he would get to know her, for she seemed to him to be the unattainable kind of girl that only the sharpest young men would know. It was obvious to him, as he looked at her for the first time, that she was completely confident of herself in her relationships with members of the opposite sex, that she knew she was a peach, and that all the men in Balham, whatever their age might be, would look at her with pleasure. She was sixteen, and her calves were bigger than they normally would be, because she was having injections in them at the hospital that made them swell: Peter thought her calves, above her feet in high-heeled shoes, were superb. Peter had seen girls like her around before, but for him they were in another world, a world that he thought that he could not hope to enter.

Peter walked away from the school, intending to catch the trolley-bus at the stop that was before the stop at the school, for the bus filled up in the town, and when it got to the school it would sometimes not stop. The stop he was walking to was by the side of the cinema; and outside that cinema always stood a newspaper-man at that time at the end of the afternoon. A long queue of people waited at the bus-stop; and Peter wandered up to the end of the queue, dreamily and leisurely. Buying a paper from the newspaper-man was a girl, and Peter watched her longingly, for she was dressed in a red coat, had long brown hair, a pretty figure, flirty eyes, and sweet, girlish sex in every movement that she made: her hair fluttered in the slight breeze that blew across the corner on which rose the old cinema; and, instead of having the urgency of most girls going home from work, she had a drifting unhurried way with her that seemed to suggest that she did not really care where the winds of circumstance blew her, and that she did not particularly care if she got home or not: as it happened, she did not have much of a home life, for her parents were dead, and she lived with her aunt who was out in the evenings and late afternoons, working as a bus-conductress; and as a result of that she did not indeed care whether she got home or not. Peter did not want to get home after school particularly, either, so they were birds of a feather. Hilda walked casually from the newspaper-man to the end of the queue, and Peter was not able to look at her any more, although he continued to think of her in a romantic manner, allowing his mind to dwell uncontrolled upon her. Hilda always went home on the 37 trolley-bus at roughly the same time in the afternoon, and that was the time when the boys from St. Elevenses who used the bus were on it. There were a number of boys who used the bus to Balsham, and they included Peter, Splay-foot Sam, Sam's long friend, Yatchjohn, and Coffee, all those boys living in the residential area of Balsham. Hilda always seemed to be on the same bus as Peter and Splay-foot Sam. Nobody from the school had yet talked to Hilda, but she was becoming a talking-point amongst the 37 bus-users from the school, for her eyes flirted with their flirting eyes; and she caught their attention partly because she was so pretty, and partly because she seemed always to be at a loose end, aimless, drifting, and not remote like so many of the other working girls who rode on the bus. She seemed almost to be waiting for someone to talk to her, although she did not directly invite that in her manner. She did not look cheap or wanton.

Peter had not yet got to know Splay-foot Sam, but they travelled on the same bus together so frequently that they were well aware of each other's existence. One afternoon the bus stopped at Balsham, and Hilda alighted from the bus, followed after a moment by Splay-foot and his friend, and a moment later by Peter, who was drinking in the back view of the girl, who was now walking casually, and very slowly, across the wide main road, to the road that crossed it, on which was the 423 single-decker bus-stop, where Hilda always waited after she had finished that part of her journey that was made on the 37 trolley-bus. Hilda knew she was being followed.

As it approached the main stop, the trolley-bus from Balham would always pass by the big, new public library that stood conspicuously on the side of the main road, less than a quarter of a mile from the main Balsham bus-stop, from which it could be seen, and at which Hilda and the three boys had alighted. The library could be clearly seen

from the windows of the bus, and any regular traveller on the
trolley-bus would be bound to know where the public library
was.

The main road was very wide at the main Balsham bus-
stop; and at that point it had an island in the centre of it, on
which was a bus-stop shelter for potential travellers who were
going to catch the 37 trolley-bus to Balham: the main road
at that point was divided by the island into two roads, one
of which was a one-way street. The two boys, Splay-foot and
his friend, followed the almost-dawdling Hilda, as they
crossed the whole double width of the road, and Peter followed
behind the two boys. Knowing that Hilda could hear what
they were saying, Splay-foot and his friend talked about her
in loud voices filled with humour of the kind to which boys
of that age are addicted when the conversation is about girls:
Hilda pretended not to hear them; and Peter followed behind,
absorbing the back-view beauty of the aimless peach that
had a rolling stone. Splay-foot Sam wore a well-preserved
satchel hanging from a leather strap on his shoulder, and Sam
had an unbalanced, slightly grotesque body, with gigantic
calf-muscles: he walked behind Hilda in his usual rolling
style—duck-feet splaying; knees bending; pelvis tilting, as the
balls at the end of his thigh-bones swivelled in the sockets at
either side of the pelvic-basin; shoulders tilting in opposition
to the pelvis-tilt, to keep the body balanced; and the satchel
banging against his hip, because of this complicated and
rolling gait. Sam sometimes looked almost deformed, but he
was not. Suddenly, while they were still all on the main road,
going towards the far pavement, Hilda turned round to
Splay-foot, satchel-swinging Sam, and his tall friend, and
with laughter shimmering in her eyes, and her body going in
one direction, her head looking in another, she asked them
if they knew where the public library was. Simultaneously
the two boys replied that they did not know where it was,
although they certainly did, being regular borrowers; and to
keep the sweet connection going Splay-foot looked over his
shoulder and asked Peter in a loud voice if he had any idea
where the public library was, Hilda's eyes being now on

Peter. Peter was not prepared for being related to Hilda, even in this disconnected manner, but he managed to make a fair reply, and said with dry humour: 'I haven't the ghostliest,' which Sam thought was a very witty reply to have invented on the spur of the moment, and at the hearing of which Hilda smiled self-consciously and a little sheepishly to herself, and turned her head so that it faced in the same direction as her body. The connection was terminated, and the boys followed her to the 423 bus-stop, where she stopped and waited as always, standing prettily by the low fence, a yard or more from the few people who were conventionally waiting for the bus under the canopy: Sam and his friend passed her and walked on home, and a few seconds later Peter passed her, his heart pounding because he was near such a collection of beauty all in one place, Peter then going on home in the same direction as the other two boys, but not communicating with them. Peter walked home in a state of deep emotional disturbance; and when he got home he found that the house was empty, for his grandmother was out. He walked into the gloomy sitting-room, and without taking off his raincoat, which on this occasion he was wearing, he strode to the mantelpiece, and looked over the clock into the mirror above it, to check his appearance. Very rarely he would hear a brief ringing in his head and his head would swim, and as he gazed at his reflection this happened: it was not because he was in a turmoil because of Hilda. He decided that his appearance was not all that could be desired, despite the fact that he was trying hard to look romantic, and he wished that he possessed a raincoat with leather football-buttons on it. He walked out of the house again, too disturbed to settle, and began to walk to the 423 bus-stop, hoping that Hilda would still be waiting there: he knew that she often waited there, letting the buses go by, catching the fifth, sixth, or seventh 423 that stopped. Midway between his grandmother's house and the cross-roads at the shopping centre of Balsham where the buses stopped was a roundabout, across which the huge Balham Bypass made its massive way, mocking the petty roads of the suburban residential area. Peter met

Splay-foot Sam there by accident for a brief moment, and to his delight Sam said to him that he thought that 'I haven't the ghostliest' was a very witty thing to say: Splay-foot was quite sincere.

That was the first time any Elevensinian boy had spoken to Hilda, the Belle of the 37 Trolley-bus, the girl who watched the 423's go by. Breakthrough.

.　　　.　　　.　　　.　　　.

Hilda Brown worked in Balham, in an office run by a 'nice' man who had a false leg. Her boss liked her, but he was not the forward type. Hilda felt very delicately towards her partially disabled boss, and she knew that he thought delicately towards her: but nothing at all happened, and their relationship was a strictly business one. As an extra-special treat, Hilda let him kiss her on his birthday because she was sorry for him, and because she liked him.

Hilda had no regular boy-friend, unless you could call the band-leader her boy-friend, and we don't think you could really, because he was married, and although he saw Hilda occasionally Hilda and he did not associate regularly. Hilda loved the band-leader's brown eyes, and she would go all dreamy about them, after having mentioned them in conversation: he was about twenty-five years old, and a small-time band-leader, who played at the dances that were held around Balham-Bye and Balham-Far, Hilda living somewhere thereabouts. She was very excited once because he had promised to buy her a transparent blouse. The trouble with Hilda was that she told little white lies, and you could not really be sure that her name was Brown, or that many of the things she said were really the absolute truth. She once said that the band-leader, who was 'lovely', had got her to sing in front of his band to a floor full of listening dancers, and that that had made her shy, but you could not be absolutely sure that that was true in every detail. Hilda liked to remain a woman of mystery, and she did not talk much about herself. She thought of herself as a shy girl, but compared with Peter, who had not

228

spoken to her yet, she was as confident as Winston Churchill. She would go all soft at the mention of Dana Andrews, the film-star; and you would be overdoing it more than somewhat if you called her a profound girl, for she was superficial, fresh, charming, girlish, and dreamy, but not a lady philosopher. Hilda was not sad, but her background could have made her that if she had not been so charmed by the passing scene, and by boys and men, for she had no family life to speak of, no background of security, and nothing much to hold on to. She had a job, but she did not seem to be held to that like other working girls are held to their jobs: she was a drifter, and she went where the wind blew her. However, she was not immoral as such a girl might have been, and it was very likely that she was a virgin. There was not much to Hilda, but nevertheless she was a symbol of something or other to many of the Elevensinian boys, and she was the Belle of the 37 Bus-route. If Sam had had his way, the whole world would have been changed, and run on Marxist lines, and many many people declared redundant (Winston and all the capitalists among them), but he would have not expelled Hilda from his Utopia. When she had finished work Hilda would not be in a hurry to catch the trolley-bus to Balsham from Balham, and when she got to Balsham she would be in even less of a hurry to catch the 423 to Balham-Bye, because there was nothing to do when she got home, except to put on her slacks and go and play with the children on the field nearby: so she spent her time waiting for buses, and not catching them; walking very slowly from one bus-stop to another; sometimes catching buses to places that she did not need to go to, and making circular journeys back to where she started from; and casting a few flirty glances at the boys from St. Elevenses. As a result of all this drifting, and waiting in the streets, she saw quite a few policemen, talked to them, and was admired by them: she had something in common with the policemen, for both she and they spent much time aimlessly in the streets, watching the world go by, and half wanting to talk to somebody 'nice'. Pretty Hilda with her bare legs; standing smiling in the breezes that blew along the roads; her red coat buttoned all the way down to keep out those breezes; her slightly rising chest covered from view; and her friendly attitude to the world in general: you could not help liking her. Peter could not help liking her anyway. Peter had to pass his Higher School Certificate examination when his two years in the sixth form were up, but that examination was a long way away, and while he was in 6B he felt he could take it easy for a while. But it did not matter if he passed or failed that examination, as it had mattered that he should pass the General School Certificate examination, for passing the higher examination would not allow him to stay at school any longer, and he would be forced to go into the Army whatever happened. But he had his sense of pride; it was not done for an Elevensinian to fail his examinations; and Peter intended to start work in earnest in his second year in the sixth. He did start work then, and he worked as hard as he could; but the knowledge stayed outside his pretty hair, in his text books, and in his carefully kept exercise books, and when 1946 came he failed the exam. But check: we are leaping ahead in time again.

· · · · ·

On Wednesday afternoons the sixth-form boys who were in the school rugby team played rugby in the park outside the town of Balham, where multitudes of younger Elevensinians were also playing games of rugby amongst themselves. Peter, unlike Splay-foot Sam, was not in the rugby team that played other schools, and on Wednesday afternoons he stayed in the school and worked without the supervision of a master. At times sixth-form life was irregular, and the boys in the sixth were given more freedom than the younger boys. Perhaps Peter should really have been playing rugby on Wednesday afternoons, but nobody seemed to care very much if he did not as long as he attended the school. If Peter had been another boy he would have played truant on those slackly supervised Wednesday afternoons, and he would have gone out with his girl, but as Peter had no girl, and had nothing better to do, he stayed at school. Occasionally he went into Balham on those Wednesday afternoons, and went to the pictures.

After spending one Wednesday afternoon at the school, Peter left the school, and waited for the trolley-bus outside: the trolley-bus was far from full, and there were no Elevensinians on the upper deck. But as Peter came on to the upper deck from the winding metal stairs he saw that Hilda was sitting there, in a seat behind which sat a solitary soldier. Peter's heart froze with sudden romantic emotional pressure, and he went and sat across the aisle from her, a couple of seats back. Hilda seemed unaware of anything as Peter gazed at her, and as the trolley-bus made its heavy, murmuring way past one familiar scene after another, past occasional shops, past houses on the main road, under bridges, and past hoardings. Peter watched entranced as she played idly with her red-varnished finger-nails, nails on which the varnish was chipped and applied long before. Peter stared with concealed delight, the flimsy trolley-bus ticket in his hand, at her bent and evocative brown head, behind which the tops of houses sped past on the other side of the bus window. He looked down at his own hands on his grey flannel lap, and gazed bemusedly at the backs of those hands, on which he had drawn the Elevensinian badge in blue-black ink, in moments of idleness that afternoon in a deserted classroom. The upper deck being empty except for the soldier and Hilda (Peter had almost forgotten he was there), Peter expected the soldier to lean forward and talk to Hilda, but the soldier did not: Peter was sure that the soldier must have been covetously aware of the delight that sat in the seat in front of him: it seemed to Peter that it would have been so easy for the soldier to try to get off with Hilda, as the upper deck was so empty (once again he did not realize that he was there too). The trolley-bus surged towards the stop at Balsham; Hilda rose abstractedly from her seat; saw Peter, her eyes flirting suddenly at the sight of a familiar Elevensinian (any familiar Elevensinian would have caused that reaction in her); and made her way in an aura of girlish sex down the steps to the platform below, where the conductor stood playing with his ticket-printer.

Peter knew the familiar routine by heart by now, for it had happened so often: he would follow the slowly walking girl across the road until she got to the other bus-stop, and then he would pass her waiting figure: but this time it was different, for there was only he and Hilda, only he and Hilda—not a rival Elevensinian in sight. Dare he speak to her for the first time?—dare he speak to that symbol of something or other? What ecstasy if he could!

It was different walking slowly behind Hilda across the wide main road this time, for there were no Elevensinians. Peter felt that he and Hilda were together in a silent and abstract world of their own as they walked, one behind the other, from that part of the road that was busy with traffic, on to the one-way part of the road, where one did not have to hurry because it was not used so much by cars. Hilda stepped from the vague danger of the road on to the narrow pavement that led short to the mouth of a subsidiary road that issued into the big road-crossing; and she walked ever so slowly by the high fence as Peter stepped on to the narrow pavement also. Peter did not know where he got the courage from, but before he knew what was happening he was asking her if she always caught the 423 bus, his shoulder close to hers, his face looking down at the side of her head. At the sound of his voice Hilda looked up at him with a pretty smile, half surprised that he had spoken to her. She acted as if the question was perfectly reasonable, and said 'yes' in a friendly fashion. Peter could not believe his luck, for he had thought that perhaps she would rebuff his friendly advance. They began to talk small-talk, Peter finding it surprisingly easy; and Peter felt King as he walked with her to her bus-stop. They stood there talking, Hilda with her back to the fence, and Peter standing with his back to the road, facing her. Peter did not care what he talked about as long as he was with her, and he revelled in the delight of being able to look constantly into her face. She looked at him all the time then; but on later occasions, when they stood in the same positions, she spent most of the time avoiding his eyes, and looking to either side of her, as if she wished to get away, but could not be bothered to make the effort, because there was only her empty home to go to. Peter asked her why she did not catch the 423 buses that came and went at intervals as they stood there, and she gave an evasive answer. As he was new to her this time, she was pleased to stay talking; but on later occasions she found his attentions wearing, and understandably too, for Peter loved her with a fervent and obsessive intensity. Much time passed, but Hilda made no move to catch any of the buses that stopped and started: Peter could not believe his good fortune. What did he care if his mother got worried because he was not yet home? He realized that his mother would be home by now. Why should he worry? This was the most wonderful time in his life so far: he would wait there with Hilda just as long as she stood by the fence. They did not move their positions hardly at all, except for a step there and a step back.

Splay-foot Sam and his long friend came back on the bus late that afternoon, for Sam had been playing for his school, and his friend had been watching. It was admirable that Sam, who was still only in 5A, should be playing for his school. When the two boys passed Peter and Hilda they made a few remarks, and though Peter did not turn from his vigil over her face she smiled warmly past him at the two passing boys. The evening was encroaching upon the afternoon when Splay-foot Sam's mother sent him out on his bicycle to buy her something in a shop in the centre of Balsham. Splay-foot pedalled along the main-road, and saw to his surprise that Peter was still talking to Hilda. Splay-foot rode his sports-bike in a rolling and swaying manner, his bottom tilting exaggeratedly on the saddle, and his flop-hair dancing on one side of his forehead in a manner that Hilda thought was most attractive. She smiled past Peter at the sight of Sam; and Sam, impressed that Peter had stayed so long with her, called out 'Jolly good show' to Peter, with a perplexed admiration in his unsmiling eyes.

As the evening came, Yatchjohn alighted from a 423 that Hilda made no move to catch, walked through the alighting and dismounting passengers towards Peter and Hilda, an unlit pipe in his mouth, and an expressionless look in his eyes. He knew that Hilda and Peter were looking at him, but perhaps he was afraid of the feeling of sexual pleasure that emanated from the happy pair, for he pretended not to see them, not wishing to see others enjoying themselves when he was not. Peter noted that Yatchjohn's raincoat was filthy, and that the belt was tied and not buckled round his waist, so that the raincoat was drawn in, with pleats splaying out, above and below the tightly drawn belt; but the thing that Peter noticed with envy was that the coat, though disreputable and old, was the army-style kind that he coveted, with leather football-buttons all over it, in necessary positions and also in unnecessary positions. It was ten o'clock in the evening when Hilda eventually caught her 423 bus; and the fantastic thing was that for all that time she had not moved more than a step from her position by the fence: she had leant forward and leant back; had looked down at her feet, and played one foot against the other; smiled a million times; told Peter nothing at all, though she had talked quite a lot; and looked at her finger-nails; but she had not walked even a yard from her position by the fence. Peter went home with joy; but when he got home he never told his mother what he had been doing.

.   .   .   .   .

They walked together up the bypass; a stream of cars passing them in the opposite direction to that in which they were walking; the very wide road that had not been laid so long ago looking fresh compared with some of the much smaller roads that threaded in between the rows of Balsham houses; and the houses that bordered the bypass being set far back from the monster road. There was a sense of bigness about the view up the bypass that was rare in the areas in which Peter spent most of his life—Balsham and Balham. When Peter cycled along the bypass in the direction of Balham-Bye the scale of life became changed for him, for Peter usually moved in a pygmy world of little houses and little roads, through which the giant belt of grey bypass roared, loaded with vehicles going from one city to another. When Peter wanted to breathe he cycled along the bypass; and when Peter wanted to feel alone with Hilda he walked by its plain, watched only by the passing motorists, who went by too quickly to make him feel really observed. Hilda and Peter walked away from the roundabout, and all the colours in front of them were light, except for the cars, and even they seemed light in colour, because they were going so fast that their individual colours did not have time to register: the sky came down to the road expansively; and Peter was glad to get away from the tiny roads, hemmed in by brick-red, with only a thin strip of sky. Hilda pointed to a house in the distance, a spacious house of covered bricks set back from the road, and told Peter that in a bedroom there lived a girl-friend of hers, who had left a comb with light hair-dye still in it on her dressing-table, which Hilda had combed her hair with, causing her to now have a band of gold from her temple that ran amongst the brown. They walked up and down the bypass as the hours passed, and the traffic began to thin; and it was a change from standing by the 423 bus-stop until the road there was deserted, and the hour was nearly in its teens: they had stood till the big black hours many times by the 423 bus-stop by now, and Peter had got to know her quite well.

Peter had nagged his mother so much that she had finally given in. It had cost six whole pounds, a lot of money in those days, and that was more than Iris could afford, but she had been unable to avoid buying it for her persistent son. It was exactly what he had dreamed of having: since he had met Hilda he had found it even more imperative that he should have such a raincoat, and be attired in what he considered was an attractive way: he had not much confidence in his appearance, but he had been completely confident that such a wonderful raincoat would make the most of what little he had: he dearly wanted to appear as a romantic figure in Hilda's eyes, and he had not felt that he was one when he had to wear his old blue raincoat to keep out the cold and the rain. He felt so fine with his arms and front covered over with those half-sphere brown football-buttons, that were composed of little strips of leather criss-crossing; and there were all those army-style subsidiary features on the light yellow-ochre raincoat—purposeless doubling of the material; duck-feet edging; and bits and pieces on the shoulders and on the cuffs: how proud he was of himself, and the time of day he enjoyed most was that time when he was able to wear the over-decorated and slightly preposterous thing. He would only have felt happier if he had had an army captain's uniform on underneath it. He stood, holding Hilda, by the side of the roundabout, the raincoat open at the front, and the belt hanging at his sides from its two loops. Hilda teased him about the raincoat, and began to play with the belt that she took from its moorings. Peter kissed her lips, lips from which the red had been licked off by Hilda during the course of the evening, and the scent from the powder on her face sent his senses reeling. The darkness had now enveloped them; the bypass was now comparatively empty, the cars that had been on it in the dimming daylight now immobile in garages miles away; and the high night-lights formed a regular and double procession in perspective away down the length of the bypass. When it was very late, and Hilda wanted to go, Peter found that his raincoat belt had got lost, having fallen somewhere on to the path. He was in a panic, and infected by it. Hilda helped him peer at the pavement, realizing how important it was to him that the belt should be found. Peter's panic increased; and when he eventually found the belt he was so relieved that he laughed with intense and charming joy into her startled and newly made-up face, lunged playfully at her curving hips with his hands, and kissed her passionately, so that she had to re-do her mouth, before she went home amongst the watching people in the 423 bus that she would catch. Hilda liked him more, when he kissed her in the joy of having found his belt, than at any other time during their whole acquaintanceship; and there was more warmth and response from her, at that moment when he kissed her, than ever before or after. Hilda generally treated his advances fairly coldly, letting him kiss her, but keeping her mouth closed as he did so; waiting with him for many hours, more because she had no better alternative than because she found him attractive; looking past him as he talked fervently to her; taking his hand quickly from her overcoat-covered chest when he placed it there; and never telling him that she liked him: it was a strange relationship, and it developed because she had nothing better to do with her after-work time: she spent most of her evenings with him now, just standing, and part of her nights, and this would seem to indicate that she found him attractive, but it was not that way at all; for she would much rather have stood till the buses stopped running, and she had to walk home, with Splay-foot Sam, if he had been able to stay out as long as Peter was able to stay out. Splay-foot had got to know her by now, and the three of them would stand and talk until Sam had to go home to tea, and it was only after that that Peter had her to himself. Sometimes she waited until eleven-and-a-half and caught the last bus home, and sometimes she waited until the clock chimed twelve over the buildings, and then she would walk home, Peter accompanying her part of the way, although she kept telling him that it was not necessary for him to do that. Another reason for the many hours was Peter's persistence, and the fact that he was glad to be with her regardless of how she treated him, and regardless of how late the hour might be, and sometimes she found it difficult to get away from him. Peter told his mother that he had been doing a bit of fire-watching at the school whenever he came home late after having waited with Hilda, and Iris had to accept this explanation, although she did not really believe it to be the truth. Once, and only once, Peter stayed with Hilda until one o'clock, waiting, standing, face to face, kissing and talking, as the world around them left the streets and went to bed: Peter lived a lot, during those months, in a world of silent and deserted streets, daytime-crowded streets that became their own as the hours passed, and the people gradually relinquished their possession of the streets and went indoors. Peter did all of the loving. The first wait they had

had together had been different from all those that followed, because Hilda had been intrigued with the new experience, but after that familiarity bred contempt, and Peter's unreserved and undignified worship of her increasingly bored her the more she received of it. Tired by the weight of his love and admiration though she was, Hilda was never nasty to him, for it was not in her nature to enjoy an atmosphere of disagreeableness: she just bore with him, tolerated him, was unresponsive, and teased him—when Splay-foot Sam was present. No relationship between boy and girl could have been more odd. Waiting for eight hours every evening with a boy she did not find attractive, slightly hypnotized by the intensity of his attention, unable to stir herself into going home, and being, in her unresponsive way, kind to the boy who loved her—too soft-hearted to deny him the joy of her company, and too weak-willed to break away from the everlasting wait.

· · · · ·

Splay-foot Sam walked duck-footed below Peter; his curling hair uncurling from the hair-line, where it was in tiny frizzy waves, till it was in one long, wide, loose wave that flopped over half his wide and narrow forehead; his shoulders swaying contrariwise to the swaying of his wide pelvis; his big blue eyes laughing with Hilda—shared mockery of Peter the temporary clown (Peter took this mockery, for he was too old now to reply to it with force, as he had replied to the treatment of him by Coffee); his uncreased grey trousers swirling round his fat gastrocnemius muscles; his mind free for a while from thoughts about Marx writing his book in the British Museum; and when he was not talking he was whistling an improvisation on a jazz theme. Sam's friend had been on the trolley-bus with them, but he had left them after they alighted from the bus, walking loftily away; and Hilda, Sam, and Peter were drifting slowly past her 423 bus-stop in the direction of the roundabout, away from where Hilda caught her bus, away from where Sam usually turned off to

go home, and in the direction of Peter's home: it was just
something to do, and just somewhere to walk, for Sam could
easily retrace his steps home, and Hilda could catch her bus
at another stop. Hilda always intended to catch her bus
early, but always she just stayed on, after Sam had left them,
with Peter, until everywhere was as deserted and sad as the
streets of the City of London abandoned by the fickle commuters. When Sam, Peter, and Hilda were together the other
two often teased Peter, inventing a vast girl-friend for him
called Agatha, whom they said was so fat that when Peter put
his arms round her waist his hands did not meet behind her.
Hilda, though she stayed so long with Peter in the evenings,
acted always, when Sam was present, as if she had no connection with him at all; and all the time she was alone with
Peter she was always on the point of going home.

Sam said it was time he went home to tea, and he waddled
away from them over the grey pavement, turning to wave
sweetly at Hilda when he was fifty yards away. Hilda was
left with Peter and his devotion for her, and she resigned herself, and stood, as he talked, her eyes smiling, not at him,
but at the world as it passed by. They walked these days, and
only now and again did she wait immovably at her 423 bus-
stop nearby the trolley-bus stop.

Time drifted past, the darkness came once more, and
Hilda and Peter were left alone again in sole possession of
the formerly lively streets. They stood in a side road, by a
horse-trough filled with water, and as they looked from the
pavement where they stood they could see the 423 bus-stop
across the main-road. Hilda was talking about how a policeman wanted her to go to a policemen's ball, and she was
wondering whether she should go or not when the day of the
ball arrived: Peter was jealous, and he listened to her with
resentment. It was nearing midnight, and during the last
two hours, when the streets had been quiet enough for Peter
to try his one-sided kissing, Hilda had been more than usually
unco-operative; he had been annoyed that her mouth had been
dead when his lay on it; and he felt he wanted to do something, anything, that would evoke some response in her, that

239

would stir her apathy into life. He felt that after such a long acquaintance he deserved just a little warmth and response from her; and, although he did not show it, he was irritable and angry with her indifferent, languid, and phlegmatic attitude. It was true that sometimes she laughed, but invariably she laughed at him and not with him. Certainly she punched him playfully sometimes, and was sometimes lively, but he was well aware that she was very lively when Sam was on the scene, and decidedly dull in spirits when she was left alone with Peter. If only her lips would respond just once: it seemed so little for him to ask of her. It seemed so painfully obvious at times to him that she found him boring and unattractive, and he so wanted her to be romantically in love with him. He was sure that she would have been amorous with Sam if she spent as long alone with him as she did with Peter. She said she must go; and she said she would not be seeing him the next day, because she had to go to the policemen's ball, and his anger increased. He watched her as she put on her make-up, her head bending over the water in the horse-trough, the lamplight above her, using her reflection in the dirty and still water as an aid to cosmetic application: she always made herself up again, and combed her hair, at the end of a session, because she wanted to look respectable in the bus, or when she walked the long way home. How he wished he could leave her that night with something to remember him by during the following day when he was not to be allowed to see her. How he wished he could disturb her apathy towards him, as he was sure Sam could have done if he had been in his place. How he wished she thought of him with desire when she was not with him: he knew she thought little about him, and that if she did think of him it was as a bit of a clown, and as the boy-friend of Agatha, the hypothetical lump. She looked so pretty as she leant over the still, greeny water in the white concrete horse-trough, the lamplight glittering yellowly across her hanging hair, catching on the metal of her cosmetics, and splaying out over the water below her smiling face; and he felt a powerful but resistible desire to upend her into the trough, for then she would be disturbed by him, then she would think of him as she made her bedraggled way home, then she would remember him during the next day when he was not to see her, and then she would remember him when she was dancing at the bobbies' ball.

.   .   .   .   .

The next afternoon the trolley-bus was full of people coming home from working in Balham, and full of Elevensinians also. Peter sat in a seat on the top deck, and out of his sight sat Hilda, in a seat across the gangway and behind him. Peter had got on the bus at the stop after the one that Hilda had used, and he could not communicate with her in the crowded bus: anyway she seemed less than eager to communicate with him. He knew she would go straight home that afternoon. Hilda also knew that if she got off the trolley-bus at the alighting point in Balsham Peter would involve himself with her, and make it difficult for her to continue her journey on the 423 bus because of his pleading: so she intended to stay on the trolley-bus after Peter had alighted, getting off the bus at a later stage herself, at a stop that was not normally the most convenient (for the 423 was better for the rest of the journey, as it took her very near her home), and walking the rest of the way home, via the road that ran in a short tunnel under the railway-bridge. But when the trolley-bus reached Balsham, and Hilda did not make a move from her seat, Peter stayed on the bus: he could still not get to her because there were so many people on the bus, even though many of them had alighted at the Balsham stop. He could see that Hilda was aware that he was still on the bus, and he could see a smile of a self-conscious and outwitted nature on her face, as she pretended not to notice him and stared out of the bus window. The person who was on the outside of the double seat that Peter was sitting on left the seat, making it possible for Peter to get up and to go and sit by Hilda: he was just going to do this when a boy he knew vaguely came from the back of the bus and sat by him, hemming him in once more. The boy teased Peter about Hilda,

and glanced over at Hilda now and again. To Peter's relief
the boy soon got off the bus. Hilda was so obviously un-
desirous that he should talk to her that he could not bring
himself to approach her amongst the watching eyes of the
other passengers, and he sat self-consciously in his seat,
ridiculously worried about the fact that the bus was carrying
him further and further away from his home. The bus stopped
by the railway-bridge; and before Peter could pull himself
together Hilda had leapt from her seat, just as the bus was
starting again, run down the stairs, and trotted on her high
heels away down the pavement, by the side of the restarting
and towering mass of people-filled red bus. Peter went down
the stairs after her as if his life depended on it, and almost fell
off the bus on to the pavement as it moved away. His quarry
thought that he was still on the bus, and he saw her in front
of him, walking along a stretch of deserted pavement. Not
caring about the people in the bus who could still see him,
because they would rapidly move away with the bus out of
his life, he rushed towards her, his raincoat open and flying
behind his running and bending figure. She squealed with
surprise, and a minute amount of pleasure, as his hands
caught her waist, and she lurched forward as his body surged
against her; and, in a flurry of positional rearrangement on
the part of Peter and Hilda, she protestingly told him that
she could not talk to him, because she had to go home and
get herself ready for the bobbies' ball. But Peter was like a
leech on her as always, and he tagged on to her as she walked
under the railway-bridge. She protested some more by the
wall below the bridge, and then reluctantly he let her walk
away from the darkness of the long arch, and out into the
afternoon light in the street on the other side of the railway-
bridge.

.   .   .   .   .

Peter was no more the withdrawn boy that he had been
once upon a time; no more the thick-headed boy who alerted
into occasional bursts of violence; and he was, in the sixth

form, less of a fighter—even something of an occasional philosopher, now curious about the profounder aspects of life; and now so used to the atmosphere of the school and the nature of its boys that he had relaxed and opened himself, and become sociable—sociable with the boys he was familiar with in the school, that is—and still withdrawn when he was with people he did not know. Peter, now he was not hiding behind a protective and cold barrier from his fellow school- and class-mates, had become approachable, in a pompous and slightly absurd kind of way; his pomposity causing the other boys to treat him—as schoolboys will always treat pomposity —with laughter. But pompous as he now was, and liable to inner rage if a bus-conductress called him a boy, he was now able to make friends at the school, and he was thick with a number of the boys. He had grown heavy in his build, had broadened and matured, and he was almost fat, being some-times confused with Peebles, who was now a much-decorated senior Scout in the school Scout-group, more staid than ever before, in the lower-sixth science form, and known as 'Chubby'. Peter hated being mistaken for 'Chubby', because he knew that romantic figures were not fat ones; and also he had given up long ago his ambition to be a much-decorated senior Scout—his raincoat was decorated enough anyway, and, with its many bulbous buttons, was a good substitute for the badge-emblazoned cloth of a senior Scout's shirt. Peter was so eager to do everything possible to make himself look a romantic figure that he was quite glad he was no longer a Scout, for the wearing of a Scout's hat struck him as directly in opposition to being romantic-looking. What he wanted most now was a pair of brogues, all perforated like his father's pair had been: he had envied his father two things, both of them made of leather, and they were the belt and the brogues. But brogues were out, for Iris could not afford them for her appearance-obsessed son. He still desperately wanted to dis-tinguish himself, to be top of his form, to get an open scholar-ship to Oxford, or to be a hero on the sports or athletic fields; but his myopia prevented him from playing rugby or soccer even moderately well, his aptitude for sporting events seemed to be limited despite his good physique, and he was not naturally clever at his lessons. He was good at P.T. now because he tried so hard, trying to build up his muscles, but a chap who is good at P.T., which is non-competitive, is not a hero. He was not really fat, it was just that his pelvis was wide, and that he was not underfed: in fact he had a powerful body, with shoulders that the P.T. master had pointed out once to the whole form, but he was no good at competitive sports because his bodily co-ordination was poor. Peter had made friends, and he was no more within his shell. But when he later went into the Army he withdrew into himself again, and became exactly as he had been in the preparatory school, and as he had been when he had been in the preliminary classes at St. Elevenses. In the Army he became the idiot of his platoon, the despair of his sergeant, and as withdrawn as a tortoise. But we have not got to that yet; and he was only in the Army for nine weeks anyway, being kicked out almost as soon as he got in, either because he was an idiot, unable to put a machine gun together, or because he was hopelessly myopic: his discharge papers said it was because of myopia, and we expect it was, although his sergeant was awfully glad to get rid of him, for he could not count a row of beds properly, because his brain had seized up with fear in the unfamiliar barracks, where they cut off all his precious hair and fed him until he really was as thick as 'Chubby'. It was a pity because he did so want to be a major.

.   .   .   .   .

They had walked further than usual this time: Peter and Hilda. Hilda's legs were up on the seat; and Peter sat beside her shoed feet, his raincoat open, and, after issuing from compression below his posterior, hanging down behind the right angles of his legs. It was nearly evening, and they could see, across some allotments in a field, that the sky was becoming crepuscular. They sat at the back of a double bus-stop-shelter seat, and the seat that faced the road and the seat that faced the allotments were divided by a partition that rose to the roof of the shelter: Peter had chosen the seat for privacy, and Hilda had accepted it because her injected and swollen, but beautiful, legs were getting tired. As twilight darkened, and the daylight was gradually extinguished over the allotments, Peter lunged hopefully across the seat at Hilda, his hands caressing the flesh of her lower legs: she squirmed with little energy in an attempt to repulse his advances, but he did not feel discouraged enough to stop pawing the inflated beef of her calves, so she stirred herself, and began to struggle in earnest: her smile did not leave her face as she struggled, but she did not want him to make love to her: she was a pleasant-natured girl, perhaps a little afraid of sexual contact in a virginal manner, and even when she was putting a stop to Peter she did not look bitter or nasty: it was very confusing to Peter when she smiled as she withdrew from his eagerness. Peter had not had an opportunity until then to paw her legs, because they were normally pavement-pointing, and until she put down her feet from their resting-place on the barred seat he took full advantage of the opportunity. Hilda did not seem too worried by his hands on her calves, presumably considering that they were the least intimate part of her that he could paw, barring her feet; but she had a decidedly virginal reluctance when his hands strayed to her chest, regardless of the fact that it was covered by her overcoat. Peter was getting rather heated by now, the feel of her calves having started his blood careering round his blood-vessels, and in the privacy of the back section of the bus-shelter he increased his advances, causing Hilda to move rather violently, so that the bus-shelter clamoured with the sound of her struggling limbs against the thin metal behind the seat. Some people who were waiting on the other side of the shelter heard all the noise and the sound of her protesting voice, and thinking that a girl was being raped, or perhaps murdered, behind the metal partition, they ran round to investigate, intending to save a young girl from defloration or worse. Peter was a good boy, brought up in St. Elevenses, and by a middle-class and proper mother, and he was in fact quite incapable of raping anybody: he was merely getting a little overheated, his glasses steaming up because of a pair of inflated calves. As the people stared at Hilda and Peter, Hilda controlled her merriment, and Peter wiped his tortoiseshell spectacles with a grubby handkerchief, both of them sitting up properly side by side. Peter had heavy spectacles now, and looked vaguely like his father. Seeing that Hilda did not look as if she had just experienced attempted rape, the good citizens disappointedly returned to the other side of the shelter to wait for their bus again: subconsciously they had been looking forward to calling the police, comforting a distraught and ruined girl, and putting a half-nelson on a struggling sexual maniac. Peter felt rather offended by all this because he was an Elevensinian, and like all Elevensinians he did not care for being treated as a criminal, for it must be remembered that in all its history St. Elevenses had not produced one criminal, being primarily concerned with producing potential Prime Ministers, potential captains of industry, and mathematical geniuses (even Splay-foot Sam, with his loquacious love of Marx, was considered at that time by the staff of St. Elevenses to be in rather poor taste: and prefects who told him to cut his hair had no sympathy with him when he protested that he wanted to be 'natural'). As soon as the citizens had gone out of sight Hilda burst into girlish laughter, but Peter sat there stiffly and outraged.

When the sky was as black as a tinker's pot, Hilda rushed round the shelter and waited for a bus, leaving Peter bashfully at the back of the shelter, too self-conscious to go after her and plead with her amongst the other people who were waiting. He was now in a very hot condition, and his cheeks were dark with the risen blood of continual blushing: he wanted Hilda very badly indeed—in a restrained Elevensinian manner that is. When he heard the bus arrive on the other side of the shelter he realized that Hilda would take the bus to the 423 bus-stop two miles away, and change buses there. If he arrived at the 423 bus-stop at the same time as her bus did, he could plead with her again, and continue the evening with her perhaps. He ran from the seat, and did a Jesse Owens down the deserted suburban main road: the bus stopped frequently, and he was able to race it to the 423 bus-stop: he could run fairly well, but the reward he hoped for at the end of this race was great, and he ran as he had never run before, the sweat blown from his brow by the wind of his speed. But as he stood watching the people getting off the bus, the perspiration streaming uncontrollably from his face, he could not see Hilda amongst them, and in a state of puzzlement he walked home, trying to extinguish the fires of passion within him, and wiping his face with a soaking snot-rag. He asked Hilda about it the following day, and she told him that she had not got on the bus by the romantic shelter, because her band-leader had driven up in his car, and driven her home: she romanced about his lovely brown eyes as she told this story to the disbelieving Peter. Hilda hid among her little white lies, and Peter wished he was a band-leader with lovely brown eyes, or Dana Andrews, but he never quite made it.

.   .   .   .   .

Peter was disappointed that, despite the fact that he had spent hundreds of hours with Hilda, he could not with conviction call her his girl-friend: she had not even committed herself to the extent of saying that she liked him. He wanted to do something with Hilda that would prove to him and others that she was his girl: something that he could tell to his friends, something that boy-friends and girl-friends did together. Peter thought that going to the pictures with a girl was a very romantic thing, and that if a girl went to the pictures with a boy it indicated surely that she was fond of him: he had great faith in going to the pictures with a girl, and it was a thing he had never done, and was never to do as a matter of fact, until he took a girl he met through a marriage-bureau when he was twenty, a girl who was very frigid, and whom he never saw again. He wanted Hilda to go to the pictures with him, for once he had done that with her he felt his mark would be upon her. But Hilda would not go with him. He asked her so many times that eventually she agreed to make a date, and to meet him outside the cinema by the bus-station in Balham on the following day. But she never turned up at the appointed place; and when he later heard that she had on another occasion gone to the cinema with an Elevensinian in 5B, whom she had only just met, a racy boy with the dollies, Peter was immeasurably sad.

The summer holidays were a threat to Peter that year, because he would be at home during that time, and not be able to see Hilda on the trolley-bus journeys. But Peter's unrequited love was undauntable, and he walked from his home some late afternoons, arriving in the centre of Balham just at the time Hilda alighted from the trolley-bus, this being a disappointment to her, because she had been looking forward to a Peterless period of relaxation during the school holidays. Peter walked along the road, where it joined the roundabout, in the hot sunshine, the perspiration pouring down from beneath his armpits and under his shirt, his mind dizzy with the anticipation of meeting Hilda, and dizzy with the strong sunshine that blasted at him from above the houses bordering the main road that encircled the roundabout, and which merged at that point with the spacious and open bypass. He knew that Hilda did not want to see him. When he got to the cross-roads where the 423 and 37 bus-stops were, he knew that if he stood there waiting Hilda might see him before he saw her, and that then she might make herself scarce, getting back on the trolley-bus or walking away down the main road. So he went into a sweet shop, from the doorway of which he could see the 423 bus-stop that she would make her usual dilatory way to. He got out his ration-book, and asked the lady in the shop how many ounces of sweets he had coming to him: the lady thought that he intended to spend all his coupons, and, when she told him how much he could buy, she was very annoyed when he used up only a few of his coupons: Peter loved his sweet ration and spent it sparingly. The lady lived in the house that was next to Peter's grandmother's house, the house that sometimes contained the lady with the grey-and-red-pleated skirt, but Peter had never spoken to her before. The sweet-shop lady, who was middle-aged, had once told his mother that she thought that he was handsome, and when Peter heard this from his mother he was knocked sideways, for he did not think he was quite as good as that. He tried to believe the sweet-shop lady's assessment of his romantic potential, but he could not convince himself that what she had told his mother was true, for he was sure he had a weak chin, and he was sure that glasses ruined a boy's chances of being good-looking (girls never make passes at boys who wear glasses). There was an icy silence in the shop as the lady handed Peter his chocolate, and in front of the other people in the shop she said that he would not be able to pull a trick like that on her again. Peter had not meant to give her the idea that he meant to spend all his monthly ration, for it was just that he did not understand sweet coupons and their value, and he accepted her treatment of him as a deceiver in embarrassed silence. But he did not leave the shop, and waited out of sight from the 37 bus-stop, mingling with the customers in the now crowded little shop, watching expectantly the road outside. Hilda came into view at last, and he rushed over to her joyfully, but she was not pleased to see him, and looked as if she felt she had been tricked. Peter seemed to be tricking everyone. Hilda had seen him waiting for her on other occasions during the summer holidays and had avoided meeting him.

.   .   .   .   .

Peter returned to school in the Autumn term and entered 6A. But, when he got on the trolley-bus after school in the afternoons, he found that Hilda was not on the bus. It had not been a very successful romance, but it had been something, and, after all, beggars cannot be choosers. Peter had felt so pleased one day, months before, when a prefect who had seen him with Hilda, and who had admired Hilda, had asked him how his girl was.

A long time afterwards he thought he saw Hilda from the top deck of a trolley-bus that was near the railway-bridge, and he had strained to have a better look from the window at the figure passing from view amongst the crowds on the pavement below. He had rushed off the bus after her, but he had been too late, and she was gone. Perhaps it had not been her at all.

Even longer afterwards he had been walking one dinner-time amongst the crowds in Balham with a friend of his, and he had suddenly seen Hilda standing talking to an Elevensinian called Horsey. Hilda saw him, turned her head, and smiled with recognition in her funny way, looking at him over Horsey's shoulder, as she had looked at others over his shoulder in the past. Peter felt so disturbed that he put his head down and bolted through the people on the pavement, until he was out of her sight and round the corner. His friend caught up with him, and asked him what was the matter, but Peter could only laugh self-consciously. Hilda had meant so much to him. It was seeing her with Horsey that had turned him upside down as much as anything, since for her to be talking to Horsey was terrible. Horsey had been one of the somewhat younger Elevensinians who had coveted her from afar on the trolley-bus in days of yore. Splay-foot and Peter had known that Horsey coveted Hilda, and they had talked about that, for Horsey was a revolting-looking boy, far from up to Hilda's standard, with a dirty neck and a completely glamourless appearance; Peter had not thought of himself as being handsome, but he had thought that he was at least a hundred times better than Horsey, and when he saw Hilda talking to Horsey, of all people, he felt it was very unfair of her, and even beneath her. How could she have sunk so low?

23

The White Cross in the Graveyard

BUT before Peter went back to St. Elevenses in the Autumn term, entering 6A, another thing happened. The summer holidays were seven weeks long. During the last part of those summer holidays Peter did not see Hilda, and he took to playing tennis. Unknown to him at that time that was almost the last time he was to see Hilda, and he was also not aware that before he started the Autumn term at school he was to see the last of his mother. Iris went on a holiday in the later part of the summer, and the poor, half-blind woman needed that holiday. Peter did not want to accompany his sister Annabell and his mother down to Cornwall, and he stayed at home. When Iris and her daughter got down to the farm, nearby St. Ives, they liked it so much that Iris sent Peter a letter, asking him to come down to them after all, because it was so lovely down there. But Peter played tennis in Balsham. He should have gone, for Iris never came back to the gloomy little house filled with Victoriana in Balsham.

.   .   .   .   .

The farm had a duck-pond below the bedroom window that was as filthy as hell and surrounded with pigs. The bread at mealtimes was loaded with Cornwall farm-cream, and then loaded with home-made jam. You could get to the sea by walking through a crevice in the white rock, and there was nobody anywhere about. Iris was coming back with Annabell, who had grown up somewhat by now, from a shopping visit

251

to St. Ives, walking back over the fields. Iris was to go to St. Ives once more only after that visit, but that time she would not see the fields as she went, for she went in a coffin, and they buried her in a graveyard outside the town.

Annabell was walking on ahead over a field not far from the farm, and Iris was climbing over a stile that was in the fence that bordered the field. Annabell heard her mother calling and went back to her: Iris looked up at the girl, and, with an apologetic silly smile on her face, she said that she felt terribly tired. Annabell helped her mother back to the farm; the woman at the farm put Iris to bed; and later on, as Annabell stood at the foot of the old stairs of the farmhouse, she heard the death-rattle in her mother's throat, and poor, half-blind Iris had finished with her wasted life.

Annabell stayed down on the farm; Peter cried once because he tried to; the relations organized things; and Cousin Trevor and Peter went down to the farm for a holiday, Peter considering that to go on holiday with Cousin Trevor was a more attractive proposition than going on holiday with his mother. Ever since Iris had gone to Cornwall, for the holiday that she had so much been looking forward to, the grandmother had been staying with Cousin Trevor's mother and father. When Peter's uncle took over the funeral arrangements, he thought that it would be nice if Peter went on a holiday to ease his bereavement, and so he put both Peter and Trevor on the train.

Cousin Trevor had grown up now, and was a perfect companion for Peter, their intelligence being about equal, because Trevor was precocious and Peter was backward. With Annabell, Peter and Trevor walked over the rocks by the sea, with their shoes and socks off and their trouser-bottoms rolled up; and Annabell tucked the lower part of her frock into the elastic that supported her bloomers, and took her shoes and socks off too. They looked in the pools amongst the rocks for crabs, and Peter told them about Hilda. When they returned for tea at the farmhouse, after walking miles by the seashore, they ate lots of bread piled high with jam over the preposterously thick clotted cream, and Peter came out in spots again. But he did not care, for they were not on his face and did not mar his visible beauty, and nothing like that could alter the joy of the holiday with his beloved cousin Trevor.

Trevor's mother was worried about Trevor's father: he had not had a holiday and he was looking very tired. She sent him down with a business colleague to join the 'children' on the farm. One day the uncle and his friend arrived in the car at the farm, and that did not alter Peter's enjoyment of the holiday, for he loved the atmosphere of his uncle and his family, and was not shy of all the persons who were now down on the farm. The friend who had come down with Peter's uncle was in love with the aunt of Peter who had given Peter the American knife: the dental chappie had died, leaving Peter's aunt everything he had. Peter's aunt later married Fred, the business friend of Peter's uncle, but by then he was dying a long death, and she had to nurse him till he got skeletal and died.

Annabell did not know what was going on inside her: she was beginning to become capable of reproduction. Of course she did not know about sex, for just as Iris had not been able to face the task of telling Peter so she had been unable to tell her daughter. Annabell was now at a stage that was very similar to that Peter had been at when he first found himself disturbed by vague sexual impulses stirring within him, although she was maturing at an earlier age than that at which Peter had started to become adolescent, because girls become adolescent earlier than boys do. She found that she liked sitting on Fred's lap, though she did not know why, and for that matter did not question her subconscious impulses. She was not asked to sit on Fred's lap: she just did; and he did not repulse her, for he quite enjoyed the experience of having a child-woman giggling on his lap, for Annabell was a holiday girl, brown with the sunshine, and childishly immodest still. Nobody stopped her throwing herself at Fred, for nobody there could care less what she did with herself, it being a stag-party except for Annabell.

It was all very jolly, and in the evenings they all played

253

pontoon in the farmhouse sitting-room, Annabell sitting on Fred's lap. One day they all had a race. Peter was not good enough to win races at school, but he had a strong confidence in his running ability, and he was sure that he could win against the opposition that was arrayed on the dilapidated road outside the farmhouse: there was Fred in a pair of plimsolls, Uncle attired in holiday casuals, Annabell acting as the starter, and bare-footed Peter and Trevor. Peter was handicapped by being placed at the rear, and Fred was given the greatest start. The end of the race was a disused white edifice, at the turn of the road, by the edge of a field. There was a false start due to Peter's over-eagerness, and then they were off. Peter felt his bare feet skimming the surface of the puddled road; and as he accidentally barged his uncle, so that his uncle was nearly knocked flying, his uncle laughed as if he thought he had been outwitted by permissible unfairness, although Peter was hurt by this, for he had not intended to barge his uncle unfairly, it not being an Elevensinian thing to do at all. Peter won, and apologized to his uncle, who still thought that he had been purposely barged into the puddle. It just did not seem to Peter to be any good living by pure and honest Elevensinian principles in life, for people always misinterpreted his principled actions, and treated him as if he had no sense of what was honourable by Elevensinian standards.

When Peter came back to Balsham, and his grandmother's home, he found that his grandmother was there again, and that his mother's place in the house had been taken by his uncle Perce and his auntie Harriet. As he entered the house his auntie Harriet looked down the stairs at him, attired as she was in an overall, and told him pleasantly, with due respect for the fact that he had recently lost his mother, that she and her husband were getting his new room ready for him. His uncle and aunt were nice to him at first, for they were trying to be kind to their motherless nephew, but Peter's introspective nature, hidden behind an aggressive attitude, was not understandable to his uncle; for Uncle Perce did not understand sensitive Elevensinian products, and after some short time Peter and his uncle became enemies. Uncle Perce came from the kind of background the products of which Peter was afraid of: Peter had been moulded in the protected academic atmosphere of a good school until he was now seventeen, whereas Uncle Perce had left school at thirteen, had obtained a squashed nose in a public house, and only really understood uneducated men who put tiles on roofs or who mended the plumbing. Uncle Perce was an outsider in the family of Peter's relations, for all of Peter's relations were middle-class, and very conscious of it, tending to look down on the working classes. Uncle Perce could not have been expected to understand the inhibited and complex Peter, and it must be said in his favour that he was prepared to like Peter before he met him. Peter's reserved, snobbish, and sixth-form manner did absolutely nothing to help matters, and Peter did not try to disguise the fact that he looked down on members of the working class. Peter had no right to do this, for he was the very worst kind of nigh-public-school secondary-school product—unintelligent, completely unpractical, dependent, self-centred, and pathetically helpless underneath his assumed air of masculinity and adultness. There was no common ground at all between him and his uncle, and it might have helped if Peter had been able to talk about the insides of motor-bikes or the construction of houses. While his uncle Perce did his football-pools in the sitting-room, Peter looked on with an aloofness that he might have learnt from Not-so-Green, and thought to himself how stupid football-pools were. After some time Peter and his uncle Perce hardly ever spoke to each other.

Peter was now in the higher sixth—6A—and he considered himself to be an intellectual. He used as many long words as he could, and tried, with a self-conscious sense of superiority, to see beneath the surface of things: he was really an awful twit. Perce's wife understood Peter to a certain extent, though she did not like him very much, just because she understood why he was so difficult to live with, her loyalties being with her husband. Peter's attitude was to a certain extent the result of his shyness towards his uncle

Perce and auntie Harriet, and he hid from them beneath a
heavy veneer of gruffness, also hiding a kind of inferiority
complex beneath a false superiority complex. In a way Perce
did also understand Peter to a certain extent, for he had seen
lads come and go, and he knew well the phenomenon of a
youth aspiring to manhood, and putting on exaggerated
masculine and adult airs: with this phenomenon he justifiably
had no sympathy. But what he did not understand were the
manifestations of Peter's fear of the lower classes, and the
manifestations of Peter's extreme shyness and absurdly preposterous sensitivity, and he hated Peter for those manifestations. Perce hated Peter as a bricklayer will hate a boy from
Eton, and Peter nearly got his own nose smashed as a result
of this.

St. Elevenses came to the rescue in a very proper Elevensinian fashion. Peter had to have some money, now that his
mother was dead and unable to support him: he had to have
some money to pay to Auntie Harriet, and some money to pay
for his school dinners and his Hildaless trolley-bus fares. St.
Elevenses generously ignored the fact that Peter was one of
its most unpromising students, and from the school funds they
took some money and allocated it to Peter, giving it to him
periodically over the counter in front of the headmaster's
secretary's office: Peter was rather taken with the eyes of the
female secretary, and he liked the pound notes she gave him
even more. The people who financed the boarding school that
his sister went to (now as a full-time boarder) came to Peter's
rescue also, and he received a certain amount of money from
them, too. He had never had so much money in his life before
and it went to his head. It was more than he needed, and
what was worse it came in lumps. Peter had never forgotten
the wonderful three-speed bicycle that the teacher-lodger had
possessed, and he still wanted to possess a sports model with
a thick back hub. He found that his old bicycle was difficult
to sell, for one day when he was younger, when he had suddenly discovered to his delight that one could actually cut
metal with a saw, he had used the saw experimentally on the
cross-bar of his bike, and from then onwards it had a saw-cut

JOHN·BRATBY·FEBRUARY·1961.

in it that went halfway through the tubular metal of the cross-bar: amazingly the bar did not break when he rode the bicycle after that. But he sold the bicycle, after he had filled in the cut so that it did not show, though only for a single pound note. Then he bought a brand-new blue bicycle with chromium drop-handlebars, a thick back hub, and lots of glamorous manufacturer's transfers on it, paying for it with some of his maintenance money. One of the reasons why he had so much money to spare was that his auntie Harriet did not charge him very much at all for his food, and another reason was that his grandmother charged him no rent, despite the fact that he was given money to pay rent with. After he had bought the bicycle, Peter was still in possession of more money than he knew what to do with; and while he was in 6A, where the semi-adult sixth-formers were allowed to study during some curriculum periods on their own, even being allowed in the summer to peruse their text books on the seats outside the school building, and where staff supervision was considerably relaxed, Peter would go into the town with a friend, when he should have been at least within the school grounds, and he would buy large amounts of grapes, which he would return with, eating them outside the school building in the sunshine, and giving them with extreme largesse to all and sundry. Peter was rather fed up with his lack of prowess in the school world of sport and athletic endeavour, and because of this, and as muscles were all the rage at the time, Peter also bought an 'expander' outfit, which consisted of three chromium-plated and powerful springs joined to two handles. He would spend his evenings in his bedroom, stripped to the waist, in front of a mirror, pulling at these springs above his head, until eventually his arm-muscles became well defined, and larger than they had been before. At this time, when Peter did P.T. on the school field, he would never wear a singlet, and he would parade his torso proudly, so that anybody could see it, and perhaps admire it, if they wanted to waste their time doing such a thing.

Perce was apparently proud of his torso too, for he would do gardening in the summertime, also stripped to the waist.

Perce was well built in a manner similar to Splay-foot Sam, for he was stunted, heavy-headed, and slightly grotesque. But, unlike Splay-foot Sam, Perce had bowed shoulders, mature hard muscles, a broken nose, and a head that lolled back as he walked, this last characteristic being similar to that possessed by Not-so-Green. Perce got very brown on his torso in the summer of 1946, as a result of undressing in the garden.

At this time, just before Peter was to take the Higher School Certificate examination that he failed, Peter's enmity with Perce had flowered, and they had some rather unpleasant rows, Perce being under the very incorrect and twisted misapprehension that Peter was in love with his auntie Harriet: Perce was the kind of man who, if he lives under the same roof as another male, feels competitive and antagonistic after some time, and he was jealous because of Peter's male presence in the house. Peter had been used to warming himself by the fire in his pyjamas, while his mother had been alive, and while he had been living with her in his grandmother's house; and he did not realize that he should have acted differently now that his aunt had taken his mother's place in the house. He still warmed himself by the fire in his pyjamas, after having an evening bath, and before going up to bed; and, as he had partially the same blood in his veins as his aunt, he did not feel it was improper for him to sit near her so indecently attired. He could not understand that his uncle might resent this harmless habit, but Perce was in fact very angry with Peter about the pyjama business, and Peter and he had a row about it. The next evening, when Peter came in late after going to the pictures, he found that everyone had gone to bed, except for his quivering grandmother, who had waited up for him, and who told him with fear in her voice that Perce had been waiting all evening for Peter to come home so that he could kill him. The grandmother said she was too old to be able to stand such goings-on, and she asked Peter to go away and stay at the Y.M.C.A. Peter had not the slightest intention of doing such a thing, for he would rather have been murdered by his uncle than have had to go and stay amongst all those unfamiliar and frightening working-class residents of the Y.M.C.A.: he was still frightened of the outside world, and he was to remain so for many years, hiding in one protected atmosphere after another.

Things all came to a head between him and his uncle one day while his uncle was working in the garden, stripped to the waist. Perce had known the rough life before he finally settled down and married Harriet, and he was a man who would fight, not in the cricketing Elevensinian way, but with a knowledge of all the dirty tricks. Peter was a fool to challenge him as he did. After Peter and Perce had had a hot verbal interchange in the kitchen, Perce walked back into the garden. Peter thought presumably that he was dealing with another green Elevensinian seventeen-year-old, for as his uncle passed through the small kitchen doorway, into the sunshine beyond, he stood erect and challenging, his own torso also naked, and said: 'That's right, run away.' Perce turned with a slow menacing movement, responding horribly to Peter's challenge, and began to retrace his steps towards Peter. If Perce had fought with Peter, then Peter would have been nearly killed. Harriet knew that her husband would kill Peter, and she knew that Peter, though big, was no match for the street-fight-trained man she had married. Harriet liked Peter to a small degree, for she could understand his introspective and shy nature, owing to the fact that she had once been slightly like that herself, and she felt a certain amount of sympathy for the boy. She also liked him a little because he was her sister's son. For these reasons she did not want to see Peter killed. But the main reason she did not want to see Peter killed was this—if her husband killed Peter, he would be taken away from her, and she could not bear the thought of living without him. What was she to do? She knew that Peter thought he could fight the man, and she knew that reasoning with Peter would not prevent the fight from occurring. Peter was sure he could beat his uncle, because his uncle was smaller than he was. So she pretended to be in a great rage, rushed at Peter, and shouted to him to get up the stairs, and to go and lock himself in the bathroom.

Taken by surprise, Peter did bolt up the stairs and lock himself in the bathroom as requested. Harriet tried to calm her husband—his face had been horribly expressionless and evil with potential violence, when he had turned to Peter after hearing the challenge—and Peter could hear her through the door, talking to her husband at the top of the stairs. Time passed, and Peter had time to think in the locked bathroom, at the top of the stairs, in the tiny house. He began to realize that he was well out of the fight that his challenge had proposed, and he had time to think about the evil expression that had been on his uncle's face. He now did not want to fight any more. His uncle came to the door of the bathroom, and Peter heard his voice quietly telling Peter to come out: there was a horrible note of evil in the purringly persuasive voice, and Peter knew that if he opened the door he would lose a leg, get killed slowly in a tortured fashion, or get his fingers broken. He stayed in the bathroom, filling in the time by looking at his hair in the mirror on the wall, and soon his uncle went away. Peter got tired of the enclosure after some time, and quietly and cautiously he opened the door, and went to the head of the stairs. His uncle heard him though, and came halfway up the stairs, standing below Peter, who looked down at him, expanding his naked chest challengingly: Peter was still only a boy. Peter's Elevensinian sense of the disgrace of cowardice was with him again, and as he looked down at his impassive-faced uncle he did not intend to turn and run. His uncle, his fury cooled by now, looked up at Peter as Peter swelled his chest over him, and he saw a child from the cradle trying so hard to be a man, so with a cynical smile on his otherwise expressionless face he turned and went down the stairs again.

24

They wanted to make him a Guardian of our Liberty

J U S T as some flowers will open up in the protected atmosphere of a greenhouse, so Peter had opened up in his last year in the sixth form at St. Elevenses: however, as has been explained, he closed his soul up in the evenings when he returned to Perce and Harriet, covering his sensitive parts with petals of gruffness and making himself unavailable. But Peter needed the familiar Elevensinian greenhouse in which to flower, and out of that greenhouse, when he was in the Army for nine weeks, he was an enclosed bud, reverting to the state he was in when he was in the preparatory school, and, like a greenhouse flower put out in the cold, he might have died a death of the soul if he had been kept in the Army too long. In the platoon's barrack-room, amongst the butchers' boys and the lower-class spivs, he closed up completely, his mind ceased to function, he became the idiot of the platoon, and he had not a single friend.

Raw recruits crowded into the barrack-room, and as they stood by the beds that had been allocated to them, putting their belongings into their tall bedside lockers, the lance-corporal with the white hair, whom all the lads instinctively liked, asked them details of their appearance, age, and next of kin, writing those details down on forms for the Army files. The sergeant was a little, smart, neat, terse, brisk regular, who kept his only feminine aspect carefully combed, and out of sight beneath his cap: once his cap had fallen off as he was showing his General Service Corps raw platoon how to crawl

262

on their bellies through the grass towards imaginary enemy lines, and Peter had seen the sergeant's feminine vanity revealed: the sergeant had hastily, and with embarrassment, covered his waves over with his cap again, and continued with the practice demonstration, but the feminine side beneath his act of masculinity had been disclosed to the watching recruits. As he walked amongst the unfamiliar raw recruits the sergeant felt ill at ease, and he tried to show that he was a good chap by taking one of the boys into his office at the end of the barrack-room, and showing him his collection of swords and guns that hung on the wall: oddly enough he chose Peter, and Peter smiled stupidly at the collection, and the sergeant then began to realize that Peter was the nincompoop of the new platoon. Peter was frightened to death in the Army, and from then on he did everything hopelessly wrong, his frightened state making him a cold, closed, tense block of incapability: he held his rifle wrongly on parade on the barrack-square; he marched out of step; he fired his machine gun at the target belonging to the soldier next to him; he shaved with such a nervous hand that his chin was a mass of blood; and he could not even clean his rifle or the latrines in a manner that was satisfactory to the corporal or the sergeant. 'I don't know what to do with you,' said the sergeant after four weeks of trying to train Peter into a defender of the nation's liberty, for it was obvious to the sergeant that, if the nation was going to depend on soldiers like Peter for its liberty, the nation had had its chips. But Peter had still a vague hope within his chest that before he had finished his National Service he would be a captain with three pips on each shoulder: in fact he thought that it was so romantic to be an officer in the Army that he was quite prepared to stay on and become a major with a glorious crown on each shoulder, like the soldier who gave out the pay to the raw platoon.

At first they were not allowed to go out of the barracks for a few days, and there they stayed, being fitted up with their uniforms, many of which did not fit at all well; being issued with a rifle each; being given denims to wear when the task was dirty; being in the Naafi in the evenings, with their

civilian hair-cuts still on their heads; and then going to the
ruthless barber and having their crowning glories shorn
unceremoniously, one after another. When his precious hair
had gone, Peter gave up all hope. When they were properly
fitted out, and looked like soldiers, the raw recruits were
allowed to go into the town on Saturday afternoon. Peter
went out in his green-khaki overcoat, the wide, triangle-
tipped collar turned up round his ears in a manner that
Peter thought made him look quite a devil of a chap; and
walked round the town in a black, emotional tizzy, not
looking where he was going. In the bed next to him in the
dormitory slept a raw recruit called Ginger, and at that time
Ginger had not realized that Peter was a stupid blockhead.
Ginger was a man of the world, with blue eyes and slicked-
down hair (what there was left of it), and as Peter resided next
door to him he was quite prepared at first to make a friend
out of Peter. Ginger had looked after his widowed mother in
civvy-street, and he was independent: the complete reverse
of Peter, who still needed his mother to look after him. Ginger
went out into town on that first Saturday afternoon, determined to find himself a piece of crackling, who would entertain
him in his spare time while he was stationed for the six weeks
that they had to spend at that particular barracks. Ginger was
immediately respected by the other boys in the platoon, for
they could see that Ginger 'knew his way around' in life at
the tender age of eighteen. Ginger found a girl almost immediately that afternoon, in fact he found three, for smooth and
white-faced Ginger was 'all there' in his quiet and unassuming
way. While Peter was roaming round the streets of the
town, so completely lost in this new world of the Army that
his senses reeled as he walked, and the buildings he looked at
seemed distorted and falling, charging pointlessly down one
side-street after another in a futile attempt to get away from
people, Ginger was talking to three pieces of crackling behind
a section of low wall that separated him from the pavement,
his little sexy group being beneath the wall of a large grim
building: Ginger had found a little sanctuary from the bustling
crowds, where he could flirt with the girls in peace. Peter

came from his side-street wandering, and braved the main street, not because he wanted to, but because he came into it unawares: Peter walked through the Saturday-afternoon crowds on the pavement, and then he heard his name called. Peter glanced out of the corner of his eye and saw Ginger and the girls, and then, frightened by the girls, he pretended not to hear his name being called, even though Ginger called it three times in a very loud voice, as Peter passed on looking the other way. Ginger told him afterwards that he had called to him, and it was obvious that Ginger had been puzzled by Peter's lack of response. Ginger told Peter that he had wanted Peter to meet the girls, so that Peter could have one of them for himself, Ginger finding three rather more than even he needed. Ginger told Peter all this as they stood between their beds in the barrack-room dormitory, preparatory to going on parade; and Peter hated himself for not having had the courage to go over and talk with the generous Ginger and the girls, for he knew that chances came his way seldom, and that that had been a chance for him to get a girl to go out with in the evenings while he was stationed at the barracks: Peter would have loved to have a cheap, tarty shop-girl or factory-girl to go around with, and to kiss under the outside of the barrack wall. From then on Ginger began to realize that Peter was a twit-type lad, and after that he left Peter alone.

Peter hated going out amongst the crowds on a Saturday, but he felt he had to do something with his Saturday afternoons, for if he stayed in the barracks there was nobody there, and it was deadly grim. All the other members of his platoon seemed to have found girls in the town. The following Saturday evening Peter came back to the barracks rather late, and when he entered the dormitory he found most of the lads asleep in their beds in the darkness. He walked none too quietly to the side of his bed and began to undress. He felt very lonely, and he put on his pyjamas feeling that he had wasted his Saturday afternoon. He felt sensitive inside himself, all introspective and self-pitying, wishing that he was back in the sixth form again, but physically he did not feel sensitive, for he had been walking the streets for hours, the only part of his body he could feel being his feet, which were painful with walking, and he felt vigorous and hard bodily: after becoming a concertina on the pillow, he dug himself beneath the tightly tucked bedclothes, more like a horse than a human being, and lay beneath the harsh grey army blankets, staring into the darkness above him, his mind empty but for a yearning after something too unattainable to be definable. There was a rustling from the beds across the aisle: Peter did not know that some of the others were awake, waiting, listening. Peter settled into his bed, and sensitivity returned to his body as it began to relax. He shifted slightly, and then came to him the rather unpleasant realization that in bed with him was his army rifle. 'The bastards!' thought Peter, and he lay without moving for a while, letting the realization that a joke had been played on him sink into his consciousness. Then the side of his body told him that also in bed with him was the barrack-room broom; and later he realized that another rod-like object was on the far side of the bed from that side from which he had entered it. He investigated the far side of the bed and found a second rifle. It was just not Elevensinian! 'The broom must be dirty,' thought Peter; and as he had been brought up to hate dirt, his fury became cold in his mind with intensity. As he lay there with his bedfellows, not moving a muscle, it occurred to him that he was in an innocent position; and he traded on this, for he knew no one could blame him if he threw the bedfellows out of the bed, and left them there. He threw the rifle out first and the others followed, making a great deal of noise as they hit the floor. He was glad to observe that no one had laughed: apparently they were now worried about the incriminating evidence that lay on either side of his bed. He felt he had scored. He went off to sleep very quickly after that, and when he woke in the morning the rifles, the broom, and the unidentified object had gone from the floor.

Peter found communication with girls, and making contact with girls, in a person-to-person manner, practically impossible because of his embarrassment, but there was one way he could make contact with them, or communicate with them, without embarrassment on his part, and that was by letter: the distance between his place of writing and the girl's letter-box was a distance that relieved him of the torment of blushing, and Peter, the great protection-seeker, felt protected by that distance. Two things that happened to him in those nine weeks in the Army caused him to write two letters to girls he did not know, when he was demobbed, in a desperate attempt to get hold of a girl for himself. Both letters were encouraging, passionate, and absurd requests for a meeting: one was addressed to 'The Girl With Brown Hair And A Friendly Nature To Strangers, The Ironmonger's Shop, The Street By The Barracks, Danderstown-upon-Hab'; and the other, probably delivered, was addressed to 'Cynthia Bloom, 7 Oldham Street, Arnotstown, Surrey'. When Peter wrote the letters he was desperate, and he was willing to try anything, however unpromising it might be; and also it was obvious that he had great faith in the G.P.O.—too much faith, in fact, regarding the letter to the girl he had been smiled at by, in the ironmonger's shop outside the barracks. He had felt sure that Cynthia would reply to him, for he had seen her name written in pencil on a lavatory wall in the barracks, accompanied by encouraging information suggesting that, if one wrote to Cynthia at that address, it would be a profitable thing to do, because she was extremely eager for love: to be perfectly honest that was not exactly what was written on the lavatory wall about Cynthia, for the information was actually presented in somewhat more colourful terms, but as it says in our publisher's contract that we must not include matter of an obscene nature in our manuscript, we are rather restricted. There were many other notices on the lavatory wall around Cynthia's address and particulars, and some of these were of an extremely imaginative nature, illustrated in a startlingly vivid, if not professional, manner. Peter spent a long time there, looking at the walls, and before he left he wrote down Cynthia's address, on a scrap of paper and with a pencil-stub, very hopefully.

A transformation had occurred in Peter. It may be difficult to conceive in the mind the idea of a youth who had been the escort to nowhere of Hilda; an integral part of 6A, and to a slightly lesser degree 6B; who had been able to pass the General School Certificate examination, if not the later higher examination; who had been a sixth-form character; and who had had friends with whom he talked on an intellectual level, and with some intimacy; changing, in a few weeks after entering Danderstown-upon-Hab, into a perfectly moronic green soldier; treated with a certain amount of contempt by his platoon-mates; friendless and useless; the despair of his sergeant; isolated and characterless: but, conceivable or not, Peter was such a youth. He was now in the outside world that he had dreaded so much when he was at St. Elevenses, the effect being that he was frightened and frozen, afraid to open up and be what he had been in the previous eighteen months. Only once in his life had he experienced anything like this before, and that had been when he had been taken from the protected family atmosphere and put in the hospital, and later put in the preparatory school. But he had been very young then, and now that he was eighteen one would have expected him to be adult enough to be able to take the displacement from one way of life to another without such preposterous results manifesting themselves in his character and behaviour. The explanation lies in the fact that Peter was always so sensitive that his sensitivity was abnormal, and he was permanently in a state of psychosis, and was a psychiatric case: but nobody had ever thought of sending him to a psychiatrist, least of all Peter. Even in later life Peter never became a normal person in this sense, for he always hid from life; sought protected atmospheres; was intensely self-absorbed and introspective; hid from life in his marriage; was antisocial; and was eccentric. As he grew older, before and after his marriage, he hid behind many things, one of these protective barriers being a tendency to laugh at himself; a habit that made other people laugh at him too, of course. But when he became a professional man he expanded and lived a fuller life through his work, work that did not bring him into contact with people very much, putting his hitherto frustrated and twisted energies into his work, it being obvious then how enormous those frustrated energies were, and how difficult it must have been to contain them when they had no outlet, for he became a tremendously hard worker: those energies, when they had no such outlet, such a time being when he was in the Army, went foul within him, and caused him to live in a state of psychosis.

Peter was scared of the rough confidence of the semi-educated youths in his own platoon—youths who were confident with girls. There were one or two fellows he was not so scared of. There was the other platoon imbecile—a clumsy great oaf, with untidy hair, a huge mouth, stupid rolling brown eyes, and huge hands—who accidentally barged Ginger's bed every time he walked down the aisle, while Ginger was trying to read a letter from his mother, stretched out on the top of the bed; until one day the quietly confident, unassuming, and long-suffering Ginger, who was not very big or naturally aggressive, rushed at the oaf, and sent him sprawling down the dormitory, to the encouraging shouts of: 'That's right, Ginger: teach the silly b—— a lesson.' And there was the ex-sixth-former, public-school product, who obviously had officer-potential, and who realized that Peter and he had a link of sorts amongst the uneducated scum, because they both had the same superior airs, and could both talk about psychology and philosophy; although Peter's contributions to the conversations were comparable to a musician playing by ear, were clichéd and not properly understood, and were parrot imitations of what Peter had heard Splay-foot Sam talk about on so many occasions. But mainly Peter lived with no means of contact with the other members of his platoon; and as a result of seeing his behaviour on the rifle-range, and on the parade-ground, they treated him as an even bigger insanity-case than the oaf who jogged Ginger's bed when he went by.

Peter did the preliminary course in the barracks, and after that course the boys would be assigned to their regiments. But Peter never got as far as being assigned to a regiment.

The platoon was to have a passing-out parade, but as Peter could not march in step he was left behind to wash out the latrines, for the sergeant was proud of his record regarding the training of raw recruits, and he did not want it smudged by Peter doing something during the passing-out parade, such as dropping his rifle or sticking his bayonet in the side of another member of the platoon. Peter protested when he found he was to be the only one left out of the passing-out parade, for he had his Elevensinian pride. But the lance-corporal (the one disliked by the platoon, not the white-headed corporal) told him that he was no good at marching; that he was a regular threat (for example, the time when he had nearly blown the whole platoon up on grenade practice); that it would be better for the platoon if Peter stayed behind; and that anyway the latrines were dirty and needed cleaning. Very resentfully Peter went and stared at the urinals with his bucket and mop. And, when his platoon were doing their stuff on the parade-ground, Peter watched them from the inside of the building through an upstairs window. Peter was outraged: how disgraceful for an Elevensinian to be left out of the platoon's passing-out parade.

Peter was again left behind after all the other members of his platoon had left the training barracks to join their regiments; and three weeks of idling around, waiting for his discharge, followed. The army opticians had decided that Peter should never have been let into the Army in the first place; that the medical examination he had had for the Army when he was in civvy-street had been faulty; and that Peter's extreme myopia made him absolutely useless to the Army, for if while in battle he had lost his glasses he might have been so short-sighted that he might have thrown a grenade at part of his own regiment, or run into the enemy trenches thinking that they were those of his own platoon.

They kept Peter in Danderstown-upon-Hab barracks; and Peter spent his time divided between eating Naafi cakes in the rear portion of the quartermaster-sergeant's office and doing odd jobs, like rolling up blankets for a filthy old A.T.S. girl, who told him that she was sure he would prefer to be rolling girls instead: she was right, of course, but that was not the way to talk to an ex-Elevensinian.

Peter did not belong to any corps, platoon, or regiment now; and he was put in a dormitory with a number of other oddments the army authorities in Danderstown-upon-Hab barracks did not know what to do with at that time. When the sergeant-major asked him one day what he was doing, Peter tried to sound educated, by saying that he was waiting for his discharge because he had myopia: Peter knew the sergeant-major would not know what myopia was. But the sergeant-major, an ugly tempered war-veteran, just said: 'What the hell's that?' as if Peter was talking rubbish, and walked away.

It was during this last three weeks of his nine weeks of army service that Peter became a policeman for two days, and he felt very important: he nearly let the prisoner escape, but that was the sort of behaviour that the Army now expected of Peter: why they made him a deserter-escort will for ever remain a mystery, no doubt.

Peter went over to the cookhouse, to get some food for the journey to where the deserter had been temporarily detained before being escorted back to Danderstown-upon-Hab barracks by Peter and the blond, and good-looking, corporal. Peter had in his hands two mess-tins, gleaming flashily, one being his and one being the corporal's; and he looked round the door of the cookhouse tentatively. Inside was a massive man in an apron, who had a shock of red hair in a rather elevated position, and a pair of steel army glasses somewhat lower but still far above Peter. (Simple Simon met a pieman . . .) Cautiously Peter prepared to speak to the vulgar fat giant amongst the kitchen activity and smells: Peter thought he might get his head bitten off when he asked for some food, for he was not acquainted with this cookhouse man, and knew from a previous experience that some of the gentlemen in the cookhouse were extremely irritable, and prone to deliver invective at the slightest provocation. But this particular one turned out to be very generous, and not at all as Peter had expected. 'Hold out your two mess-tins,' roared the giant scullion; and into each tin he slapped a sandwich of vast proportions, consisting of two preposterous chunks of bread-and-butter, enclosing an equally preposterous layer of meat-roll (1946, American type), the obscene pink meat-roll being drenched in tomato ketchup. Peter felt very grateful, even though he hated tomato ketchup; and with the two loaded mess-tins in his hands he went outside into the late-autumn sunshine that bleached the parade-ground.

The blond corporal did not know Peter, and so he treated him at first as if he were a perfectly normal human being: this treatment pleased Peter, for he was convinced that he was indeed a perfectly normal human being. They left Danderstown-upon-Hab, took a train, and arrived in the late evening at the barracks where the deserter was being kept. As they passed through the barracks entrance-way, the corporal, who had up until now seemed to Peter to be a sensitive chap, shouted to a. member of a group of soldiers hanging around: 'Hey, cocker! Where is Block B?' Peter then realized that the corporal was not a subtle, sensitive, and gentle soul, and he realized why the man had been made a corporal. They slept in neighbouring beds in a dormitory filled with regular soldiers, and Peter's forehead was all that was visible above the army blankets that covered him: a sergeant came in, and thinking that Peter was the usual occupant of the bed Peter was in, the usual occupant being a regular soldier of a mature age, he addressed Peter in a friendly and familiar way, soon realizing his mistake good-naturedly when the corporal put him right: Peter was inordinately pleased that he had been mistaken for a mature regular who was one of the boys, for he was usually mistaken for a cretin.

Peter shaved in the morning, unable to exactly locate with his razor the position of the side of his face in space, and very disturbed by all the unfamiliar faces that peered, on either side of him, into the long horizontal mirror, the result being that his chin was very raw as he walked from the wash-rooms to the dining-hall in the fresh morning air. The corporal was sitting alone at a table in the deserted dining-hall, and as Peter sat down beside him he ordered Peter's breakfast. Peter enjoyed that breakfast, eating with a non-commissioned officer who occasionally addressed remarks to him: Peter felt this was a more fitting way for an ex-Elevensinian to eat his breakfast, infinitely superior to eating with a mass of stripeless scum, who had no proper respect for an ex-Elevensinian. The corporal had still not discovered that Peter was an imbecile.

The deserter did not seem to be any older than Peter. It turned out that he was a newly called-up National Serviceman, who had been stationed at Danderstown-upon-Hab, when he ran back to his mother because he was so frightened of army life: it appeared that Peter was not the only delicate soul who had been frightened by army life. He was not the only boy who, having lived in a protected atmosphere, found army life too much for him. Peter had expected the deserter to be a tough criminal type, but he found the boy was silent and frightened. The corporal sat with Peter and the deserter in the back of a huge, grim, dark, covered lorry, that bumped along the roads through the town, from the barracks to the railway-station. Peter looked out of the back of the dark lorry at the breezy and light town-scenes, that changed rapidly as the lorry rumbled on. One hand of the deserter and one hand of the corporal were handcuffed together.

It appeared that Peter had been to a certain extent right about the corporal, when he formerly judged him to be a sensitive man, for before they got on the train the corporal took away the handcuffs, because he thought that it would have been embarrassing for the young deserter to have to sit amongst other people with the handcuffs on, and that the handcuffs might have frightened any old lady who might be in the compartment in the train. In the carriage Peter sat opposite the deserter and the corporal, and, telling Peter to watch the deserter carefully, the corporal dozed off to sleep. After a while the deserter asked Peter if he could go to the toilet, and he asked with such a sense of self-righteousness that Peter let him go. While the deserter was out of the compartment the corporal awoke, and when he saw that the deserter was there no more he asked Peter about it in a very worried way. When Peter explained the position, the corporal actually blushed, because he was embarrassed by Peter's idiocy, and from then onwards the corporal realized what all the other army personnel had realized at Danderstown-upon-Hab— that Peter was mentally deficient. Fortunately for Peter and the corporal the deserter returned to the compartment.

. . . . .

The dormitory that all the oddments were in was in the shape of a letter 'L', and was presided over by a friendly young corporal, who had pin-up girls on the inside of the tall door of his locker. Peter found himself amongst a very peculiar bunch of bits and pieces indeed.

There was the 'Herbert' for instance. He firmly considered that he was the best-looking fellow in the dormitory, and he said as much frequently, as he walked down the dormitory advertising his talents. He was a big oafish chap, similar in some ways to the imbecile who had continually barged into Ginger's bed when Peter was in the General Service Corps. Why he considered that his lumpish head was beautiful Peter did not know. The Herbert boasted that in his home town he had not only had a girl, but he had two girl-friends. This certainly impressed Peter, who did not have even one, but he came to the conclusion that the Herbert's girl-friends must have been very ugly.

And then there was Jew-boy Bernstein. Jew-boy Bernstein seemed to have been in the Army as a National Serviceman for a long time, for he knew the ropes, and said so frequently in his boasting, egotistical, garrulous manner. Jew-boy wore gold-rimmed glasses; had a dark, small, concealed face beneath dirty black hair; was small; and vital in his grubby and unclean way. Jew-boy would always be pleased to tell you the best way to do anything, for he considered that he knew it all: he would not have found life at St. Elevenses very congenial or sympathetic to him. Jew-boy had a mild business going on in the dormitory: he had a clothes-pressing service.

He worked hard at his business as a Jew will; but what did not seem to be characteristically Jewish was the fact that the remuneration he received for the pants-pressing that he did in the evenings was far from sufficient to make him into a millionaire. On Friday evenings he did most of his work on an ironing-board placed in the aisle in everybody's way, for some of the chaps wanted their uniforms to look nice for the Saturday-afternoon dances in the town of Danderstown-upon-Hab. But Jew-boy Bernstein had not reckoned with Peter providing competition.

Peter had a certain amount of Jewish blood in his veins, that came from Arthur's side of the family, although he had no idea it was within him at this time. And, as we well know, Peter had great experience in founding business enterprises. But Jewish as he might have been, Peter had no instinctive sympathy for Bernstein, for he had been brought up as a pure Englishman, and he loathed the appearance and manners of the grubby, egotistical Bernstein.

The boys in the 'oddments' dormitory were not doing any kind of training, and, unlike the boys in Peter's former platoon, they were not interested in proficiency in army training: some of them were waiting for discharge like Peter, and goodness knows what the others were doing. They were not so aware of each other as the boys in Peter's former platoon had been, and they were not interested in judging Peter as an idiot. In fact, as they did not have any opportunity to see Peter making a fool of himself in training or on the parade-ground (these activities had finished for Peter and for them now), they were unaware of the fact that Peter was dumb. Another important fact was that a number of these boys in the oddments dormitory were also useless characters like Peter, and there was a general atmosphere of imbecility, in which imbeciles went unobserved and uncriticized. Naturally Peter felt more at home in this atmosphere, and he did not feel so self-conscious or reserved. In fact Peter showed a little initiative for the first time at Danderstown-upon-Hab barracks while he was in the oddments dorm.

Peter's hair had grown by now, and he wore his army beret

at a rakish slant on his head, the beret being pushed back to reveal some of the hair-line and a carefully placed kiss-curl. In an imbecilic way he was becoming an old stager at the barracks, which was mostly filled with raw recruits who had not known Danderstown-upon-Hab barracks as long as Peter had. Sometimes Peter would give patronizing advice to chaps who had just been called up, and who had only been in the barracks for a week or less. Only oddments and the training staff stayed on at Danderstown-upon-Hab barracks for more than the six weeks' preliminary training period. Peter felt a little confidence growing within him, but if he had been sent to another barracks, amongst unfamiliar surroundings and unfamiliar faces, he would have closed up completely again, and his brain would have seized up into stupidity. However, confident to a small degree as he was now, he still acted in a moronic manner.

Peter had had to iron his own trousers when he had been living with Harriet and Perce; and as he watched Jew-boy Bernstein ironing away at the ironing-board at the end of Peter's bed, Peter considered that he could do that, too. As the iron and the ironing-board were the property of the dormitory, and not the property of any one individual, Peter took over on some evenings, undercut the Jew-boy price-wise, and ironed out rather badly the trousers and tops of some of the chaps. The Jew-boy poured scorn on Peter's creases, but, as his creases were actually no better than Peter's, Peter stayed in business. Jew-boy Bernstein did not like Peter at all.

Peter was easily influenced. He was put in more than one dormitory of oddments while he was waiting through the final three weeks for his discharge, and in those dormitories he came in contact with some undesirable characters. Peter began to forget Elevensinian standards as he listened to some of the stories that were told to him. He had been influenced to the good at St. Elevenses, and now the impressionable and gullible Peter was being influenced the other way. The imbeciles talked to him, for he was one of them. These are some of the stories that Peter heard, that made him think that to have Elevensinian standards was perhaps not the best thing.

A tall, twenty-three-year-old ex-lorry driver, who slept in a
bed next to Peter's: 'I went on this army P.T. course: they
wanted to train me to be a P.T. instructor, but when I got
there they decided I was not well-muscled enough, so they
sent me back. I must have left my muscles there, and I'm
waiting for them to send them back to me by post in a parcel.'
And: 'That chap over there wanted to urinate in the night,
but as he could not be bothered to go out to the latrines he
did it out of the window, by which window his rifle was
leaning at the time, and when he woke up in the morning and
looked at his rifle he found that he had mis-aimed, and that
the rifle-barrel was full of urine.' Or: 'I was driving my lorry
in an area I did not know, and as I had lost my way I knocked
on this woman's door to ask her the way: her husband was
away at the time, and she said she liked me, and asked me
in, but as I had to get my lorry back to my boss I could not
afford the time to stay: she was quite nice, and I often wonder
what would have happened if I had stayed in her house.' A
younger and imbecilic boy asked Peter to write a letter to
his mum for him because he could not write, and for some
reason he told Peter this: 'There was this woman-friend of
my mother's in the house, you see, and as she had not had
it, she got me—I was very young, and did not know what it
was all about—to go into the bedroom, and give her what she
had not had recently.' As he told Peter this his eyes were
full of wonder, as he remembered the woman's behaviour, and
he smiled at Peter from his weak blue eyes. These were not
the kind of stories that Elevensinians told, and they suggested
to Peter that the world was not only as he had seen it from
within the walls of St. Elevenses. Peter wished that he had
been a lorry-driver, and he wished that his mother had had
a friend like that. He began to think that a depraved life was
the thing, and that is why he wanted to steal the watch that
he found on the wash-basin.

While he was in the dormitory that Bernstein was in,
Peter went late one evening to have a wash and a hair-do
in the empty combined wash-room and urinal-room. He
arranged his hair, and then just as he was going to leave the

white-tiled room he saw a fine and flashy watch on the wash-stand next to the one he had been using. Peter had never had a watch, and with his mind filled with bad influences he began to covet the watch that he fondled in his hand. It was certainly too late to give it to the corporal, for the corporal was asleep by his locker full of pin-up pictures, so Peter put the lovely watch in his pocket. But Peter was not a thief, and the criminality of his intentions worried him. Another boy from the oddments dorm came into the wash-room, just as Peter was leaving, and Peter could not restrain himself from showing the watch to the boy, and telling him that it was the property of someone else. Peter was sure that all the boys in the lower-classes had no moral standards, and he was sure that the other boy would think that to steal the watch was the only sensible thing to do in the circumstances. As they returned to the sleeping and dark dormitory, Peter went up to the other boy, and in a whisper told him not to tell the corporal about the watch: the boy looked embarrassed at this blatant and unashamed confession of evil intentions. Peter thought about the watch as he lay in bed, and when he gave the watch to the corporal the following morning he felt he had been weak: he was sure the corporal would keep the watch for himself, and perhaps he was right in thinking this.

.   .   .   .   .

Peter still walked alone in Danderstown-upon-Hab town on Saturday afternoons, but now he felt slightly more con-fident, and he hoped that the kiss-curl that issued out from beneath his back-worn army beret, and which decorated his forehead, would get him a cheap Danderstown-upon-Hab girl. But he wandered the streets until it was very late without ever picking up a girl. One evening, when it was almost time for him to return to the barracks, and when he was approaching the barracks, his mind full of the memories of the 'girl and boy' scenes he had seen so many of that after-noon in the town, Peter felt rather desperate, and was ready to make an effort. He felt that he just could not return empty-handed to the barracks again. He looked round him for a girl, and saw one ahead of him who seemed quite suitable. He quickened his heavy step, and began to catch up with the girl. As she heard him marching after her she probably felt frightened. She quickened her own steps, and turned down a side-street. Peter turned also from the empty road that led up the hill to the barracks, and heavy-footed it down the narrow and deserted street after her. She probably thought that he was another Jack the Ripper, and she hurried her high heels in a way that should have put Peter off. But Peter was too desperate to be put off by an unencouraging manner; and anyway he was used to sensing unencouragement in girls. He came up behind her, and said: 'Excuse me,' in a hoarse and passion-choked voice: she stopped and turned to him, but her reaction was not as Hilda's had been when Peter first spoke to her. 'Yes?' said the girl questioningly, obviously scared out of her few wits, and wishing that the boy-friend she had just left in the town was with her now. She was quite a nice girl, but eager to get away. 'Would you come out with me some time?' asked Peter, his desperation having given him courage. 'No, I'm sorry,' said the girl, without being nasty, and she went on down the road, leaving Peter to make his way dejectedly and wearily up the hill to the barracks. Why couldn't he get a girl like the other chaps did?

.   .   .   .   .

Peter was going to get demobbed. He had been in the Army for nine weeks, but he was to be fully outfitted with demob clothes, and he was even going to be given a civvy-street hat. Peter wondered how Harriet and Perce would receive him when he returned, and he decided to buy a present for Perce. Peter did not smoke, but as he could get cigarettes at Naafi prices he had once sent home to Perce a packet of cigarettes. Now he intended to go a bit further. He was allowed, on demob, to buy a large quantity of cigarettes at the Naafi at the usual low Naafi prices, and he bought his full quota, intending to give it all to Perce as a gift.

.   .   .   .   .

They were all going on the train from Danderstown-upon-Hab to the demob clothes-centre—Peter, Withered Arm, and Veteran. Withered Arm had been in the Army only as long as Peter, but Veteran had been in a long time. Veteran explained to the other two in the railway-carriage compartment that he had been mixed up with a nymphomaniac, and he told them that she had been too passionate for him. Peter wondered how any man could turn away female sexual advances, for the girl that the veteran described seemed just what the sexually frustrated Peter wanted: he had been frustrated so long that he could have taken on a whole army of nymphomaniacs, and then some. Withered Arm was a tubby youth who was being discharged from the Army because he could not use his arm, but Withered Arm had been crafty when he always dropped his rifle on parade as if his arm could not lift it, for Withered Arm could lift a kit-bag easily with that arm that got him out of his National Service. Before he had been called up, when he was working in the factory, Withered Arm had made a £5 bet with a work-mate that he could get out of the Army by pretending that his withered arm was useless. Withered Arm had acted a good part when he got in the Army, dropping everything from his withered arm, and now he was to be demobbed he told his story to the veteran and Peter with restrained pride and a subtle smile that never left his pleased eyes. Withered Arm was looking forward to getting back to the factory and collecting his five quid winnings. He had fooled all the army medical examiners, and he was quietly proud of it. He certainly had been clever. His arm was indeed withered, and the bicep was shrivelled, but although it looked useless it was in fact quite a strong arm. It was probably the first time his withered arm had come in useful to him; and in his earlier days he had probably never thought that his arm would do him a service one day. Withered Arm had had his shrivelled limb from birth, and as a young boy he had probably bemoaned the fact that he was not physically like other boys; but now his deformity had paid a dividend at last. As the train got nearer the demob clothes centre Peter gave some thought to the pre-army-entry medical examinations, that were sometimes so badly done that people like him were sent into the Army, only to be medically discharged again after they had been medically examined once more when they were actually in the Army. Obviously the pre-army-entry medical examiners had not believed Withered Arm when he told them that he could not use his arm, which had been perceptive of them rather than slack; but when Withered Arm got on the the parade-ground he played such a part that the army medicals were forced to believe that the arm was useless, whether they liked to or not.

The demobilization clothes centre had long tables in a vast room, on which were piled various articles of clothing. Peter and the other two soldiers walked along by the tables, choosing what they wanted. The other two chose their clothes fairly quickly and waited for Peter for hours outside the building, because Peter, unaware that they were waiting for him, took an interminable time choosing his overcoat and sports-coat from the racks that were in enclosures at the far end of the table-filled room. With all their demob clothes in three big cardboard boxes, one box each, the three soldiers got on the train again to go back to Danderstown-upon-Hab. A girl got in the compartment and sat opposite Peter. Unable to look at her, and embarrassed by her gaze, Peter pretended to go to sleep.

25

Civvy-street

In his army uniform, hugging his box of demob clothes to him, and with a parcel containing all the cigarettes he intended to give to Perce, Peter sat in the empty railway-carriage compartment, as the train took him from Terminus Cross station to Balsham. A man and his young son got in the compartment and sat opposite Peter: Peter was looking out of the window, by the door with the big leather strap in the middle of it. The man looked curiously from Peter to the familiar box that lay on Peter's lap, and then, his curiosity getting the better of him, he asked Peter if he had just been demobbed, for he thought that he recognized the type of cardboard box that Peter had.

Peter felt rather gay as he walked down the slope from the railway-station to the main road that ran through the shopping centre of Balsham; but as he looked to his right he remembered Sally, who lived in that direction, and a wave of nostalgia swept over him, But his nostalgic sadness soon disappeared as he walked through the small town, for he was overjoyed to see all the familiar scenes again, the shops he knew so well, and the pavements he had trodden so many times in so many different moods.

He stood outside the door of his grandmother's house, and, feeling that his homecoming was a dramatic occasion, he knocked on the door. His grandmother opened the door and looked at the army figure on her doorstep without recognition. Peter looked so different that she did not see that it was he at first.

Perce hardly welcomed Peter at all, for he had thought that when Peter went into the Army he would be rid of him for two long happy years. Harriet made a meal for Peter, and Peter ate it alone at the table, as Perce sat morosely by the fire listening to the radio. When Peter had finished his meal he put his bare elbows on the table, and sat there happily in his army shirt with rolled-up sleeves, feeling that he was the centre of interest, and revelling in it. He was not a soldier home from the wars, but he was a soldier come home, and he felt that was dramatic enough.

Peter intended to make the most of his peace-offering to Perce, and, with an acute sense of his own generosity, he asked Perce if he would like a large number of Naafi cigarettes —his demob quota. Perce did not know whether he was being asked to buy them, or whether they were a gift, so to be on the safe side he said to Peter, his face peculiarly fierce and confused: 'Yes, I'll buy them from you, Peter, if you want to sell them'—as if he was doing Peter a favour. Peter was stunned, for he thought that his gift was being refused, and that Perce was not willing to accept a peace-offering. Peter was so disappointed that he could not bring himself to tell Perce that the cigarettes were meant as a gift, and in a stunned manner he sold them to his uncle.

Peter went back to his seat by the table, and looking up from his empty supper plate he asked Perce if they would mind if he stayed there in the grandmother's house. Peter did not expect any difficulty with this request, for he was sure that they would realize that he had nowhere else to go, and that to get diggings would be terrible for the dependent Peter. Peter was terrified when Perce said: 'We will have to ask your grandmother. If she says you can stay then you can: it is her house.' His uncle's hate of him was made obvious to Peter; he had thought that nine weeks' absence would have healed everything. Later on, in the evening of the following day, Perce told Peter reluctantly that his grandmother had said that he could stay.

But Peter was not to live at his grandmother's house as he had lived before. His upstairs front bedroom, which had been quite spacious, had been taken over by the little daughter of Perce and Harriet, and Peter was put in the tiny room that his grandfather had once used as a book store. Peter hung up his brown demob overcoat in the wardrobe opposite the window, tried on his civvy-street hat, and sat down disconsolately on the bed beneath the window, looking, with a sense of claustrophobia, at the two feet of floor that separated the bed from the wardrobe.

Peter had to get a job. A job in the outside world. He was qualified for no job except labouring, and it was a frightening prospect. The Army had been bad enough, but now he really would have to face the outside world, a world with not even the barrack walls around it. His poor, sensitive, and raw soul. Could he manage to find courage enough to expose that soul to the outside world? Peter would have done anything to avoid going out to work in the cruel world, but as he had no money he had no alternative—he would have to go to the labour exchange in Balham.

WHARFLAND

Peter stood by the circular saw in his army uniform, and fed wood into the voracious steel teeth. Peter did not talk to anybody, and barriered off from the others he handled the wood with hands covered with massive gloves. Amidst the machinery of the saw the engineer could be seen, covered in grease. Peter stepped aside, and let the slick-haired young man, who lived only to 'get up the apples and pears, and have a kip', take over from him. As the labourer fed wood along the conveyor-belt, to the teeth, Peter collected more wood for the labourer to feed, and then, when there was a goodly pile, he waited idly and watched, or, with one hand in his pocket, handed single logs to the labourer. The company director was an angry man with dark hair, a dark face, and glasses: he reminded Peter slightly of his father: the company director wanted work from the men his firm paid wages to, and when he saw Peter with one hand in his pocket he yelled at him through the deafening noise that the vicious and ever-ravenous saw was making.

Peter could lift the sacks of logs on to his back, but he made strained faces as he did so, and the slick-haired labourer looked on with contempt, thinking that Peter was not very strong. Peter took each sack to a coal-hole, and emptied the wood through the hole, the logs tumbling down a long way on to the floor of the boiler-room below. Peter let the logs accumulate into a huge pile in the room below the coal-hole, and he could just see a man looking at the accumulating pile—a man who tended the boiler, and who was in the room below. Peter was letting the logs spread out in confusion on the floor below, and the boilerman looked up at Peter with hate in his eyes: Peter should have emptied the sacks so that the logs piled neatly, but of course Peter was disconcerted by his new job, and he did it clumsily. When Peter went back to lift another sack on to his back, the labourer contemptuously shouldered him aside, and began to hump the sacks himself: for Peter's grimaces as he had lifted the heavy sacks had made the labourer quite sure that Peter was not strong enough for the job. Peter felt slighted, and told himself that he was a very strong lad. When he got home that evening he took out his muscle-building springs, and strained at them in the confines of his tiny bedroom. When he had had enough exercise he knelt on his bed and looked through the bedroom window at the occasional girl who would go by along the pavement in front of his grandmother's house.

They moved Peter to the company premises that bordered the River Limber, just below the bridge at the end of the town. On Peter's shoulder was a leather pad, but that did not prevent the huge stacks of timber that Peter had to carry on his shoulder from making a sore place there. But he bit his teeth, six long lengths of unplaned timber on his shoulder, his thorax driven down into his pelvis with the weight, as he carried the wood from a wood-pile on the water's edge by the barges, to a wood-pile on the other side of the wood-yard. Peter longed to be asked to carry wood from the moored and loaded barges, along bouncing planks that led from the barge

to the wharf, to piles near the water's edge. He envied the bare-torsoed and heavily muscled labourers he saw running with their shoulder-loads along the springy gangway from the barge that was low in the water to the shore. How their muscles became defined as the labourers bounced with the spring of the gangplank below their heavy feet, the ends of the planks piled on their shoulders clapping as they ran: they earned their money, and their muscles were hard as the wood they carried. But Peter was not allowed to do that work, and he sorted piles of timber with the slick-haired blond labourer, who often quoted his father as if his father had been an oracle, holding on to one end of a number of planks as the blond man held on to the other end, one at one end of the wood-pile, and one the other end. They were sorting the planks into piles of the same lengths of wood. Peter was so idiotic in this strange setting that he handled the wood badly, not synchronizing his movements with those of the labourer, and later Peter heard the blond man complain that Peter must have something wrong with his hands. By one side of the yard stood an old man, who had been kept on by the firm after he had become useless, because he had been with them so long. He did odd jobs around the yard. He spent all the time shouting angrily, and with a furious face, at the others, telling them that they were doing everything wrongly. His language was bluer than the water by the still barges, and the labourers told each other that he was senile and soon to cross the Stygian ferry. During his dinner-break Peter went out of the yard to a cake shop, bought a large bag of fattening cakes, and ate them at the water's edge, looking up at the girls passing across the bridge that arched high above him. Before he went home he would go to the public baths in Balham. As the bath filled with hot water Peter watched it nakedly, and fingered the blood on his raw shoulder. He decided that he could not keep the job up much longer, partly because his shoulder was becoming so bad, and partly because he could not stand the company of the crude men any longer. What did those crude oafs know about philosophy? thought Peter to himself, as he rubbed the tiny cake of soap over his muscle-hardening body. They treated him as if he was the idiot, but his inner thoughts told him that it was really the other way round. How he longed to be in academic company again—back in the sixth form at St. Elevenses. Gingerly he applied the soap over the wound on his shoulder, and his body stood in the bath, white, strong, and healthy.

26

Monastic Sanctuary Again

P E T E R had an inferiority complex because he had failed the Higher School Certificate examination. Only very inferior Elevensinians failed their examinations, and Peter wanted to have another try at the examination. He had been well educated, had passed the G.S.C. examination, and was academically superior to the labourers and to the boys he had met in the Army; but he did not look at it that way, and only saw it as his headmster would have seen it, for Peter's headmaster would have looked upon Peter as a failure. Peter felt that before he went into the outside world permanently he must pass the exam he had failed.

Also Peter wanted to postpone a permanent existence in the outside world as long as he could, and he wanted to hide again within the walls of his old school. Desperately he racked his brains after he had left the wood-yard, having worked there for only a few weeks, for he wanted to escape from the workaday world, having had quite enough of it since he left the school at the end of the previous summer term.

Peter longed to return into the form called 6A: all his acquaintances who had been in that form when he was in it had left the school now—Coffee and the others; and the constitution of 6A would now be changed, but Splay-foot Sam would now be in that form, and they would be Elevensinians there, and that meant a lot to Peter. He wanted to return to hold on to the apron-strings of Saint Elevenses.

.   .   .   .   .

Peter went to the school to see the headmaster. Peter waited outside the secretary's office, his army trousers showing below his overcoat. The old headmaster was going to leave the school that term, and he was waiting for his replacement to take over from him, so that he could retire, go for leisurely walks with his stick, and die in peace, away from boys. He was an Elevensinian institution. The Spring term had started, and it was in the month of January. When the headmaster let Peter into his office he thought that Peter was on leave from the Army, and had just come back like all the other recent school-leavers to pay a brief visit, to go round all the classrooms, and to have sentimental chats with all the masters. When Peter told him that he wanted to come back to the school to retake the exam the headmaster smiled as if he knew that Peter wanted sanctuary, patted Peter on the shoulder, and told him that the new headmaster would take care of him. Peter did not know that the new headmaster was an ex-brigadier, who was to establish army rule in the school.

. . . . .

They gave Peter a further grant of money, and the club that Arthur had belonged to continued their grant also. Peter closed his eyes to the outside world with a feeling of relief, and determined to pass the examination even if it killed him: Elevensinians did not fail exams—it was an unheard-of disgrace.

Peter had to do revision. He did not have to take the 6A classes again. His exercise books were full from the previous year's teaching and what he had to do was to revise. He asked Grate if he could work in the bookroom that was next to Grate's room, and in the narrow room surrounded by the school's supply of text books Peter established himself.

Peter now felt that he was above the authority of the prefects, and almost above the authority of the staff. He felt arrogant. Was he not older than the other sixth-formers, an ex-service man? And how could he be expected to take orders from the new prefects, some of whom had been nippers when

Peter had been fifteen—when Peter had been a respected fighter? Why, Peter felt he was a man: those junior prefects had been almost babes in arms when he was fighting heroic battles with Smithers or Packagger. He lived a retiring life in the extreme sanctuary of the bookroom, glowered at everybody, and considered that it was beneath his dignity to speak to anybody but members of the staff or the older sixthformers.

Peter came to school late now, for it was not for a man like him to come to school at the proper time—the school morning assembly was for the children. Peter approached the back door of the school one morning, after the school had started, and while from the big hall came the sound of mass hymn-singing. The names of late-comers were being entered in prefects' notebooks at the back door; and there was a small queue of bad boys leading to the back door that was used by late-comers, that being the prescribed method of entry for such criminal types. There were two prefects standing just inside the back door; Welling and a priggish boy who was a junior prefect, and who had been so young when Peter was fifteen. Peter was not going to take orders from that priggish kid. Peter barged past Welling and the junior prefect without giving his name. Welling did not care: he respected Peter because Peter had been willing to fight him in the boxing finals on a previous occasion; and anyway he was a tolerant prefect who did not have to force his prefect authority to obtain respect as the junior prefect did. Peter charged gloweringly along the deserted corridor, arrogantly ignoring the calls of the junior prefect. Peter dashed up the long curving stairs that led to the upper floor where was his bookroom sanctuary, and the junior prefect caught up with him on those stairs. Peter refused to come back to the back door to have his name taken down in the regular manner, and he brushed rudely past the indignant junior prefect, and haughtily continued up the stairs in a kingly rage. What did they think he was—a schoolboy? Later on the form-master of 6A came to the bookroom, and told Peter that the junior prefect had made a complaint to him, and asked Peter to apologize to the junior prefect. The form-master was not a master who was respected by the boys, and although he was a nice chap he was considered to be soft, and his discipline was poor. Peter absolutely refused to lower himself to apologize to the little-policeman junior prefect, and the form-master weakly accepted his arrogance. When the master had gone, Peter fumed all morning in the bookroom, and did not do a scrap of work until dinnertime. These puffed-up junior prefects—they had no respect for age.

Peter's house had a meeting in their house-room, and Peter was supposed to attend, but even that was below Peter's dignity, and he stayed in the bookroom. The house-meeting was held in the 6A form-room, the room that belonged to the soft master just mentioned, and the meeting was presided over by that master. The roll-call was taken, and, when it was discovered that Peter was absent, a boy was sent to the bookroom to tell Peter to attend the meeting. But Peter was now afraid to attend, for if he went along he would have to enter the room full of boys who would be waiting for him, the meeting being held up by Peter; and if Peter entered the whole roomful of boys would look at him, a thing that Peter could not bear, because, under all his act of manliness and aggression, Peter was a shy and embarrassed soul. Peter haughtily told the boy to tell the master that he was too busy, and gleefully the boy returned to the house-meeting, to tell the master, in front of all the silent and waiting assembly, that Peter had said, sir, that he was too busy.

THE READING OF THE WILL

For a month or so now Grandma had been confined to her bed, and every day a nurse came to her bedroom to help her perform some natural functions. The old lady had nothing to live for now that her husband had died, and soon afterwards she went up there to find him.

Some time after the old lady's death the whole family of relations assembled in the small sitting-dining-room at the back of the house, to hear the will read by the generally accepted head of the family—Cousin Trevor's enterprising father. How they all got into the room together it is impossible to say. Chairs were brought from all over the tiny house, and the family sat all round the room. Very seldom did the family assemble in such force. Cousin Trevor's father was the only one who stood. He was to read the will, and he stood, with a certain delight in the importance of his position, warming his arse in front of the fire. On occasions like this they always called on Cousin Trevor's father. He was the most respected member of the family; he had made more money than any of his brothers; and his children were the most intelligent children. He was in his 'evening at home' clothes: a dark, nautical-looking blazer with shiny brass buttons, and grey flannel trousers. There was Cousin Trevor, who had shot up recently until he was taller than either his father or mother; there was Auntie Myrtle, looking glamorous as usual; there was Auntie Maggie, looking exactly the opposite of her sister Myrtle; there were Maggie's two daughters; there was, of course, Auntie Harriet, and Uncle Perce telling himself that he was quite as good as the rest of them; there was Cousin Trevor's sister, looking like a beetroot, and Cousin Trevor's mother, looking upper-middle-class, and educated; and there was Uncle this and Auntie that, and some of their children. The will-reading was begun. Harriet and Perce got the house—for as long as the lease held out, and that was not for long. Perce and Harriet had expected that, and they felt they deserved it, considering that they had looked after the old woman at the end of her life. There was not much else to leave. The rest of the will was concerned with the giving of various articles to various people. Cousin Trevor's father came to the end of the will where a small bequest was made to Peter. He was to get the battered wireless, because he had listened to the dance-music on it so much, and because the old woman thought that he loved it so. But Peter was not present, and Cousin Trevor's father sent the tearful Auntie Maggie to find Peter, so that he could hear of the bequest that had been made to him.

Peter was scared. He was afraid to go down into the room where the family gathering was. He was too embarrassed. He looked out of his bedroom window at the row of cars parked outside the house in the darkness, and he fearfully listened to the sounds in the lower half of the house. He was damned if he would go down. He tried to hide his fear beneath an arrogant fury, but the fear would not be submerged. He pretended to himself that he was busy, and did something as intensely as he could, but he was unable to keep the sounds from below from entering his ears.

Auntie Maggie knocked on his door and told him to come down, with a tearful sense of righteous indignation, annoyed that Peter was not showing proper respect to the dead. Peter hoarsely called through the locked door that he was not going down, and Auntie Maggie, her eyes filled with tears, went downstairs again. But Peter was not to be let off so easily. Auntie Maggie came up again, and with a new authority in her voice told Peter to come down, telling him, to add strength to her request, that his family-head uncle wanted to see him, and that he must come down. Cousin Trevor's father was not to be disobeyed. Peter respected two people despite his arrogance, and they were his headmaster and his successful uncle. Everybody in the family respected the opinions and wishes of Cousin Trevor's father. He was God.

Peter, frightened to death at the prospect of having to go down into the crowded room, opened the bedroom door, and found his auntie Maggie outside. He had never seen his auntie Maggie with tear-filled eyes before, and as he looked at her he told himself that she was being silly. 'I think you had better come down, Peter,' said his middle-aged aunt, 'your uncle has something to say to you.'

Peter opened the door of the sitting- and dining-room, and his innards quailed as he saw the size of the gathering. He went in, and looked round for somewhere to sit. In front of the fire, where his successful uncle stood, was an uncrowded space; and the will-reading having been finished, the uncle was silent. Harriet and Perce sat, with slightly bent heads, to the side of the fire; and when Perce saw Peter he looked at him unpleasantly, his thoughts about Peter being decidedly unpleasant. Peter was desperate. He stood in the room, with all eyes upon him, casting his eyes fearfully and angrily around him, trying to find a seat. He just had to sit somewhere; to become part of the seated crowd: he could not stand much longer, isolated and watched. There was the high-chair that belonged to Harriet's baby son: it was not big enough for Peter's posterior, but it was all there was. Peter squeezed his bottom into the chair, and sat, leaning forward, his hands on his knees, his face red, the wood of the high-chair pinching his bottom, trying to pretend that he was not there at all. He looked round the room furtively, and saw his uncle Perce looking angrily at him because he was probably ruining the baby's high-chair. Peter was too agonized to care what his uncle Perce thought. Peter wished the father of Cousin Trevor would say to him what he had to say, so that Peter could then escape from the room, and rush to safety up the stairs to his tiny bedroom, but his successful uncle did not say anything. Peter looked with sweating terror at the semi-circle of relatives to one side of him, and saw in the middle of the semi-circle of seated figures his cousin Trevor, his overgrown body taller than the others. Cousin Trevor caught his eye, and slightly patronizingly, and with some sweet friendship, he said: 'Hullo, Peter.' Nobody else had said 'Hullo' to the self-pitying Peter. Peter could not stand it any longer, for he could not sit it out any longer either: he felt a complete idiot sitting in the baby's high-chair. Forcing his croaking voice across the room at Cousin Trevor's father, Peter said, with desperate aggression: 'I was told you wanted to speak to me.' Cousin Trevor's father was disconcerted by Peter's aggressive voice, and his eyes tried to laugh away his unease. Peter was surprised to see that he had disconcerted God. 'Well, it was only that . . .' said his uncle, with a little false laugh, '. . . your grandmother left you her wireless in her will.' Peter did not care what he had been left. He just turned and ran. Out of the room and up the stairs. He locked the door of his bedroom behind him, and stood, thanking his stars that it was all over.

27

A Pseudo-Intellectual

St. Stairs was a pseudo-intellectual, and he and Peter got on fine. St. Stairs was in the A.T.C., and the anti-militant Splay-foot Sam directed a warlike fusillade of verbal vitriol at St. Stairs's disconcerted face, but St. Stairs continued to join the others in blue after afternoon school. St. Stairs, a plain-faced, brown-haired, not brilliant boy, talked to the real intellectuals in the sixth; and intellectually he was the link between Peter, who intellectualized stupidly, affectedly, and pretentiously, and the chaps who would soon go to the university—senior prefects, who spent a lot of time socializing in the school library, and who really could think in an adult manner. St. Stairs was not so intelligent as the pre-university, third-year sixth-formers, but they let him talk with them, and when St. Stairs wanted a rest from the strain he would go to Peter, and repeat impressively what they had said—such remarks as: 'You can't believe what you read in the papers—you have to read between the lines if you want the truth.' Peter loved talking about Freud and inhibitions and complexes with St. Stairs, and they analysed each other and themselves very seriously, and at great length. But, much talk as there was about Sigmund, Peter had only a vague idea of what it was all about. He just felt adult talking that way: it did not matter if he understood it all or not. For a while he got *The Times* every day, and carried it about with him, but he did not read a word of the unsensational small print, for he could not understand it: but the *Daily Mirror*—that was another story; and if Peter got hold of that he would read it all—sneering at it loftily afterwards to St. Stairs, for they were above that sort of thing. Peter was in a quandary about Splay-foot Sam. He felt that Sam's interminable intellectualizing, as they walked from the 37 bus-stop after afternoon school (without Hilda now), was just the job, although he did not follow 99 per cent of it; but his loyalties were divided, because some of the more adult sixth-formers laughed at a chap who would wear a red tie if he could, and Peter did not know which was the right intellectual attitude to take towards the oft-uttered brain-activity of Splay-foot Sam. One thing Peter could have been sure of, and that was that he was one hell of a fraud when he was in 6A for the second year running. Oh, he did feel so superior to Perce: why, Perce had probably never heard of Freud.

Peter was a year, or perhaps less, older than St. Stairs, and this made Peter feel that he deserved a better friend, but St. Stairs was all there was really, apart from Sam, and so Peter and St. Stairs became close friends. At breaktimes they would stand in a secluded part of the playground, away from the vulgar crowd, feeling very dignified and superior, and talking intensely about their sexual frustrations and inhibitions, getting what enjoyment they could out of them, by applying Freud to them, and wondering what had happened in their childhood that had made them grow up afraid of girls. St. Stairs was only half as scared of girls as Peter, but that still left him with complexes and inhibitions, as one can readily understand. Peter worked hard in the bookroom from January to July, for he had to pass the exam this time; and when he was not working he was talking superior nonsense to St. Stairs in the bookroom, playing tennis, or walking with St. Stairs through the town, eyeing the girls, wanting them, and despising their tiny shop-girl brains. And Peter did not stop glaring and glowering in the university atmosphere of the upper sixth.

THE YOUTH-CLUB GIRLS

Peter became a member of a marriage bureau. He did not want to get married—Elevensinians did not get married

while they were at school—but he hoped to meet a girl that way. He received various descriptions of girls, but as he wanted a tarty type he rejected them. Peter made it difficult for himself, because he did not want a wallflower: he wanted a girl who attracted men—a girl whose photograph he could show proudly to the chaps in the upper sixth—a girl they would whistle over. He hated the thought of being mixed up with a girl who was a plain Jane. Hilda had been all right; and Cynthia, the girl on the latrine wall, could not have been a wallflower according to the recommendations given to her in pencil below her name and address. Peter wanted a girl that other boys would like; and he felt that if he had a wallflower it would only make clearer, to the world around him, that he was not any good at 'boy-girl' stuff, for only wallflower-boys got wallflower-girls in Peter's book. He was still young enough to be an idealist regarding potential girl-friends; and it was only later on that he abandoned his idealism, after even more years of sexual frustration, and took anything he could get, regardless of whether they were wallflowers or prostitutes. He got a photograph from a very nice girl, who wrote to him as a result of the marriage bureau, and she was willing to meet him. But in the photograph she had wooden beads round her neck, and wooden beads suggested unattractive spinster aunts to Peter, and he did not consider that glamorous girls wore wooden beads. Wooden beads were for the blue-stocking type, and, after all, can you imagine Betty Grable wearing wooden beads round her neck? Peter could not. Peter was in a bit of a fix. The wooden-beads girl had replied to a letter from him, and he had to find a way of putting her off. He wrote her a letter saying that, as he was studying for his examination, he could not allow himself to go out with her, for he said that he should spend all his time studying. She wrote back a nice letter saying that she quite understood, and Peter threw it contemptuously in the waste-paper basket. Wooden beads, indeed—ugh!

St. Stairs went to a youth club. He came to Peter one day and suggested a solution to Peter's problems. St. Stairs could arrange a blind-date for Peter with a girl from the youth club. St. Stairs would come too, and another girl would be St. Stairs's piece. St. Stairs was falling in love with his youth-club girl. The idea was that they should all meet up in London on a Saturday afternoon, when the girls had finished work, and then they would go to the pictures. Going to the pictures with a girl, thought Peter: just the job. Peter felt that his girl-less years were coming to an end, and he asked St. Stairs if his (Peter's) girl was any good. St. Stairs said she had her points, and Peter began to drool with expectation inwardly (it was not done for Elevensinians to drool outwardly, of course).

St. Stairs met Peter in Balham early after dinner, and they went on the train to London together. They were to meet the two girls in a large concrete yard, where the cinema queue would end, and where the two girls would be keeping a place in the queue for Peter and St. Stairs. Peter and St. Stairs came to the queue, and Peter saw the girls. St. Stairs introduced Peter, and Peter looked at what he had got. St. Stairs's girl was passable even though her rubber mackintosh smelt powerfully in the hot sunshine in the big and crowded yard, which Peter did not think was very glamorous of her, because the smell reminded him of a clothes-hanger rack in a musty and gloomy hall by a front door. Peter looked at his blind-date, who was smiling winningly up at him, and he realized that St. Stairs had played a joke on him. Thin, lip-stick-red lips in a fat, plain face. Tiny, too-bright eyes that were close together. And—horror of horrors—she had a figure that was as fat as Peter's disappointment. Peter thought that he did not deserve this: but there was no escape now. The queue began to move, and Peter and the other three moved out of the yard with the slowly moving queue, and came to the front of the cinema, afterwards entering the foyer. Peter paid for his girl, feeling that he was throwing money away.

Fatty sat next to Peter in the half-darkness, and Peter put his feet up on the back of the seat in front of him, and felt he was too good for Fatty. The film had not started yet, and the dim lights were still on. St. Stairs grinned at Peter from his seat by Smelly Mackintosh, and Peter hated him. Fatty took off her overcoat, and Peter looked down out of the corner of his eye. The fact that he saw that she had a forty-two-inch chest bulging her light-blue thin wool sweater made no difference to his dislike of her, for she had similar preposterous dimensions all over her body. She liked him glancing at her chest, and she was smiling at him all the time, but Peter felt that so she should, considering that he was so much better-looking than she. The lights went out, and the film started. St. Stairs kissed his girl in the darkness, and Peter knew that Fatty expected him to kiss her: but he was not going to sink that low, and he set his face and stared at the screen, shifting his bent legs, feeling that it was all a waste of time. The film became tense, and Fatty gripped his arm intimately to suggest that she needed a man's protection from the horrors and strain of the film. But Peter was coldly unresponsive, and he only thought how revolting her contact with him was, and how unpleasant was the pinching grip she had on his arm, a grip that was supposed to be sexually exciting, no doubt.

When the films had finished, and they walked up the aisle, Fatty was still not discouraged, and she still smiled her too-bright close-blue eyes at Peter, and held on to his arm. Peter looked down at her, and hoped that nobody would notice that he was paired with such inferior material. St. Stairs, who had been keeping an eye on Peter during the films, called over his shoulder to Peter in a sporty manner: 'You are being rather slow, aren't you?' Fatty smiled encouragingly at Peter when she heard that, but Peter kept his face set.

They walked by the Serpentine in the darkness, and Peter allowed himself to trail behind, leaving Fatty to talk to St. Stairs and her girl-friend. They walked along the Bayswater Road, and Peter was still behind on his own, preferring his own company to that of the very available Fatty. Peter wanted out. He looked round for a means of escape. A bus pulled up at a bus-stop just by where he was walking. Peter looked at the three figures walking along the dark pavement in front of him, and then, as the red, humanity-packed, orange- and yellow-lighted bus began to move away, he slipped unobserved on to the bus. Fatty walked on with St. Stairs and Smelly Mackintosh, thinking that Peter, who she told herself defensively was a shy boy, was still behind. When Peter saw St. Stairs on the following Monday at the school he indignantly complained; and said accusingly that St. Stairs had said initially that Peter's blind-date was all right. St. Stairs threw back his head and laughed his blooming head off. Peter glowered like James Mason used to do, and remembered Fatty's mean, thin, red lips and monstrous figure with distaste. What a dirty trick to play on a fellow intellectual! But of course St. Stairs was all right: he had a girl now.

SO-LONG SANCTUARY?

Refuge and asylum. They were soon to disappear. Peter just scraped through the examination that summer, and with that he had to leave St. Elevenses and face the outside world. He had wrapped himself in cotton-wool for as long as he could, and now he had to allow the wrappings to be ruthlessly torn away, revealing his naked and defenceless soul to the cruel world. Peter tried not to think about the future. But there was worse to come.

Perce and Harriet let Peter stay in the house they had inherited: they let him stay until he had taken his examination. But when the summer holidays started, and he was no more away at school during the daytime, they decided that it was time for Peter to go. It was their house now. And they did not like Peter. Harriet told him that he must find diggings. Peter was out in the cold. He could no more hide in the familiar atmosphere of his dead grandmother's house. He could no more hide within the walls of St. Elevenses. And he had to find a permanent job. There was no escape. Or so it seemed to him at the end of July. He did not realize that Life is incalculable.

Peter's weakness was so great that it led him into one protected atmosphere after another for the rest of his life.

He hid in an apprenticeship. And then he hid in his profession. And he hid in his marriage. During the rest of his life he never showed his vulnerable sensitivity to the outside world of Philistines, except on one or two occasions when he was off his guard. The cotton-wool was periodically replaced, and his weakness found him asylums. But he was not so different from the rest of us. For we all hide from life in one way or another, in our professions, behind false faces, behind acts that disguise us, using crutches of one kind or another, and only facing life when it catches us off our guard. The soul will always find a hiding-place. And the more it needs one the more hiding-places it will find. It is only the zombies who need no hiding-places. And perhaps, in reality, there are no soulless, insensitive zombies.